THE
BODY
INSTITUTE

D1490575

THE BODY INSTITUTE

CAROL RIGGS

Entangled Publishing, LLC
2614 South Timberline Road
Suite 109
Fort Collins, CO 80525

Entangled Teen is an imprint of Entangled Publishing, LLC.

Visit our website at www.entangledpublishing.com.

Edited by Stacy Abrams
Cover design by Kelley York
Cover photograph brain © Alex Mit/Shutterstock
Cover photograph city/road © wavebreakmedia/Shutterstock
Cover photograph girl 1 © Dean Bertoncelj/Shutterstock
Cover photograph girl 2 © Vladimir Gjorgiev/Shutterstock
Interior design by Jeremy Howland

Print ISBN 978-1-63375-125-5
Ebook ISBN 978-1-63375-126-2

Manufactured in the United States of America

First Edition Septmeber 2015

10 9 8 7 6 5 4 3 2 1

~With love to my husband, Dennis, and my daughters, Janelle and Megan.~

CHAPTER 1

Five more reps, and I should be done with this body for good.

I pull the weight bar down to my chest, working my biceps. Here I am, flat on my back once more, communing with my old buddy the Fluid Resistance Machine.

Twenty-six…twenty-seven.

Man, I can't wait to get back into my own body and be myself again. Hanging out with my friends, spending time with my family. Dancing. Urban paintballing. Messing around with kinetics experiments at the Catalyst Club.

Out of the corner of my eye, I catch the jog-pump-stride of other Reducers toning and slimming. Hard workers, these ladies: 100 percent keyed in to their jobs. Above us on the third floor, I'm sure a bunch of men are exercising just as hard in their own gym.

A chirp signals the end of my programmed reps. I ditch the machine and do cool-down stretches while it resets for the next victim, then take a brisk shower and head to the first floor for my weigh-in.

I shake a rush of tingling nerves from my fingertips. If my

stats are on track this morning, I can finally check out of the Clinic. I've toned up Shelby Johnson's body, plus kept her weight stable this past week. Imagine—fifty whole pounds, sweated off in three months. Soon, Shelby's Before and After images will spring up in vidfeeds everywhere, peddling the Institute's new client group, teens fourteen to eighteen.

Put an end to obesity before you reach adulthood, the ads will shout. *Look fabulous in three to six months!*

I'm happy to say I've made important progress for Shelby and the pilot program.

The scanner in the Weigh Center doorway blinks as it reads the ID chip in my hand. This early, the garish green waiting chairs hold only a few Reducers. I nod to another arriving worker, a guy who has about ten pounds left to lose. Before I can start up a conversation, an electronic voice near the ceiling intones, "Morgan Dey, report for weigh-in."

In Admittance, I step toward an available tech. "Hey, how's your day going?"

He grunts and barely looks at me as he waves me onto the scale, like Reducers are a bunch of faceless cogs on an assembly line. "Morgan Dey in the body of Shelby Johnson," he verifies for the data streamer. He records my vitals and steps to the wallscreen readout. "Your assignment is complete. Restoration is scheduled for oh-nine-forty-five today in the administration building. Arrive at least ten minutes early at Mr. Behr's office."

A wide grin takes over my face. In one short hour, I can shed my Loaner body and go home. I exit the Weigh Center and take the stairs two at a time back to the second floor. With a hasty handprint, I access my dorm room. After I dictate a log entry of my morning workout, I grab my Institute phone so I can send a voice-to-text message to Mom, Dad, and Granddad. I word the message carefully, since Leo Behr, the director, screens everything a newbie Reducer sends.

Or so he says. Personally, I think it's a bluffy scare tactic he invented to keep his workers in line.

> Coming back today! Restoration at 0945. Home
> after that. See ya.

I dash off similar messages to Blair and Krista, and I'm ready to reclaim my body and leave this place. Forget the monumental pay. Nothing is worth the constant sweating, sore muscles, and hunger pangs I've endured for the past eighty-nine days. For my next job, I'll find an easier way to earn credits. But I need to clue in my other self. Because when I wake up in my own body after it comes out of suspended animation, I won't remember thinking this way. I send myself a memo.

> Never sign up to be a Reducer again. It's awesome
> tech, but a torturous way to earn credits.

For extra insurance, I send another to Blair and Krista:

> If I ever say I want to be a Reducer again, PLEASE
> tell me to find a different job.

I can count on my two best friends to stop me from joining a second time, since they weren't too fired up about me being gone so long this time. Blair also didn't get the point of the job, since credit shortages aren't part of *her* family's vocabulary. Not that I've exactly told her or Krista about my parents' financial problems. Just my dreams for attending tech school. I don't want to sound like I'm asking for pity—or worse, bragging about helping Mom and Dad pay the bills.

Downstairs, I slip into the fresh morning light of summer and breathe deeply. *Farewell forever, tedious Clinic.* Added to that cheerful thought, twelve thousand lovely tax-exempt credits will soon be auto-deposited into my account, not to mention the eight thousand that will go into my parents' account for their share of my underage earnings. So fantastic.

At the administration building, I pass under the program's motto, lasered into the metal above my head.

THE BODY INSTITUTE:
TAKING THE WORK OUT OF YOUR WEIGHT LOSS

The ID scanner verifies me with a subtle flicker.

Turning left, I head to the director's office. Leo's waiting room has plush chairs with built-in gamevids on the armrests. My shoes make no noise on the sound-insulated tiles. As Granddad would say, it's government extravagance at its best—spending the people's hard-earned tax revenue. He's not impressed one teensy bit that Congress is helping fund the Institute to create a healthy future.

I flinch when an electronic voice speaks before I have a chance to sit down.

"Morgan Dey, the director will see you now," it announces from concealed speakers in the wall.

Speedy response times this morning. I like that.

As I walk through the autodoor into the office, Leo rises behind his desk, his trim build matched with an equally trim mustache. A broad salesman's smile spreads across his face as he shakes my hand.

"Morgan, you've done well. Shelby will be delighted with her new appearance."

"Thanks, Leo." I smile at his exuberance. "Will I get to see a vid of her reaction?"

"No. We only reveal your client's name and show you progress vids so you have a record of your success. Shelby's allowed to send one text message of thanks, which we'll forward to you. I'll take your Institute phone now, please."

I hold it out, and he whisks it into a desk drawer. I eye his crisp shirt and black suit. Impressive. As usual, he looks like he belongs to this office as much as the mahogany desk, the high-tech desktop screen, and the Italian landscape on the wall.

"Will Shelby be able to keep off the weight I lost for her?" I ask.

Leo gives a rather fierce smile. "The reintroduction program involves a strict year of maintenance exercise. The hardest part will be changing her eating habits, and we'll help her make that transition."

I hope that works out for Shelby. At least her body is free of junk food cravings now. She's already healthier, and she won't have a bunch of tax fines for being overweight.

"If that's all your questions, I'll send you on your way," Leo says. "Your real body is already emerging from suspended animation, so there shouldn't be more than a half-hour lapse between Transfers. The solution is leaving your body's bloodstream, and the stasis gel is evaporating from your skin. See you on the other side."

It's strange to hear him talking about my body as if it's a separate entity from me. I leave the office, and a hostbot shaped like a bell glides up. Flutters of nervousness and excitement cascade over me as I follow the bot's silvery form down the hall. It's almost time for the big switch.

We pass a door that slides open, and a voice leaks from

the room like dissipating gas, low and almost hissing. "Then get rid of him, if he knows too much," a man says. "Send him to Seattle."

I sidestep as a man with narrowed eyes and a dark goatee rushes out, pocketing his phone.

"Excuse me," I say. The man strides off, saying nothing in response.

A soft whistle comes from the rolling hostbot. "This way, please," it says.

I stumble behind the bot, the hairs on my arms standing upright as I stare over my shoulder after the man. What was *that* conversation about? It sounded hostile or threatening, but I guess I'm hearing the words out of context. I shudder. None of my business anyway, I suppose. By tomorrow, I won't remember one syllable of that man's odd conversation.

I can't decide if that's a good or a bad thing.

In the Transfer wing, I find a nurse with an angelic face. She's the same nurse who helped insert my brainmap file into Shelby's body at the beginning of my assignment.

"Morgan Dey?" the nurse asks in a gentle voice, checking her chart reader. "In the body of Shelby Johnson?"

"Yes. Hi, Irene."

She scans my ID for verification. I trail her across the room and check the beds we pass to see if my real body is in any of them. Most are empty, while the rest are curtained off for privacy. We come to a section with two beds, one of them occupied, and a shock zings through me. *Yes! There it is.* My own self—my true body. My dark brown hair is splayed across the pillow, and tubes and sensors are attached to my torso under the gown. I look pale and lifeless. It's eerie to be standing in front of myself like this. Knowing there's nobody home inside.

After three months of seeing Shelby's face reflect back at me in mirrors, my real features on that pillow look as if they belong to someone else.

I rub the goose bumps from my arms and stretch out on the white-draped bed, the one next to my very still body. The sharp odor of rubbing alcohol hits my nostrils, and the prick of Irene's IV needle stings my forearm. Nerves scramble like crazed insects in my stomach despite my attempt to focus on the swirly patterns on the ceiling.

Electromagnetic Resonance Transfer, or ERT, is an incredibly complex process. Sure, I trust the geniuses who developed it, but if it hiccups or glitches, I'm in huge trouble. If my brainmap doesn't leave Shelby's body the way it's supposed to, I'll be stuck forever in the body of a blonde with blue eyes. I don't care that she's seventeen like me and has a pretty face. I want my own body, and the life that comes with it.

Even worse, if for some reason my original brainmap won't reinstall into my real body, I'll be stranded as a data file with no consciousness.

No, stop. I just need to breathe and relax. The ERT process worked great before, and there's no reason it shouldn't work now. There hasn't been a problem with any Transfer since the Institute opened. The risk of failure is microscopic. I'll be fine.

Irene pulls a divider curtain between my real body and me, and a thin doctor, as gaunt and sunken-eyed as Death himself, stands at my bedside. "You've received your anesthetic, Miss Dey," he says, attaching monitoring sensors to my torso. "In a minute or two you'll drift off. When you become conscious in your own body, you'll remember nothing of your experiences as Shelby Johnson. This is normal, since we'll be using your original brainmap file and not the one you've been using in Shelby's body."

I squint up at him. Right. I know all this from my initial briefing, but now that I'm about to experience it, it sounds creepy. I'm on the verge of losing three months' worth of memories in a matter of seconds. My current brainmap will be gone forever, wiped out in the name of patient privacy.

Irene leans over. Her calm face floats in front of me, her features beginning to appear swimmy. "Start with one hundred and count backward. Restoration ERT will begin shortly. It's like going to sleep. After a short nap, you'll wake up in your own body."

I take a deep breath and blow it back out. Here goes nothing. Or rather, hopefully, here goes something.

I begin counting. *One hundred, ninety-nine, ninety-eight...*

My eyelids start to grow heavy.

Ninety-seven, ninety-six...

Naptime. Like going to sleep.

Ninety-five...

Except if this were a real nap, I'd be more certain I would wake up on the other side.

CHAPTER 2

A whirring noise flutters the air like pigeon wings in flight. It wafts into my consciousness and skitters around in my head, as though it's finding the lost borders of my mind. I discover my face, or at least the feelings of a face. Chin muscles twitch, nostrils flare. My eyelids feel crusted over, as if eye-goo from a long sleep has dried on the lashes.

"Morgan, wake up," comes a voice from a muffled tunnel. "Can you hear me?"

My head jerks in response. I inhale a rush of air that fills my nose with traces of rubbing alcohol, disinfectant, and the smell of latex exam gloves. My mouth opens, dry and stale. As my eyelids break free of the crusties, I peer at a much-too-bright world.

"Welcome back," a male nurse says. "You're in the recovery room. Take deep breaths and drink some water before you start moving around."

I groan. Move around? I don't think so. My body tingles like stone trying to morph into flesh. Breathing is easier than moving. I'll stick to that.

After some of my stiffness has melted away, I turn my head and discover a window. Sunlight seeps through the cracks in the autoblinds. Where am I, anyway? The last thing I remember…Oh yeah, I'm at the Los Angeles branch of The Body Institute. I did this on purpose. Went into suspended animation so I could help a girl lose weight and earn some serious credits. The doctors stored my brainmap file and inserted a copy of it into the Loaner client. A Shelby someone or another. Johnson, that was it. Shelby Johnson. I hope I worked off the fifty pounds she needed to lose. I have no idea, but Mr. Behr warned me during my initial briefing that I wouldn't be able to remember anything.

More minutes filter by while a monitoring machine whirs behind me. I order the head of the hospital bed to rise, and sip from a cup of water on a stand. If my assignment is over, this must be the end of June instead of March. A big gaping hole in my life, just like that. It doesn't feel like I've been out of it that long. I wonder if Shelby is having surreal feelings of her own right now. Waking up fifty pounds lighter, as if by magic. Spending three months of her life on blank hold, stuck as a data file with no consciousness at all. So bizarre.

The nurse reappears, checks my vitals, and removes my IV and sensor monitors. "When you're ready, step into the bathroom and shower. Your duffel bag with your clothing is in there. Any stasis gel not yet dissolved from your hair will wash out easily with shampoo."

I swing my legs over the edge of the bed and wiggle my toes. Everything seems to be in working order. I shuffle to the shower, where the hot water revives me to my normal self. I dry off and slip on a red T-shirt and my favorite comfy jeans.

The nurse has already stripped the bed by the time I exit the bathroom.

"Mr. Behr is expecting you in his office," he says. "A hostbot will take you there."

"Thanks." I trot behind the hostbot, squinting at its wheeling mechanisms and wondering how it's programmed to move. Does it ever malfunction and guide someone to the cafeteria instead? Maybe Blair and I should do our next Catalyst Club project on robotics.

I reach the director's waiting room, where the hostbot drifts away. One other person is there, a lanky guy whose dark hair hangs across his forehead as he bends over his phone.

"Are you waiting to see Mr. Behr, too?" I ask.

He whips his head up and grins to reveal a pair of adorable dimple dents. "Hi there," he says in a smooth, earnest voice. "No, I'm way early for my initial briefing. You're first in line."

"Uh, thanks." It's a dumb response, but it's what pops out. My newly awakened brain waves skip and dance in my head as I match his grin, my unused cheek muscles protesting with an achy cramp. Man, he's *cute*. I edge toward Mr. Behr's office. The guy still has a grin plastered across his face, his dimples dissolving all sane thoughts from my mind. Something shines in his eyes that makes me want to stay there all day to find out what his life is like—who he is, what he does, what he thinks about.

I fumble near Mr. Behr's door. The scanner confirms my ID, and the door opens.

"There you are," Mr. Behr says from across the room, glancing up from his deskscreen. "I trust you're feeling all right."

"I'm fine." I step inside and let the door close behind me. I do feel fine, despite going fuzzy brained from seeing that hot dimpled guy. "Did I help Shelby lose weight, Mr. Behr?"

He gives a triumphant smile. "You certainly did. I knew I'd spotted a winner when I saw your application last fall. Have a seat and I'll show you the vid. And please, call me Leo, like you have been for the last three months."

"Okay…Leo." I can't believe I called this brisk, intimidating man by his first name. A lot can change in three months, I guess.

I sit as his screen flares to life with footage of what must be me inside Shelby Johnson, while Leo calls me Morgan and I respond. Hard to believe that's truly me, talking in a different voice, moving around in another body. Fascinating. The scenes change as I exercise and transform Shelby's body into one that's slender and toned. My Shelby self asks Leo questions before Restoration, and the images vanish.

"Nice," I say with a laugh. "I'm impressed with myself."

"You should be." Leo whisks a finger across his screen. "Nevertheless, when you see the promotional ads, don't forget you'll be subject to a fine if you publicize that you were part of Shelby's weight loss. You're only allowed to say you've been working for us in general. Contact between Loaners and Reducers is forbidden, and any focus should be on the client, not the Reducer."

"I remember that," I say, even though I'd love to be able to tell my friends and family.

Leo swivels the screen to face me. "Your parents are standing by, ready to sign off your contract after they confirm you're alive and well."

Of course. The parental stamp of approval, since I'm not eighteen yet. Too bad Mom and Dad couldn't take time off to be here in person as I'm checking out, but oh well. I'm a big girl and don't need them to hold my hand. Besides, they have to work and keep earning those credits. I wave my fingers at the images, which show a pleased Dad and an enthusiastic Mom.

"I'm done with my Reducer job," I say. "Back to the normal me."

"I can't tell you how good it is to see your face," Dad says. "I was beginning to think all those texts and emails were from an automated system."

"An auto-system can't fake my thoughts and personality, Dad."

"You look super, honey," Mom says. "I'm glad you're done. I can't wait to see you after rehearsal. Are your muscles weak from being in suspended animation for so long?"

"Nope," I say. "Animation's more like being flash-frozen. I'm the same as when I went in."

"That's a relief." She looks around for Leo. "We're ready to sign, Mr. Behr."

"See ya, kiddo," Dad tells me. "I should be off work by the time you get home."

Leo takes care of their bio-signatures. When he returns the screen to me, Mom and Dad have vanished, replaced by a lengthy page of legal jargon. "Your turn."

The computer scans my ID chip, and I press my hand onto the bio-pad.

"Your earnings have been deposited," Leo says. "We've also already removed Shelby's temporary ID authorization from your personal and email accounts. They're all yours now, and you're ready to head home." He rolls his shoulders a little, as if he's tense. "As you leave the grounds, steer clear of the protesters from WHA by the front gates. The past few weeks, they've been gathering to discourage people from joining the program. If any of them tries to engage you, say 'no comment' and keep going."

By WHA, I assume he means the Warriors of Humanity Alliance. But I don't know why they'd object. "What's the Institute have to do with human rights violations? Did I miss some big newsflash?"

"It's just an unfounded rumor."

"About what, exactly?"

He throws me a stony look, similar to the kind my science teacher gives me when I ask too many questions. "That the Institute was involved in an identity situation. The WHA is simply inventing lies and exaggerating them."

I have no idea what an "identity situation" means. I start to ask, but the preoccupied look on his face stops me. Obviously he has other things to do and doesn't want to elaborate. I'll check it out later online or ask Granddad. He keeps up with conspiracy-type news like that.

Leo grips my hand in a vigorous shake. "It was a pleasure working with you. You've helped make the teen pilot program a roaring success. We need more driven, strong-willed people like you in the world."

My face warms with a pleased flush, even though I know he's overdoing the praise. "Glad to help out."

"This teen program will increase our need for Reducers. If you're interested, we can contact you for future work."

I shrug. Why not? This seems easy enough, and besides, being on the list doesn't mean I'm locked into it. "Sure, although I have to study and get back into my classes first."

"Of course. I'm sure you'll easily resume your schooling, since you were ahead of most other students. That's why you were a perfect candidate."

I reclaim my bag and move to the door. "Thanks for everything. See ya."

"Stay fit," Leo says.

As the door closes behind me, the lanky guy in the waiting room rises to his feet.

"All done?" he asks.

"Yep. Going home now." A powerful warmth races through my veins as he hovers near me, and I don't think it has anything to do with my circulatory system still gearing up. Our glances lock and stick as if instantly melted, fused into one gaze. Gorgeous. He has a pair of infinite-soul, puppy-dog eyes. "Is this your first Reducer job?"

"Nah, this will be my third."

"Sounds like you really like the gig."

"I'm thinking about making a career of it. The pay's good, too."

I tilt my head. "You want to spend your whole life in other people's bodies?"

His half grin makes the corners of my own mouth go up. "I know, it's strange," he says. "But I love helping people lose weight." He takes on a dramatic pose, pressing one hand over his heart. "I'm helping eliminate obesity in the masses, slowly but surely, one person at a time."

I laugh because he's making it sound melodramatic on purpose, yet deep down I know how he feels. It *is* for a good cause. We're improving the world, helping people become healthier. He understands.

"How much weight did you lose for your Loaner client?" he asks.

"Fifty. You?"

His expression goes a little shy, which is utterly endearing. "Fifty the first time, seventy-five the second. Aiming for fifty again this round."

Awesome. He's good at this job, and not bragging about it, either. "Sounds like you're an ideal worker."

"Yeah. Leo can't wait to Transfer me again." His voice is lower now. Softer.

We mirror another inexplicable grin. He moves closer, and my face just might crack from smiling so hard. Not that we've said anything earth-shattering, but there's an undercurrent in the space between us, as if we're talking about more than we're really talking about. A hidden beat, a yearning kind of rhythm.

My phone blings in my bag, cutting through the thick fog in my brain. I wrench my thoughts back to reality. "Sorry, I gotta go," I say without much breath left in my lungs. It's time to leave, head home. "Have fun with your body-snatcher career."

"Wait." He reaches out and touches my forearm. His fingers press against my skin, soft and sizzle-electric at the same time. "If you're on TeenDom, we could chat there."

A powerful gust of surprise and delight blows through me. He wants to connect on Teen Dominion? How totally sly. "Sure thing. I'm on there. We can do that." I try to stop sounding like I'm babbling. "My handle's @geektastic007."

The dimples appear again. "Cute. Don't laugh, but mine's @superguy."

"I'd never laugh at something that serious." A chuckle tickles its way up my throat and tries to escape through my teeth. "Chat to ya later."

"Sure thing. Enjoy your real life."

His gaze follows me out the waiting room. It gives me a surprising tingle, the wake of something warm and extraordinary.

Whew. I pull out my phone and bring up my text. It's from Blair.

> Yay! Got your own phone back yet? About time you finished that job, Morg. Let's hang out SOON.

Excellent. I can't wait to do exactly that.

I cruise out the main doors, humming a song and squinting up at the warm June sun. A perfect day—and even better, no one's around to hear me singing off-key. It was a terrific idea to put my name on that Reducer candidate list last year. I may seriously think about doing the job again if Leo calls me. It's hard to beat winking out of consciousness one moment and bursting back into life the next with loads of credits and praise.

Not that I want to do it as a career or anything, like Superguy with his intriguing dimples. I can't imagine that. Being someone else for months or years, not able to live my own life. No thanks.

My song fades as I approach the Institute gates and find myself near a group of six determined-looking men and women carrying signs. These must be the WHA protesters.

A balding man with a fringe of stringy gray hair spots me as I pass through the gates. His flashing e-sign reads: PUT AN END TO GOVERMENT CONTROL. I avert my gaze from him and his poor attempt to spell "government."

"Are you a Reducer?" the man asks me.

"No comment." I keep walking.

"You have to be a Reducer," a stout, wavy-haired woman says. "I bet you let the Institute use you for the new teen program, to help the government force people to be thin. And I bet you don't even know what they had you do."

A skinny girl, not much older than I am, steps closer to me.

"Last year I was a Reducer. When I was done, I had no idea what my Loaner body did. They showed me a vid, but that didn't prove anything. Someone could've pretended to be me while they recorded it."

That's crazy. I give a terse exhale and dodge a bearded man. His sign flashes at me.

REDUCER, WHERE IS YOUR SOUL?

All at once, the sun doesn't feel as warm or bright.

"No comment," I say again. "Just leave me alone, please."

The protesters crowd around me, scowling, following me. The stout woman almost bumps into my arm. Words from their signs flash in my face.

ERT: FUTURE ASSASSINS AND IMMORTAL-WANNABES.

BRAIN SWAPPING: A CRIME AGAINST HUMANITY.

PUT AN END TO IDENTITY SHUFFLING!

STOP BODY THEFT.

I slow down. Okay, what's their deal? From their signs, it doesn't sound like they know what they're talking about.

No matter what Leo advised, I have to take a few minutes to set them straight.

CHAPTER 3

I point to the brain swapping and body theft signs, and catch the balding man's eye.

"What's that even mean?" I ask. "ERT doesn't swap actual brains, just brainmap files. And with the clients' permission, so there's no 'theft' going on."

"Close enough," he says. "It's not natural to separate people's minds from their bodies and mingle them with someone else's. We don't know if those things can be separated cleanly. It's like dissecting a person when we're not sure where the cutting lines are."

I shake my head. More ungrounded fears than science, just as I thought. "Our minds are different from our bodies, and our brain waves are easily extractable. Obviously the Institute is separating the two cleanly, and it has been for the past four years."

The stout woman grunts. "You're brainwashed. You have no idea whether it's clean or not."

"I'm done with my assignment, and I have all my thoughts back. I'm totally me again."

"At least you *think* so," the balding man says with a stern look. "Even if that's true, you're involved in a program that throws a giant wrench into the security of ID chips. It's not right for people to become each other and have access to someone else's identity."

"I'm the only one who was in my Loaner's body," I say. "To help her lose weight. Period. And now her ID belongs to her again."

The stout woman jabs a thumb toward the ex-Reducer girl. "How about what she said—maybe it wasn't you doing the assignment. What if someone else lost the weight instead, and used the Loaner body for an assassination one day?"

My patience is fading fast here. "That's ridiculous. We're busy at the Clinic all the time. We're on constant camera. We dictate daily logs of what we do."

The bearded man speaks up. "They could replace your mind in the middle of the night. The new person could commit murder, then your mind could be put back in to do the weight loss before you woke up."

I laugh. "Seriously?" I'm wasting my time with these people. Leo was right about their claims being way off base. A person has to have an IV and be unconscious to undergo a Transfer. Sensors, monitors, everything. These people have no idea how ERT works.

Time to head home. I pick up my pace and hear scattered grumbles behind me.

"We'd better not see you back here," the stout woman yells after me. "Don't be a part of the problem!"

I stride away down the sidewalk. Man, for a human rights group, the WHA should be thrilled about the Institute improving people's quality of life by helping them lose weight and be healthier. Apparently not. The world is a baffling place sometimes.

At the sleek crimson overhang of a Metro-Transit shelter, I scan the onscreen schedule. The next Metro-Transit Express to the Yellow Zone arrives at 1420. Great timing. As Dad predicted, he should be home when I arrive in an hour. When the MT pulls up with a low thrumming noise, I sit near the window. I scan my email on my phone, catching up with what's gone on for the past three months—messages I've sent as well as received. It's spooky, since I can't remember any of them. It's like reading someone else's mail.

I relax in my seat. It'll be great to hang out with Blair and Krista, especially with my account so nicely padded with credits. Most of that will help pay Gramma's never-ending hospital and funeral bills, but I can spare a bit to do fun things. Like treat my two best friends to a game of paintball. Or I could finally get that *Ultimate Tech* subscription I've been wanting. It'd also be amazing to stash a few thousand toward attending the Pac-West Technical Institute someday, but with the government grant I applied for in January and will *hopefully* get, I shouldn't need to.

I scroll through the rest of my messages, hoping for an email from the grant program. I see nothing. So frustrating. Government bureaucracy works slower than a one-armed robot.

My TeenDom message board pings. The tightness in my chest fades as I tap up a chat request.

Accept @superguy as Link?

Well, well. Mr. Mesmerizing didn't waste much time asking to connect. I smile and tap "yes." Almost immediately, I get a message back.

> @superguy: cool to link with ya! off to be briefed by
> Leo. ttyl

While I stream music and enjoy the perma-grin on my face, the network of transit rails crisscrossing the city whizzes past my window. High rises and megacomplexes flash by, the vidscreens on their surfaces strategically placed to flaunt ads to MT commuters. Crimson shelters give way to the dull mustard shelters of the Yellow Zone. All is peaceful—until the zealous faces of the WHA protesters buzz back into my mind's eye.

REDUCER, WHERE IS YOUR SOUL?

I shift in my seat, chewing my lip. That sign was the only one that really bothered me. My soul…good question. Well, if a soul equals the core of my being, my guess is that during ERT it hitched a ride with my brainmap, transferred into Shelby's body as a unit. Wherever my consciousness exists, my soul has to exist. Right?

I did the research before putting in my application. ERT didn't work until the Institute scientists realized they had to cancel the brain activity in the original body before inserting the brainmap file into another body. Maybe because the brain waves in the map are connected to a non-replicating soul.

I snort. That guy with the fringe of hair and his "goverment" control sign. I don't get his problem. The government manages everything from health care to transportation, and it all works fine. It's great the president and the lawmakers care enough about their citizens to fund businesses like the Institute. The protesters are as paranoid as Granddad, who's always insisting things like public security cameras and ID chips violate his freedom.

A minute later, the MT arrives at the Yellow Zone shelter nearest home. I hurry to my megacomplex, which rises fifty floors upward, jutting into the sky as though straining to reach a section of unused airspace. The ground-level autodoor opens and sucks me into its vast mouth of recycled air. I skirt the outer aisles of the superstore on the first floor, but a few holo-ads find me anyway, springing up to advertise glow-in-the-dark hair color and pedometer shoes. Neat stuff, but right now I don't have time to look.

"Later," I say, dodging them and taking the first available elevator pod to the seventeenth floor. I press my hand onto the ID pad by my apartment door.

"Welcome home, Morgan," it greets.

At last. Now I can relax and be me, 100 percent.

The door slides open to reveal Dad, his long legs stretched across the couch. Granddad sits in a nearby recliner, his wiry arms folded and his eyes closed as a snuffling, holographic water buffalo stampedes across the TV viewing platform.

Dad jumps up to gives me a giant squeeze of a hug. "Good to see you, kiddo. Sorry I couldn't get time off from work to ride home with you. Mom will be here later. She's doing a gig at The Lounge tonight and said she'll come home for a quick howdy after they run through a few songs."

I've been trumped by a sound system? Wow. And yet I shouldn't knock Mom's latest attempt at a big singing break. She's working hard doing what she loves, and we need credits any way we can get them. A cameo appearance from her is better than nothing. I peer around the image display. "Hi, Granddad."

Granddad's eyes snap open. "Morgan!" He unfolds from the recliner. "I didn't hear you come in, with this noisy TV spewing buffalos in my face. Come give me a scrunch."

I drop my bag and step into his outstretched arms.

The bristly ends of his beard scruff up my face as he hugs me. "You hungry yet?" he asks.

"Not really. I'll wait for Mom."

Granddad grunts. "There's a starvation plan if I ever heard one. Valena said she'd pop by around four thirty, but when's she ever on time when she has a gig?"

"You mean sixteen thirty," I correct with a soft smile. I don't know if he's becoming more forgetful lately or if he's simply being stubborn about things that have changed since he was young.

Dad sinks back onto the couch and pats the cushions. "Let's hear what you've been doing while you were gone. Your emails were pretty vague."

I sigh and sit next to him. Of course my messages were vague, because I wasn't allowed to share details about my assignment. And *now* I can't remember them. He should know that. Parents. I love them to death, but I swear, they never pay attention. Speaking of which, I suppose Mom's mind will be whirling with performance details, and she won't think to pick up special food on the way here. We'll be eating frozen dinners or SpeedMeals tonight.

The usual fare, but at least I'm home.

The next morning, I jog along the path that winds through the Yellow Zone's East Park, finishing the last lap of my run. As I pass other joggers, I savor the springiness of my leg muscles, the energy of my lungs. I relish the snap of my ponytail on my upper back. What a rush. I can't fathom being in Shelby's body, starting out my Reducer job fifty pounds overweight, not able to enjoy this kind of exercise. That must've been rough.

As much as I love having been part of the Institute's cutting-edge technological program, the whole amnesia thing does bother me. Still, if I'd hated the experience, I'm sure I would've sent myself a message saying not to do it again. I've thoroughly checked all my emails and messages, and not one single negative sentence is there. So it couldn't have been too bad.

But I should research that WHA "identity situation" Leo mentioned. I'll check it out when I get home.

Reaching down to my jogging belt, I peek at my phone. Nothing from Blair to finalize plans for the day, although Krista called earlier. I leave the park and ease into a walk, recording the end of my jogging session on my exercise app. That causes my linked Health Points account to go up sixty notches. Nice. At this rate, I'll be able to enter the grand prize drawing, not just the smaller monthly drawings. It'd be great to win some pedometer shoes.

My TeenDom board pings a private message alert. I snatch up my phone.

> @superguy: good morning! i'm in my Loaner body at the clinic dorm. weight loss & training here i come. what r u doing?

I type a text, trying to watch the sidewalk at the same time so I don't trip or bump into someone.

> @geektastic007: jogging the park. do u like jogging?

> @superguy: paintball's way better.

> @geektastic007: i love paintball! hopefully i'll do some with my friends soon.

> @superguy: super jealous. too bad there's no
> paintball in the clinic.
>
> @geektastic007: we gotta bug Leo about that.
> exercising can be FUN. like hover skating or
> basketball or other sports.
>
> @superguy: at least there's a pool here. which i'm
> about to dive into.

My mind-circuits light up all at once, envisioning him in a swimsuit. His real body rather than a Loaner body. Lean, lightly muscled, tanned…oh, *yeah.*

> @geektastic007: have tons of fun, fishboy. PS,
> my name is Morgan!

We sign off. I'm almost skipping as I enter my megacomplex. It's a curious thing—for such everyday words, that exchange felt pretty momentous. It's way too soon to know, but maybe this guy could end up as a boyfriend. I think I might finally be ready for a serious relationship again, after breaking up with my longtime boyfriend in February.

At my megacomplex, the elevator pod zips me up to my apartment. Before I forget, I go to the deskscreen in my room and search for "WHA identity conspiracy." I click on a vid by Walter Herry, the head of the WHA. A man materializes onscreen, his large nose pointed at the camera, his eyes intent as he ticks off government rights violations on his fingers. About midway through, the vid zeroes in on The Body Institute.

"People of America, we're in deep trouble," Herry says. "The government is funding this program, and over the past year there's been a dramatic push to use it to get people to lose weight and ease the workload of National Health Care. This is due to the strong influence of the new director of the Los

Angeles branch in California, Leo Behr. At first glance this ERT program seems admirable, but now the government is pressuring people to join by piling on increasingly heavier tax fines."

Interesting. I didn't know Leo was that involved. But it makes sense. The system is bogged down by a flood of overweight and obese people with health problems, all waiting to see doctors. It's costing health care too much to treat them. Getting the Institute on board is a great way to solve that messy problem. It's much easier just to eliminate the weight.

"After these overweight people are admitted," Herry continues, "their minds are stored in a computer while strangers take over their bodies. Even the Reducers themselves aren't sure what goes on during this time, because their pre-Reducer brain waves are reinserted at the end of the job instead of the ones that have carried out the weight loss. Are they truly in those bodies?"

I shake my head. This is the same nonsense the protesters were spouting.

"There's no end to dark possibilities here," Herry says. "If you were a Loaner, would you want your body used for unknown purposes? To sabotage a company, spy on your neighbor, or steal ideas or possessions? Perhaps even kill someone?"

Yeah, right. Herry makes it sound like the Institute is using client bodies for sinister purposes in some illegal underground network.

Herry wags his finger at the camera. "It has also come to our attention that the Institute might be using Loaner bodies for *permanent* body switches. A woman from Iowa reports she visited her brother after not seeing him for two years, and he is definitely not her brother. He doesn't know her. His mind is someone else's. It seems the Institute has put someone else's brain waves into his body—"

I close my connection. He means *brainmaps*, not brain waves, and I've heard enough far-fetched conspiracy theories. On my initiation tour, I went to the Clinic with Leo and talked to Reducers who were hard at work the very same day they got downloaded, losing weight for their clients. No one else was in those Loaner bodies. No spies, no agents on secret missions. No one stuck IVs in their arms in the middle of the night to perform an assassination.

Enough of this. No wonder Leo isn't worried about the WHA's claims.

I head to the kitchen to rehydrate.

Mom wanders in, wearing a fuzzy blue robe and ratty slippers. Her eyes and mouth are smudgy, like she fell asleep without removing her makeup again. It even looks like she's wearing the same eyeliner I saw last night during my hour-long visit with her. Music gigs must be brutally exhausting.

"Morning, Cupcake," Mom says.

I resist an urge to roll my eyes. I've way outgrown that nickname. "Morning, Mom."

Granddad shuffles in, his bushy hair looking freshly Einstein. He clatters his breakfast dishes into the autowasher and takes a pack of cigarettes from his shirt pocket.

"Not in here!" Mom says. "You know what it does to my throat, and I have to be able to sing tonight."

Granddad waves her off. "I know, I know. I'm heading to the balcony lounge, so stop fussing." He leans close to me and kisses my cheek with a loud smack. "Good morning, young lady," he says, and shuffles out the front door. It whooshes shut after him.

"I never know what he remembers from one day to the next," Mom says, worry lining her forehead. "Have you eaten yet, dear? I'm having a breakfast shake."

"I ate with Dad." I pour myself a glass of water from the purifier. Granddad doesn't seem *that* much more forgetful, but I haven't been back long enough to notice much. I hate to think of his mind fading as he gets older.

Mom shakes out a packet of pink powder into a glass, her eyes going dreamy. "You should've seen the crowd last night at The Lounge. I sang 'Tears on the Rooftop,' and they pounded on the tables when I finished. The manager booked us Thursday through Sunday for the rest of the month." She begins singing a verse from the song, her husky voice winding around the kitchen like a bewitching serpent.

I wait to speak until she's done. "That's fantastic. Too bad I'm not twenty-three, or I could come hear you."

"Please!" Mom shudders as she pours milk into her powder. "Don't rush to get to drinking age. It makes me feel old." A mischievous twinkle appears in her eyes. "You know, we should splurge a little with our new stash of credits, take the MT to the mall. I could buy something dazzling to wear for this weekend, and I bet you could use some new school clothes."

My mouth opens, then closes. Dad won't be happy if she spends too many credits on non-basic things. It'll make our debt stretch on forever. Not only that, even though we haven't seen each other for a while, Mom and I *so* do not shop at the same kinds of stores. Too bad Blair hasn't called, to give me a solid excuse for having other plans.

"Shall we?" Mom smiles, her spoon whipping milk and powder into a pink fizz. It's weird how her hair is a couple inches longer than before my Reducer assignment. While I was frozen in time, everyone else kept on living. The hair on my *legs* didn't even grow.

"Uh, I was thinking about hanging with Blair and Krista today."

"Don't worry, we'll be done by early afternoon, fourteen hundred at the latest."

I let out a prolonged sigh. Oh, all right. Maybe she'll be smart about her spending. She's well aware of our shaky credit status. Besides, how can I say no when she's standing there with her face all eager and shiny?

"Fine," I say, trying to keep my voice pleasant.

At 1415, Blair dashes into the Danger District lobby and over to the café table where Krista and I sit. Wisps of her honey-colored hair have worked loose from her clips. I stand and let her attack me with a crushing hug.

"Sorry I'm late," she says, sounding anything but. "What'd you two do all morning?"

Krista shrugs, her orange mouth pursing. "The usual. Slept in. Watched a vid."

"Mom dragged me off to go shopping at the mall," I say. "I mean, how many dresses can you watch your mother try on? Luckily she let me look for jeans while she got her nails done."

Krista slurps her drink. "At least you have a mom to do stuff with, Morg. Even when your parents are gone, your grandfather's around."

"True." Poor Krista is alone in her apartment most of the time while her dad works. Her mom's been back east ever since the divorce last year and doesn't call much. I reach over and rub Krista's shoulder.

"I can't believe your grandfather hasn't moved into that retirement home yet," Blair says.

"The waiting list is miles long. It's a government home." Which Granddad hates, but he has no choice. Private care homes cost twice as much as his labor pension.

Blair leans in, smiling. "I hope you got that health care improvement stuff out of your system. I really missed your smarts at the Catalyst Club on my circuitry project."

"I'm actually trying to decide if I should do the program again," I say. "For me, it went by in a flash, and I woke up with a ton of credits."

"Please," Krista says. "Let's not talk about it right now. I know you love the science thrill of it all and doing big favors to society, but you just got back."

Fine. Even though I can't recall missing them, I'll let the subject drop. I check my mascara on my phone's mirror setting and clip my phone to my belt. "So, are you both ready to play some night-vision paintball?"

"Absolutely," Blair says. "I'm going to imagine you girls are my last two ex-boyfriends."

Krista hoots. "Watch out! She's in serious walloping mode."

Ten minutes later, we stand outside the Nightglow Field 3 entrance, geared with marker guns, night-vision masks, and compressed-air ammo pods. I activate my exercise app and give Blair and Krista a thumbs-up.

Ready for combat.

We enter, scattering like deadly viruses in a strong wind.

It's fabulous to be me—doing what I love and hanging with Blair and Krista.

CHAPTER 4

It's August, and in the middle of a school term after only two measly weeks of vacation. I missed the first four weeks of break by being on my Reducer job. Sometimes I wish classes were set up like Granddad says it used to be, with the entire summer off instead of year-round school with alternating breaks.

I flick through my phone's messages with lazy fingers, but the girl sitting in front of me jiggles one leg as sweat starts to form at the nape of her neck. Alison must be reacting to the announcement of our upcoming Health Check weigh-in. I doubt it's U.S. History that's sending her into freak-out mode, even with the six-page essay Mr. Bernstein is assigning.

Across the aisle, Blair and Krista take notes on their deskscreen interfaces. As if she feels my gaze, Blair lifts her head. "Only five more minutes of Mr. B.," she whispers.

Alison trembles. She's trapped. No one can predict when these weigh-ins will happen, unlike the mandatory annual physicals that National Health Care schedules. Unfortunately, it looks like she's carrying more than the twenty extra pounds the government allows. She hasn't lost any weight since I saw her before my Reducer stint.

I pocket my phone. Mr. Bernstein is replaced by a trio of blue-uniformed workers carrying registration readers, digi-scales, and body mass index devices. Alison runs a shaky hand through her short black hair. Row by row, we file up to the front of the classroom. Alison shuffles off to a stern-looking guy for data collection. A tall woman in blue, moving like a rusty android, scans my ID chip.

"Morgan Dey, verified." She ushers me onto the digi-scale. My poundage readout along with my height, bone density, and personalized Body Mass Index assessments are sucked away into some government data-file netherland, recorded for dubious posterity.

The woman's wire-thin eyebrows arch. "Excellent weight and muscle tone, Miss Dey."

By the time I reach my seat again, Alison is also back, a weeping mess of mascara. Krista crouches beside her.

"Just start slow," Krista says. "Twenty minutes of walking every day, and get one of those exercise apps for motivation. Morgan uses hers all the time, and look how toned she is."

"I won't be able to lose this weight," Alison says. "Not by the time I have a two-month checkup. I haven't been able to exercise much since my grandma broke her hip, and I've been helping take care of her. She went home with my aunt yesterday, but I still can't lose that much weight, that fast. My mom's gonna be so crimped about having to pay this fine."

Blair hovers nearby. "How many pounds do you have to lose?"

"All twenty-four of it! Not just the extra four. It's unfair."

I grimace. Poor girl must've been on National Health

Care's radar. If people keep excessive pounds on longer than six months, serious fines start happening. Routine tests reveal physical reasons like low thyroid problems, but when those come up clear, the government accepts no excuses for being overweight.

Krista adds a fresh layer of orange lipstick. "You can always let a Reducer handle it. Morgan was a Reducer and helped a girl lose fifty pounds. All you have to do is check in, put your brain waves on a data file, and let someone lose weight for you. Easy-peasy."

"My mom can't afford something like that," Alison says.

"The Institute has an adjusted pay scale," I say. "If your income is super low, you might not have to pay anything."

Alison blinks. "Really?"

"Yep." I'm a freaking walking advertisement for the program. So is Krista. Although I suspect Krista is honing in on the two hundred Health Points she'll get if she convinces this girl to join the program. The Body Institute rewards well for referrals.

"How's it done?" Alison asks me. "How do they put some-one else in my body?"

Krista holds up a hand. "Keep it simple and non-techy, Morg."

I laugh and give a brief sketch of the program.

"Cool." Alison wipes her face, which now reflects a glim-mer of hope. Blair hands her a tissue. I think we may have a convert. Krista gives me a thumbs-up behind Alison's back.

Being healthy is a lot easier if people help each other out.

In another handful of minutes, we're dismissed, and since neither Blair nor Krista is in my next class, they fade off down the hall. U.S. History is the only session we share. Which makes the rest of the day about as exciting as Granddad's twentieth-century tech.

I duck into my Political Awareness classroom. The teacher sets up a holovid about presidential speeches and retreats to read an e-book. I poke around on my phone to multitask, gathering site references for my U.S. History assignment.

I'll do my essay on National Health Care. I can ramble on about how independent doctor offices got replaced with affordable government services. How health care almost went bust at first, covering so many unhealthy people. Smokers, couch spuds, that sort of thing. I could even sneak in a section about how the Reducer program was developed to help people change their lifestyles instead of just slapping them with tax fines.

Granddad always talks about life before nationalized health care. I'll use him as a reference. He's a little hazy on chronological details, but I can cross-check his info online.

My TeenDom account pings, scattering thoughts of National Health Care far and wide. It's Superguy! My heart goes into instant rat-a-tat-tat as I read his words.

> @superguy: greetings, geekling. i'm feeling monstrously proud of myself right this sec. got 32 of my targeted pounds melted off me as of this morning's weigh-in. i love being a Reducer.

Amusing how he said "me," as if it's his own body he's losing weight for. He's making major-league progress if he's lost that much in eight weeks.

I dart a glance toward the teacher. She's still absorbed with her e-reader, so I type out a response. It's actually perfect that the TeenDom site doesn't use a voice-to-text app, since I need to be in stealth mode.

> @geektastic007: congratz! u r good at it for sure.

> @superguy: aw, shucks. thanks.

> @geektastic007: i'm doing essay research... snoooore. hey, how about we meet up when ur done with ur job? we can do stuff that's way more FUN than clinic exercise. like there's this skating complex near my apt with a cool holo-obstacle course.

> @superguy: call me weird, but i always liked writing essays. not enough to make me want to be back in school. i'm glad I got my education cert & all that studying is behind me. Having my own apartment rocks, too.

I frown, my fingers poised over my phone. What? He totally blew off my question about getting together, the same as he did last week. Does he want to be stuck with chats on TeenDom for the rest of our lives? Getting together in person would be way more exciting. Unless he doesn't like girls asking those kinds of questions—maybe he wants to call the shots, make the first moves. Maybe I should chill for a while.

> @geektastic007: yes, u r weird. essays r not exactly joyful things.

> @superguy: too bad i'm limited to this Institute phone. i found this hilarious joke image i want to attach. u would get a huge kick out of it.

> @geektastic007: it's a drag u r stuck with only text & email.

Regular voice calls and visual mode are always disabled for a Loaner's privacy. No vids, no attachments, either. Too bad. I'd love to see his joke image, as well as hear his voice again once he gets back into his own body...if he even *wants* to call me. I don't know what's going on in his head. I can't even get him to tell me his real name or where he lives when he's not Reducing. His TeenDom profile lists his location as "galaxies beyond."

So not helpful.

When I log off, I pretend to watch presidential speeches for a few minutes. Then I check my email and stare down at the screen.

There it is. A message from the Government Need Grant Program.

I suck in a quick breath, tap it open, and skim the words.

> Dear Miss Dey:
>
> We have now processed your application for educational funding from our program, and your request has been carefully considered. While your father's income is certainly below the national average, we regret to inform you that his total wages remain above the ceiling amount for our funding criteria. We wish you the best in your—

I flick off the display. No way. My application was refused because Dad pulls in too many credits. Do I have to be on the stinking welfare rolls to get a grant?

Rot it all, and *major* sludge. I chew on my knuckle. There are only a few months left of school before I earn my graduation certificate. Without that need grant, I'll be working years and years before I can save enough credits to afford tech school. Not to mention there's still a massive pileup of Granddad's debt left to pay.

My head sinks to the table, and my forehead hits with a thump. I don't know why the world has to be set up like this, needing all these credits in order to live. The rest of my life stretches out like a murky and dreary road.

At 1500, Political Awareness finally ends. I commute home and drag myself down the sidewalk through the heat.

Bling! My phone announces a text.

I stop short in the middle of the sidewalk. Hmm. It's a message forwarded from the Institute. I tap it open.

> Hi, this is the client you were a Reducer for. I love what you did with my weight loss, and 8 weeks later, I'm keeping it off! Thanks SO much. My whole life is changing.

It's obviously from Shelby. I gape at the words. An odd bubble of wonder forms under my ribs, and my mouth curves into a smile. Whoa! I, Morgan Dey, have changed someone's life. The thought rushes over me like a sudden and refreshing wind. I hardly feel the wavering heat around me as I finish my trip home. The holo-ads on the superstore perimeter babble at me, a flurry of excited blurs that might as well be speaking an alien language.

When the front door opens, I stroll into the living room. As soon as Dad catches sight of me, he orders the TV off. Highly unusual. A talk-show host fades in a gritty smear of color and sound.

"Hi there, sweetie." Granddad enfolds me in a surprisingly tight hug.

"What's up, guys?"

"Nothing,'" Granddad says. "I told your dad you're not going to do it."

Dad presses his mouth into a taut line and throws Granddad an irritated look.

"Do what, get groceries?" I ask. "Make dinner? I don't mind that stuff."

"No," Dad says. "I got a call from The Body Institute an hour ago. Mr. Behr said if we're interested, he has another job for you. Starting the first of October. For a girl who's a hundred pounds overweight."

My jaw goes slack. "That's a lot of weight to lose."

"No kidding," Granddad says, balling his hands into fists. "It's preposterous. This body swapping stuff just isn't right. Why can't the government leave these people alone and let them decide how much they want to weigh? At least let them lose their own weight instead of shuffling them off into this program."

"It's promising new technology," Dad says. "Losing weight is hard to do, and it's an honor Morgan's been chosen for something like this."

Granddad grunts. "They could just use a diet pill. Save everyone a lot of trouble."

"Diet pills aren't a healthy way to lose weight," I say. "And the program tones up a person's body at the same time. Pills can't do that."

That line of reasoning reduces Granddad's objections to a throaty grumble.

Dad turns to me. "Anyway, kiddo, I told Mr. Behr I'd talk it over with you and Mom."

"That's a massive number of pounds, but it sounds like a

cool challenge—"

"And I have no say in this?" Granddad asks. "You didn't tell her the rest, Gregg. She'll have to be gone six months this time, instead of three."

"Yes," Dad says mildly, "and there's also forty thousand credits for payment."

"Wow!" My future explodes with renewed possibility. With forty thousand, we could wipe out Granddad's debt entirely. I'd even have some left over to put toward tech school tuition.

"Money's not everything, you know," Granddad says.

"I realize that," I say, knowing he means *credits*. "Dad, what do you think?"

"Six months is a long time, especially to interrupt your schooling. And a hundred pounds is a lot of weight to lose. On the other hand, you did well last time, and though I hate to say it, the extra credits would be nice for all of us."

Granddad points a bony finger at his son-in-law. "You and Valena will only get two months' share of that money, since Morgan turns legal age in December."

I keep quiet. He doesn't need to know I'm contributing to his bills, or that I already donated my last earnings to the family debt—all but what I spent on a pair of jeans and one round of paintball. He's embarrassed enough as it is with his daughter and son-in-law helping him. He wouldn't be happy to know I badgered Mom and Dad into letting me share in the payments.

"We have to do something, Bob," Dad says. "Not only are the collectors siphoning off your labor pension, yesterday they threatened to garnish *my* wages if we don't slash the debt in half by the end of December. We won't be able to afford to live here if they do that."

I exchange a panicked look with Granddad. That's a nasty development. If we lose this apartment, our only choice will be to live in the Yellow Zone's low-income district — The Commons. Heavily patrolled and run-down, those old high-rises only have a tiny bathroom plus an open room where everyone eats, sleeps, and lives. I think the buildings used to be hotels or something.

"Then I really should take this job," I say.

"Hold on a minute," Granddad says. "No need to involve Morgan. I'll be in the retirement home soon, and there'll be fewer expenses. You can put that savings toward the bills."

"I don't think that'll make enough of a difference." Dad sighs. "Let's wait to see what Valena says." He steps into the kitchen and thrusts his head in the freezer, presumably to inspect the selection of frozen dinners.

Granddad faces me. "It's a bad idea, and you should look for another job. What if that out-of-shape body has a heart attack while you're exercising in it? You'd be dead."

"I'd be fine." I walk over and pat his shoulder. "They keep a copy of my brainmap for backup. If the overweight person's body dies for some reason, they'd just bring my body out of suspended animation and put my backup file into my own body again."

"I don't get it." He blinks. His pale blue eyes look confused in the midst of his wrinkles. Old. He's so old and out of touch with a world that's changing around him.

"First, they record my brain waves to make a brainmap," I explain, trying to word it simply. "That's the backup. Then they prep my body for suspended animation by making an opposite signal of each brain wave in the map, and insert those into my body. The opposite set blanks out everything except my basic brain functions, the ones in the medulla that keep my heart beating and stuff. They don't map or cancel those."

He shakes his head. "Spare me the techy jargon, sweetie. It sounds like they're destroying your brain waves and turning you into a vegetable."

"Sort of. Except it's temporary and reversible. My body is put in suspended animation, and when I'm done with the assignment, the backup brainmap file gets returned to my body. The real me goes wherever my active brainmap goes, and I only exist in one body at a time. It's not like my mind can be cloned or anything."

"Sounds fishy to me. It's playing Russian Roulette with your life. You shouldn't go around separating parts of yourself like that."

"It's all scientifically tested and safe, Granddad. The Institute also sends copies of the backup files to their national headquarters branch in Denver."

"What if they leave out a few brain waves and you forget your mom or dad? Or me?" he asks in a quiet voice. "You might not really be *you* anymore."

"The Institute wouldn't do that. I'm not going to forget you, don't worry." I pat his shoulder again. There's no convincing him at this point, because he'll just get more upset. "We can talk more later. I'm heading to my room to do some gaming."

For a couple of hours, Masters of the Cyberverse claims my half-hearted attention while a cloud of bleak unease hangs over me. We can't be teetering on the brink of going to The Commons. A girl in my calculus class lives there, and she says it's like some sort of prison or internment camp. Mandatory quiet hours. Enforcers can search bags and backpacks. The units have security cameras posted in the halls, like hundreds of watching eyes. Sure, it's safer that way, but that type of surveillance belongs in superstores, MTs, and other public areas. Not inside a residential building. We *can't* live in a place like that.

I take a short break for a SpeedMeal dinner of chopped beef in a watery gravy, then return to my room for more gaming. I've just guided my silver elf into a deadly forest when I hear Mom come in the front door. While rabid lizards snap at my elf's heels, agitated tones fill my ears. Mom's questioning lilts at the end of her sentences. Granddad's raised voice, Dad's lower voice in response.

What are they saying out there? I let my silver elf rest at a mushroom shelter.

"Save. Exit," I command. The screen goes dark.

I cross my legs and tap my foot against the side of my desk. In a way, I don't care what Mom and Dad decide. This new job is a great chance to wipe out the bills and keep us from losing our apartment. It's bettering people's lives. It meshes with National Health Care's vision of healthy people. If I can get a tech education someday and become an electronic engineer, I won't be stuck forever on a financial hamster wheel like Mom and Dad.

Dad's job at Rourke Robotics involves sitting in one place for eight hours a day, quality checking the machines that solder circuit board components. That'd be enough to make me run screaming from the building after one week, let alone the sixteen years Dad's been working there. I've *got* to get a more interesting job than that someday—a higher-tech job, one that's not drudgery assembly line. One that uses my brain.

There's nothing in my life that can't easily be put on hold for six months. If Mom and Dad say no, I'll ask Leo if the assignment can start in December when I'll be eighteen and able to sign my own contract. That'll work unless the client doesn't want to wait that long, and the Institute finds another Reducer to do the job. That would be annoying.

Granddad knocks and summons me to the living room. I walk out and find Mom in Granddad's recliner, her smooth legs crossed, her burgundy nails draped over the chair arms.

"Hi, Cupcake," she says. "How was school today?"

"Boring. I need a change, a challenge. Besides, Dad says they might garnish his wages after December. There's no way I'm letting us live in The Commons." I throw a careful look at Granddad. I need to stick to the truth but not admit my involvement. "You and Dad need all the chances at income we can get."

Mom scrutinizes me, head to toe. "There *are* other jobs out there. Although it sounds like you really want to do this Reducer assignment."

"Absolutely." I wince as Granddad erupts with a loud, scornful noise. "For one thing, it earns a lot more than other jobs. If I were eighteen, we wouldn't be having this discussion."

"You sound pretty certain," Dad says.

"I haven't been this certain since I bought my first electronic kit."

"Honey," Mom says, "you're close to graduating. I think it'd be better if you finished your schooling first. You must only have about five months left."

"Three and a half. But even with a six-month break, I'll still get my certificate before my friends. In fact, maybe Blair and Krista will catch up while I'm gone and be in more of my classes."

Granddad paces to the dining table and back. "Why can't

you finish school while you're in this other girl's body? It'd be your brain waves doing the learning."

"Yes," I say, "except when I get back into my own body, I won't remember a thing." I don't even try to explain the amnesia bit that goes along with that scenario. "Besides, if I'm in this other girl's body, I'll have her handprint and ID chip. She'd get certification, not me. The Education Board doesn't allow exceptions. I checked last time with Mr. Behr."

"Stupidest thing I've ever heard," Granddad says, sputtering.

"You know, I think Morgan's right," Mom says. "She's ahead in her schooling, and she could use the credits. We all could, especially with the penalties and interest they keep adding onto the bills. Plus this added threat of losing our apartment." She plucks at her new dress, making a face like she wishes she'd never bought it, and sends a sharp glance to her father. "We wouldn't even have those bills if *someone* hadn't refused to sign up for National Health Care in the first place."

Granddad starts to bristle, and I hurry to jump in before he skids off into a tangent about the "evils" of government medical care and the inflated fees of Gramma's final week in the hospital. "Right, Mom. I'll be a Reducer again so you and Dad can whittle down the debt. It'll be free and easy credits for you."

Rubbing his hand across his forehead, Dad groans. "At your expense."

I step over and give him a sideways hug. "I don't mind. I'll use my share of the credits to go to tech school." Lower, to keep Granddad from hearing, I add, "Seriously, with this job I can help you *totally* pay off the bills. Please. You can't let us get sent to The Commons."

Dad closes his eyes. He's wavering, I can tell. When he

opens his eyes, he exchanges a look of resigned agreement with Mom, and nods. At the same time, Granddad cries, "No!"

A thrill of victory zings through me. The votes have been cast, three against one.

In five weeks I'll be an Institute employee once again. I can't wait. By the time I finish this job in April, my family will be completely out of debt.

CHAPTER 5

The night before I leave for the Institute, I hang with Blair and Krista one last time. As the holographic Swiss Alps on Blair's TV fade at the end of our movie, the clear keening of a flute filters into the room. The ending credits fall like lazy snowflakes.

Krista sighs, a long, drawn-out sound. "I just love that he tracked her across the world to Switzerland. Gotta get me that kind of devotion in a guy."

"Me, too," Blair says. "We must be doing something obscenely wrong."

Images of Superguy's lean-muscled arms and teasing mouth spring into my mind's eye. I shoo them away fast, kicking out my legs while I stretch. He's still being charming yet weirdly uncommunicative these days. His name and zone location remain a big mystery. "I don't think they make guys like that in real life. Only in chick flicks."

"Killjoy." Krista throws a pillow at my head and misses by a yard. Blair giggles.

"Thanks for the *dee*-licious pizza," I tell Blair. So much

for adding Health Points to my account tonight, but it was worth it. It's great Blair's parents bought our pizza, since as "junk food" it's highly taxed and way expensive. I scoot off the couch and begin picking up napkins and plates. "Guess I'd better head home soon."

"Stop doing that," Blair says, flapping her hand at the party debris. "I didn't invite you over for your last food splurge to watch you clean up."

Krista slumps. "The rest of fall break won't be the same without you, Morg. And it sucks you won't be here for the holidays."

"Sorry, can't help that." I shrug into my sweatshirt and zip it, her words dampening me. "It's too bad you both can't do the program with me."

Krista blanches. "That's *your* thing, girl. I don't care if it pays a million credits. You're not gonna catch me stuck in someone else's body doing squats and treadmills. I'm aiming for beautician school, period."

"We totally need our education certificates," Blair says. "I have to wrap up trig before I move on to calculus. I'll never get into tech school if I can't pass basic courses."

Yeah. That, plus Blair can afford to attend whichever tech school she wants after she gets her basic certification—and after she explores France this summer. I move toward the door, deflated further. "I guess we'll be split up soon anyway. I'm only bumping that up a few months."

Blair tackles me with a hug. "Quit being so freaking practical," she says, her words pepperoni-scented on the side of my face.

"Miss ya already." Krista likewise squeezes me tight. "Good luck with the job. It's your kind of sweet, humanitarian thing. You sounded like you really got into it last time. Send us loads of messages after you switch bodies, okay?"

"Duh. You'll see so many texts and emails you'll get sick of them."

"Doubt it, loser."

We share one last laugh. To my surprise, my voice cracks on the command for the front door to open. Outside Blair's megacomplex, the cool night air hits me like a slap as I hurry to the MT shelter. Everything feels larger than life right now. Looming new experiences. Changes. Leaving my current life for an entire half year…all at once it feels a little too momentous.

How can I run off like this? Ditching my friends and family, even if they are being supportive about it. I walk a little faster, trying to leave the ache and nervousness behind. Concentrating on the negatives won't help me do what I need to do. I have to power through this doubt. Being a Reducer does have its positives, but I could do without the heart-wrenching parts.

Tingling zaps and zings race over me. Yes, I need to focus on the positives. Tomorrow I'll head to the Institute, and though it probably makes me a certified schizo, that idea also sounds incredibly sly. This job will push me to new limits. It'll be a great challenge.

When I board the MT, I tap up Leo's initial email and read it for the millionth time.

> Hello, Morgan,
>
> Here's more information about your Reducer assignment. This time, you will be residing offsite. We have strict requirements for this kind of

setup; your Loaner's parents have requested this arrangement and have been approved for you to live with them. They have a personal gym and employ a live-in cook who will provide meals for you.

It's more challenging for a Reducer to lose weight outside the Clinic, but after your exemplary success with your previous assignment, I'm confident you'll be able to handle the extra work and responsibility. It's a definite privilege, since not many Reducers are allowed to live offsite. I've already discussed these things with your parents; if you have any questions or concerns, please call or email me. I'll arrange a briefing meeting if your answer is yes.

As a final note, payment for a six-month assignment is provided in two installments: one at the end of three months, the second upon completion of the job.

Regards, Leo Behr

As the MT travels along, I watch the city lights wink at me with eyes of red, green, and gold. This stint will be trickier than last time, I'm guessing, and with tons more responsibility. When I first toured the Institute, I saw the Clinic with its dorm rooms, gyms, indoor pool, and cafeteria. That setup clearly worked for me before. I hate to mess with success.

Yet how hard can it be to work in a different setting? It'll be cool to have the privilege of doing something not many other Reducers are allowed to do. Leo thinks I can handle living offsite, and so do Mom and Dad. A change in location shouldn't make any difference.

And it's perfect that I'll get paid half the wages after three months. That'll be right in time for the collectors' December deadline.

Yes, I can do it. I *have* to be able to do this assignment.

There's too much at stake for me to fail.

The MT deposits me onto the sidewalk at my usual shelter. When I walk inside my apartment, I blink, finding the lights low and Mom home with Dad. Soft music plays from the TV platform, the visibility turned off. My parents recline on the couch together, gazing at our wall screenpic that's set to a tropical beach.

"Hi, kiddo," Dad says, mellow. "I trust you had a good time with Blair and Krista."

"Yeah, I'll miss them a ton," I say. "Done with your gig at The Lounge, Mom?"

She pushes her dark hair from her forehead. "Unfortunately, we've been replaced by a couple of twenty-four-year-olds singing retro country. Can you believe it? Richard was so mad I thought he was going to heave his drum set across the dance floor."

I try not to smile at a mental image of Richard doing that. "Sorry, Mom. I bet you'll find another gig soon. Hey, is Granddad awake?"

"He was five or ten minutes ago."

I leave them to enjoy the rhythmic waves of their beach and move down the hall. When I knock, Granddad's door opens to his command. He looks up from his oversize chair and presses his finger on a large printed book to mark his place.

"Welcome home, sweetie."

A lump clogs the back of my throat. After tomorrow, it'll be six long months before I can return home. No exceptions. I step over a wadded T-shirt and a stray sock and squeeze into the chair beside Granddad. The springs creak under the plaid cushions. A fragrant and sweet aroma drifts up from his mug on the bedside table. Blueberry herbal tea, his nightly drink.

"All pizza'd out?" His bushy hair wiggles as he scratches his head.

"Never. But it'll probably be my last pizza for a while." I scrunch lower, until I can lean my head on his shoulder. I touch the crisp pages of his novel. It's a thick book, the edges of its brown cover frayed and well-loved. "Is this what I think it is?"

"Yep. *The Count of Monte Cristo*."

"Again?" A smile creeps across my lips. I remember when he started reading it aloud to me. I was twelve. When Dad protested I was too young for a novel like that, Granddad told him we switched to *The Wonderful Wizard of Oz*. We really did switch, but only for a couple of days.

"It's a magnificent book," Granddad says.

Minutes of silence pass. Memories swirl in my head, of how his spoken words conjured up clashing sword fights, passionate romance, cruel betrayal, and deep dark revenge. I'm sure Granddad is entertaining similar thoughts.

Granddad rouses himself with a sigh. "You'll be off to your own Chateau d'If tomorrow," he says, his bristly beard prickling the top of my head.

"Being a Reducer isn't like being in prison. I'm *choosing* my destiny."

"No, you'll still be imprisoned—in someone else's body. You won't be you."

"I'll be me no matter what I look like."

"Your looks are an important part of who you are." He winds a lock of my hair around his finger. "You wouldn't be who you are, the same personality, if you'd grown up looking different. You're a blend of your body *and* your soul."

"I guess. I never thought of it that way."

"Don't do it, sweetie." I hear rather than see his pained expression.

I sit up and twist to face him. "I have to, Granddad. It's the only way I can go to tech school, since I can't get a grant. It's my future we're talking about here. Plus I'm helping someone, improving her life."

"You could always get a normal job and save up the old-fashioned way."

"That'd take forever. Years. Tech school is expensive."

He looks at me with mournful eyes. "I hope you don't regret this."

"Don't worry. I won't." I lean over, give his wrinkled cheek a gentle kiss, and hand him his mug of tea before I leave the room.

I see signs for the Red Zone whip past the MT window and straighten in my seat next to Mom. We're getting closer. The Institute lies about five minutes ahead. The butterflies in my stomach perform a hot-footed little dance. Today I'll be installed in a new body, and my rigorous six months of weight loss will begin.

I'm ready and up to the challenge.

I send a quick TeenDom message to Superguy.

> @geektastic007: almost there! strange i'm
> starting up 1 day after u ended ur job.

Which is a definite downer. We had a microscopic window to get together — which we missed — and now it'll be impossible to meet for six months. Assuming he even wanted to in the first place. Oh well, no use sniffling about it. At least we'll be able to keep chatting. He won't remember the texts we sent each other while he was a Loaner, but I'm sure he's read them all by now.

There's only a one-minute lapse before he sees my text and answers.

> @superguy: GO, u! i'm sure u will do great. let me
> know when ur done morphing.

> @geektastic007: gotcha. ttyl.

Morphing. Funny way to put it.

I throw a glance at Mom's cheery profile. This morning I watched a newsvid about the WHA ramping up their protests. They insist the Reducer program violates ID security, infringing on people's rights by letting others use their bodies, blah, blah, blah. I didn't share the vid with Mom or Dad. The WHA's claims are ridiculous. In fact, I watched another vid that debunked the "identity situation" of that Iowa woman's brother who didn't know her. Come to find out, her brother was never overweight or a Loaner. There's no way the Institute could've permanently replaced his ID, because his body and brainmap were never in the system. He just got caught sneaking around in the data file room of the Institute's Kansas City branch. I bet his sister made that silly claim because she was ticked off about his arrest.

The WHA should do its homework before it reports

things. If they want to share a legit claim someday, like some valid identity snag or a Loaner rights issue, no one is going to listen.

As the MT decelerates, an overly courteous e-voice announces, "Red Zone. Now arriving at Alameda Street." I shoulder my bag and glimpse my reflection in the security camera above my head. Mom did a great job braiding my hair, and I love the new white jacket that Blair bought for me last week as a going-away present. I'm a traveling Reducer-to-be, about to embark on an important assignment.

"We're here, Cupcake." Mom's frilly laugh sounds like notes to a song. "How exciting."

I give her hand a squeeze despite the juvenile nickname, and she squeezes back. We step off the MT and head down the sidewalk. I take long strides, breathing in the rich smell of fall leaves. Puffs of whipped-cream clouds squat in the sky, peeking around office buildings at us. The taste of adventure sits on my tongue.

Approaching the Institute grounds, however, I suppress a groan. Ahead is a milling cluster of protesters, more than a dozen this time, carrying signs and blocking the sidewalk to the entrance gates. The WHA. I should've expected this. They'll probably hassle me again, and Mom too. I tuck my phone into my bag and try to hurry us past the group without being noticed.

No such luck.

They see Mom and me, and they rush at us like stray filaments toward a pair of magnet-bots.

CHAPTER 6

"Where are you two going?" a blustery voice calls. The demand belongs to the WHA sign-maker who can't spell, the balding man with stringy gray hair I saw this summer. He marches over and plants himself in front of Mom and me. "If either of you plan to join the Institute to be a Reducer, you're making a mistake."

"Who said we're going to be Reducers?" I ask. "Maybe we're meeting my sister who just finished her assignment."

The balding man hesitates, his e-sign wavering in his hands. I go around him, only to find the stout, wavy-haired woman blocking my path. "You little liar," she says. "I remember seeing you leaving here a few months ago. I warned you not to come back."

I look to see Mom a short distance behind me, blocked by a couple of protesters.

"That's a rude thing to say!" Mom exclaims. "My daughter's not a liar, and she has a right to go wherever she wants."

Before I can respond, someone's finger jabs me in the shoulder. "Ow," I say, and spin to frown at the bearded man who did it. "Don't poke me."

The balding man gets up in my face, scowling. "You're helping the government abuse people's rights. First it taxes and controls overweight people. Then it funds this Reducer program to force people to change their bodies. What's next, targeting ethnic groups? Permanently stripping brain waves from people with low IQs, or from people they decide are lazy or unproductive—or maybe from people they just don't like?"

"Exactly," the woman says. "ERT is a dangerous procedure. The Institute could delete anyone's brain waves and give their bodies to someone else."

"That doesn't make sense," I say. "They're trying to help people lose weight. That's all." I find myself hemmed in. Trying to move, I bump into the balding man. Still behind me, Mom asks someone to step out of her way. I glance toward the Institute gates and see two Enforcers standing thirty feet from us, exterior-grounds guards supplied by the government. They're eyeing the WHA group, like they're making sure the protesters don't cross some imaginary line. The sight of their bright blue uniforms is reassuring.

"Let us through." I make my words as firm as I can.

"Sorry, we can't let that happen." The woman shoves my shoulder, making me take a step backward.

What the haze? I hold my arm out to keep her at a distance and start to walk past.

"Oh, no you don't," the bearded man cries, swinging his sign at me. "You can't bully your way in."

I duck, but not fast enough. His sign hits my face, and the frame crashes against my mouth. Pain explodes across my lower lip and jaw. Someone pushes me, hard. I drop to one knee. It smacks against the concrete. A woman shrieks—it

sounds like Mom. Someone slams into my shoulder and I fall
to the ground, sprawling sideways.

"Stop!" I yell, curling into a protective ball while angry
shouts surround me.

"Halt." A thunderous voice penetrates all the other noises,
echoing into the air. "Step away from the girl and place your
hands on your heads. Do not try to run."

A voice amplifier.

The protesters' shouts stop. I raise my head to see the two
Enforcers standing in the street with their legs braced. They
aim long-range stun guns at the protesters. My hands shake
like a frail old woman's as I scoop up my bag and stagger to
my feet. The rusty tang of blood spreads across my tongue.

The balding man and the stout woman glare at me. I limp
away toward the entrance gates as Institute workers stream
from the administration building. Two security guards dash by,
one of them barking orders into a phone.

Mom hurries over and flings an arm across my shoulders,
her teeth chattering. "Are you okay? Oh, honey, your lip is
bleeding."

I touch my mouth and find it slippery. Blood is smeared
across my white jacket. My other hand tightens around my
bag handle. Fanatical jerks. I hope they get locked up for a
long time and are charged huge fines on top of it.

A male nurse with a shaved head jogs up to me. "Are you
hurt? Any bones broken?"

"I—I don't think so." I let him guide me by the elbow
along the walkway. Mom flanks my other side, murmuring
and exclaiming. I hear her words as a distant stream. *Those
people ought to be ashamed of themselves. I'm thankful those
Enforcers were right there. Oh my, you're bleeding so much. I*

just can't understand why those people did that—

Inside the administration building, the nurse leads us to a medical room. He helps me out of my jacket and cleanses my lip wound. After that, he runs diagnostic scans and discovers I have no concussion or broken bones. Not surprising, but I have plenty of bruises, along with my split lip from the sign and a mess of abrasions from the concrete. My lip and knee hurt the worst.

I take a shuddery breath. So insane. I don't know why that bearded guy bashed me with his sign. No one has hit me unprovoked like that since I was nine when Gramma and Granddad took me to the park by their apartment. There I was, swinging from the monkey bars, back and forth in the sun, having a great old time. When I jumped down, some kid reached out and punched me in the nose. I never found out why he did it. I just remember the pain. The confusion. The scary red blood. Granddad's soaked cloth handkerchief, and Gramma scolding the boy.

My lip is bleeding almost as much as my nose did that day. I blink watery eyes. In less than a minute, the world has twisted into a scarier and less safe place. It's freaky how fast those WHA people got riled up and aggressive. Their emotions are too closely tied to their beliefs, I guess. If they keep up this kind of violent stuff, no one will want to be a Reducer anymore.

Even *I'm* tempted to turn and head home. Go back to my daily jogs, my classes, my normal life. But that wouldn't solve anything. With the debt collectors' threat, my life is going to change one way or another. So I'll stick with my original plan to avoid The Commons. I want to be a Reducer, and I'm not going to let a bunch of fanatical protesters ruin that.

Mom strokes my shoulder. Her breathing is more even now. "I'm glad you don't have serious injuries, sweetie. I was really frightened there for a bit."

"I'm damaged goods for this job now." My words are distorted from my lip, which is swollen. "I hope my ERT won't be canceled because of this. Are you still letting me be a Reducer?"

"I'm really unhappy about those people shoving and hitting you." Mom's voice is unsteady. "But you're not hurt badly." She leans closer to my ear. "This job is our only chance to keep the apartment. Let's see what your father says."

That's not promising. I'm sure Dad will be more likely to cancel than Mom. The nurse lifts a container to a wall nozzle and dispenses a blob of clear jelly. He applies the jelly to the scrapes on my hands, and a smell similar to fingernail polish fills the room.

I wrinkle my nose as the odor settles in my sinuses. "What's that?"

"Protective sealant. It keeps the stasis gel in the suspended animation tank from penetrating. We put it on scratches or broken skin."

"Can I do the suspension and ERT, all bashed up like this?"

"Mr. Behr will be the judge of that. I'm applying it just in case."

He dabs sealant on my lip. As he removes ice wraps from my kneecap, the autodoor whisks to one side. Leo charges in through the opening.

"I've read your injury report, Morgan," he says, his face etched with tense lines, his brow furrowed. "How are you feeling?"

"Sore. Can I do the Transfer, or do I have to wait until I heal?"

Leo gives an abrupt laugh. The lines on his face soften, although he shoots a careful glance at Mom. "I love your dedication. No, you won't have to wait. However, realize that healing is nonexistent in suspended animation. You'll wake up in six months with these same injuries."

"I can handle that." I ease into a standing position. "I'm just worried about what my dad will say. Mom's okay with me continuing, but Dad might cancel everything."

"You're underage," Leo says, looking unhappy about the fact. "I'm required to notify him, which I already have. I assured him you're fine and showed him a video clip of you here in the nurse's station to prove it. Although he hasn't withdrawn his signature, he wants you to call him."

Oh, Dad. Don't change your mind. He can't pull me from the program before I even start.

I take out my phone and select visual mode. Dad picks up before the first ringtone dies away, even though he's at work. His face appears onscreen.

"Are you okay?" he asks, worry drenching his voice. "I knew I should've taken the morning off from work to go with you and your mother."

I aim for a casual tone. "I'm fine, Dad. See my face? My lip is cut, but it looks worse than it is. You know how lips bleed. The protesters are the only dangerous things around here, and they're gone. Enforcers were right there at the entrance and arrested them fast."

"I don't want you to push yourself to do this job because of the credits."

"I'm fine, honest. I only ended up with a few scratches and

a split lip." I try not to wince as my mouth throbs.

"What does your mother say?"

Mom moves closer to be visible on the screen. "We're shaken up. But I think Morgan can make the call, and she wants to do it."

Dad frowns. "I wish we didn't have those blasted bills to pay off. It'd be an easier decision. I don't like weighing Morgan's safety against a bunch of credits."

"Dad, please. No other job pays this well."

"We'll manage."

Words stick in my throat. No, we won't. We'll end up living in a place with faulty plumbing, drippy faucets, and peeling paint. Watched by a fleet of security cameras in the halls. Sleeping and eating in one cramped, prison-like room.

"We made our decision weeks ago, Gregg," Mom says. "This doesn't change anything."

Leo steps closer. "If it helps, Mr. Dey, from now on Enforcers will be dispersing protesters from the area. The WHA or any other group won't be allowed to loiter. They've forfeited their right to protest near our property."

"Did you hear that, Dad?" I ask. "The danger's gone."

"I heard." Dad rubs his face. "All right. I can't believe I'm saying this, Morgan—and I'm not totally comfortable with it—but I know how you have your heart set on making the world a better place. Sometimes important things like that come with a few risks. Be careful, kiddo."

"Thanks, Dad." I smile, despite the ache of my lip, and tap off the connection. All systems go, before Dad changes his mind. I face Leo. "I'm ready to sign and be briefed whenever you are."

His salesman smile returns. "I was hoping you'd say that.

You're quite a trooper."

Mom clasps me in a careful yet heartfelt hug and kisses my cheek. "Bye, honey. I'm so proud and grateful you're doing this for us."

"It's because you all are important to me," I say. "I'll text ya later."

I follow Leo out the door and eye the back of his immaculate head, noting how every dark hair obeys his precise styling. In his office, I sink into a guest chair. The deskscreen springs into action, displaying a very overweight girl with long, curly brown hair. The girl is shown talking to Leo in his office, her face listless and pasty. She wears faded navy sweats and a resigned expression.

"Meet Jodine Kowalczyk, your Loaner for this assignment."

"Jodine what?" I lean closer.

"Kowalczyk," he repeats, making the last part sound like *wall chick.* "You'll find the name in your briefing file when you get your phone. Have you ever seen or met this girl?"

"No."

"Good. It'd be unlikely, since she lives in the Green Zone. How about her parents?" The vid of Jodine fades, replaced by one of a trim couple looking intellectual, well-dressed, and sophisticated.

"I haven't seen them, either."

Leo nods toward the image. "Mrs. Janeth Kowalczyk is a well-known techfree artist, and Dr. Charles Kowalczyk is an esteemed research physicist whose mother was the inventor of the PlasmaWave oven."

"Caroline Mahoney?" I say in a near squeak.

He smiles. "I thought that would impress you, with your interest in science. The Kowalczyks are high-profile, busy people. Yet they've brought Jodine to the Institute in person and will escort you to their home when the Transfer is complete."

"Cool." Imagine that. The guy is related to *Caroline Mahoney*, and I, inconsequential quark-like Morgan Dey, will be staying with her son for the next six months.

"The Kowalczyks' living arrangements should be conducive to your success," Leo says. "Their rooms are on an upper floor, yours on a lower. You'll respect their privacy and only interact with them when they initiate contact. Is that clear?"

"Yes. No spying, prying, stealing, or dealing."

Leo flashes a rather intimidating smile. "Which includes no drugs, acts of violence, sex, cigarettes, illegal activities, or anything else prohibited in your contract. You'll sleep in Jodine's room. Her privacy will be assured by bio-blocks on her electronic accounts, games, email, and online shopping sites. If you violate something in your contract, your assignment will be immediately terminated. You'll receive no pay."

"Right." The usual serious stuff.

"It works both ways, Morgan. If there's anything in your living arrangements that puts you in danger or makes you uneasy, report it. We thoroughly screen offsite applicants, but if a problem arises, or if it's too difficult to lose weight there, we can switch you to the dorms."

"That's good to know."

"Be sure to use your Institute phone for all communications, and verify your activity with the exercise app. Using any other phone is prohibited. Any questions?"

"Nope." Same rules he drilled into me before my last assignment. I dart a look at a security camera on the wall. It's documenting proof that I've been advised and warned.

After I complete my bio-signature, Leo escorts me out the door and toward the services of a waiting hostbot. At the Transfer room, I dress in a thigh-length hospital gown, and Irene greets me. I settle on a white-sheeted bed and watch her ready an IV.

A familiar gaunt doctor joins us and adds sensors to my torso. "Your mind is being prepped for Transfer, Miss Dey, and your body for suspended animation. Let us know if you're uncomfortable in any way."

I nod. Dr. Gaunt-as-Death again, exactly like the first time I went under to become Shelby. For all I know, he and Irene might've also been around to handle my Restoration when I left Shelby's body. What I *do* know is that right now, I'm ready to ditch my own body and get on with my assignment. I have a pounding headache. My knee throbs, my hands sting, my lower lip feels thick. I'll deal with these battle wounds in six months. At the moment, I want to begin my assignment and start blasting a serious trail toward my family's debt obliteration.

The miraculous drippings of my IV begin to take effect. My aches fade, and less intense drumbeats pound my skull. I lose the sensation of my mouth and head. No skin, no heart, no bloodstream. A melting away, a warm blurring and floating off into a great expansive nothingness while my thoughts grow farther apart...less coherent...distant...

Like a ghostly murmur inside my head, I breathe, *Goodbye, Morgan Dey.*

Heaviness. I try to budge under a thick, sloggy mass. It's as though piles of sandbags cover the length of my body, a suffocating weight. Where are my lungs? I struggle to breathe as an acrid taste fills my mouth. Murmuring voices penetrate my ears, and the scent of rubbing alcohol shoots up my nose.

My eyes pop open, and I find Irene smiling down at me. She's removing the IV from my arm. "Wha—what happened?" I ask. My voice sounds odd, rounder and more melodic than normal. "Did it work?"

"Everything went fine," she says. "You now occupy the body of Miss Kowalczyk. Your adjustment will be faster than coming out of suspended animation, so you should be able to sit up in a minute."

I'm not so sure about that. I shift with an effort, and the sandbag sensation lessens a fraction. A white ceiling with panel lights floats above me, shedding stark brightness into my eyes. I move a leaden arm and hold a hand in front of my face. Five pale, rounded fingers stretch out in my vision, the fingernails bitten down to ragged nublets.

I crack a half smile. Not cool, Jodine Kowalczyk. Fingernails are not good nutrition, or good for tooth enamel, either. I move a leg, a larger and heavier leg. It's like I'm testing out some sort of high-tech exoskeleton robot. My inner self seems way too small to move my limbs.

Nevertheless, I need to try. This is what I have to work with.

With considerable exertion, I prop my new body into a sitting position. I squint, seeing flashy spots before my eyes. Careful. Too much altitude, too soon. I survey my wider hips and thighs, along with the thick legs in navy sweatpants that hang over the bed. Irene arrives at my elbow to help me scoot off and stand.

"There you go," she says. "You'll get used to moving around soon. Once you're ready, Miss Kowalczyk's parents and Mr. Behr are expecting you in Mr. Behr's office."

"Thanks. I'll head over there." I marvel again at the strange voice that comes out of my mouth. Beautiful, in a shy, ultra-feminine sort of way. I cross the room with awkward steps and make it out the door. Another ubiquitous hostbot greets me. I maneuver down the hall despite being winded in less than twenty seconds, and halt when I reach Leo's office.

I inhale a huge lungful of air to steady myself. Here I go. Time to meet some high-society, famous people—my faux-parents for the next six months.

CHAPTER 7

Before I'm ready, the door slides open.

Leo and his smile appear in my line of vision, along with the stately figures of a man and a woman sitting in the office's leather chairs.

"I'd like to present Morgan Dey," Leo says with a flourish of his hand. "Morgan, this is Dr. and Mrs. Kowalczyk."

I greet them, and the man stands and circles me like an alert Doberman in a charcoal-gray suit, his gaze probing mine.

"A pleasure to meet you." He shakes my hand—Jodine's hand. "It's quite disconcerting to think you're not my daughter, standing there in her body."

Mrs. Kowalczyk gathers herself into a graceful stand and steps closer, the rose color of her high heels the exact shade of her stylish dress-suit. "How do we know it isn't Jodine?" she says with a faint smile. "Perhaps Mr. Behr has merely programmed her to lose the weight on her own, and then let her toddle back in here."

Toddle? I toss a wary glance at her. "Trust me, Mrs. Kowalczyk, I'm not Jodine. I have no idea where you live or what your apartment looks like. But I'm really psyched about spending six months with someone related to Caroline Mahoney. She was a brilliant scientist."

Something exultant flickers in Dr. K.'s eyes. "There's your proof, Janeth, on more than one level."

"I see." Mrs. K. shakes my hand at last, her fingers strong and slender.

There's clearly something I don't know about the proof of my identity.

"Guaranteed, it's Morgan in there." Leo hands me an Institute phone. "I'm always available by email or cell. Do any of you have questions before we part?"

Dr. K. and I shake our heads, but Mrs. K. nods, looking at me in Jodine's body as though I resemble biowaste. "Does Morgan know her schedule for weigh-ins, and will she be able to get here reliably on her own?" she asks.

"I believe so." Leo gives me a pointed look.

"Mondays at oh-nine-hundred and Thursdays at fourteen thirty, at the Clinic," I recite. "I'll take the MT Express here and back, and Leo has set up a special limited account that'll be accessed when the scanners read Jodine's ID."

"Very well." Mrs. K. retrieves a rose-tinted purse from her chair and moves to the door with her husband.

Feeling like a non-matching accessory, I follow the pair from the room. I'm puffing and panting by the time we arrive at a parked ebony vehicle outside. After Dr. K. seats his wife in the front, he holds the back door open for me. I squeeze in, conscious of my new bulkier figure.

"It's awesome you have a car," I say as he gets behind the wheel. "I've read a lot about them, but I've never ridden in one."

"I find driving relaxing," Dr. K. says. "It's a fine machine, and I like interacting with it." He voice-commands the vehicle to start. It moves forward, silent and powered by compressed air.

How mega-sly. When I was twelve, I loved it when these kinds of cars replaced gasoline and hybrid-electric ones. I wrote a science report on how the manufacturers made the tanks safer, designing them to crack instead of shatter in a collision. Not that many people in the city even have cars. Too expensive, too unnecessary. I wonder if Dr. and Mrs. K. ever take the MT.

I squirm under the autobelt that's stretched across my waist and torso. It doesn't seem to be made for overweight passengers. A boisterous rumble comes from my belly, and I glance at my new phone: 1100. Apparently it's close to Jodine's usual mealtime.

Mrs. K. lightly pats the sides of her upswept brown hair, and her shoulders relax as we leave the Institute grounds. "I can't tell you what a relief it is to be finally doing something constructive about Jodine's weight. She's ruining her body. I thought I'd go out of my mind trying to deal with it. It was beginning to hamper my creative art flow."

I can't tell if she's talking to me or to Dr. K.

"This ERT program should be successful." Dr. K.'s tone is confident.

"It had better." Mrs. K. half turns toward me. "For every additional twenty pounds Jodine gained, we were taxed at a higher rate. The rates have also gone up each year she's kept the weight on, and this past year even the base rates have doubled. Can you imagine the stress?" She shakes her head, which wiggles the tiny pearls dangling from her earlobes.

"Yeah," I say carefully. "The government doesn't like

obesity."

"Well, it burdens the health care system," Dr. K. says. "Too much time and funds are spent treating diabetes, heart disease, strokes, and high blood pressure. I hate to see Jodine putting herself in danger of those illnesses. Advances in genetic engineering don't do us any good if people insist on making their bodies unhealthy."

"Yeah," I say again. Jodine chose to keep overeating, despite all the rules we're taught in school about diet and exercise. Despite all the reward points for staying fit. Still, it doesn't seem fair to listen to the Kowalczyks complain behind Jodine's figurative back.

We drive along, with the Kowalczyks discussing national health and the quality of city streets. It's a perfect time to message Superguy.

> @geektastic007: i've morphed! can't tell u details of course, or i'd have to kill u.

His response comes after six long, boring minutes.

> @superguy: excellent, 007. u could make a career out of being a Reducer.

> @geektastic007: i'm not as dedicated as u. i like my life & enjoy being myself.

> @superguy: i like myself perfectly fine, thank u. i just like helping other people while i'm at it. pay's darn good on top of that.

> @geektastic007: aha. the REAL reason. lol

> @superguy: i gotta admit, it helps. hey don't work too hard. i'm off to get groceries cuz it's like Mother Hubbard's cupboards around here at

my apartment.

@geektastic007: enjoy. later, gator.

I grin and stare out the windows without seeing anything. More fun nonsense. I don't know why I get such a kick out of writing everyday stuff with this guy. Blair and Krista advised me last week that I need to find a "real" boyfriend—one who actually tells me his name and wants to meet up with me—but I haven't exactly seen anyone I mesh with at school or while dancing at the Flash Point club. It doesn't matter anyway. Now that I'm in this body, I'm not allowed to have a live relationship. Texting will have to be good enough.

We drive for almost forty minutes. As Dr. K. guides the car through an ornate set of iron gates, I flick Jodine's curly hair away from my face and check out a smooth concrete drive leading toward an impressive whitestone building.

The Kowalczyks' *house.*

Their home isn't an apartment at all. It's practically a mansion, decked out with gables, pillars, and windows galore. And these look like *real* windows. In my megacomplex, outer window units cost more, which is why we have a screenpic instead that alternates from beach scenes to forests to tropical fish. I wonder if the Kowalczyks' windows actually open to let in outside air. That would be stellar. The windows at Blair's luxury apartment don't even do that, since she's way up on the twenty-sixth floor.

In front of the house, an automower cuts a stretch of lawn that must be real grass, not artificial turf. I've never seen this much green growing outside a city park.

The car glides into a garage, and Dr. K. orders the vehicle to stop. He turns to his wife. "I'm heading upstairs to work. Can you show Morgan around and have Nettie send up lunch?"

"Of course, Charles." Mrs. K.'s stiff posture contradicts the agreeableness of her words. "Follow me, Morgan." She aims for a door while Dr. K. vanishes into an elevator pod.

I nab my new phone and try to keep up. Inside, I walk into a spacious dining room in which a classy chandelier hovers above a table flanked by high-backed chairs. Cream-colored tiles grace the floor. Through an archway, I glimpse the curve of a stairway leading to the second floor. I have a feeling the faster elevator pod is used more than the stairs.

"Lights on," Mrs. K. says, and the chandelier springs to glittering life. "Please call Nettie to the dining room."

She seems to be speaking to a house system computer. Very cool.

A large painting of a banquet hangs on the wall by the dining table. In dabs of colors so thick I can almost taste them, a feast spreads out before my eyes. Hot buttered rolls that are toasted golden brown. Roasted chicken, olives both green and black, bowls of steaming potatoes, plump links of sausages. Crisp lettuce and tomatoes and cucumbers. And to top it all, a juicy apple pie sits in the center, like a queen surveying her minions.

The food looks insanely real. My insides gnaw themselves to shreds, like sharks in a sudden feeding frenzy. I wonder if I felt this hungry when I was in Shelby's body.

A gnome-faced woman about five years older than Mom appears in the archway, crinkles forming at the edges of her eyes and mouth as she smiles. She cradles a bag of potatoes. "Is this Jodine's new trainer?"

"This is Morgan Dey, the Reducer." Mrs. K.'s words sound rushed. "Morgan, this is Nettie Reynolds, our chef and housekeeper." As Nettie shifts her potatoes and shakes my hand, Mrs. K. adds, "Nettie, please show Morgan around and send up lunch for Charles and myself. We're both extremely anxious to get back to work."

"Yes, ma'am."

Mrs. K. crosses the floor to the elevator pod, which swallows her and her rose-colored heels in a flash. Nettie—not seeming to mind I've been unceremoniously dumped on her—motions to her right with a jerk of her head. "The kitchen is this way."

I shadow Nettie through an autodoor. She dumps the potato bag onto a counter island and swats at a floating green robot. The bot is round and a few inches thick, the size of my hand.

"Scat!" she tells it. "Go filter someplace else. Higher."

With a soft noise that sounds like a purr, it ascends, oddly childlike. I watch it rise. It must be an airbot. I've never seen one in real life, only holographic ones on TV.

The cavernous rumblings of my stomach echo into the room. Nettie points a knowing finger. "I heard that. Never fear, I've fixed you lunch. We'll eat first and tour later."

"Thanks." I check out the marble counters and sunshine-yellow walls while Nettie slips two plates into a small elevator shaft and voice-sends them upstairs. A cinnamon-red sink by a window overlooks a backyard, framed by red-striped curtains. The kitchen even has a garbage incinerator like the ones the government puts in public places.

I close my gaping mouth with a snap. "Gorgeous kitchen."

"Mrs. Kowalczyk let me redecorate it a few years ago. I like my kitchen to be a cheery place." Nettie winks. "Now, I hope you like roast beef sandwiches. Jodine does."

"Do you mean the thin-sliced packaged beef, or SpeedMeal

beef sandwiches?"

She gives a chuckle that almost sounds like a guffaw, and slides two plates of sandwiches onto the counter island. "Neither. Homemade bread with leftover roast beef that's been simmered with onions, garlic, and sherry. Don't worry, it fits in with the dietary list that the Institute sent. I'm going to enjoy introducing you to some truly tasty food."

I sit on a stool covered by a bright red cushion and check out my thick sandwich. Is this roast beef fattier than what goes into a SpeedMeal sandwich? Is that why Jodine gained weight? I watch Nettie take a monstrous bite of the other sandwich, and shrug. I do need protein, calories, and healthy carbs to work out, and Nettie and Jodine's parents eat this food and aren't overweight. I just need to practice moderation.

Besides, the urgings of my new body's stomach have already drawn my hand to the plate almost before I realize it's there.

CHAPTER 8

Hands on Jodine's hips, I survey the horde of stuffed animals on her flowered comforter. Bears, giraffes, cats, and puppies lounge there, with a dragon and two parrots thrown in. Who knows how Jodine sleeps here. There's barely room. Sure, I've owned my share of stuffed animals, but I exiled them to a bin in my closet years ago. At thirteen, Blair, Krista, and I redecorated our rooms with gaming maps, earring trees, and star constellations.

"Sorry, you guys are history," I inform the animals and begin moving them to the window seat. I'll return them to the bed at the end of my assignment.

The furry critters have a great view from their new location. Trees, hedges, and emerald lawns. I pause to play with the voice-activated openers for the windows and blinds, letting cool autumn air flow into the room. The breeze is exhilarating, although it produces an appearance of the round green airbot from a vent near the vaulted ceiling. It drifts above my head, busily extracting pollen and dust from the invading air.

When I complete the stuffed-animal migration, I explore

the walk-in closet.

Decently cute and fashionable clothes. Plus-sized, obviously, but quality-made. However, nothing looks like it fits my current body except the faded navy sweats I wear. That makes the nifty wardrobe coordinator on the wall totally worthless. I turn to leave and catch my reflection in a full-length mirror on the inside of the closet door.

The eyes reflected there widen. My new body is broad, with lots of extra padding. I have light brown hair to my waist, with curls cinched as tight as a poodle's. How will I wash and comb that for the next six months? And wow, the freckles sprinkled across my face. This whole body seems overrun with freckles. Poor Jodine. I wonder if her curvy, wide mouth has ever been kissed.

My gaze drifts up. Above the closet doorway hangs a picture of an indistinct cluster of purple grapes, a crooked white vase, a petrified pear, and two plastic-looking apples. I step closer. The picture has brush strokes like an actual painting. It's an odd place to hang a picture, where no one can see it.

There's also a trio of initials huddled in one corner. Before I can decipher them, a scene flashes in my mind. It's the window seat in the bedroom, with a canvas and an array of paint tubes scattered across the cushion. Sketchy gray lines indicate skeletons of fruit and a tall vase. A hand holds a paintbrush. My hand. A blob of red wavers at the end of the paintbrush, and I dab it onto an apple outline.

My first spot of color. Blatant. Frightening.

Thrilling.

The painting in the closet whips back into focus. My initials in the corner sag, as if leaning on each other for support: JNK.

Jodine Nora Kowalczyk.

I drop my gaze to my hand and shake my head. No, not *my* hand. Not my initials, either. Weird, how I imagined Jodine painting that still life. That's *so* not supposed to happen. All her memories should be neatly canceled out of this body. I sure hope there wasn't a glitch in the ERT procedure.

Wait, *wait*. How do I know Jodine's middle name?

Is that a memory, too?

No…that's impossible. I bet Leo told me, or I read it in my briefing file. But whether Jodine's middle name is Nora or not, I'm afraid the painting isn't a very good one. Some people just aren't artistic.

I leave the closet. That freakiness about the painting aside, what I need to do now is throw myself into some serious weight loss. No one expects me to start officially working out until tomorrow, the first of October, but looking in the mirror has motivated me to get a head start.

I find a hair tie, contain some of the kinky mass hanging down my back, and leave Jodine's room. Nettie has some lively music going, along with kitchen-related clinks and clanks. A smoky, meaty aroma drifts through the living room. Nettie must be making early dinner preparations. It smells a little too heavenly.

I'd better not let Jodine's stomach get any ideas. I flee to the downstairs rooms.

For the next twenty minutes, I use the Kowalczyks' personal gym, working myself into a sweat on various resistance machines. My arms and legs tremble as I grab an electrolyte drink from a wall fridge and stagger out the door. Next to the gym is a huge room like the grocery section of a superstore, filled with rows of chilled produce, bright jars of liquids, and freezers filled with who-knows-what. Necessary stuff, I guess, for a chef who cooks food the Basic way.

During her tour, Nettie also showed me a third room down here, which promises to be the best one in the house: the game room.

I can't help grinning as I enter. A HoloSports Center takes up one wall, with image selectors for 3-D bowling, tennis, baseball, and boxing. Two chairs border a table for voice-activated holo-chess, checkers, and cards. A karaoke machine and a synchronized sound system sit next to that.

I'm *so* gonna like it here.

In a comfy chair at the karaoke machine, I scroll through the computer list until my heart stops pounding, and I cool off. I select one of my favorite songs. Drumbeats careen into the room from hidden wall speakers, and I punch a button to generate a 3-D audience. Tapping my foot, I sing a line as the technoguitars join in. A crashing thrill leaps in my chest. This girl has an incredible voice! Rich, resonant, and velvety. It gives me the absolute freaking shivers.

Too bad Mom can't hear me. She'd be impressed.

I finish the song. The audience, set to react to the singing quality, gives me a standing ovation. As the background track and applause fade, I lower the microphone and catch a glimpse of my new body. The wondrous spell fades.

Oh, creepy. I let myself get carried away, big time.

I shudder. Being able to sing like that is really cool, but it's way warped. I'm much too different from my usual appearance and off-tune-singing self. I need something familiar, a hint of Morgan Dey. Maybe some fresh outside air for my next round of exercise. I toss my bottle into the recycle chute and trudge back upstairs. Nettie sits at the kitchen island reading recipes on a reader screen, her reddish-brown hair pulled into a short ponytail. Something sizzles in a pan behind her.

"What's that?" I walk over and peer into the pan. The aroma wafts into my nostrils like a siren song made for noses. My stomach roars approval.

"I'm sautéeing onions and mushrooms. Want to give them a stir?"

I grab a nearby spoon and stir like I know what I'm doing, my salivary glands going into turbodrive. "Hey, is there a city park nearby for variety in my exercising, and do you think it's okay with the parents if I go? I don't think Leo expects me to be stuck in the house all the time."

Nettie twists to look at me. "You sure are different from Jodine. The park isn't far. At the gate, turn left and walk one block, then turn right and walk three blocks. I'll double-check with Mrs. Kowalczyk before you go." She hits an intercom button on a panel near the food elevator.

"Yes?" comes Mrs. K.'s voice, sounding more than a little impatient.

"I'm sorry to bother you," Nettie says. "Morgan wants to know if she can walk to the park. Does she need to check in with you or Dr. Kowalczyk when she goes somewhere?"

"Not as long as she notifies you where she's going, abides by her contract, and doesn't leave the Green Zone. Except for her weigh-ins at the Red Zone, of course."

"Thank you." Nettie signs off and turns to me. "Dinner will be ready in about an hour, if you can be back by then."

"No problem." I escape before I snatch a savory mushroom right from the pan.

The Green Zone's North Park looks a lot like the park by my megacomplex at this time of year. Benches, bushes, and winding paths meet me there. Rust-hued leaves cling to the trees. A scattering of loose leaves lie on the ground, not yet scooped up by the sweeperbots that emerge in the pre-dawn hours.

With my phone's exercise app turned on, I try to jog around the path, but the effort comes out more like a bouncing walk. My knees ache. My lungs go into hard labor. Feeling winded and as heavy as concrete, I slow to a careful walk.

A man and his leashed dog approach me, trotting in tandem. I nod hello. The man passes me as though I'm a dull hologram. Another thirty yards ahead, three teenage girls sprawl across a bench. They're howling like a pack of wolves, while a fourth girl wearing retro glasses tosses an electronic boomerang disc across the grass, out and back, out and back. None of them have the radically pierced, razor-shaved appearance of Edge chicks, yet something about their postures seems brash and hazardous. A bleach-blonde on the bench looks my way. Her arm springs out into a rigid point.

"You, Monstro!" she yells. "Didn't Noni tell you to stay clear of this part of the Zone?"

My steps falter as the other girls swivel in unison, affixing me to the path with their stares. It sounds like these girls know Jodine. Not good.

The girl with glasses raps her fist on the disc. "Yeah, I told her, Tibs. Looks like she has a bad memory."

Biting back a snappy retort, I resume walking. I'd better ignore these girls. Not only is fighting prohibited under my contract, I'm not exactly inhabiting a body that can fight back. Or sound tough, for that matter—not with this melodic voice. Heck, I probably can't even run far if things get dicey.

Tibs, the bleach-blonde, uncoils from the bench and strolls toward the path. "The North Park is off limits, Kowalczyk. You hurt our eyes. Bad enough we have to look at you in class, let alone on break. Just because you can afford to pay your tax fines doesn't mean you can flaunt your fat body in public."

"I'm leaving now," I say, trying to sound calm.

"You're leaving, all right," Noni drawls, pushing her glasses up the bridge of her nose. "But first we're gonna teach you a lesson, and beautify the park while we're at it." She gives a wicked grin, drops the boomerang disc, and pulls something slender from her jeans pocket. "Right, girls?"

The others chuckle and whoop, loping across the grass toward me.

My heart does a hard double flip. I don't wait to see what Noni pulled from her pocket. I break into a clumsy, heaving run.

CHAPTER 9

Stomping footsteps and feral howls of glee pursue me down the park path. Adrenaline spikes through my body. I gulp sharp breaths and toss a look at a security camera posted on a light post. Will I be attacked and bloody before auto-intervention kicks in and Enforcers are alerted?

"JO-dine, JO-dine," one girl chants behind me, while the others hoot and make wolf calls.

A pain in my side increases. I try to go faster but can't get past a rapid walk. Noni and her pack lag behind, obviously not trying hard to catch me. They're toying with me, relishing my panic.

I shriek as one of them yanks on the hem of my sweatshirt. A handful of something scratchy and crackling gets stuffed underneath, next to my skin. Another handful scrapes me at my neckline. Ouch, what the—

Leaves. Dead, dried leaves.

"Stop it, you android losers!" I yell as they herd me off the path. They cram more leaves under my clothes and shove some into my hair. They laugh, pushing and pulling on me. I stumble. They press me the rest of the way down, rolling me face-up. Two of them drape themselves across my arms while Noni bends over with the object she pulled from her jeans pocket. She snaps the cap off and waves the object in my face.

A tube of glaringly red lipstick.

I thrash. Better than a switchblade, but not something I want to be assaulted with. I work one arm free and swipe it at Noni, sending the retro glasses flying across the grass. Tibs leaps closer and helps pin down my arm. I kick, but my legs are as useful as a pair of worms dangling from an apple.

Noni gives a bark of a laugh. "You're feistier than normal, J." She attacks with the lipstick, scrawling and scribbling across my face and down my neck. "Oooh, much better," she says in a waspy voice.

Her pack titters. Noni caps the lipstick and hops off to retrieve her glasses while the others release my arms. They scamper away, their rowdy laughter reverberating around the trees and across the park grounds.

Lying on my back, I gulp for breath. When I can speak, I ravage the autumn air with a few expletives. Then I sit up with a groan and pull crackly leaves from under my sweats by the handfuls, and shake more from my hair. Disgusting, not to mention humiliating. Being helpless like this sucks. All the control over my body and my life, stripped away in a single instant. At the complete mercy of those girls' twisted whims.

I blink back some tears, finding it annoying I have them in the first place. I've never been this low on the social ladder before. Talk about the mucky basement bottom. I can't believe Jodine has to put up with this kind of thing.

I don't know why those girls think they can boss Jodine around, or treat her like she's worthless. I'm out here trying to exercise and help her be thinner. They could've just ignored me. Jodine should've warned Leo and me about the girls in her disclosure report, or at least about not venturing into the North Park. I should report this incident. There are rules about this sort of thing.

Although if I do tell Leo, he'll transfer me to the dorms instead of letting me stay with the Kowalczyks. Then I won't be able to find out if Dr. K. is anything like his genius mother. I won't be able to try out that rockin' HoloSports Center, not to mention the humongous holo-platform for RPGs in Jodine's room. With that big of a slide-out, my silver elf will be a foot tall rather than six inches. I'll lose my room with a window and a great view.

No, I'm not going to let those punk girls scare me into the dorms.

I'm not giving up that easily.

I limp back toward the Kowalczyks' house, loosening my hair and hiding my face with it. I feel the ghostly pressure of the lipstick tube across my cheeks as I walk. It lingers there, along with images of the protestors. Shoes kicking, hands shoving, voices shouting. Unbelievable. And flippin' scary. I've been attacked *twice* today. This job is hazardous.

What next? This is only my first day. I don't know how I can finish my assignment if things like this keep happening.

Inside the house, I aim for Jodine's room, but Nettie enters the living room before I get there.

She gives a strangled cry. "What happened— Is that blood?"

"Lipstick," I say past a clogginess in my throat. "I'm not hurt, just crushed and degraded. Please don't tell Jodine's parents or Leo. I'll just go to a different park from now on."

Nettie's expression shifts to pleased. "I like your spunk. Poor Jodine took to hiding in her room after mean pranks like that. I helped her find some assault support sites online a couple of years ago. Bullying help groups, prank resolution. If you want, I'll show you later."

I smile, which comes out shaky. "Thanks. I'm gonna clean up."

"Come to the kitchen to eat. We only use the dining room when Dr. and Mrs. Kowalczyk have time to join us."

I scrub up in Jodine's private bathroom off her bedroom. Or try to. The lipstick leaves a stubborn ruddy tint, making me look like I have a slight sunburn.

On my phone, I text Superguy. I need his sympathy even if I can't describe details.

> @geektastic007: having a bad day. whew, major
> trauma time.

Every ten seconds, I check my phone for a message. He doesn't answer before I leave for dinner. Very disappointing. I guess he's in the middle of doing something else.

The aromas in the kitchen pull me by the nose through the living room. Nettie bustles around the bright kitchen and sends two trays upward in the food elevator.

"Want help with anything?" I ask.

"I'm done, thanks, but you're welcome to cook with me anytime. Jodine loves doing that."

I inhale as Nettie places a steaming plate of food in front of me. Mmm, thick, buttery smells. Some sort of potato, chicken, mushroom, and onion dish that looks awesome.

"Dig in." Nettie settles herself on a stool. "The Institute tells me you need calories and protein to work out, so your body doesn't go into starvation mode and hinder your weight loss."

I eat in pure rapture. "I can see why you cook Basic, even though it's a lot of work. Do you *ever* serve frozen dinners or SpeedMeals?"

A horrified grimace contorts Nettie's face. "Never. I'm a purist. I was trained by my uncle in Basic ways, and there's no comparison to SpeedMeals."

"Except you can't beat SpeedMeals for convenience. Ten secs in the PlasmaWave, and presto!—dinnertime. It's cheaper, too."

"I have plenty of time, and the Kowalczyks aren't concerned about the credits."

"As tasty as Basic food is, I can see why Jodine has a hard time being slender. Why aren't you and her parents overweight?"

Nettie shakes her head. "It's not my place to tell Jodine to stop eating. Her problem wasn't necessarily what she ate. It was how much. She ate extra servings and snacked in between. Plus she didn't exercise. It adds up after a while."

I let that soak into my mind. That could be true, but I didn't grow up eating this kind of food. It'll make my weight loss way more challenging to have such tasty meals available. While Nettie may look like a friendly gnome, she cooks like an evil sorceress. "It doesn't sound like Jodine tried very hard."

"It was a vicious cycle. She'd eat to feel better, get discouraged from weighing more, then eat to feel better again."

My forkful of potatoes takes on a new meaning, and I marvel at it. I can sort of see what Nettie means. This food is already making me feel a lot better. Warmer. Safer. Funny how eating can do more than just satisfy hunger. Maybe it isn't always a lack of will power. So complex.

It's a good thing the Institute developed the Reducer program to help people out.

"How long have you lived here?" I ask.

"I was hired as a chef and nanny combo when Jodine was seven." Nettie chuckles. "She was a quiet little girl, curious and smart. Now, we have some great times in the kitchen, and she wallops me good at holo-chess. Quite often."

All at once I feel like an intruder, galaxies out of place. "It must be weird for you to see someone else in her body."

Another long exhale. "It's for her own good. She'll be back in six months, and maybe she'll be happier when her body matches what everyone wants it to look like."

Maybe she'll be happier?

I know she will—she has to be. That's my goal as a Reducer, the master plan. A chance to improve not only Jodine's appearance and self-image, but to change her whole life. I won't let her down.

The HoloSports Center in the game room displays a high-quality 3-D net and tennis court, and my ponytailed opponent hunkers down for the final serve. I brace for the shot.

Whack! My opponent serves a fast one, slicing across the court. I shift to a backhand, but not fast enough. The ball whooshes past me and a bell dings to signal the end of the match. Winner: my opponent.

Trounced again by a hologram. I command the game to shut down. It's hard to maneuver in this body, especially when

I have sore muscles from exercising for the past two days. I need to quit and prepare for my official welcome dinner with the Kowalczyks anyway. Nothing in Jodine's wardrobe fits besides what I'm wearing, but there might be time to put my sweats in the laundromachine if I hustle.

Wrapped in a fluffy pink robe that's a size too small, I sit in the laundry room while the machine gurgles and spins. I send messages from my phone while I wait, one to Blair, one to Krista, and one home. My best friends don't seem to be having any problem enjoying the rest of their fall break without me. Krista met this hot Italian guy at the Flash Point, and he introduced Blair to his older brother. Both Blair's and Krista's messages for the last few days have been absolutely staccato with exclamation marks, breathless dashes, and intense italics.

And here I am, stuck in a body that can only fit into one pair of sweats.

A hurricane of hot air blasts around inside the laundro-machine as the wash cycle switches to dry. In contrast to my friends' lives, there's not much new at home, except Granddad says the cost of cigarettes has doubled with the new health tax. It sounds like he's seriously going to try cutting back on the cancer-sticks so he can pay more on his bills. That's great, because it'll be way better for his health.

I wish I could see everyone, not just text them. Granddad and I both started reading e-books of this creepy science fiction novel called *Alien In The Machine*, but I'm sure discussing it on our phones won't be the same.

Enough sad stuff. This calls for a mood-boosting text session with Superguy. I re-read the message he sent an hour after my park attack, and some of the sharp edges melt from the ache of my homesickness.

> @superguy: major trauma deserves a major hug.
> [[[(hug)]]] hope ur night is better than ur day.

He's super hot *and* thoughtful. What a great combination. Too bad I can't exchange his cyberhug for a real one. His fingers on my arm in Leo's waiting room were soft and electric...what would it be like with both his arms around me? Shivery and outrageous, I bet. I type a new text.

> @geektastic007: i have sore muscles today u would NOT believe...or maybe u would.

I only have to wait one and a half minutes before he logs on and answers.

> @superguy: poor geekling! yep. part of the job so get used to it.

> @geektastic007: have u listened to Beatn Golden yet? u like?

> @superguy: yes & they are awwwwesome. i dunno why i hadn't heard them before. love the technoguitar dude—he's stellar.

> @geektastic007: they're a new band. on the net-stream all the time now.

> @superguy: that explains it. i haven't streamed much music lately. last night i went out for sushi with friends. u like?

"Drying completed," a honeyed voice informs me. The laundromachine. I snatch out the sweats before they're dumped onto the auto-folding table, and return to more exciting activities.

> @geektastic007: haven't ever tried it. my grand-father says all fish have worms so my mom is too

grossed out to buy it.

@superguy: lol. never? wow. u should try it sometime, live a little.

@geektastic007: i might someday but not while i'm Reducing.

@superguy: sorry, my friend Rajeev is here at my apt. gotta go.

@geektastic007: ok i'm off to eat dinner anyway.

Always too short. I wish we could keep messaging for hours. It'd be nice if we could set up an uninterrupted time to text, but I've asked him before and he never answers. Does he not *want* to chat for more than a few skimpy minutes? Does he have such a hectic schedule that he can't spare an hour?

I scurry off to get dressed and fix my hair. This morning I washed Jodine's curly locks for the first time, and to tell the truth, I still feel vaguely homicidal from the battle of combing it out.

In the dining room, Dr. and Mrs. K. are already seated.

Nettie walks in alongside a servbot that carries steaming platters of food. The servbot is a tiered cart on wheels, plain and serviceable. "Stop," Nettie says, and it halts beside the table.

I try not to drool on my plate while we pass food. What a spread. Garlicked lamb chops, baked stuffed butternut squash, a fruit salad, sliced pickles, and herbed rice. All nourishing calories I can work off, I'm sure.

"This looks great," I say. "Thanks, Nettie."

Mrs. K. sips from her wineglass, a distant look in her eyes. "Yes, quite lovely. I do hope this brainmap shuffling will bring about some results."

"Give it time, dear," Dr. K. says. "We'll know in a few

weeks. Right, Morgan?"

"Right." Man. Nothing like a little pressure.

"It'd be wonderful if things go back to how they used to be," Nettie says. "More fun and relaxed, like when I first came here. I remember Jodine laughing more."

Mrs. K. pats her mouth with a napkin. "I'd like a change, too. Somehow it doesn't seem fair. We decided to have one child, even though we were approved for two. I always thought I'd have more in common with a daughter, and that's why I selected to have one. I certainly can't relate to a daughter who's a hundred pounds overweight."

"I've never had much in common with her." Dr. K. chuckles. "Then again, I'm not a female."

That squirmy, fly-on-the-wall eavesdropper feeling again. I sincerely doubt my parents dissect me like this in front of dinner guests. When the conversation turns to politics, I eat fruit salad and stay mute. Even Nettie seems well informed. Thankfully, the conversation shifts when Nettie asks Mrs. K. how her new painting commission is coming along.

Mrs. K. brightens over a forkful of squash. "Quite well. The composition is sketched out, and I've begun blocking in the colors."

I start to ask what kinds of things she paints, but Dr. K. speaks first.

"I wish my dilemmas could be solved as easily as yours, my dear. I've hit countless dead-ends on my ion thruster theory—"

"You simply cannot compare your physics to art," Mrs. K. says with a frayed edge to her voice. "I don't know why you even try."

Nettie clears her throat. "Is anyone ready for dessert?"

She places plates on the servbot and instructs it to fetch the next course.

As the servbot rolls away to his loading station, I toss a curious look at Dr. K. "What do you want your ion thruster to do?" I ask, the question mild and tentative in Jodine's melodic voice. "Something tricky with space probes?"

It's Dr. K.'s turn to brighten. "No, I'm experimenting with electromagnetic fields and ion propulsion, trying to bypass barriers of friction, mass, and gravity. If I can do that and increase the total thrust potential, I can create an ion engine for passenger airlines."

I stare at his clean-shaven face. Ion thrusters are notoriously slow accelerating. Dr. K. is either a genius like his famous mother—or a lunatic. "Is that possible?"

"That's what I'm exploring. After dessert would you like a brief tour of my workspace?"

"Sure!" I notice Mrs. K.'s rigid expression and curb my enthusiasm. Obviously there's some sort of awkward conflict or competition thing going on here between her and Dr. K. That's not something I want to get in the middle of.

The servbot returns with a tray of pumpkin cake squares adorned with dollops of whipped cream. Nettie passes the plates. The first bite slides down my throat, pumpkiny and creamy.

Oooh, decadent shivers.

Mrs. K. frowns. "Should you be eating that, Morgan?"

The next bite freezes halfway to my mouth. All at once the dessert seems as appealing as sawdust and shaving cream. *What am I doing?* I'm not getting paid to sit around and eat pumpkin cake. I'm getting paid to lose weight.

"You're right. I shouldn't be." I throw Nettie an apologetic look.

"I don't know what you were thinking, Nettie," Mrs. K. says. "Desserts have to be nonexistent or extremely low-cal while Morgan's staying with us."

"I'm sorry, Mrs. Kowalczyk." Nettie stares at her plate. "Pumpkin is nutritious, and I was thinking of this as a special occasion."

I twirl whipped cream with my fork while everyone else finishes eating.

After a murmured good night, Mrs. K. disappears into the elevator pod. Dr. K. motions to me and strolls off. As I follow, my glance skims the painting on the wall. My gaze slips from the roasted chicken, bounces over olives and sausages, and settles on a signature at the bottom right edge.

Janeth Kowalczyk, the signature reads.

I gape. Mrs. K. *hand-painted* this feast the old-fashioned way, with brushes and actual paint? I don't know why I didn't figure that out. No wonder Jodine hides her muddy little picture in the closet. With a mother who can paint like this, it'd be intimidating to try any artwork, let alone hang something where Mrs. K. might see it.

It doesn't make sense, but looking at that painting makes me feel...bad. Off balance. Like something isn't right about me, some sort of special *something* that I'm missing.

I hurry to join Dr. K. at the elevator pod, a flush of nervousness spreading over me like a bad rash. This entire household is packed with colossal intellect and talent. Even Nettie has her super cooking abilities.

Does Jodine ever feel this insignificant?

CHAPTER 10

The elevator pod returns, and Dr. K. and I step inside.

"Up," he orders. We rise to the next floor, where I follow him across a polished entryway. He signs us in to a huge workroom. Long tables hold tangles of batteries, coils, and electrical equipment. A large oscilloscope sits nearby. Wallscreens display advanced mathematical equations. It's a cluttery mess, but it looks like an industrious and happening place.

"Super," I say, and catch sight of something familiar on a nearby wallscreen. "Hey, that's the formula for quantum energy."

"Very good. I'm impressed you know that."

"I learned it in an extra credit physics class. I love science and math."

"Excellent." Dr. K. steps over to a boxy-looking device and pats it with a geeky gleam in his eye. "Along with developing a booster to solve the acceleration problem, this is what will make my theory work. An antigravity module." He describes its inner workings, and I actually follow three-quarters of what he's saying.

"Wow," I say, the science gears in my brain spinning.

"What projects have you been involved with?" Dr. K. shoves aside a voltage meter and leans his elbows on a table. "I like to hear what inquiring young minds are doing."

I try not to panic. After what he's just revealed, my fiddlings at the Catalyst Club seem trivial. "My science club did a project on electromagnetic energy. We messed around with transformers, connecting them to vacuum globes and making plasma. It was fun, watching the lightning bolts zap and fizz when we touched the globe."

"Gives a satisfying tingle to the fingertips too."

I laugh. *Satisfying.* Yeah, right. I'm glad he's not as intimidating as I thought he'd be.

Dr. K. gives me an intent look, then smiles and shakes his head. "You're clearly not Jodine. She doesn't care for technology or science, or being known as Caroline Mahoney's granddaughter. She's more of a right-brained, artistic type like Janeth."

Having seen the klutzy still life in her closet, I doubt that. I murmur a neutral reply.

"ERT's such an astounding procedure," Dr. K. says. "To be able to gather the consciousness of one person—everything she said or did or remembered—and compact that into a transferrable data file."

"Yes!" I say. "The tech is what got me interested in the program. I was researching neurons and how the scientists chemically activated trillions of synapses to fire, to release memories. I was amazed how after they recorded the brain waves to make a brainmap file, they came up with the idea of making an opposite signal to cancel out the ones in the body."

"Well, it's more like rendering them inactive than

canceling," Dr. K. says. "It's loosely similar to sending radio waves, using a transistor to mix the waves and their opposites together."

"Right, which makes your body prepped for either suspended animation or insertion of someone else's brainmap, depending on whether you're a Reducer or a Loaner." I'm sure my extreme grin is making me look giddy. It's fantastic to talk with someone who understands inverse polarity and ERT technology.

Dr. K. straightens and surveys his lab. "I'm sorry to say, I should get back to work. I'm admittedly single-minded during a project. We'll talk another time."

My excitement swirls away. I really hope there will be another time. He accompanies me out the door and across the entryway.

"Thanks for the mad scientist tour," I say.

The sound of Dr. K.'s chuckle follows me as I step into the elevator pod.

In Jodine's room, I stream some music and dance to shake off tension and burn calories. After two songs I flop onto the bed. Not much endurance power with this body. This is going to be a long, long six months.

While my breathing settles and the music rocks on, I check out the Masters of the Cyberverse posters and deduce that Jodine's game character is a half-tiger, half-fairy creature called a liegerdeen. The green airbot emerges from the ceiling vent, and I watch it drift for a bit before I cross to the desk and sign into the game. I guide my silver elf on a jewel quest. When I reach the treasure, a crawly sensation of being watched ripples down my back. I whip around to find the airbot behind my left shoulder.

"Go higher, you little pest," I say. "What're you filtering? Do I have bad breath or something?"

It drifts a few inches upward and gives an abrupt mechanical purr.

"Come on, float higher."

It tips a little to one side, as if contemplating my words.

"*Higher,*" I say, my voice firm. "Or I'll be tempted to solder your little vent door closed."

It floats off.

Silly heap of circuitry. The critter is too curious for its own good.

After I dictate my daily activity log, I change into a worn crocodile-cartoon nightshirt and lie on the bed with the lights off and the blinds open, watching the night sky shimmer with stars. The stuffed animals on the window seat huddle in a furry cluster. I wish they were people instead of toys, so I'd have someone to talk to. The words of Blair and Krista and Superguy only exist in cyberspace, and I can't see people I know in real life. I'm not allowed to mingle with any of Jodine's friends, either. I'll have to ask Leo if I can make new friends while living offsite.

I don't want to be stuck with six months of near-nothingness for a social life.

That, to say the least, would be brutal.

The Monday of my fifth weigh-in arrives, my seventeenth day on the job. I ride the MT until I see signs for the Green Zone's west section. I want to get in a good walk before I go to the Institute, and I've found a new park where I can exercise without fear of bumping into wolf-girls.

A motherly looking woman sitting across the aisle gives me a warm smile, and I smile back. It's great to get a reaction, and a positive one at that. Hardly anyone interacts with me on the MT anymore. When I was in my own body, businesswomen smiled, guys checked me out, and chicks scoped out my clothes. Now, it's usually like I'm not worthy of a glance.

I rub my hands over my face. My *freckled* face. Right now every neuron in my brain shrieks for normalcy, for looking slender. For being smooth-haired, brown-eyed Morgan Dey. The real me. I just don't feel like myself in this body.

After I get off the MT, I jog along the park paths, passing benches and gazebos. In a short time, however, my knees start to creak and ache, and my feet begin to tingle. Pain lances through my chest. I stagger and clutch the front of my sweats. Maybe what Granddad fears is a real possibility. At the moment it sure seems like this body's going to die on me.

Even if not, it doesn't feel good.

I slow down and try to catch my breath. Air in, air out. Easy does it. I just need to cool down, and I'll be all right. If I don't panic, I should be able to work through the tingles and the aches and the thundering percussion under my rib cage. I pull out my phone in case I need to call for help. After about seven long minutes, my chest pains subside. My heart—Jodine's heart—finally thumps at a more normal pace. I take a shuddering breath.

From now on, I need to pay closer attention to overload signals in this body. I can't jog at full speed like I used to with my own body.

A muscular middle-age man runs by, intent on his course. Most people I've seen here are a bunch of athletic types focused on their own bodies, not interested in chatting with other joggers. Seventeen days is a long time to be on this job with only Nettie to talk to, but Leo didn't like my idea to make new friends. Apparently friends cause "potential complications" and are prohibited. He warned that any contacts must be kept extremely casual and told me not to bring anyone to the Kowalczyks' house.

He's also paranoid about me possibly seeing someone who knows Jodine. The more I stay inside and keep to myself, he said, the simpler things will be. I didn't tell him about my run-in with Noni and her wolf pack. I refuse to be housebound or shipped off to the Clinic for the rest of my assignment.

Okay, back to work. Taking a bracing breath, I glance up and notice a guy in gray sweats moving along the path ahead of me, slow and steady. He has short brown hair. His body looks even heavier than mine. Puffing a little, I close in on the guy.

Whether he's friendly or not, I'll soon find out.

CHAPTER 11

I catch up and walk beside the overweight guy. "Hi," I say, breathless. "Having a good walk?"

"Good? I dunno if I'd use that adjective." The guy's words are wedged between huffs and puffs. "I've barely made it a tenth of the way around the park. And I'm bushed."

"Want company? I need to finish a lap myself."

He really looks at me, then. "Hey, that's nice. This is my first day of serious exercising. I need all the support I can get."

In return, I really look at him. Brown eyes with a mischievous glint. A longish nose. A wide face with a double chin. Hmm. But he seems friendly, and I need someone to talk to, not a movie actor or a male model.

"I'm trying to lose weight," I say. "I've lost about a dozen pounds out of a hundred."

"I'm jealous!" the guy says, wheezing. "I need to lose a hundred thirty pounds. Not gonna try jogging yet. Walking's enough for me right now."

"Yeah, don't overdo it. I don't want to have to call for a medic."

He flashes me a look of amusement. We approach a bench, and he waves an arm at it. "Mind if we sit? Gotta catch…my breath."

The metal bench creaks as he sits down, and it creaks more as I sit next to him. Our thighs touch a little on the seat. I try not to think about it.

"I'm Matt." The guy holds out a sweaty palm. "Matt Williams."

I shake his hand with my own clammy one. "I'm Mor—Jodine." Oops, almost messed up there. "Jodine Kowalczyk."

"That's a complicated last name," Matt says. "How do you spell it?"

I laugh to stall for time while I try to remember. "With way too many z's and k's."

"Okay." He laughs, too. "Here's my ever-so-flattering bio. I'm nineteen, live on the forty-fourth floor of a nearby megacomplex, and teach primary school part-time. Last but not least, I'm turning over a new fitness leaf. By the end of summer I plan to be a lean, mean, handsome machine. Or as close to that as I can get."

"Nice." I hesitate. He's so fresh and open and honest. I'm not sure what to say about myself. I can't pretend I've earned my education certificate, because then I'd have to invent an occupation. And I'd be violating confidentiality rules if I say anything about the Kowalczyks, where I live, or being a Reducer.

"I'm almost eighteen," I say. True, since Jodine's birthday is in March, mine in December. "I live in north Green Zone, and I'm doing my schooling with a private tutor."

Matt nods. "Nice. Tutors make for faster learning."

I give a weak smile and stare across the grass. What a

way to start out an acquaintance, by inventing a lie or two. Like Granddad always says, relationships should be built on honesty and trust, not fabrications. I'm pretending to be someone I'm not…a definite negative of the Institute's offsite assignments. But that should be all the fibs I need to tell. If I ever see this guy again, I'll stick to impersonal topics. Like the weather.

"Are you ready to walk again?" Matt asks. "I have to get rolling, or I won't be able to squish in a shower before work."

"Ready when you are." Another lie. This encounter didn't last nearly long enough. I love having real-life company, especially someone as nice as this guy. I suppress a sigh and accompany him for six laborious minutes until we reach the far corner of the park.

"I come here every morning except Thursdays," I say, thinking of the one weekday when I walk after my afternoon weigh-ins. "Maybe I'll see you again."

"I plan to be here every day, Miss Fitness," Matt says, and waves vigorously.

I smile as I watch him go down the street. Yes! My gray October day has just been radically improved by a very friendly guy named Matt Williams.

If we do end up meeting every day, I'll just have to keep him a secret.

When I reach the Institute grounds, I pause to catch my breath after my hike from the MT shelter. At the gates I see Enforcers are keeping the entrance clear of WHA protesters. Good. Not to sound uncharitable or anything, but I hope the protesters who attacked me are rotting in jail cubicles somewhere.

At the Clinic, I enter the Weigh Center and sit in one of the horrid green waiting room chairs until my name is called. The usual data streaming commences. I'm informed I've lost twelve pounds to date. That jives with the scale in Jodine's bathroom so it's no surprise, but I leave the building feeling more like fifty pounds lighter.

To celebrate, after I reach the Kowalczyks' and eat lunch, I text Granddad. If he's bonding with his cigarettes on the balcony lounge, I hope he has his phone with him.

> Hey, Granddad. Are you there?

He responds after a few seconds.

> Hi, sweetie. Let's see your face. Call me.

> I'm not allowed to do that.

Hopefully he hasn't forgotten already.

> My screen mode's been disabled for privacy. I can only do texts and emails. How are you feeling?

> I'm feeling like I'm not talking to my granddaughter. How do I know it's you? Can't you do an old-fashioned call with just voice?

> No, I can't use my Loaner's voice.

I hate these limitations. It's like living in a box with my eyes poked out.

Granddad's response scrolls across my phone.

> That's absurd. It's bad enough I'm talking to a brain clone who thinks she's my granddaughter—who's really some computer file downloaded

into some overweight girl.

Ouch. That's a terrible way to put it. Trying to quit smoking must be making him irritable.

> I'm not a brain clone. My consciousness is just hanging out in someone else's body.

> If your brain waves are copied, you're a brain-washed copy who thinks you're Morgan. You're not Morgan.

> Then how would I remember my memories, who I am and who I know?

> Copied. You're programmed to remember, to think you're the real thing.

He's so stubborn, he's making me feel like I'm not myself. I don't know how else to convince him. Time for a new topic.

> What have you been doing lately?

> Trying to avoid a bunch of pesky holo-ads for a free year's supply of electronic cigarettes. Can't even walk by the superstore without being harassed. I keep telling them I'm already cutting back on the regular kind.

I hate to think how crispy and blackened his lungs must look while he exercises his so-called right to smoke the real things. Using e-cigarettes is a lot healthier, especially since they don't have nicotine in them anymore. It's too bad the ban on smoking didn't work a few years ago—people just started growing their own black-market tobacco. I sigh. At least he's trying to cut back.

> Have you read any more of Alien In The Machine?

Uh, nope. Sorry, can't get into it. I got a new sci-fi
novel yesterday. Androids infiltrating humans by
taking over their minds. The people started up
this massive underground revolution. Guess I'll
get back to it. Talk to you later.

As he disconnects, a painful swell surges through me. I
exchange a glassy stare with a stuffed cat on the window seat.
Granddad has abandoned our discussion book, and I know
why. No voices to hear each other's excitement. No faces to
show our emotions. No blueberry tea and roasted sunflower
seeds, the scents mingling in the air with our shared words.
He's avoiding the feeling of loss. Withdrawing.

To distract myself from those depressing thoughts, I flop
in front of the deskscreen and navigate to a physics game site.
The numbers soothe me. The formulas stimulate my brain. Yet
one persistent corner of my mind keeps ricocheting back to
Granddad's words. A more serious distraction is in order.

I tap up the TeenDom site.

@geektastic007: hellooooo, r u there, superguy?

Five minutes creak by. Man, I hate being stuck with online
relationships only. I try again.

@geektastic007: feeling like the last humanoid on
the planet. anyone home in ur galaxy beyond?

I wait ten more draggy minutes. No use. Superguy's probably out dancing or watching holovids with friends. I'll try a
game instead. I sign in and zone out with my silver elf, hiking
around a mountain village. As I enter a clearing, a rumbling
cyber-roar splits the air.

Dragon.

I need to hide—fast. My wings unfurl and my tiger legs

propel me upward into the branches of a tall tree, and none too soon. Massive scales and wicked claws pass me by within inches. After another tense moment, the dragon's roars fade.

Triumph washes over me. Score!

A chirruping breaks my concentration. The airbot. I shake my head and squint at its green shape hovering nearby. Then I stare at the crumpled form of my silver elf lying dead on the snowy RPG platform. Burned to a crisp from dragon fire.

What? How did that happen? I just flew into the air and landed safely in a tree—

Hold it. My game character doesn't have springy tiger legs or fairy wings. I'm a silver elf, not a liegerdeen. And I can't have accessed Jodine's character, because she has blocks on her account. *What is going on?*

With my heart in high gear, I order the platform off. I push myself back from the deskscreen, chair wheels skidding.

This can't be right. I saw the tiger-fairy jump into the tree, I really did. It's as if my brain experienced a hallucination in liegerdeen-land while the actual game dragon annihilated my silver elf. Whatever that means. Did Jodine play this part of the game before, and somehow I've tapped into that memory?

It makes sense. In a twisted, I-think-I'm-becoming-certifiable way.

I grab my phone and access Leo's number at the Institute, praying he's available. My prayers are answered when his text pops up onscreen.

How can I help you, Morgan?

I just had something scary happen, and I need to know what's going on.

I'm surprised the voice-to-text app can keep up with the

words tumbling from my mouth.

> Take a deep breath, slow down. Tell me your
> problem.

I draw in air, latching onto his calm words.

> I think Jodine is haunting me.

I describe the liegerdeen vision and the dragon-perpetrated homicide.

> Do you know what's happening?

Leo's answer scrolls out.

> What you've experienced is a residual memory.
> Sometimes a stray memory or 2 hides in the
> recesses of the Loaner's brain during mapping,
> so there's a potential for a Reducer to experience
> them. It's not a big deal.

My trust in the Transfer process experiences a 6.5-magnitude quake on the Richter scale. I stare at his words.

> This is NORMAL?

> It's rare, but yes, it's fairly normal for a Reducer
> who lives in a Loaner's environment. That kind of
> setting seems to trigger stray memories, if there
> are any.

I don't know what to say to that. It doesn't fit with my black-and-white view of science and Electromagnetic Resonance Transfer. It's messy and vague, not as clean as it should be—like I told the protesters it was. It should involve tidy packages of memories, swapped with precision and no overlaps whatsoever.

Well, even though I won't keep her memories, since my original brainmap will be put back into my own body, I DON'T like experiencing them.

The flashes may be unnerving, but that's it. I'm sure you'll be able to adjust.

Yeah, sure. I fight to keep my words polite.

What if a few of MY memories are missed at the end of my assignment, when my current brainmap is generated so it can be canceled out of this body? The memories would be stranded in Jodine's brain.

There's a much less likelihood of your waves getting stuck in her brain recesses, since they're not hers. The mapping should be quite complete.

Only *if* no waves of mine are hiding out somewhere. It doesn't sound like an absolute certainty.

I would've liked to know about these residuals in my briefing. Are there any other secrets I should know?

The residuals aren't secret. They're mentioned in your contract. Fine print. You have an e-copy that you can examine any time.

The steam of my indignation fizzles. Guess I should do that, although I *have* been busy trying to lose weight.

I guess that's all, then.

One more thing while I have you on the phone, Leo says.

> Please study the file on workouts. I've checked
> your log, and you could use some variation in
> your weight training. Alternate between upper
> and lower body to give your muscles a chance to
> recover and then build themselves up. One day
> for upper, the next day for lower.

How embarrassing to be lectured about my regimen. I mumble an agreement, and hang up before I say something I'll regret later. He could've warned me about this residual memory stuff. Maybe it doesn't happen often, since not many Reducers live offsite, but I don't like it. I also don't like the slight possibility of Jodine ending up with a memory or two of mine, even if I keep all my original memories in my own backup.

Those memories aren't something I want to share. They're *mine.*

I wonder if that painting session I saw while in the closet was also a residual. Did any memory flashes happen when I was in Shelby Johnson's body? I'll never know. The whole concept of residual waves is more than simply "unnerving," as Leo calls it.

But one thing I do know. Jodine is way stellar at Masters of the Cyberverse. She can leap into a tree ten paces from a dragon's snout and not get incinerated. Though I don't want her memories, I wouldn't mind channeling some of *that* skill and timing.

Heaving a sigh, I look down at myself. I'd love to ditch this body and go back to my own self, pronto. But I want to help Jodine and be a part of the Institute, and no one said it would be easy. Not even Leo. It's time to get my chin back up, go downstairs, and work out.

Maybe I can fit into something different, now that I've lost some weight. That'd be a great shot of encouragement. I rummage around and find a grass-green sweat suit. It's snug across my stomach and thighs when I pull it on, but I'll go for it. Wearing the same sweats for nearly three straight weeks is beginning to give me navy nightmares.

I find Mrs. K. in the gym wearing a bright pink tank top and shorts, toning her legs on a resistance machine. She looks quite fit for her age.

"I can come back later," I say.

"No, I'm finished." Mrs. K. swings into a sitting position. "I'm usually out of here by now, except today I got a phone call—" Her brown eyes go deer-startled. "You're wearing green. Have you lost that much weight already?"

"Twelve pounds. These sweats are pretty tight, though."

"Where are those navy sweats—in Jodine's room?" A look of zeal takes over her face. She tears out of the exercise room, knocking over an empty water bottle.

I frown as the bottle spins on the floor. Has the woman gone crazy? I run after her to see what the massive deal is.

When I reach the living room, Mrs. K. emerges from Jodine's room clutching the navy sweats with a ferocious gleam in her eye. I trail her to the kitchen. She marches to the incinerator receptacle, stuffs the sweats inside, and orders it to lock. While the incinerator checks for human tissue and blood to prevent foul play, Mrs. K. spins toward me with a jubilant expression.

"I've been wanting to do this for eight months," she says. "I was sick of those sweats. They're the only thing Jodine wore. Her Fat Outfit. I refused to let her buy anything larger, even though it was mortifying to let her go to school that way."

"I was pretty tired of them myself," I say, appalled at her

intensity. I'm also appalled that this act of cremation leaves me stranded with the green sweats, which will be uncomfortable until I lose more weight.

The incinerator gives a rumble and a whoosh, and the navy sweats are history.

Hands on hips, Mrs. K. glares at the machine. "All Jodine would do was sit around. Read, play games, watch vids, and *eat*. Those sweats symbolized her laziness. Her failure. I hated them every time I saw them."

I take a step backward. Whoa. Talk about intense motherly ire. Poor Jodine.

Nettie ambles in with a bag of flour and lifts her eyebrows at us.

"We had a burning ceremony," Mrs. K. explains. "To celebrate Morgan's success. She's fit Jodine's body into something besides those repulsive navy sweats."

"I see," Nettie says, wisely noncommittal. As Mrs. K. strides out the autodoor, Nettie turns to me. "I could tell you'd lost weight already. Good job."

"Thanks." I glance at the incinerator, and another wave of pity rises up for Jodine. How sad that her mother punishes her for her weight. Mrs. K. also made it sound like Jodine spent all her time in her room, alone. "Doesn't Jodine have friends to hang with?"

"One main friend," Nettie says. "She comes over every week or two, or at least she did before Jodine signed up at the Institute. Shy mouse of a thing, very sweet. A few years ago Jodine had a daily visitor, a loudmouth brat named Noni. I wouldn't call her a friend. Dr. Kowalczyk ended up forbidding her to come over after some things went missing around the house."

Noni, as in the leader of the wolf pack? That's a shock.

But the banishment explains part of Noni's bristly treatment of Jodine. A lonesome wave splashes over me. "I wish I could see my own friends, Blair and Krista."

A memory of Blair's ten-year-old upturned nose and pixied hair pops into my mind's eye. One spring day she arrived in reading class, assigned to sit next to Krista and me. We didn't get much classwork done that morning. We were too busy setting up colonies on our desks with these adorable little cartons of protein-and-fruit snacks from Blair's backpack. The treats came in the shapes of robots and space shuttles.

My swell of homesickness rises higher.

Nettie smiles, and it's a tender expression. "You can help if you'd like." She pats the bag of flour on the counter, sending a puff of white upward and the red airbot downward. "I'm making a low-calorie quiche. I'll let you roll the crust."

"Cool." I'll hit the gym after we finish.

Nettie measures flour and instructs me in the fine art of using a rolling pin. I push up my sleeves and plop the dough onto the counter, smiling as the stuff squishes under my fingers. It reminds me of fooling around with play-dough in primary school. Good times. I like experiencing my own memories instead of Jodine's. That way I know I'm still myself.

The red airbot filters overhead as I poof flour into the air. The green airbot rushes in from the ceiling vent with a small chirp, ready to help purify the breathing spaces for humankind.

A few seconds later, I glance up and flinch to see the green bot hovering by my shoulder. "Hey, twerp. What's your deal?"

Nettie gives a smirky smile while stirring something aromatic on the stove. "It likes you."

"No. Really?" I snort. She makes it sound like the critter is alive.

"I'll let you in on a secret. Dr. Kowalczyk had that one re-programmed to react to Jodine. He thought she could use a friend, since she spends a lot of time in her room."

My shoulder muscles tense. No way. Its sensors must be really confused, then, unless it's just responding to my appearance. "It thinks I'm Jodine?"

"Yes, and she doesn't have a clue it's been tweaked. She loves the silly thing."

I eye the airbot, trying to imagine what's going on in its tiny circuitry brain. "It's cute, but it's kind of a pest. It keeps invading my personal space."

The airbot trills, sounding almost indignant.

"Here, taste this." Nettie holds out a wooden spoon with a dab of quiche filling on it. "Does it need more oregano?"

"I doubt I can tell." I take a taste anyway. The flavors explode in my mouth, dancing on my tongue. Lusty onion. Fragrant herbed zucchini. A pungent medley of garlic, basil, and oregano.

And somehow, I *know*. My taste buds—Jodine's taste buds—decide for me.

"Almost perfect," I say. "It needs this much more." I grab the jar and shake out a precise dash over the pan.

As Nettie stirs it in, I stare at my hand and back away.

Freaky, freaky, freaky. Did some renegade residual memory make me act on autopilot?

Because *that* was most definitely not me.

CHAPTER 12

The next morning, I walk from the MT shelter to the park, anxious to see if Matt will show up as he promised. Already he's the lighthouse in my life's monotonous sea of strenuous exercise. Which is kind of scary, and maybe also pathetic. Poor Matt. He's unwittingly signed on as my one-man social committee. That'll teach him to be friendly.

I scan the area while I jog-walk. Where is he?

One-third into my lap, I spot him ahead on the path. I hurry to catch up, gaining on him easily.

"Hi, Matt! It's so sly to see you again," I call out. No, that sounds too eager. *Keep it light and easygoing, girl.* I reach him and match his pace. "I'm surprised you showed up, since you had such a hard workout yesterday."

Matt gives me an amused look. "I'm serious about losing weight. I even got myself a handy little exercise app, to help nag me on my walks." He pats the side pocket of his sweatpants, where a phone clip is attached.

"I have one of those on my phone, too." Further words flee from my head. I want to be witty and kind, approachable and worthy of being a new friend. If I say something stupid, he might not want to hang out with me.

"If you live north of here, why do you come to West Park?" Matt asks.

"Trouble with some classmates. They banished me from North Park."

"Is that why you're not in regular classes?"

"Yeah." Mostly and indirectly true.

He throws me a searching look, a smile playing on his lips as he scans my hair and face. Funnily enough, it's almost as though he's checking me out, and liking what he sees. "What other exercising do you do? I take it you haven't lost a dozen pounds just from park walks."

"Nope. I do HoloSports, treadmill, and resistance machines. My, um, parents have those at home. I never used their gym much, up until a few weeks ago." I chew my lip. I don't know if I'm crossing a line giving out this info. It implies my Loaner family can afford things like that. So does the tutor fib, actually.

"I joined a city gym near my apartment."

"Nice." I concentrate on my breathing. There's a soundless hum between us, a vibrating space that's empty yet full of *something*. What is it, mutual interest? Sheer awkwardness? My frail psyche, overly worried about ending up with a big fat zero for a social life?

I shake my head to dislodge the feeling. Matt mentioned joining the city gym. I wonder if he'd be interested in joining the Reducer program instead. He doesn't have to go through all this torture himself. Or…maybe I don't want to tell him. Then someone else would be inside his body, losing weight for him at the Clinic. That'd be the end of my walking buddy.

After another quarter-lap, he motions to a bench. I sit with him, bunching my legs so our thighs won't bump this time. I watch a cluster of pigeons peck in the grass, their self-important struts making me smile.

"Do you like your job at the school?" I ask. Lame question, very lame.

He shrugs. "It's a job. I teach nine- and ten-year-olds. It's more like occasional directing, since the online curriculum does most of the work. All I have to do is play babysitter and keep the little squirrels on task. I'm also getting some reading done, and if I use a portable screen, I can trek around the classroom for exercise at the same time."

"That's smart." I scuff at the ground with the toe of my sneaker.

Matt's impish brown eyes study me. "What about you? After you get your certificate, are you landing a job or going for more education?"

"Not sure. I might try tech school once I save up enough. Last year in my spare time I worked in a warehouse shipping online orders, like transistors and circuit boards and wiring, but I'd rather have something more challenging."

"Me, too. I don't think I'll stick with teaching. Not sure yet what else I want to do."

"Yeah. Tough to decide."

He shifts. I scratch my arm. We watch the pigeons for a few more minutes.

I clear my throat. Okay, I'm going to ask, for his own good. Because I'm feeling strangely attached to him already, and I care about his ultimate health. If I say this right, maybe it won't sound rude. "Um, have you ever heard of The Body Institute, and their Reducer program? They have a cool thing going on for weight loss." I wince. Not subtle, but hopefully inoffensive.

He grins the biggest grin I've seen him make so far, which transforms his face into something quite captivating. "Definitely. They bombard me with zealous ads every time I get a fine notice. But I've decided to do this myself. To prove I can."

"Impressive," I say, and mean it.

Matt glances at his phone. "Whoops, I'd better get going. Class awaits."

No way. He can't leave already. I'm not ready to go back to the efficient emptiness of the Kowalczyks' personal gym for the rest of the day. "We should walk sometime when you don't have to run off to classes," I say on impulse. "Are you done working by around fifteen thirty? On Thursdays I'm here in the afternoon instead of the morning."

His grin reappears. It's dizzying, somehow personal, and directed at *me*. "I only teach Monday through Wednesdays. So I could meet you here Thursday afternoon. If you want, afterward we can go to a café, and I'll buy you something low-cal to drink."

"That'd be really great." I keep my voice calm, even though all my nerve endings have sprung into a haywire dance. Awesome! He wants to see me again. An official friendship has been born, despite my bumbling attempts at casual conversation. Who crimping *cares* what my contract says about not making friends. It's worth the risk. This guy's nice, and somehow on my wavelength. What Leo doesn't know won't hurt him—er, me.

I walk the rest of the path with Matt, my steps infused with a bounce. It's hard to believe, but I have a date of sorts with this teacher guy—and boy-oh-boy, am I looking forward to it.

In the middle of Wednesday night, the blustery patter of rain hitting my window awakens me. I flop onto my back and moan. No, not rain! It has to stop. Matt might not meet me at the park if the weather is like this. A frown gathers on my forehead as I lie under Jodine's comforter. The minutes crawl by. As the last shreds of sleep desert me, a mighty rumble starts under my belly button and roars around my abdomen.

This traitorous body is hungry again. Not merely hungry, but starving. Famished, ravenous, and out-of-control crazy with the desire to bite into something crunchy or creamy or salty. If only I had a big bag of chips. Or a chunk of that drooly-looking lasagna I saw in the freezer yesterday, something Nettie must've made before I became a Reducer.

Yeah, the lasagna!

I bolt upright, wadding the comforter between my arms. No, wait. I can't do that. Nettie might wake up if I make noises in the kitchen. I'll be busted for sure. I also have a Clinic weigh-in tomorrow morning. Very bad timing.

I lie back down, close my eyes, and try to count sheep. A herd of woolly sheep, standing in a field. The first one jumps over a fence. *One.* Another one joins it, as fluffy and creamy as the first. *Two.* A pair of sheep now, standing together with soft ricotta and mozzarella coats, mixed with a little oregano and basil—

I bunch my pillow over my head. Why so much trouble tonight? I've been hungry before and haven't ever been this close to giving in. My defenses are way down. I know it's partly from the rain possibly messing up my plans to meet Matt. The other part is doing this job. I'm tired of trying to lose weight, fed up with deprivation and sweating. I miss seeing Granddad and having our cozy book discussions.

Okay, that does it.

One small square of lasagna. I'll be extra quiet. Then I'll come back to bed and sleep.

I throw on my robe, pad out the door, and skirt a vacubot attending to the carpet. Its circular lights make it look like a low-flying UFO, snuffling back and forth across the living room. In the kitchen I snag a piece of lasagna and shoot a guilty glance at the autodoor leading to the hall where Nettie's bedroom is located. I tiptoe to the PlasmaWave and slip my plate inside. The ending beep makes me cringe.

I listen. Hearing no footsteps, I snatch a fork and a tall glass of chocolate milk, and hustle back to my room. The lasagna goes down like soothing medicine, warming and filling my empty spots. The milk makes a rich, chocolaty finish. I hate doing things I know Jodine has done in her past, since it blurs the line of differences between us, but I can't seem to help myself. I think I know exactly how she feels living in this house, in this body. The last thing I see before I fall asleep is the round shape of the green airbot drifting over the stuffed animals on the window seat.

Morning comes too early. My room alarm chides me, sounding freakishly like Mom.

"Wake up. Third reminder," it says with zeal. "Thirty minutes past initial alarm."

"Turn off," I growl. I sit up and push a tangled mass of hair away from my face and neck. My stomach sloshes. Worse, the memory of my midnight failure sits like a horrible weight in my lower gut. How could things as blissfully tasty as that lasagna and that glass of chocolate milk give me this much grief? I'm no better than Jodine, while doing this job in her body. I tromp into the bathroom.

"You are *totally* bad," I scold myself. "You're stronger than this, I know you are."

I spend the morning punishing myself with healthy food and strenuous workouts. By the time I board the MT for my afternoon weigh-in, I feel a little more like I deserve the right to hold the title of Reducer again.

A man in a business suit flicks me a wary glance as I settle onto a seat. I ignore him by tuning in to some music on my phone, using the built-in earbuds. Since the rain has stopped, I assume all my paranoia last night about not seeing Matt was for nothing. It figures. I fast-forward my thoughts to my upcoming "date." Let's see. After I finish at the Clinic and reach the park, we'll share a sweaty, puffing walk, followed by an awkward chat in a café. Yep, I can live with that.

It's a shame Matt and Jodine can't meet each other in April, although they might not bond as well if they haven't lost weight together. Hmm, what in the megaverse am I going to tell Matt at the end of my assignment to explain why I won't be around anymore? I don't know. I guess I'll just have to see if we're still hanging out by the end of March.

I hum along to the tune I'm streaming, a song of lost love kept alive by the memory of one golden afternoon by a river. My humming grows into soft, bittersweet words as office complexes flash by my window. The song and I trail off a dozen seconds before the MT arrives at the Red Zone shelter. Across the aisle from me, the businessman stands and brushes lint from his suit. He gets off right behind me. When we reach the sidewalk, he touches my shoulder with a light hand.

"You have an exceptionally lovely voice, Miss," he says, and walks away.

"Thank you," I call out after him. I'm crazily pleased, which makes no sense. After all, it's not *my* voice he complimented.

But it buoys me up, just the same.

I'm *so* not used to getting positive attention for my singing. I love this part of being Jodine.

I walk to the Institute grounds, humming the same song. At the double autodoors to the Clinic building, a redheaded Reducer gives me a broad smile as she exits.

"Keep losing that weight," she says. "Don't give up."

"Same to you. You're looking good." I meet her eye, and in the process I bump into another, heavier Reducer coming out the doors. "Sorry," I say, turning toward the guy.

"No worries," the Reducer says.

I focus my gaze on him. Mischievous brown eyes, long lashes, double chin.

"*Matt?* Are you— Oh my gosh, you're a Reducer!"

Matt's mouth goes slack, and he gives an incredulous laugh. "You're a Reducer, too? So your name isn't Jodine."

"No." I grin. "It's Morgan Dey."

"Morgan." He blinks as if he's trying to get his mind wrapped around the word. "Nice to meet the real you. How bizarre. I'm Vonn Alexander."

"Vonn," I say, likewise dazed.

"Are you weighing in? I'm done, but I could wait for you and we could head to the park together."

"That'd be great." I can't wipe the drunken smile off my face as we walk down the hall to the Weigh Center. We have more in common than I thought. *Nice.* I peek at his profile as he sits next to me. I'm dying to know what he really looks like.

I'm not sure I can ask, for confidentiality reasons. Maybe we shouldn't have even swapped real names.

Vonn leans toward me, looking into my eyes as if he's trying to see *beyond* them, at the real me inside. "I started losing weight for Matt on Monday, the day we met in the park. When did you start?"

"This month. Lost twelve pounds since October first."

"Inspiring. I'm on a nine-month program, squeezing in the part-time teaching. Matt would've lost his job otherwise."

At that point, I hear my name called for weigh-in. "Be right back."

I walk into Admittance. To my mortification, I've lost one measly pound since Monday. The midnight lasagna is likely the culprit, along with taking a slower pace around the park this week with Matt—I mean, Vonn. I return to the waiting room, making a heroic effort to keep my expression pleasant, hoping he won't ask how I fared.

He rises to his feet. "Now we get to puff and pant our way to the MT. Oh, boy."

We set off down the sidewalk. I want to know more about him. The only thing I know for sure is that he's nineteen like the real Matt, since that's how the program works. "My parents are okay with me doing this job, but my grandfather hates it. Are your parents and friends chill with you being a Reducer?"

"Some friends yes, some no. My mother thinks I've lost my mind. My dad passed away when I was twelve."

"Sorry to hear that."

"Thanks. I'm mostly glad Matt's a loner, although that sounds terrible. He has no social life except for the teachers and kids where he works. I like being able to live offsite without worrying about running into someone he knows. Leo's hyper about that sort of stuff."

"I can relate." Noni and her friends being a distasteful exception, of course. I give a sudden laugh. "Oh, man. I actually asked you if you wanted to join the Reducer program."

"Pretty funny. But you were just doing your civic duty, helping round up people who stress the health care system."

Even though he's right, something about his statement hits me as wrong. The recruiting sounds a little insidious, phrased like that. I nibble on my fingernail, then stop and stare as I realize what I'm doing. Gross. Fingernail chewing is Jodine's habit, not mine. Where is this *coming from?* Is Jodine's body affecting my mind—like some sort of muscle memory—or are her residual memories taking over?

I don't like either explanation. First the residual memories, then more blatant things like sprinkling oregano, snacking at midnight, and nibbling on fingernails. This job is sliding from bad to worse.

"I'm slowing you down," Vonn says as we reach the park and begin walking. "You're not getting as good of a workout."

"I'll make up for it later." I concentrate on my breathing so I'll quit thinking of chewing my fingernails.

Vonn nudges me with his elbow. "What would you be doing if you were in your own body? A bit of snogging down at the dance clubs?" He slips into a British accent for the last sentence and winks.

I burst out laughing. Why yes, maybe I would be doing that, if I found someone I wanted to be with, someone to kiss. "Dancing is great exercise and gives me serious Health Points. I also belong to a science club. Oh, and I have about three months of schooling left. The tutor bit was a lie, sorry."

"No worries. I had to pretend I wasn't a Reducer. One

of *my* favorite things to do is indoor wall climbing at Rock Mountain."

"Rock Mountain's a blast! Although it's spendy and way out in the Orange Zone."

"I hear ya. It's a long way even from the Blue Zone, where I normally live."

We keep up an easy conversation. The words rush out now, as if an unseen dam has broken. After we finish our park loop, we walk two blocks to a café decorated in electric blue and lavender. *Half-Moon Café*, the sign says. Edge music strobes over the small tables and curved chairs. Aromas of toasted bagels, cinnamon, and mint drift into my nose.

"Cool place," I say, eyeing a wallscreen TV that mutters to some customers on our left.

Vonn ambles toward the counter. "The fruit drinks here are tasty. They'll make any blend you want—" He whips his gaze left.

I follow his stare to the TV. A flash news report has materialized, showing melted synthetic bushes, broken glass, and blackened sidewalks. Back east, there's been some sort of minor bombing. The newscaster paces beside an electric fence, her face sober as she describes two people as injured. She reports that the four attackers who threw a series of handmade bottle bombs have been apprehended and are in custody.

The incident happened at The Body Institute's eastern branch in Boston.

CHAPTER 13

Vonn and I sidle closer to the TV, drawn as a single unit. He swears under his breath.

Two people injured. Oh, no.

"Who'd do something like that?" I ask.

"I bet it's the WHA. They're getting extreme these days." Vonn looks as grim as I feel.

The newscaster gives a brief background of the Institute and its five branches. I check out the images of three men and a woman in one corner of the holoscreen. The alleged bottle bombers. Sure enough, the caption for the attackers scrolls up as "known WHA members."

This is bad. The protesters are becoming more and more violent. I won't be able to finish my job if they keep pulling stunts like this. Man, I just want to hurry up, lose my targeted weight, and be done with this assignment. "The Institute had better make sure something like this doesn't happen again," I say.

"They should at least add more Enforcers outside the grounds."

A servbot rises from behind the counter. "I'll take your order when you're ready."

Vonn accesses his account on an exchange screen. He places his order, and I choose the same blend. My brain cells are having a hard enough time trying to process the newsvid details. After the servbot mixes our drinks, Vonn and I sit, huddling over a dainty oval table.

His gaze meets mine. "The WHA is really ramping up their campaign against the Institute. Boston's not the only place they're targeting. Did you see the newsvid last week about the Reducer caught trying to sabotage ERT equipment in Seattle, Washington?"

"No. Why the haze would a Reducer do that?"

"Undercover work for the WHA. She pretended to agree with Institute ideals, got selected as a Reducer, and tried to sabotage the system from the inside."

I have trouble swallowing my juice. "That's serious. Without ERT, there'd be no Transfers until the equipment is rebuilt. We'd have to wait to get back into our real bodies."

"Loaners would, too. But Leo said not to worry. They caught this woman before she damaged anything, and he said it happened because of a one-time screw-up in the selection process. The Seattle director knew the woman had strong ties to the WHA, but he okayed her application since her membership was more than three years ago. Bad judgment. He got fired."

I'm positive Leo keeps a tighter rein on things than the Seattle branch director, but it sounds like he's downplaying things again. Like he did with the residual memories.

"Fire bombs and attempted sabotage make me nervous," I say. "I don't want to worry about getting hit with a bottle bomb every time I go to the Clinic—if my parents even let me keep the job." A hard pressure forms in my throat. I don't have to be a proverbial rocket scientist to know Mom and Dad might pull me from the program, even though this attack happened back east. Granddad will also put extra pressure on them to cancel.

Vonn fiddles with his unopened straw. "I think you and I are safer, since we live offsite."

"We still have to go to the Clinic. Before my Transfer, I got attacked by WHA protesters right at the front gates."

"That's…terrible. Is your real body okay?"

"Mostly scraped and bruised." Vonn's concerned, how sweet. And he's level-headed enough to discuss this bottle bombing without freaking out. I like this guy. A simultaneous, depressing thought flies up and smacks me right between the eyes. I wince. "Vonn, you know what? When we become ourselves again, we won't remember meeting in the park. This café. Exercising together. The things we're talking about right now."

He looks stricken. "That sucks."

"Seriously. I doubt I missed anything when I stayed at the Clinic, but this time I'm doing new things as a Loaner. Meeting people, like you." I study his face as he nods, trying to imagine what he looks like when he's not in his Loaner body. When I open my mouth to ask, I lose my nerve. I don't want him to think I'm only interested in his looks. "Do you think if we met as our real selves, we'd mesh?"

"One way to find out." Vonn rips the paper from the end of his straw without taking his gaze from my face. "I'll be done being Matt in August. We could get together, even if we don't remember each other or what we've said and done. We'll just have to find a sneaky way to set up a meeting so our jobs aren't terminated. Carrier pigeons or secret code, or something."

He's serious about this, and amazingly, he wants to do it without even knowing what I look like in real life. I smile a full smile this time, despite the news of bottle bombs thrashing inside me. "Kind of like arranging a blind date for our other selves. I like that."

"Then we'll do it," he says, and blows his straw paper across the table at me.

When my phone announces a message that night, I fortify myself with a deep breath and a shoulder roll.

> Morgan, are you there? We'd like to discuss something with you.

> How are my favorite parents?

I'm glad I'm using text instead of voice so I can cover up my jitters. Mom answers first.

> Upset. Have you seen the newsvid about the fire bombs?

Dad chimes in, his words a different color on my screen.

> At the Institute's Boston branch, protesters threw cocktail bombs before getting stunned and arrested. They set bushes on fire and gave two people minor burns.

> I saw that.

I hurry to speak a rebuttal text.

Did you get Leo's message talking about how they're going to do searches and bomb detection in a two-block radius from the entrance gates? They'll do that at all five branches. And more Enforcers will patrol outside the fences.

Do you honestly think that's going to solve the problem? Dad asks.

I don't see why not. No one except workers will be allowed inside the gates.

Oh, sweetie, it's not worth it, Mom says, and adds more objections.

You can't predict what the WHA will do next. You can earn credits another way. We'll get paid for October, and that will be enough. The band and I are planning to hit it big next week in Philadelphia anyway.

I can't believe she wants to trade a sure chance of credits for an uncertain one. The music industry is such a gamble.

We don't know if that'll earn enough to pay half the debt by the December deadline, Mom. And I'm not done losing weight for my client. She really needs this to happen.

Dad's words scroll out fast.

Morgan Renita Dey, you can't be serious. As much as we need to make a huge dent in the bills, this is sounding dangerous. We can't let you continue. I don't think I have to tell you that Granddad agrees.

But I'm living offsite! I only go in to the Institute twice each week for about 10 minutes for my weigh-in and vitals. My Loaner's parents aren't thrilled either, but they're not pulling her from the program. They think the extra security will be enough.

Sounds like they're being naïve.

I hear the grumble behind Dad's words.
Mom's line appears under Dad's.

Maybe we should give Mr. Behr a call and tell him we're through.

We can't do that.

No. I can't quit now. Besides our looming remaining debt and my needing to help Jodine, Vonn and I haven't even hatched a plan to meet up after our assignments are over. I won't know how to find him when he becomes his real self.

Please. I want to do this. I need to. You supported me helping to change the world before, even with risks. I'm turning 18 soon, and if you take me out now I'll just sign up again after I'm legal age.

Mom jumps in.

She has a point, Gregg. She's old enough to make her own decisions.

We're responsible for her until she's 18, he counters.

I speak my text, clipped and hard.

Are things going to be suddenly different on December 10th? The situation will be the same, and I'll feel the same.

Dad is silent. Stewing.

I'm going to think about this for a little while, he
finally says.

Three days later, I recline on my back in the park grass with
Vonn, thankfully still on the job despite its very real risks.
A crisp breeze swirls around us while dense grass tickles my
bare arms and feet. My toes wiggle next to Vonn's. Bumpy
clouds drift overhead.

"Werewolf munching on a hamburger," Vonn announces,
pointing.

"Are yours always about food?" I ask. "The one above the
oak tree looks like a little girl riding on a lion. See, her hair is
whipping back, and so is the lion's mane."

"I sort of see that."

A flying insect darts into my ear, making me bolt upright.
"Dumb bug! Flew right in like it knew where it was going."

Vonn sits up beside me. "Is it out?"

"Yeah. I'm getting cold, though. Cloud watching works
way better in the spring." I grab my sweatshirt and pop it over
my head.

Vonn's smile is shifty as he reaches for his sweatshirt.
"My mom would get super uptight if she saw me lying on the
ground in a short-sleeved shirt. In November. Without socks
or shoes."

"Is she afraid you'll get sick?"

"Of course. Is your mother as coddling as mine?"

I shake my head. "Mine's more relaxed, and she's usually concentrating on her singing career. She works nights, so my dad and grandfather keep tabs on me more than she does."

"My dad was the busy one in my family."

"Was he gone a lot?" I ask carefully, remembering his dad has passed away.

"He traveled and job-hopped a lot. It drove my mom nuts. Extreme jobs, too. He was a stunt man for some minor vids, then he was an aerosuit tester out over the Grand Canyon. His last job was racing jet-cars at the Speedway…"

Something tightens in my gut as he trails off. Oh. That must be how his dad died. "I assume that's why your mom's coddly, and why she isn't thrilled with you being a Reducer."

"Right. Dangerous stuff. I should stay in my own body where I belong."

"She sounds like my grandfather." I smile. Vonn's great about sharing serious things. To tell the truth, we've shared more lately than I ever did with other guys. With my last boyfriend, I spent more time dancing and kissing than talking. While that was a blast, I'm getting to know more about who Vonn really is beneath his skin. And I like what I'm learning.

I grab my sock and snap his arm with it. "It's time to power-walk back through the park for our next session of laps."

"Slave driver." Vonn grunts as he tries to put on his socks.

"I love how you're spending nine whole months to get Matt into shape. Now that's dedication."

"He'll appreciate it. Leo and National Health Care will too."

Leo. I yank my socks on and add my shoes. I had another residual flash last night while doing karaoke. There I was, finishing a song by my favorite band. As the last notes died away, I watched my fingers select a song I've never heard before. I sang an entire stanza on autopilot before I lost the thread of it and stared at the screen. That memory affected my actions for half a minute before I realized what was happening.

There's a ghost inside me—a Jodine-shaped ghost. It gives me shivers every time I think about it. I hate the residuals, and I hate Leo's lack of concern about them. They're definitely getting worse. It's like I'm trapped in some paranormal vid, or an episode of "Freak Out or Believe." There *has* to be a logical, scientific reason behind it. Is it easier to access the residuals, the longer I'm in Jodine's body? Or maybe I'm just unlucky enough to run around triggering her deep-seated memories.

"Vonn," I say. "Have you had any memory flashes, or thoughts that could be Matt's and not yours?"

He throws me a startled look. "Last week I saw an old woman by the elevator pod in my megacomplex and knew I'd talked to her before. Except I *haven't* talked to her. I also had a fleeting image of a green and yellow parakeet."

"I've had flashes at least three times." I tell him what Leo said about the stray memories.

Vonn frowns. "Wild. Here I thought I was alone in this body."

"Sometimes I feel like my soul's merging with Jodine's."

"Nah. It'd only be a few brain waves mingling, not your soul." Vonn helps me to my feet, and brushes grass and leaves from my back. "Even if there *is* some blending going on, it doesn't make any difference, since they reinsert our original file back into our own bodies. You'll be the same you after this is over. It's all part of the job."

I start walking with him. "That's what Leo said."

Yeah. In fact, Leo's said a lot of things. He downplayed the

Seattle sabotage incident to Vonn. He doesn't care that ERT isn't accurate during the brainmap-generating process. I know he wants the Reducer program to do well, but I'm starting to wonder whether he bends a few rules to keep it working. Or at least looks the other way when it's used for questionable things. He's much too glib and hedgy about the residuals.

I glance at Vonn puffing beside me. "Humor me for a bit. You know that Reducer woman who tried to sabotage the Seattle ERT equipment?"

"What about her?" He reaches over, snags my fingers with his, and smiles.

I struggle to concentrate. Wow, he's *holding my hand*. His touch is warm, surprisingly electric, and very distracting. "She had a hidden agenda, and used a Loaner body to get into the Transfer room. What if the Institute assigns offsite Reducers to do undercover work? They could be losing weight at the same time they're doing stealthy activities."

Vonn tosses me a look that implies I'm unhinged, which isn't surprising, since that's how I'm starting to feel. "You mean the Institute would hire them to do secret spy missions?"

It does sound silly when he puts it like that. "Sort of. In a Loaner body they could watch what's going on in a company. Copy files, steal ideas, ruin programs they don't like. Or spy on a boss or a coworker."

To his credit, Vonn doesn't laugh. "I doubt it. All the Institute wants to do is market their brilliant ERT program and make a profit. It's a business. One that's doing well, especially now that the government is fining people and digging up clients for them. It's a mutual partnership."

"You have to at least admit undercover things like that are possible."

"I guess, but I don't think it's happening. At least as far as Leo and the Institute getting people to do their evil bidding. That's wacko conspiracy theory material."

He sounds so sure. I wish I could dismiss these concerns as easily as he can—as easily as I did at the beginning of my assignment. My nagging seeds of doubt are growing into a suspicious little vine. I shouldn't have talked to those WHA protesters or watched Walter Herry's dumb vid. What shady things have I accidentally become a part of, by agreeing to do this job?

"Besides," Vonn says, "not many Reducers are allowed to live offsite. Ninety-seven percent stay in the dorms, and it'd be almost impossible to do anything undercover there."

"True. I'm probably just being paranoid." I guess I need to let it go, but the possibility that it's true is unsettling. As the days of my job go by, the Institute seems to be warping more and more into something unrecognizable. With an effort, I shove those dark thoughts to the back of my mind. "I think what I really should be worrying about is how to keep myself from having seconds and thirds of dinner tonight. I swear, food tastes a hundred times better when I'm Jodine. Even fruits and veggies have more flavor now."

"Maybe Jodine has more taste buds than you do."

I laugh. "Right."

"It's true. Some people have more, and they taste things better. Jodine must be cursed with a ton of them."

"*Cursed* is definitely the word." I roll my eyes as we start walking. "It's not fair."

Vonn launches into song. His voice comes out sturdy and baritone, his words to a popular tune as bright as the sun. "*Life's not fair, got no hair. Roll me out the door, Ma.*"

He's exactly the remedy I need, what I should be concentrating on so I can get through this assignment. I join in on the chorus, and we laugh and keep holding hands as we hike through the park.

Our voices blend perfectly.

CHAPTER 14

I shift in one of the Clinic's green waiting room chairs and try to cross my legs. My thighs refuse to oblige. I glare at them and leave them uncrossed. Amazing, the things I used to take for granted.

A guy with a buzz cut snickers next to me.

"Not funny," I say, wishing I were already done with my afternoon weigh-in and on my way to the park to walk with Vonn. "I bet you think it's amusing because you're almost done. What do you have left, six weeks? Less?"

"Four." He sounds proud....and relieved. "When I'm done, I'm gonna buy a car and move out of the city. There's this sensational dark blue convertible at—"

A blaring siren interrupts his words and reverberates around the room. I clap my hands over my ears. The alarm blares from the walls through my palms, the sound slicing into me.

"Emergency," Buzz Cut yells over the noise. "Could be a fire."

We leap up. I hustle with him and two female Reducers

toward the nearest exit. The siren volume lowers a notch as a mechanical voice joins in.

"*Do not panic,*" the voice says. "*Please proceed to the nearest exit. This is not a drill. I repeat, this is not a drill.*"

I hurry behind Buzz Cut. He orders the exit door open and dashes through the opening. I follow, bursting out on the east side of the Clinic. The two female Reducers join us. I scan the grounds, and a shock jolts through me.

Protesters are swarming through the entrance gates, shouting, "Down with the Institute! Stop body swapping!" They hit people with their signs and attack the four Enforcers there. Some protesters lie crumpled on the ground, likely hit by stun guns. Guards at the administration building brace themselves to intercept a group of charging rioters. Battle cries rend the air. Reducer victims shriek. More protesters pour across the lawn, closing in on the Clinic.

"It's an attack, not a fire," I shout. "Get back inside."

Buzz Cut and I dart back toward the exit with the female Reducers. One of the women squeezes through before it closes. The other woman smacks up against the door's surface, pounding her fists on it. "Somebody, please," she cries. "Activate the door. Open, open!"

Nothing happens. The exits aren't meant to be accessed from the outside.

Buzz Cut swears. "We're stuck out here. Run!"

I whip around to see two protesters hurtling toward us, and I scramble away from the building. Buzz Cut and the woman race with me. I'm breathing hard. My legs burn and strain. I thud across pavement and fake grass. Crazed shouting erupts behind us. This is a nightmare, one that feels much too real.

The shouts grow louder, closer. Panic rips through my

body as I try to run faster.

Will the protesters beat me up, or can I fight back? Is *any* kind of violence forbidden under my contract, even self-defense?

I lag behind Buzz Cut. He grabs my arm and pulls me forward as the female Reducer stumbles and falls. Behind me, she screams.

"Stop being a Reducer!" a man shouts.

"I will, I will," the woman says, sobbing. "Just don't hit me again."

My steps falter.

"We have to help her," I cry out to Buzz Cut. He shakes his head, his eyes frantic. In another moment we reach the electric fence enclosing the Institute grounds. I hear it hum, a low warning drone. *Trapped.* The only thing we can do is keep running along the fence line.

I look back to find a burly protester on our heels. He barrels up and swings his sign at Buzz Cut, who ducks and rolls across the turf. The protester stamps after him. This is my chance to escape, but my feet won't obey. I can't leave a fellow Reducer here to get mangled.

"Stop!" I throw myself between them, poised to kick. "We haven't done anything to you—"

The protester cracks his sign against the side of my head. I stumble to the ground, pain shooting through my skull. My vision blurs. I try to roll away, but the protester grabs a thick wad of my hair. He raises his fist to punch me; I squeeze my eyes closed and scream. A searing charge ripples the air, making the hairs on my arms and neck stand up. A heavy thud sounds. My eyes snap open to find the burly protester beside me, convulsing on his back, while an Enforcer with a stun gun stands thirty feet away. Gulping air like I've just come up from water, I untangle my hair from the protester's slack fingers.

"Are you two okay?" the Enforcer asks as he strides closer.

"I — He hit my head with his sign." I wince, my head throbbing. The artificial turf goes in and out of focus.

Buzz Cut helps me to my feet. "I'm okay," he says. "Thanks to this girl. She threw herself in front of that guy when he barged toward me."

The Enforcer slaps restraint-cuffs on the unconscious protester, scans our IDs, and dictates a report into his phone. I glance toward the grounds entrance to see an entire fleet of squad cars has arrived. The bright blue of official uniforms is infiltrating the grounds. Enforcers with stun guns are taking down protesters everywhere.

It's over. I hide my face with my hands. Buzz Cut wraps his arm across my back, and I welcome the comfort.

An ice compress soothes my aching head as I sit in the nurse's station. Some Reducers have been whisked away to the hospital, while others have returned to their regular lives at the Clinic. The nurse on duty is gone, scurrying off to replenish her supply of bandages and compresses.

I breathe in the calmer air, soaking in the quietness, the lull after the storm. This is extreme—the third attack against me in a month. Once with Noni, twice with protesters. This job is jinxed.

My soul feels as if a thousand evil boots have stomped across it.

The hate in that burly protester's eyes keeps burning

through me. So much savage anger directed at the Institute and its workers. Directed at *me*. Why such venom? What did I do to deserve it? I have no idea why the WHA can't protest their rights infringements in a more peaceful way. Even if they have one or two valid objections—which I'm beginning to think they might—they're going about it all wrong.

A whisking noise sounds as the autodoor opens. Slow footsteps enter. It's Leo in a dark suit. He rolls a chair over and sits facing me. Something about the lines around his mouth and eyes makes him look vulnerable, more muted than usual.

"Checking out my injuries this time around?" I can't help saying, to lighten the mood.

His expression doesn't change. "The nurse says you should be fine. I've notified the Kowalczyks, and they're standing by in case you're able to finish your assignment."

I frown and wish I hadn't, because it makes my head hurt. "What do you mean, 'in case I'm able to finish my assignment'? You just said I'm fine."

"I'm pretty sure your parents will revoke permission for your job when we tell them you've been injured again. Put yourself in their position. If you had a daughter who got attacked twice in one month, you'd probably pull her out of the Institute as fast as you could."

"You're right," I whisper. I won't even have a choice. Mom and Dad were upset enough the first time and worried about the bottle bombs on top of that. There's no way they'd let this happen to me and do nothing about it. A huge lump materializes in my throat, making it hard to breathe. My bill-paying and tech school dreams start dissolving at quantum speed. We'll end up in the prison camp of The Commons for sure now. And I'll lose my contact with Vonn.

Leo's gaze meets mine, then slides away. "You haven't been Reducing for the Kowalczyks very long. I assume you don't want to give up already."

"No, I'm not a quitter. But even if a miracle happens and my parents let me keep going, Jodine's parents will probably pull her out of the program."

"That's not the case. Even though the Kowalczyks are incensed, the issue of Jodine's extra weight must be addressed or their tax fines will continue. They don't have much choice. Plus, I've assured them that security will be boosted by mounting cameras on all surrounding streets to monitor large groups. Backup Enforcers will be called before any groups larger than eight people reach the grounds. That way the Enforcers at the gates won't be overpowered."

"So you're going to replace me with another Reducer?" I try to say the words without a wobble, and fail.

Leo adjusts in his chair as though his suit chafes him. "I'd prefer not. With your experience and dedication, you're the ideal candidate for this job. I'd like to avoid the hassle of finding a suitable replacement. As well as wanting to avoid poor public relations with your mother and father. Since your parents will undoubtedly withdraw permission when they hear you were part of this incident, I suggest we not tell them about it."

I stare at him and give a strangled cough. *"What?"*

"It's better if they don't know. I can send them a broad report, as I will to all families, without mentioning that you were onsite at the time. Think about it. Your parents don't know your weigh-in schedule, and they think you're living safely offsite. We could even tell them your weigh-ins and health checks from now on will be done at your Loaner house rather than at the Clinic. That way the news will come across as a more distant, less alarming concern."

A flood of relief rushes through me, along with a tornado of misgiving. Leo Behr, gatekeeper of all that is restricting and protocol-adhering, is suggesting I lie to my parents. Should I go along with it? Not only that, do I really *want* to keep being a Reducer after I've been attacked again?

Curse this job. It's growing too complex and confusing. My goals of helping others and bettering the health care system are starting to pale next to the risks and disadvantages. It doesn't seem like such a great idea to be involved with the Institute anymore. And yet, I have to be.

I trade a wary look with Leo. He knows I need those credits. It just doesn't feel safe to keep going. "Can't you send out a tech to do my weight checks for real at the Kowalczyks', so I won't have to go to the Clinic? I'd feel loads better about continuing the job."

"Believe me," Leo says, "we're going to make the grounds a lot safer after this. I'd rather not assign someone to drive all the way out to north Green Zone merely because you're feeling skittish."

Skittish, indeed. He's certainly not very sympathetic, which means I'm stuck putting up with potential added risk, depending on how well his safety measures work. But he's taking a risk with me, too. "You must trust me a lot. I could go running off to the WHA and start a viral vid about how you're trying to get around parental permissions. It'd be really damaging publicity for the Institute."

He gives a cagey return smile. "I doubt you'd do that—especially if you wanted to get paid. It'd be your word against mine."

A short laugh of disbelief escapes my mouth. Whoa, deviousness. I can't believe he's saying this to me. Threatening my wages goes way beyond glib and hedgy. "You're kinda scary, you know?"

"Does that mean your answer is yes, and you'll continue your assignment?"

"Yes." When he breaks into a wide, boyish grin, I return a weak smile. Even though I hate this method of saving my job, all is not lost. I can keep earning those all-important credits for my family. That's the most important part.

I just need to survive the next five months. Work hard at my weight loss. Pay off the bills, stay out of the prison camp of The Commons. Then—and only then—I can relax.

"One more thing, however," Leo says.

"What's that?" I hope he doesn't want me to lie about something else.

"The Kowalczyks don't know you threw yourself into the path of an enraged protester. While the act was heroic, your duty isn't to protect others while you're in a Loaner body. It's not yours to take risks with. You must protect Jodine's body at all times."

Wow. I didn't know it'd be against the rules to help someone in danger. That's not the kind of person I want to be. "Am I allowed to use self-defense, or is that considered violence?"

"Good question, one that's actually in your contract. We certainly don't want Reducers provoking a situation they could claim was self-defense. If there are no other options and the Loaner's life is in direct danger, you can consider self-defensive actions. Nevertheless, it's better to flee, hide, or try other things first."

I really need to take more time to get familiar with my

contract. "Why did the alarm message tell us to go outside, anyway?"

"Standard recording. The technician punched the button before she had all the information. She should've sent the building into lockdown instead. By the time she switched tactics, it was too late. A lot of Reducers had already run outside."

I watch him stand and send his chair rolling back across the room. "I guess I'm ready to be picked up," I say. "Or I can ride the MT."

"The Kowalczyks have insisted on escorting you home," Leo says. "I'll walk you to where they're waiting."

No lowly hostbot escort for me this time. I'm rating high today. I brush a renegade coil of hair from my face and walk beside him down the hall.

"You're trying to raise credits to attend technical school, along with helping pay off family bills, right?" Leo asks.

I meet the gaze of his sharp gray eyes. "I'm surprised you remember that."

"That's partly why I chose you to be a Reducer. You're selfless, hard working, and you want to make something of your life. I had personal goals when I was young, and I continue to have them. Are you familiar with the history of ghettos or slums?"

Random change of subject, but I'll humor him. "Ghettos or slums were miserable places with gangs. Poverty. Drugs, street fights, and starvation."

"Exactly. I grew up in a neighborhood the locals called the White Slash District. I was fourteen when my best friend got killed in a knife fight." He pauses for a moment, jaw muscles tight. "At that point I knew I had to change my life. I saw my chance to get ahead by joining National Health Care. After years of rigorous work, here I am, director at a branch of a prominent, government-backed institution."

"That's amazing," I say. I can't fathom what it'd be like to lose a friend in a stabbing. All at once his determination, his drive, and the precision of his business suits take on a new meaning. He's gone from the violent streets of the slums to the high-tech, sleek office of upper management. That's inspirational. It makes him sound a lot less scary and ruthless.

At the autodoor to a room marked *Private Guests*, Leo rests a hand on my shoulder and slows me to a halt. "Don't be discouraged by this attack, Morgan. You're tough and adaptable. I encourage you to do whatever it takes to reach your goals, as I have. Make sacrifices. Work long and hard. You're the one in control of your future."

Behind the shrewdness, there's a glimmer of sincere pleading in his eyes. He *really* wants me to do a good job as a Reducer. Not only for myself, but for him. For his Institute.

"Thanks, Leo," I say. "I'll do that."

Exuberance flares through me as I walk through the auto-door. Yes, I *am* in control of my future. By deciding to continue this assignment and stay in this body, I'm making sacrifices to get where I want to be in life. Where I want Granddad and my family to be in life—debt free. My struggles will be worth it in the end.

I have dreams. I have important goals.

CHAPTER 15

The metallic whir of motorized gears enters my ears, and I sense what must be the motion of the Kowalczyks' vehicle easing through the autodoors of their garage. I open my eyes, surprised to find I've dozed off during the ride home. The painkiller the nurse gave me must've been more potent than I thought.

"Stop. Turn off," Dr. K. commands the car. He whisks out, opens my door before I finish unbuckling my seat belt, and offers me his arm. Mrs. K. hovers by my other side.

"I'm okay. Just an ugly bump on my head." I pause. "Or Jodine's head."

Mrs. K. makes an indignant sound. "If those protesters had severely injured you, they would've had a lawsuit on their hands. I'm tempted to call a lawyer as it is. I don't know how the WHA can claim to protect citizens' rights while they run around harming people."

"I've never liked that Walter Herry," Dr. K. says. "Not even before he resorted to violence to make his points. He's getting desperate and ruining a perfectly useful organization."

The house door opens to reveal Nettie standing with her hands clasped into a tight ball. "I've saved dinner, if you're hungry. Morgan, how are you?"

"Not as bad as everyone thinks, but it hurts some."

Nettie gives a motherly cluck of her tongue. I let Dr. K. seat me at the dining table while Nettie scoots off to the kitchen. In a few minutes, the servbot appears with plates of broiled halibut, brown rice, and broccoli. As I listen to conversation about the attack and how the world is filled with violence, a shivery sensation crawls over me like a mess of spiderbots.

The protesters could've seriously injured me today. Not just a simple twisted ankle that would set me back weeks or months and stop me from getting my assignment done in time. I could've ended up with an intensive-care-unit type of injury. Worse, would the burly guy have stopped beating me once I was unconscious, or would he have killed me?

A bite of fish catches in my throat, and I grab my water glass to wash it down. How awful to think that Jodine's body could've died, and I could've died a painful death without really dying. I shudder. Dying isn't something I want to do more than once. Those protesters believe in their cause a little too heartily.

Stop body swapping. That's what they were shouting. While it's true being in Jodine's body is causing me a swarm of problems, and this job is more bizarre than I thought it would be, it's not worth killing anyone over.

Nettie scoots a bowl toward me. "More broccoli?"

"No, thanks." As I set my glass down, my phone announces an incoming text from home. "Excuse me. My mom's messaging."

A chorus of understanding assents follows me as I leave. I speak a return text.

Are you still there, Mom?

Honey, did you hear about the protester riot at the Institute?

I take a steadying breath. Here go the lies.

Yeah. Good thing I'm way out here in the Green Zone. Leo—Mr. Behr—says not only are they posting more security from now on, but I won't even have to go to the Clinic anymore. The health checks can be done here at my Loaner parents' house.

Oh, what a huge relief! This time your father was going to put his foot down and say you were finished, no matter how much you objected. I—I don't know what we'd do if something happened to you, baby. You're my Cupcake. My little girl.

Her tender mood is catching, even though I can't hear her voice. I slip into the quiet of Jodine's room and sit on the bed, knees weak.

It'll be okay now, Mom. Just concentrate on how great it'll be to wipe out our debt.

I shift the conversation to a non-Reducer subject, and we talk for another ten minutes before signing off. The room seems barren without Mom's caring words. I hate lying to her. If Leo's willing to lie to get what he wants in this situation, what else could he be lying about, to me or anyone else? It's not a thought that settles well in my mind. I glance over at the stuffed animals on the window seat. Their return stares are accusing.

"Don't look at me like that," I tell them. "It's for a good

cause. The quality of the rest of my life—my *whole family's life*—depends on this."

They gaze back at me, silent. I groan and stretch out on the bed.

I know it's really me I'm trying to convince.

I settle myself onto an MT seat and squint against the mid-morning sun that slants through the windows. October is almost over. The tender lump on my head is nearly gone. Today's weigh-in at the Clinic went well; I've met a tremendous goal. Even so, a sense of desolation presses upon me, as if I've finished a big race and discovered there's nothing on the other side of the finish line. I pull out my phone and speak a message to Mom, Dad, and Granddad. The accompanying text scrolls up as ghoulish lettering in honor of the holiday.

> Happy Halloween! One month down. Lost 22 pounds. Eat some chocolate for me. Miss ya.

I send another message to Blair and Krista.

> You dressing up for the party at the Flash Point? Don't have too much fun without me, okay?

I sign off. I'm not happy about missing the club's annual costume party. Last year I dressed up as a cyborg with a horned cap, metallic-green miniskirt, and flashing arm bands. I racked up major Health Points with Blair, Krista, and a trio of more extroverted Catalyst Club guys. We stuck to a cheery geek theme, dancing like robots and drinking fruit punch that we dubbed "battery acid." This year I want to hang around friends like that, to get out and do something fun.

This is one of those moments when, as Granddad says, "money" isn't everything.

I stare down at my green sweats, which fit looser than ten days ago. It really doesn't seem important right now how much weight I've lost. My options tonight involve doing things like playing HoloSports bowling or Masters of the Cyberverse. Vonn plans to hunker down on his couch with a tray of celery sticks and have a *Zombie-Cyborg vs. Alien* movie marathon. He suggested I fake an activity for my log and join him, but I had to tell him my Loaner's parents probably wouldn't allow me to go anywhere alone at night. Especially after the riot attack last week.

I won't be able to hang with Nettie, either, since she took the day off to visit her brother in the Red Zone. She prepared plates of leftovers for dinner and won't be back until tomorrow. Unbelievable. Even the house chef has more exciting plans than I do.

It's too bad Superguy hasn't answered me about having a long texting session tonight.

I check my TeenDom account again. Aha! There's one message there now. My heart speeds up. Maybe I can do something epic tonight after all.

> @superguy: hey 007, howzit? haven't heard much from u lately. i've been busy getting used to a new job & i'm amping up for some scary Halloween stuff tonight. how about u? can u do much at the clinic?

I purse my lips. I'm probably not allowed to tell him I'm living offsite, but I guess it doesn't matter. He obviously has better things to do than a texting session. Not one teensy mention of me asking him to do a longer chat. Honestly, I'm not sure why he bothers to keep messaging. Even if he's waiting until I'm done being a Reducer before we meet up and get more serious, it's discouraging he doesn't want to text more meanwhile. Do I *want* to get together with him in April, now that I've been hanging with Vonn every day and holding Vonn's hand? That's the zillion-dollar question.

Superguy may be as hot as all-blazing haze, and he writes sweet and flirty texts, but he's keeping me at a distance for some reason. There's no substitute for positive, mutual, real-life male contact.

I'll leave my options open, I guess. We did have an amazing connection that day in Leo's waiting room. So hypnotic and electric. I hate to toss that potential away like a pile of unrecyclables. I type a quick response.

> @geektastic007: i can't go out = a BO-ring night.
> still working hard on my weight loss tho. good
> luck with ur new job & have a super week!

There. That's somewhere in between wild encouragement and a complete brush-off.

I lean back in my seat and ride for a while. Three young teen boys in costume sit diagonally across from me, erupting in steady outbursts of laughter, belches, and pseudo-spooky noises. Their unimaginative outfits consist of a vampire, a red devil, and an oval-eyed alien. They heckle a quiet girl sitting near them who looks about thirteen, until she sidles away to another seat.

The vampire scans the other passengers and zeroes in on me. "Dudes, check it out. This chick's already dressed up." His voice cracks with fluctuating hormones.

"She could go partying as a giant pickle," the devil says, chuckling devilishly.

"Or a green circus tent." The alien gives a raucous laugh.

I roll my eyes and mouth "help me" at the security camera. Dude. I am *so* not in the mood for this.

"How about a green whale?" the devil says.

"The Mediterranean Sea!" The vampire barely gets the words out between cackles of laughter.

"Good one, Marco." The alien scoots closer to me, his eyes darting like underground bugs behind his oval-eyed mask. "Or maybe she could go as a megacomplex."

"A sonic boom," the vampire suggests, cracking himself up.

I blow out a forceful sigh. *Oh, ha ha ha. Good one, Marco.* My fuse is growing shorter and shorter. "How about *you* guys could go as parasites?" I say. "A three-pack."

The vampire's eyes widen, then narrow to battle slits. "Bloated toad."

"Lobotomized frogs," I shoot back.

The alien hoots. "Hot air balloon!"

"Rotten eggs," I snap, barely taking note of the MT slowing and announcing the next stop. "Malignant tumors."

"Nuked countryside." The devil's contribution.

I glare. "Obstinate warts. Unstable molecules. Burned-out circuits."

The trio gets up to leave as the MT comes to a standstill.

"Want more?" I ask. "Pus-pimples on society, belligerent biowaste—"

Sending catcalls and belches over their shoulders, the boys hop off the MT.

I sink against the back of the seat and close my eyes. Little freaking snots. I know some people think overweight people are second-class citizens, but that doesn't mean those boys have to poke at me like litterbots at a pile of trash. Do they think I'm less of a person because I weigh more?

By the time I get off the MT, my battle with the boys begins to bother me in another way. Uneasy twinges needle my mind. Maybe I shouldn't have given those boys such a hard time. I'm as bad as they are—I stooped to their level.

Would Jodine want her body used to do something like that?

I don't think so. I'm not liking the person I'm turning into while I'm in this body. Nibbling on my nails, arguing with rude boys, and sneaking fatty foods in the dead of night. Looking like Jodine must bring out the worst in me.

I snort. Or maybe that's a thin excuse for caving under pressure, letting myself be weak and mean and snarky. I should be able to control myself better than that.

When I arrive at the Kowalczyks' house, I wander into the dim, unoccupied kitchen, my stomach making loud protests at its own emptiness.

"Lights on," I order, and assemble myself a sandwich for lunch. I'm stalled when I run out of mustard. Muttering, I trudge downstairs to the superstore-room and comb the aisles. I discover rice, noodles, and flour. Boxed and jarred food. I turn a corner, and halt as if flash frozen.

Incredible. A small section of popcorn, nuts, candy bars, and chips.

I begin drooling like Pavlov's dogs, as if a deeply buried fountain has sprung a leak. What's Halloween without chips and maybe some chocolate? It can't hurt to have a bit of comfort junk food. I'll exercise hard later to make up for it. After all, my Halloween is shaping up to be pretty dismal. I tuck a bag of

Doritos under my arm and a candy bar in my sweatshirt pocket. Finding the mustard on the next aisle, I also grab that.

Smuggler-style, I bounce up the stairs and stash my treasure in Jodine's room. I add my finished sandwich and a glass of milk.

Food at last. I chew, eyes half closed. Hooray for Jodine's wondrous taste buds. I savor crisp lettuce, smoked turkey, and tangy mustard. The sweet chocolatiness of the candy bar greets my tongue after that, and when that's gone, I open the Doritos bag and inhale. Ah! Salty, cheesy crunchiness, how I've missed it. Not that I ate a lot of chips and candy while in my own body, since they're highly taxed, but once in a while I indulged at Blair's apartment.

The chip bag accompanies me to the deskscreen, where I surf and chat with another player in Masters of the Cyberverse about the best places to mine ore in the Gorgonlands. Virtual connections are better than nothing, especially since Blair and Krista aren't in-game, and Superguy is off doing some fabulously cool Halloween thing. Like maybe club dancing as a dimpled goblin king or cultivating mega-chills at a haunted house.

When I sign off, I glance down at my Doritos bag and gasp. No way. I've eaten more than half of the chips while fooling around online.

Bad Morgan. Very bad Morgan.

I crumple the bag closed and glance around as if the walls have built-in security cameras. An imaginary graph line of my Health Points takes a major nosedive. I should toss the rest of the bag, but the Kowalczyks might catch me incinerating it in the kitchen. I'd better hide it here in Jodine's room somewhere.

Pawing through the window seat drawers, I can't find a

large enough place to conceal the bag. In the closet, boxes line the top shelves, so I nudge a stepstool over and peek inside some of them. Careful. This is borderline nosey. My contract specifies not to snoop. I take down a large white box and throw a furtive look out the closet door. I'm sure the Kowalczyks won't enter unless I voice-open the bedroom door, but I check to see if all is clear anyway.

I slip off the lid, remove a red sweater that's much too small to wear, and stare goggle-eyed at what lies inside.

CHAPTER 16

Hypertension, sugar-rush, and cholesterol, oh my!

Bags of chips. Cartons of hard candies, caramels, and chocolate bars. Packages of nuts and slim pepperoni sticks. PlasmaWave popcorn.

If Jodine stockpiles this stuff, no wonder she can't lose weight. I glance at my own chips bag, and guilt sloshes over me. Yeah, just like *I'd* been trying to do. With a hiss, I toss the bag and the red sweater inside the box.

A button on the sweater goes *chink!* against something metallic. I frown. What was that? I push the sweater aside to uncover a silver case four inches thick, about e-reader-size. There's a square bio-lock on top. I shake the case. It doesn't rattle. A strange, pleased warmth grows in my chest, making my fingers curl around the silvery edges. I'm not sure where the happy vibe is coming from. This is just a silver case, plain and functional.

I stare at the bio-lock, fingers twitching. My mouth turns into a giddy smile.

Oh, my gosh! I adore this case—or at least, the secrets inside this case.

I hiss in a breath to clear my head and yank myself back to reality. No. This case is Jodine's. I'm snooping, big time. I shouldn't even be messing with this white box. I reach out to shove the red sweater back over the case.

No one knows what's in here, not Mom or Dad, not Nettie. Not even Helena, and she's my best friend. Am I a bad person for hiding this from Helena? For wanting this all to myself?

My right index finger swoops down and presses, deactivating the bio-lock. A password prompt and virtual keypad appear on the screen. Letters form in my mind. But I don't type anything. I don't have to. I already know exactly what's in the case: a dried red rose and a lined spiral booklet written inside with an old-fashioned ballpoint pen.

It's Jodine's diary. Her small, loopy handwriting materializes across my mind's eye.

May 24.

> *He's amazingly awesome! After we sang together (oh my GOSH, we blended outrageously well) the voice director said we sounded excellent, and turned around to make notes on her e-screen. That's when Gavin leaned over, KISSED the side of my face, and whispered that I sang better than anyone he'd ever—*

As fast as I can, I haul my mind back to the walk-in closet where I crouch on my knees, breathing fast. No, no, no!

Flipping realms of schizophrenia. Not only do I know what's in Jodine's personal diary, I know her actual thoughts about this memory—I *heard* them in my mind. I shiver as I slip the case back under the sweater. There are way too many residual memories left inside this body.

Can I last five more months of this without going crazy?

I replace the box on the shelf and rush downstairs for a much-needed sanity break. Music. I need music to drown out the echoes of Jodine's mental voice. While I work the resistance machines, I crank the tunes in my streamer to crashingly loud and let it blast through my mind. Once I'm finished and back in my room, I force myself to read a section of mind-numbing Reducer contract info. My eyes blur after a short time.

I glance at the closet. Unbelievable. Jodine has a boyfriend, and I assumed she didn't. What does that say about me? I shouldn't be surprised she has one, but I am.

Jodine's residual revealed something about myself, not just her.

It must've been difficult for her to decide to become a Loaner, and leave Gavin to wait for her for six long months.

Okay, obviously I can't stop thinking about this. No sense fighting it.

Time to take action.

I bring up the ERT science site and click around. There must be a reason why brainmapping would miss these residual memories. Are they stronger and therefore harder to dislodge when the synapses are chemically activated during mapping? The visions I saw were tied to important events in Jodine's life, linked to powerful emotions. The nervous excitement of painting the sad fruit picture. That forlorn but stirring song she sang at the karaoke machine. The glorious high of evading the evil Cyberverse dragon. Her unexpected kiss from Gavin.

Although it's fascinating research, I find no answers. In fact, I find no mention of residual memories at all. There's also no data on things like personalities blurring or Doritos cravings being passed on. Though frustrating, it makes sense. Most

Reducers stay in the Clinic where memories aren't dredged up, so it doesn't happen often, plus the Institute wouldn't publicize them. If word got out the ERT procedure wasn't as controlled or accurate as it's supposed to be—like the WHA protesters were ranting about—it would be really bad publicity.

I drum my fingers on the desk. The WHA. It's hard to believe they might be *right* about their claims. Some of their wilder accusations have already been debunked. But what if the WHA is correct about this one single thing? It's a disturbing thought.

Somehow, I need to get concrete and accurate information about all this. There's more going on with the Institute than I realized. What's the truth? I don't think I can count on Leo to give me an honest rundown. Even though he insists the residuals aren't a problem, I hope someone is directing Institute scientists behind the scenes to fix the sloppy gaps of ERT.

Just as I'm pushing away from the deskscreen, my Institute phone sends out a message alert from Granddad. The text reels out fast and furious across the screen, like it's on warp-speed.

> What on God's green earth are you trying to pull, Morgan Renita Dey? If you were younger and here at home, I'd take you over my knee and paddle you. Gramma would be having a conniption if she were still alive. She wouldn't approve, believe me!

I grip the phone, frowning as I speak my text.

> Wait, WAIT, Granddad. Slow down. I have no idea what you're talking about.

> You don't, do you? Well, give a good long think about what you did with the earnings of your last

Reducer job—and what you plan to do with this
job's earnings.

Oh, haze it all. Somehow he's found out that I'm helping
pay off his bills.

Please don't be upset. They're my credits, and I
want to help.

It's not your responsibility. You have tech school
to save up for, to use for your own life. Blast this
whole confounded situation. It's bad enough your
mom and dad are having to bail me out of the
bills. You can't use your money for this. I won't
let you.

I should just tell him I won't, then slip credits toward the
debt behind his back. But I'd like to keep things more honest
between us than that.

It's either I help pay, or we get sent to The
Commons. I don't think you want that.

Of course not.

The words stop scrolling for a handful of tense seconds.

Doggone it, I don't know what to do. At the very
least, I'm going to pay you back.

No, please don't worry about doing that. We'll
figure out something.

Meanwhile—all because of me—your real self is
a vegetable, and a copy of your brain waves is
stuck inside someone else's body.

I don't know what to say to ease his guilt. I really wish he hadn't found out.

I'll be all right, Granddad.

You'd better be. Bye, sweetie. I'm going to go nuke some popcorn so I don't nab another blasted cigarette. Already had my quota for today.

His screen goes blank.

Swinging my arms, I blow out a monstrous sigh. Well, that was uncomfortable, not to mention intense. More pressure about this job is *not* what I need right now. I know Granddad doesn't like me helping pay the bills, but doesn't he see that I think he's worth it? Even with all that's been going on lately—the residuals, the bottle bombs, and the numerous attacks—I have to keep this job. For him. For our whole family.

There are so many expectations and complications with this assignment. I'm trying to hold it together, but I can feel the strain, the cracks starting to form on my psyche.

Even slabs of concrete can be broken up after repeated and incessant slams of a jackhammer.

Shaking the tension from my arms and fingers, I drift into the living room and command the TV on. A talk show about recycling materializes. After a few minutes, an ad for a new model of car zooms over the platform, flaunting its holographic stuff as Dr. K. strolls into the room wearing workout sweats.

"There's an ingeniously designed vehicle," he says. "Nice aerodynamic lines. That same manufacturer pioneered the analyzing system to prevent drunk driving. No voice-activation if the driver's breath count is too high."

"That's cool."

"It's technology, protecting us from ourselves."

The car ad vanishes and is replaced by the image of an

overweight blonde, her face glum. A lively narrator speaks of ERT while the image melts into Shelby Johnson's smiling, thinner self, like the vid I saw in Leo's office. The transformation looks fabulous.

"The Institute has great ads," I say. Pity I can't tell Dr. K. that I created Shelby's slim new look.

Dr. K. sits on the other end of the sofa. "I'm glad they extended the program to include younger teens, so Jodine could join up sooner."

"Maybe being thinner will make her happier." I order the TV off, dematerializing a bunch of skiers.

"I have no idea." Dr. K. rakes a hand over his close-cropped hair, hair that might be as curly as Jodine's if it were longer. "I know Janeth and I haven't spent much time with her the past few years, due to work responsibilities. We certainly appreciate your efforts to help her. I just wish the WHA would reign in its members and switch to more peaceful ways of protesting."

"Yeah, what's their problem? The Reducer program improves people's lives. That ought to count for something."

"Partly, the WHA doesn't want the government to make regulations. They want the people to have the right to decide things like how much to weigh and whether or not to smoke."

Put an end to "goverment" control. Yeah, I remember that sign, the one Mr. Fringe-of-Stringy-Gray-Hair carried. "But people are turning themselves into walking time bombs by overeating and smoking. Congress is just protecting people from their own bad choices. Just like the car with the breathalyzer system."

Dr. K. gives a somewhat weary smile. "I guess it's a balancing act of how much control and regulations we should have, versus total freedom and choice. No one wants to compromise." He stands. "On that cheery note, I'm going to work out. I'll talk to you another time."

The living room seems doubly empty after Dr. K. leaves. His words bounce around in my head. I don't know why anyone would want to join the WHA. I saw Walter Herry's vid, with him ranting about "taking rights back" and "using force if necessary."

Yeah. Like attacking teenage girls and tossing bottle bombs onto Institute property help get people's rights back.

I sigh. There's about an hour until it's time for dinner leftovers. I'll give Dr. K. privacy in the gym, and I don't feel like doing HoloSports, especially since I've already showered. Maybe I'll do karaoke instead. That sounds more fun.

It shouldn't be a problem if I take the rest of the day off for the holiday. I'll invent something for my log entry to keep Leo happy, and say I forgot to turn on my exercise app. One evening won't make a difference in my overall assignment.

The next day dawns as a fresh month to chase away the bleakness of Halloween. Or at least that's my goal. It's time to exercise hard and purge any remaining evidence of Doritos and candy bars from my hips. I'll keep dogpaddling in the stormy sea that working for the Institute has become. When I get back to the house, I can do some more online searches and try to unearth what's really going on—even if I have to sort through the conspiracy hype of the WHA site.

I meet Vonn at the park for our usual morning laps before he goes to work.

"Who triumphed, zombie-cyborgs or the aliens?" I ask him as we're puffing along.

He throws me a mischievous look. "Can't tell you. I don't believe in spoilers."

"Who said I'll *ever* watch that movie?" I ask with a return smirk.

"You have to. It's a classic, perfect for a Halloween shriek-fest. Maybe next year we won't be Reducers, and we can watch it together."

I marvel at him, with his nut-brown hair and the impish glint in his eyes. He hopes we'll still be hanging out next October? Surprising, but I like the idea. A lot. "We still haven't figured out a way to let our real selves know about each other," I say. "It's not like we can text one of our friends to tell us to get together."

"Not with Leo and the auto-system screening our every word. He'd delete our messages, and we'd get immediately axed."

Yeah. If Leo knew how much we were hanging out, meeting every day for walks and going to cafés and holding hands, our contracts would be erased in one single, terrible instant. Faster than we could say, "I've just lost all my hard-earned credits." I'm extra careful when I dictate my daily logs. I never mention I've changed parks so Leo can't tell my location is identical to Vonn's.

I always thought it was an overblown scare tactic that Leo screened our communication. Maybe I was mistaken, like I'm discovering I'm wrong about a lot of other things about the Institute. Not a pleasant thought.

"I could leave myself a note in my school locker," I say. "Or tell my friends in person. The problem would be getting to the Yellow Zone to talk to them. I'm not supposed to ride the MT that far, or let anyone see who I'm Reducing for."

"We have a few months left to figure it out."

I slip my hand in his. He's level-headed, and as warming to my soul as a bowl of Nettie's turkey-celery soup. Familiar and welcome. Even his appearance…but that's crazy. Months from now he'll be the same personality, but I can't get used to him looking like he does now. In August he'll animate his own body again, not Matt's. How weird will *that* be?

"Hey." I halt on the path. "Do you have a photo of your real self that I can see on your phone, so it's not suspicious I'm checking it out? I don't care if it's against the rules to share. I'm really curious."

Vonn pulls his Institute phone from his sweatshirt pocket and accesses his CyberFace profile. "It shouldn't be prohibited. I think we just have to keep quiet about our Loaner info."

I lean in to see what he's got. Photo One: a close-up of a smirky dark-haired guy with a slightly hawkish nose and dimples at the edges of his smile. Photo Two: a distant shot of his lanky figure doing a handstand next to a few right-side-up guy friends. Photo Three: a crooked shot of him fiddling with his phone and giving the photographer a jovial thumbs-up.

I grin. "You're freaking cute in real life. Kind of a joker, though, aren't you?"

"Absolutely not," Vonn says in mock outrage.

Wait a minute. I look at the first photo again, and my mouth falls open. Those dimples look seriously familiar. Is he the hot guy from Leo's waiting room—*Superguy?* A wave of dizzy joy hits me.

"We've already met in real life," I say. "Back in June at the admin building."

He cocks one brown eyebrow. "No way. Let's see your pics. Cough 'em up."

Heart thumping like mad, I bring up my photos on

CyberFace. Smiling with Blair and Krista at a science expo that I dragged them to. Standing at home with Granddad's arm curled around me. Cracking up with my old boyfriend at the Flash Point. Oops, I forgot to delete that last one.

"It's you!" Vonn says. "You're @geektastic! You were wearing black jeans and a bright red T-shirt. Your eyes are big and dark brown, like a gazelle's. So adorable."

"Impressive you remember my outfit." I fight a blush that creeps onto my face. His whole description of me is flattering, to tell the truth. "Wow, crazy how we've been messaging each other all this time and didn't know we were the same people."

"I'm officially blown out of the water." He looks it, too. His eyes blink, unfocused, and he fumbles his phone as he pockets it. "Who's the lucky guy? I can't believe you left a boyfriend behind to do this job."

"Ex-boyfriend," I'm quick to say. "It's been over since February. And I had a blast with our TeenDom chats." It was a frustrating kind of "blast" at times, but that's beside the point.

Vonn clears his throat. "So…if your thing with your ex is totally over, why didn't you ever want to get together with me? I kept asking, real polite and all, and you never answered."

I stare into his eyes so long and stony, it's a wonder he doesn't flinch. "Excuse me? I didn't answer *you*? I must've asked at least a dozen times in a dozen different ways if you wanted to meet up. I asked what your name was, where you lived. If you wanted to set up a time when we could text longer. You totally blew me off. Never answered me once."

"No way." He grabs my hand. His grip is intense, almost frantic. "If you sent things like that, Morgan, I didn't get them. I asked you about your name, too. I told you I'd take you out for your first taste of sushi. I said I'd hop an MT and hang out in the Yellow Zone with you anytime you wanted. After a while I just stopped asking, since I never got a response."

"I didn't get anything like that from you. It can't be a site malfunction either, not with just parts of our texts missing." The words drag from my mouth, thick and heavy. Something ugly is going on. I don't know what, unless…a single, bitter thought spears me. "Oh, man. I think I know what happened. When we first started texting, you were doing your summer Reducer job, using your Institute phone. Then I started this job as Jodine, using an Institute phone. That's what happened. I bet Leo deleted those lines."

"What the haze for? We weren't violating privacy restrictions." Vonn's voice is a growl, a rumble of dark thunder. "Our personal relationship is none of his business. It has nothing to do with being a Reducer and having a forbidden real-time relationship on the job, like we're doing now."

"He didn't want us to meet for some reason." I try to think back to what I said, how I said it. "I do remember texting that it'd be way more exciting than Clinic exercising to go dancing or paintballing or hover-skating. Maybe he thought we'd start hanging out so much, we wouldn't want to be Reducers anymore. He really needs dedicated workers."

"Selfish son of a—" Vonn's eyes glint with a white-hot heat. He starts walking off down the path at full speed, and I scramble to catch up with him.

We remain wordless for a few minutes. I let him cool off, and try to process what Leo's done. Even as director, he had no right to delete parts of our personal messages. It's one more thing added to my growing list of complaints against him. I can't trust him about anything, it seems. I wonder if he installed tracking software on Jodine's home computer…

maybe it's not a smart idea to scour the WHA sites while I'm on the job. I'd probably get flagged.

Crimp it all. Roadblocks everywhere.

I'm too limited with what I can do as a Reducer.

Although wow, Vonn is *Superguy*, the guy I met in Leo's waiting room, and he really *does* care. He wasn't ignoring me all those times I asked to get together with him.

Vonn slows his stride as his infuriated energy winds down. "We could've arranged to meet before you started your current assignment, if it weren't for Leo's meddling."

"We only had one free day. At least now we've met, even if we are in different bodies. That thwarts Leo, big time." Gee. I'm so practical, I'm annoying myself.

"I guess." He blasts out a sigh, and throws me a sideways look. "You know, your real body is top-notch awesome, Geekling, but your Loaner's pretty cute, too."

"Not with this hair and freckles."

"Nothing wrong with curly hair and freckles." Vonn flips a coiled strand across my shoulder.

I roll my eyes, and he cracks a more relaxed smile. We link arms during our final lap.

"Same time tomorrow, same place," I say as we finish.

"You got it, Slave Driver." Vonn salutes and sets off for work.

I wave at his receding figure. My smile clings to my face as I board the MT and ride to the Red Zone. It's mind-bending that I just walked the park with Superguy. No wonder I've felt drawn to him, even in his Matt body. A personality that magnetic can't be muted.

Now I'm even more psyched about getting together in August when he finishes his assignment.

CHAPTER 17

Around 1430 I wander into the kitchen and discover Nettie has returned from her vacation. She is standing at the fridge studying its contents, most likely plotting dinner.

"How was your day off?" I swat at the green airbot as it hovers too close.

"Wonderful," she says. "My brother's party had a live band, apple bobbing, and goofy games. I trust you survived without me."

"I did okay." I'm not going to talk about my horrendous failings yesterday.

Nettie mumbles something about a stew and holds out a cabbage. "Can you set that on the counter for me, Jodine?"

The words skewer me. "Morgan. I'm *Morgan*."

Nettie's eyes are glazed for a moment before she focuses. "Did I just call you Jodine? Sorry about that. Habit."

"It's okay," I say through gritted teeth. But it's not okay. I may do some things like Jodine, since I have her taste buds and her voice and all, but I'm *not* Jodine. I'm myself, absolutely separate from the girl who belongs to this body. Morgan Dey, period. I plunk the cabbage on the counter. "I'm off to do some boxing, unless you need help with dinner."

"Go ahead, I'm fine," she says, absorbed with the veggie drawer again.

I withdraw to the game room. I hook and jab and punch my boxing holo-foe until my right shoulder starts to ache from the high resistance setting I've selected. In the gym I switch to the treadmill, followed by the weight machine. After that, Jodine's body goes on strike. The legs wobble, a sharp pain nails me under the ribs, and the muscles feel as limp as eight-week-old lettuce.

Enough already.

Upstairs, I shower and find a message waiting from Mom, who says she and her band are planning to fly back east to do an opener for The Gazelles. This could be her big chance to be discovered. That'd be cool. I spin toward the bed to check my other mail and come face to face with the green airbot. Its sensor lights blink as it hums by my nose. It gives a trilly little greeting.

"You're peeving me, kid," I say. "I know you and Jodine had a cozy relationship, but I'm not her. I don't need a mechanical pet to keep me company."

The airbot bobs left a few inches and hovers like a puppy panting in midair.

"Higher." I point to the ceiling.

It floats upward. As it does, I swear its hum winds into a sharper pitch, like a small whine. I ignore the guilt that mushrooms inside me. Ridiculous. The critter is a mass of wires and circuitry, and I have *not* hurt its feelings. Although I can identify with the thing. Trapped in an alien form, wanting to connect with someone...

Next, I open a message from Krista.

> What's up? The Flash Point party last night was
> a blast. Wish you'd been there! Randy is SUCH
> wild fun to hang with! We're going hover-skating
> Friday. Catch ya later. Hugs!

It's the same kind of thing Blair and Krista have been saying for the past four weeks. Fun, hot boyfriends, and slender-bodied freedom. I heave myself backward onto the bed and stare virtual holes into the ceiling. Swear words fester in my mind. I close my eyes and summon up the feel of Vonn's hand in mine, which counteracts my pity party a little.

"Mrs. Kowalczyk is here to see you," the house system computer informs me.

"Come in." I sit up as the door opens to reveal Mrs. K.'s slim figure.

"Look at you." She smiles, checking out my T-shirt and stretch jeans. "You're wearing something besides sweats. That's marvelous." She sounds giddy.

"I have a few more things I can wear now." Should I be worried? She's not usually this friendly or pleasant.

"I've finished my commissioned painting." She sweeps her arms outward as if she's hugging the entire world. "Charles and Nettie saw it earlier. Would you like to?"

My dark and stormy thoughts vanish. "I'd love to take a look."

Mrs. K. radiates delight and leads me to the elevator pod. As we rise, she bounces, swinging her hands by the sides of her designer slacks. I crack a smile. Her behavior seems unusual, but I've seen her less than a dozen times since I came here. I don't really know her.

On the next floor, we enter a door on the right. Natural light bathes the room, flooding in from a wall of windows. Rows of canvases line up like soldiers against the opposite wall, and a cabinet holds brushes and the nozzles of what must be a paint-dispensing machine.

I walk over to a giant canvas on an easel. My mouth falls open. A countryside. Perfect, as if seen in a dream. The arms of a tree stretch out over most of the canvas, the tree's foliage impossibly emerald. The grass below looks softer than carpet, almost feathery. Flowers dot the grassy borders near a small stream. The whole scene glistens with vibrant green and robust yellow, sharp white and earthy brown.

"That's brilliant," I manage to say. "I could stare at it forever. I love realistic art."

"Representational," Mrs. K. says. "That's the art term. Although what I do is not strictly true to life. That's what cameras are for."

"Yeah, your artwork's more dreamlike."

"That's the intention," she says with approval. "Have you ever done any painting yourself, at school perhaps?"

I hesitate. I've never been that charged up about drawing or painting. I appreciate art, but it's more a viewer than a participant sport to me. "Just computer art with GenieDraw and a stylus. My mom's a singer, so I've been around music more than art. She has a great voice, even though mine's awful."

"I'm sure it's not that bad."

"Trust me, it is. I fall off-tune all the time. It's like I know what the notes should be, but I can't make myself sing them right." I toss her a tentative glance. "Jodine has an amazing voice. I love doing karaoke with it."

"She does love to sing." Mrs. K. purses her lips with

contemplation or displeasure, I can't tell which. "Would you like to try painting something?"

"Really?" I have no idea why I'm feeling so psyched about this all of a sudden. The idea of holding a real brush and splotching some bright, gooey paint on something sounds terrific. Unless… it's not 100 percent me who's responding. That thought stabs me and deflates a bit of my enthusiasm. "Right now?"

"Of course." She walks to the wall and nabs a small canvas.

I follow her every move while she sets up an easel and directs the paint machine to bestow blobs of color across a palette. She produces a photo of an apple and hands me an antiquated thing I don't see often: a pencil. She points. "Sketch this apple. Basically round, you see, except flatter on these two sides."

Yeah, right. My hand shakes a little as the pencil scratches over the canvas.

"Keep your wrist loose. Pretend it's your computer stylus."

That helps. Still… "It's lopsided," I say. "It looks like an MT ran over it."

Mrs. K. gives a soft laugh. "It's not that bad. Here's a brush. We'll start with red, and add other colors. I'll tell you how to shade and make the apple look three-dimensional."

Red! I clutch the brush like it's a lifeline. An unexplained thrill roller-coasters through me as I dab the bristles into a shiny puddle of crimson. *Hue. Intensity.* Where have I heard those words? Not in class, but they fit with what I'm doing. I work under Mrs. K.'s guidance for a while, with a lumpy yet presentable apple emerging from the canvas. Then Nettie's amiable voice floats into the room through the house intercom.

"Dinner is nearly ready, Mrs. Kowalczyk. Is Morgan up there?"

"She is," Mrs. K. says. "We'll both come down. Don't bother

to set up in the dining room unless Charles joins us." She swings back to study my first-attempt apple. "That's quite tolerable for a beginner, dynamic despite the rough blending. You may have some natural talent...it's too bad Jodine doesn't. Once a few years back she painted a very wooden-looking still life with fruit and a vase."

Ugh, Mrs. K. saw Jodine's painting? That must've been humiliating. I'm glad Mrs. K. likes *my* apple. Imagine that. I might be good at techfree art. Now there's something I wouldn't have guessed—or even attempted, under other circumstances. Jodine's underlying enthusiasm must've helped push me into trying.

Along with her singing voice, it's a cool perk of being in her body. The trouble is, I have little or no control when these things happen. It's almost like I'm being swallowed alive by Jodine's abilities and preferences. Creepy to a maximum degree. It's a good thing I can go back to being totally me in April.

I can't wait to have all my thoughts and actions to myself.

Mrs. K. slips my brush into a cleaning unit, and we head downstairs. We eat at the counter island with Nettie, who has prepared an out-of-this-universe Cajun shrimp and pilaf dinner that I'd love to accept seconds on. I manage to resist another helping.

But mostly because Mrs. K. perches on the stool to my right.

The rest of the week marches by. On Friday I'm still in penance mode. I board the MT for the park early, planning to put in a concentrated dose of exercise before Vonn shows up. Brushing a stray coil of hair from my face, I catch sight of my fingernails. Nice. At least my nails have grown out beyond the stubby nublets Jodine bit them into.

My phone blings as I'm getting off the MT.

How's my favorite brain clone? Granddad asks.

I burst into a startled laugh.

I'm okay. I'm out jogging, or trying to. Do you really want to talk to a brainwashed copy of your granddaughter?

I'll take what I can get. The real Morgan isn't available.

Okay. I won't push it.

What's up?

Got some good news. Danged government retirement home emailed me yesterday. Tons more forms to fill out, but they might have an opening in a few weeks. Cross your fingers, and your toes too. Soon I'll be out of your mom's and dad's hair, and into a place of my own.

That's great!

My smile fades as the next logical thought stabs me in the heart. If Granddad moves into the retirement home while I'm being Jodine, he'll be long gone by the time I return in April. His bushy-haired self won't be sitting in the recliner, smelling of cigarette smoke and aftershave. The spare room will be cleared of his strewn-about shirts and socks and old-fashioned printed books, the guest bed empty.

But I won't get to say good-bye to you in person.

There's a long pause before Granddad answers.

That's why I'm calling, even though it's not actually
you. I wanted to feel like you knew I was leaving.
Better than nothing.

I don't bother to tell him that when I finish my Reducer
job and wake up without these memories, it's still going to be
a shock to see his room vacant. My old brainmap won't have
any preparation for this news—unless I manage to read six
months' worth of text messages before I arrive home.

I'll come see you in April, I promise. You know I
will.

The place is way out on the edge of the Yellow
Zone.

It's in the Blue Zone. Has he forgotten, or is he confused?

Doesn't matter. I'll visit you no matter what.

I bet your real self would say that, too. You know
how Gramma always said you were my devoted
little buddy. She said your arms were exactly the
right length to wrap around my neck. Ah, well.
Get back to your jogging and lose that weight so
I can have my granddaughter back.

I will. Love ya.

I tap off and stare at my phone. Having Granddad live with
us puts a strain on our budget, and sometimes he's crabby, but
in a few weeks he'll be gone. I already feel lost without him. I
don't blame him for being grumpy. He misses Gramma a ton,

and there's not much for him to do all day except read books and watch TV. When Gramma was alive, he cracked more jokes. He tickled me until I shrieked, and he played catch with Dad and me in the Yellow Zone park. He teased Mom so much that she took revenge with a flyswatter and chased him around his small apartment until he hid behind Gramma for safety.

Gosh, I miss Gramma too, singing away in her stew-scented kitchen. And now Granddad's leaving earlier than I want. Is this turning into another depressing day, like Halloween?

I clench my teeth. Focus. Back to the job I'm getting paid for, and then I can go home and figure out how to deal with Granddad living in the retirement home.

At the park, I start full-speed along the paths with other early morning risers. By the time I spot Vonn heading toward the bench where we usually meet, I've slowed from a bouncing jog into a bouncing walk.

"Hi, park buddy!" Vonn calls as he walks up. "Ready to carve off those pounds?"

"Absolutely." The edges of my worry melt a little. His enthusiasm is contagious.

I fall into step with him. After our first lap, Vonn points down the street. "Let's ditch the park, 007. I want to see something different while we work out."

"I'm game."

We swerve across the street into a land of cafés, artificial trees, and trash incinerators. Wallscreens on buildings blast their ad-vids, while vendorbots shout about hamburgers and hot dogs, shish-kabobs and coffee. Why is everything always about food? I can't get away from it.

A guy on a bicycle zips past. "I'd love to go biking," I say to Vonn, my voice saturated with longing. "I wonder if Jodine has a bike."

"Matt sure doesn't." He throws a look of pretend guilt at a security camera mounted on the corner of a building. "Oops, I hope that wasn't too personal of information. I don't want to void my contract."

"Too late. I'm turning you in. You'll be shackled in a prison cubicle for the rest of your life, with no chance of payment or parole."

Vonn winces. "No payment? You're merciless." He stops at a vendorbot, buys two strawberry juices, and hands me one. "Here's a bribe to keep quiet about my hideous lapse of protocol."

I giggle and take a long drink. "Bribe accepted."

"It's a good thing those cameras don't use audio, or we'd be flagged by the auto-system."

"We do love to live dangerously." I'm being flip of course, because the risk of losing everything we've been working for is a very real one. It's best not to think about it too much, or I'll start biting my fingernails again.

Vonn's hand rests on my shoulder, large and warm. "Look, there's an interactive vid theater across the street. Perfect for a real date. Want to go?"

"I love those! But that'll mess up our workout."

"Put your exercise app on pause. We can finish when we're done."

I need no further prompting. I stop my app, and we wait for a lone car to glide down the street before we cross. We're nearly to the sidewalk when Vonn gives a surprised grunt. He reaches out as a tall, lean guy walks by the theater. The guy comes to a halt.

"Steven!" Vonn says with a delirious smile. "My, uh, room-mate talks about how he hasn't seen you since last year. His name is Vonn Alexander. He has a framed photo of you guys goofing around at the Blue Zone shooting range. How've you been, and why haven't you answered his emails? Did you for-get the password to your email account again?"

The guy hunches deeper into his leather jacket, his eyes showing no flicker of recognition. "Sorry, I'm not Steven. I don't know anyone named Vonn, and I've never been to the Blue Zone in my life. I live in Missouri. I'm just here for a friend's wedding."

Vonn's arm flops to his side. "Missouri? No way. You look exactly like him, except maybe a better haircut and cooler clothes. You even have the same faint birthmark on your forehead. Vonn said he used to tease Steven about how it's shaped like a heart."

"Uh, that isn't me. My name's Chad." The guy gives a hollow laugh. "Maybe I have a twin brother I don't know about."

"Huh. My mistake, I guess."

The guy moves on. Vonn stares after him, looking per-plexed and a little ungrounded. I have a sudden urge to hug him, he looks so lost.

"I could've sworn that was Steven," Vonn mutters.

"Funny how people can look so much alike. Unless he *is* your friend's long-lost twin."

"Even a twin wouldn't have the exact same birthmark. I swear, that was him."

I shoulder-bump him and smile. "Maybe Chad's a Reducer who permanently stole a Loaner body and ran off with it to Missouri."

"Nah. Steven was never a Loaner. He was totally into racquetball, kept in great shape. We even went to Rock Mountain one time." He gives himself a shake, but he still looks troubled.

We cross the sidewalk. Outside the theater, we check out the holo-posters, one displaying vipers that writhe and hiss, the other featuring tentacled aliens with red pulsing eyes.

"We can be jungle spies or do sci-fi on another planet," I say. Maybe a vid will erase the deep frown-crease on Vonn's forehead. "Your choice."

"Aliens. I'm definitely in the mood to blast the tentacles off something."

We pay and enter the silent, near-dark vidroom. At this time of day, we have the place to ourselves, though the room holds about twenty seats. Our holographic vid comes stocked with wireless ray guns. As soon as we sit, the walls around us begin rippling, colors and shapes expanding into holographic forms.

A slow smile spreads across my face. We've been transported to a windswept planet. Spherical buildings float on the horizon, tethered like helium balloons to a barren desert landscape. Triple suns hang in a violently red sky. I start to sweat as the planet heats up and a surge of warm air hits me in the face. Eerie music seeps into the room.

"It's getting hot in here," Vonn says next to me. He gives a loud sigh and reaches over to enfold my hand in his. "This is gonna be fun, but I wish I were in my own body right now."

I sneak a look at him. What does he mean by that? I'm not sure if he's implying he could do this vid better in his own body, or if he's tired of being a Reducer. Or if he wants to hold my hand with his real hand. His face in the semi-darkness gives away nothing. He leaves his hand linked with mine until a dust cloud materializes in the distance and turns the color of rust.

"Watch out," he says. "Something's coming in that cloud."

We grab our ray guns from the armrests. With our fingers on the firing buttons, we wait. The cloud swirls nearer and halts twenty feet away. Hovering. Minutes trickle by. The music slows to a creepy pace.

I shriek as something whips my neck. I twist left to find a slit-eyed alien snapping its slithery tentacles at me. It spits something wet onto my arm. I plug the beast three rapid shots with my ray gun before it quivers and falls.

"They're tunneling under the sand!" Vonn yells, firing like crazy. More aliens burst into view, sending out tentacles like thin wet whips. "Ouch, take that, you slimy pile of guts—"

I keep shooting. The rusty cloud begins to disperse as Vonn and I gun down the aliens. When the last creature utters a harsh cry and flops onto the sand to bubble and froth in gruesome death throes, I holster my gun in the armrest. *Yes!* Enormous fun.

"Whew," Vonn says, breathing hard. "That was awesome, but intense."

I rub my neck and arm where I was whipped. "Yeah, what the haze? The theater's got the air streams a little too compressed, don't ya think?"

"Can't say it's not realistic." Vonn chuckles, the sound low and comforting. He slips his hand back into mine.

Nice. I twine my fingers around his, aware of every single touch receptor that my hand now possesses. My sensory neurons are going wild.

The vid ushers us into a hovercraft, and the air speeds into an exhilarating breeze to simulate movement toward one of the spherical alien buildings. I grin a maniac's grin in the golden glow of the scenery. Imagine. I'm holding hands with *Superguy.* Sure, it's Matt's body, but I can sense Vonn's personality—his soul—in the way he moves his hands and in the way he's lightly breathing. How he's holding his mouth in that charming, satisfied smile.

I glance at his profile. Once we're our real selves, will we have the same great connection? Vonn likes the Morgan who met him at the Institute and texted him on TeenDom. He also seems to like the Morgan I am now, inside Jodine. This version is the one he's spent actual time with and gotten to know in real life. Am I different from my usual self? I'm *not* Jodine, but I've certainly been affected by her residuals and by aspects of her body—her taste buds, her song preferences, and a deep love for art and the color red.

Scary. Jodine could be rubbing off on me in ways I don't even realize. Maybe Granddad was right when he said people's appearances are a crucial part of their personalities. Vonn and I *both* might be different people when we're in our own bodies.

How much different?

I don't have time to ponder it further. An ambush party awaits us in the floating alien building. We escape by plunging down the building's tether shaft and find ourselves in an underground passage filled with roaring fire.

Even so, it's hard to drag my gaze from Vonn's intriguing mouth. The thought of a kiss with him is much more tantalizing than the imminent danger we're in.

CHAPTER 18

My footsteps are infused with a giddy bounce by the time Vonn and I leave the vid theater. No kiss has materialized, but the heady sensation of his hand in mine warms me from the inside out. We walk back toward the park, passing cafés and clothing boutiques and vidgame shops. One trendy café features a scattering of outdoor tables. The aromas of blueberry muffins and sweet coffee swirl over me, sending a pang through my gut, taking some of the air out of my giddiness.

Blueberry. Like the tea Granddad always drinks.

I wish I were heading to my own home right now. Except for hanging with Vonn, I'm far away from everyone I want to be with these days.

My glance sweeps over people seated at the café tables, and I lock gazes with Chad, the guy Vonn swore was his old friend Steven. That heart-shaped birthmark. The athletic build. His expression goes tight. A long-haired guy sits with him, and his glance ping-pongs from Chad to me.

Thoughts of kisses fly from my head. For Vonn's sake — and my own suspicions about what the Institute is doing behind the scenes—I have to find out what's going on. I stride over to Chad, pulling Vonn with me, and prop one hand on my hip. "Spill it. No two people can have the exact same birthmark. You have Vonn's friend's body, and I want to know how and why."

"You watch too much science fiction," Chad says. "People can't switch bodies."

"Loaners and Reducers do."

He squints. "Nah. I wasn't part of some crazy fat-reducing program. I've heard of it, though." He rakes his attention over me, head to toe. "Are you in it? Looks like you need to be."

The long-haired guy lets out a sputtery laugh. Great. Not the direction I want to go with this conversation, with the spotlight on Jodine.

Vonn gives Chad's friend a hard look and pins Chad with an even harder one. "She's talking about you, not her, and we're not leaving until you tell us how you ended up with Steven's body."

"You're both certified nutso." Chad fiddles with the paper on his blueberry muffin. "I've been in this body all my life."

"Yeah, right." I release Vonn's hand, pluck out my phone, and tap up a certain fanatic rights-advocate site. "Want some free publicity about this? I'm sure the WHA would love to hear the gory details, because they jump on stories about body swapping. I bet it'll go viral in less than twenty-four hours. Oh, look, here's their contact number—"

Chad leaps up and places a tense hand on my arm. "No, don't do that. I can't have any spotlights on me." He scans the café area and ducks closer to my ear. "I'll tell you. My buddy here already knows. Just promise you won't say anything to anyone else, because I could get in seriously big trouble. You know how illegal this is."

Yeah, because Transfers are only sanctioned for weight loss, period.

"Start talking." I'm not promising anything.

He lands back in his chair with a thump. "Okay, so...I was dying in Missouri. Multiple myeloma—bone cancer. Four stinkin' years of radiation, chemo, and a megacomplex-load of meds. All for nothing." His voice is low, almost a murmur.

"Oh." This isn't what I thought he'd say. I'm not sure what I expected, to tell the truth. I step closer to hear him better. Vonn does too, re-gripping my hand as if he's anchoring himself.

"My mom couldn't handle that I was gonna die before I reached twenty-five." Chad swallows as if it's painful. "My dad left us a lot of money when he passed away, and since she works for National Health Care, she managed to find a place that did ERT procedures...for a price. The body I'm inside of now was on life support, brain dead because of some sort of bad accident in the Blue Zone. My mom said his foster parents agreed to have him taken off the machines and let me have his body. His life, swapped for mine. All I had to do was have my last name changed since I looked different, and get my ID chip tweaked."

"A place that does ERT. You mean The Body Institute?"

He shrugs and flicks a glance at his friend. "I don't know. In February I woke up in a hotel in Seattle with my mom. It could've been a black-market operation for all I know. Anyway, I didn't think I'd run into anyone from the Blue Zone when I visited my friend here. Guess I should've covered up the hazin' birthmark."

"I guess so," I say, unable to think of anything else. A black-market ERT operation...that doesn't seem likely. The

Institute's genius tech is highly advanced and safeguarded, and I'm not sure anyone else could build the equipment and develop it properly, even if he or she knew the basic know-how. But that means the Institute would've done the procedure, and that doesn't make sense, either. Especially since tweaking IDs is high-level illegal.

"If all of that's true," Vonn says, "why didn't I see anything online about Steven being in an accident?"

Chad shrugs again. "Heck if I know. I don't control the news or social media."

I'm not sure this helps Vonn much. I don't know if discovering Steven's mind is gone forever hurts any less than always wondering what happened to him.

"Thanks for the explanation," I say to Chad.

Chad grunts, staring at his latte cup. Vonn and I leave him with his long-haired friend and the other half of his blueberry muffin, but it doesn't look like he has much appetite for his food anymore.

I squint down at the bathroom scale, past the set of toes parked there. Here it is, two-thirds into the month of November, and I've only lost ten pounds. I'm behind schedule. Last month I lost a total of twenty-two, a whole five pounds beyond the call of duty. I can't waste my entire head start. A curse on Nettie's kitchen being cheery and welcoming, and a curse on Nettie for fixing such wondrous meals.

To make things even worse, Thanksgiving is coming up later this week.

Honestly. Holidays should be banned out of respect for

people trying to lose weight.

I wolf down some breakfast and hustle off to meet Vonn. When I arrive at our usual rendezvous bench, he checks his phone and waggles a finger at me.

"About time, Miss Fitness." He gives me that smile of his with its irresistible energy, aiming it straight at me. "You're forty-six seconds late. If you're constantly late, how can we squeeze in a decent walk before I go to work and you go to the Clinic?"

I beam some energy right back. "I'm terribly sorry. It won't happen again."

"It better not, or I'll report you to Leo."

We laugh, even though in reality it's a scary thought. I *can't* lose my walks with Vonn. He's the only thing that keeps me sane while I'm in this body.

"I'm glad you're doing this with me, 007," Vonn says, his fingers strong around mine as we walk. "It takes pure grit to be out here every day."

"Beats the gym any time, and the company is better."

Vonn blows out a heavy sigh. "You know, I'm still having trouble accepting that Steven is gone. Or that his foster parents gave his body to someone else. Permanently. I'm really pissed off at the Institute right now for doing that. Just let the poor guy rest in peace, not farm his body out to strangers."

"I agree, although we don't know the Institute had anything to do with it." While it's great Steven's body is allowing Chad to live, it's awful to think about what it means for Vonn. If I saw Blair and Krista on the street one day and they didn't know me, I'd be freaked. Even if Steven was for all practical purposes dead already, it's weird to recycle his *whole body* like a transplanted lung or liver or heart.

Way ugly thoughts. No wonder Vonn's having a hard time processing the news. Some serious comforting is in order right now.

I stop Vonn on the path and wrap my arms around him. His arms curve around me. We tighten the hug, and I bury my face against his shoulder.

After a few minutes, Vonn relaxes. When I raise my head, he leans down and gives me a soft kiss on the mouth.

He smiles, then sobers up. "I hate to say this," he says, "but I'd better head off to work. The squirrels await."

I smooth my hand over his shoulder, my head spinning from the touch of his lips. Fireworks and warm fuzzies! He kissed me. He *kissed* me! A short one, yes, but really gentle and full of feeling.

We clasp hands and walk to the far edge of the park.

"See you tomorrow, Superguy," I say as our fingers slide apart.

"I hope I can kiss you again when we're in our real bodies." Vonn's voice is low, but intense. "I've been wanting to do that for a while and decided I couldn't wait."

I smile into his eyes. "Well, I'm glad you quit waiting."

We hug again, and I hike back to the MT shelter.

I board the Express bound for the Red Zone and ride while streaming some exhilarating music, replaying his soft kiss in my mind. It's kind of strange being in Jodine's body while kissing someone, but hopefully she—or Leo—won't ever find out. I look forward to when Vonn and I are ourselves again, and we don't have to worry about that anymore.

As the MT slows and nears the Alameda Street shelter, people around me begin peering out the windows, murmuring and pointing. I turn to see an accumulation of smoke or some kind of grungy haze looming in the sky about a quarter mile away. It doesn't quite look like weather clouds, and it seems like it's hanging over the Institute.

My heartbeat quickens, and I scramble off the MT. A vidscreen on a nearby building shows a reporter standing in front of a huge pile of rubble. Like daggers in my ears, I catch the words "The Body Institute."

Oh, no. The scene looks like the scorched grounds of the Boston branch. Only on a much larger scale. At a near jog, I take off for the Institute grounds.

What I see when I get closer isn't encouraging. Enforcers swarm the street, and barricades block the entrance. Onlookers gawk while a news team transmits on my left. I pass a knot of reporters.

"—occurred at oh-seven-twenty today," a reporter is saying. "The explosion originated inside the suspended animation room, where it demolished everything there and ripped toward the front. At the time of the blast, the Institute was not yet open for the day, but casualties include six staff members and two guards who were on night duty. Three other workers experienced severe injuries and have been admitted to the Alameda Hospital. No one at the nearby Clinic was harmed, though the building itself has sustained damage to the roof and exterior from airborne debris. The fire from the initial explosion has been extinguished, and as you can see, the destruction is quite extensive—"

Floating black cinders whirl above my head. A charred odor hangs in the air. It's of melted plastic, scorched wood, seared metal. I taste the stench in my mouth and gag. To my far left, the Clinic building stands damaged and debris-littered, with dozens of Reducers huddled and weeping on its walkways. My gaze swings across the grounds to the remains of what used to be the administration building.

I squeeze my eyes closed, then open them again. The scene is the same. It's clear this was the work of one incredibly massive bomb. All that's left of the building are shattered mountains of glass, heaps of rubble, and charred stubs of support beams. Hunks of sheetrock lie across the lawn, and twisted fragments of furniture jut from the debris. Wisps of smoke rise into the sky like dark serpents.

Has the WHA done this terrible thing?

I reach a barricade and lean against it. An Enforcer shouts and motions for me to back off, but right then, the total impact of what I am seeing hits me full force, and my legs buckle. My knees thud to the pavement. The entire administration building—*and its contents*—have been destroyed.

My body, my real body, was in that building.

CHAPTER 19

"No," I say, the word coming out as a thin croak. "No, *no*."

"Please, miss, move away from the barricade," says an Enforcer with the eyes of a Basset Hound. He pulls me to my feet. As I teeter there, I glimpse a man on the other side of the barrier. He's a trim guy in a dark suit, clawing one hand through his hair and surveying the scene with wide, distracted eyes.

Dust smudges his suit. It's Leo Behr.

He catches sight of me and gives an exhale so short and pained it sounds like a huff. "The Clinic is closed today, Morgan. Everything else is gone, including the backup files. And I'm afraid Denver's files were also sabotaged."

"What do you mean?" My head swims, heavy and constricted. His words crash in my head, not making any logical sense.

No body. I have no body. My body was in that building.

"I mean, everything is destroyed," Leo says. "There's no suspended animation room anymore. No backup files for you or your Loaner. You won't be able to return to your old appearance."

His words clear and settle, sinking in like knife blades. "I—I'm Jodine now?"

A frown wrinkles his forehead. Dark hollows shadow his eyes. "Please. Go to the Kowalczyks' and stay there. I have a lot of things to take care of right now."

He can't dismiss me like that. Not right now. Not after telling me in a few horrible sentences that my whole life has ended, and Jodine's too.

My insides loosen, start unraveling. I suck in a lungful of burnt air. "I can't go. I just died in that building, Leo. *Died.* And now I'm stuck in someone else's freaking body!"

Leo shakes his head. "Nothing can be done about that. Please don't make a scene."

"You could have prevented this," I say, glaring, my breath coming hard and shallow. "You posted more Enforcers, added more security! No one should've been able to walk into a high-security area and set off a huge bomb."

News reporters turn my way. Leo catches the eye of the Basset Hound Enforcer, and jerks his head toward the far sidewalk. The Enforcer clamps his hand on my upper arm and starts to steer me from the grounds.

I twist back toward Leo. "This is all your fault!" I scream, knowing he knows what I'm talking about, the safety he promised me. A sturdy female Enforcer rushes up to help escort me past the camera crew. "You helped *kill* me, Leo Behr!"

"You're not thinking straight, miss," the Basset Hound Enforcer says in a rumbly voice. "We don't want to have to cite you for causing a disturbance. Go back to your Loaner house and wait until the director messages you. Give yourself time to cool off."

I moan, which comes out chalky and weak. I moan again,

for a different reason. These vocal chords are now mine.

My muscles sag, and the two Enforcers release me.

The Basset Hound pats my back. "There you go, take it easy. Mr. Behr will contact you later with more information."

I stumble off. The sidewalk to the MT passes under my shoes like a desolate treadmill. This can't be happening. It *isn't* happening. I don't want to be stranded in this body…for good. I can't live this way. It's a cruel joke, a twisted nightmare I'm sure I'll wake up from soon.

My lip trembles, and I bite it to keep it steady.

I plod toward the MT shelter. Before I reach it, I sink onto a street-side bench in a heap. Nearby vendorbots and ads shout. Men and women in business suits pass by, along with teens on Thanksgiving break and mothers with children. They move around me, their lives far, far from me.

Pressure grows in my throat. A force behind my eyes makes them prickle. I spring twin leaks, and tears run down my face and plop onto my sweatpants. I dash the tears away with my fingers, but they keep coming.

Gone. Dead. I've died.

The words circle inside me like a broken merry-go-round, taunting me, splintering me. Last night my real body lay in peaceful suspended animation. Unsuspecting. Deep-sleeping and secure, until 0720. Then, the explosion. My body was consumed, ravaged by the blast. Did it happen all at once? Limb by limb? I envision the flare devouring my long brown hair, roaring over my hipbones and protester wounds. Incinerating that little scar on my leg that I got when I was ten and flipped Granddad's pocketknife in the air and missed catching it.

Gone, completely gone.

It's not just me, either. Tons of other Reducers are in the

same situation. Vonn's lost his body, too. No more Superguy. He'll be stranded as Matt Williams for the rest of his life. His lanky figure and those adorable dimple dents have been snuffed out.

And Jodine. My gut lurches. Jodine's parents have lost her forever. If Denver's backup files were sabotaged, her brainmap file with her consciousness and her soul is gone.

All she'd wanted to do was lose weight, and now her life has been destroyed.

So not fair.

The words Vonn and I sang last week mock me, pound holes in my head—

Life's not fair, got no hair. Roll me out the door, Ma.

I'm a complete idiot. If only I'd listened to Granddad when he said this job was too risky. If I hadn't lied to Mom and Dad after the riot attack and not been stubborn about continuing my assignment, I'd be restored to my own self by now. My body would still be alive.

Now it's too late.

After an unknown length of time, I force myself to get up and trudge to the shelter. When the MT arrives, I sag onto a seat, hunching away from the invasion of the security cameras. I shouldn't have trusted Leo and his added security measures, or the fail-safe plan of the backup files. It was all too risky. If the Institute and ERT hadn't existed in the first place, I wouldn't be in this situation.

With stiff fingers, I send a text home, along with texts to Blair and Krista. I ask if they've heard the news, and tell them yeah, I'm alive, even though my body has died. That I'm not sure what will happen now and I'll try to come back home soon.

I cry through the rest of the ride, until the MT deposits me in the Green Zone. The walk to the Kowalczyks' and down their drive stretches light-years, the balconies and pillars of the house rising up like something in a surreal dream. My body feels disconnected. At the door, I press my hand onto the ID pad, and cringe. Have the Kowalczyks heard the news yet? I don't want to be the one to tell them.

Broken sobs fill the air as I walk into the living room. Mrs. K. sits on the sofa with Nettie, weeping into a wad of tissues, her usually sophisticated face blotchy. Crumpled tissues lie scattered across the TV platform and the carpet.

Nettie looks up at me, her eyes red-rimmed. "Did you—" She stops, her mouth open but no words coming out.

"I saw the building when I went for weigh-in," I manage to say.

Mrs. K. glances up. She scans me, and then bursts into a fresh storm of tears.

I bolt to my room. Shaking, I stumble into the bathroom and splash water on my face. I can't even imagine how Mrs. K. feels, seeing Jodine's body when her daughter doesn't exist anymore.

I'm so out of place, so blatantly wrong here. But I can't help being where I am, inside this body. I don't *want* it. I'd give it back if I only could. I don't want to go home to live with Mom, Dad, and Granddad, looking like someone else. How can I hang out with Blair and Krista when I look this different? How can I finish school? Being a Reducer was only bearable knowing I'd be able to return to my own body when I was done with my assignment. To be myself. Totally. I can't be me without my own body. It's too much a part of the real me.

I blot my face with a towel and stare into the mirror. For

the rest of my life I'll look like this. The hazel eyes in the mirror grow watery. Even if I manage to shed sixty-plus pounds, I'll always be freckled and kinky-haired.

Haze it all, this *gnarly hair*. I refuse to live another minute with this much of it.

I yank open a drawer in the sink cabinet and snatch up a pair of scissors. I hack away, sending coiled brown chunks onto the counter and into the sink. When I finish, my hair hangs nearer my shoulders than my waist. I shove the severed curls into the garbage chute and make a beeline for the closet.

My stomach's growling, and I'm going to thwart it for good.

I seize the white box and cart it through the living room. Luckily, Nettie and Mrs. K. have vacated the sofa. They aren't in the kitchen, either. I thump to the incinerator and set aside the red sweater and the silver case. Candy bars, nuts, popcorn, chips, and pepperoni sticks whoosh into nonexistence in seconds.

There. No more temptation in this box.

I wonder if the Kowalczyks are aware of that small but dangerous section of high-fat, mega-calorie snack food downstairs. Tempting things like that shouldn't even exist when someone in the house is dieting.

Back in the bedroom, I toss the box with its reduced contents back into the closet, and discover a message flashing on my phone. I sink to the bed. It's from Krista.

> Oh. My. Gosh. Blair and I have been bawling all morning. What will you do? What do you LOOK like?? See you soon. Let us know when. Love ya.

I barely finish reading that when my phone rings. It's Dad.

> I heard the news, Morgan.

I picture his face, warm and familiar as a well-loved sweater, and nearly disintegrate into tears again.

Daddy?

I take a sharp gulp of air. *Daddy*. I haven't called him that in years. My throat constricts as I read his words.

> I don't know what to say, honey. I got your text, then a message from Mr. Behr. When I came home, I found Granddad watching a newsvid of the bombing with a horrible look on his face.

> You're off work?

> I took the rest of the week off. Mom's here, too, even though the band wanted to start up a new local gig since Philadelphia didn't work out. Granddad's off smoking on the balcony. Everyone's worried about you. How are you holding up?

I try to breathe through my nose, but my nostrils seem way too small.

> My body's gone.

> Yes. But you're alive, and that's all that matters. Mr. Behr says you'll be able to come home soon.

> I'm still overweight, Daddy.

My voice falters on the last word, and the dam of my control breaks. I sob into the phone. The voice-to-text app writes [Crying.] and goes motionless.

Dad lets me cry. After a while he texts some more.

> I love you, kiddo. No matter what your body looks

like. As soon as Mr. Behr gives the okay, I'll come meet you and ride home with you on the MT. He said probably tomorrow morning. Is that all right?

Yes. I love you, Dad.

After our good-byes, my eyes fill again. I want to go home *now*.

Noon comes and goes. I skip lunch, staying in the bedroom. I could play Masters of the Cyberverse, but nothing on my silver elf's agenda sounds appealing. Instead, I stare out my room's auto-windows and watch winter freeze the hedges and bushes. I wish I could text or call Vonn for some needed word-hugs, but I can't. All I have is my Institute phone, and Leo would see our messages. I'm stuck with being in isolation right now.

An hour past normal dinnertime, I venture into the kitchen. It stands vacant with a single light glowing above the sink. An e-note flashes on the screen by the food elevator. I trudge over. Nettie apparently placed a plate of leftovers in the fridge for me.

Right as the PlasmaWave oven beeps, Nettie walks in and slips a glass into the autowasher. Without saying a word, she enfolds me in a hug. I throw my arms around her, and we stand together for a moment or two until her arms fall away.

"Good night," Nettie murmurs and leaves the kitchen.

I wonder if the hug was for me or Jodine.

Emptiness descends again. I pick at my meal at the counter island. It's no use. I put down my fork. For once, I'm not hungry. I scrape the remains into the incinerator and return to the bedroom. As I slip into a nightshirt, I hear a message alert on my phone.

It's an official email from Leo.

> To Reducers, and the families of Loaners and Reducers. My deepest condolences. Our Reducers in the Los Angeles branch have been affected by the bombing of the Institute's administration building, by the deaths of their bodies in suspended animation. Our Loaners have been affected by the loss of our data files and the simultaneous corruption of our backup files in Denver. Because of this latter sabotage, no Loaner will be able to reoccupy his or her rightful body. They will each be pronounced deceased. Condolence settlements for the families are being arranged.

Jodine. *Deceased.* Blinking, I look across the room for a while before I can keep reading.

> Reducers, you will now permanently reside in your Loaner bodies. You will be paid for the weight you've lost up to this point, plus a condolence settlement. Since your real bodies and ID chips have been destroyed in the bombing, your files, accounts, and education certificates will be officially reset to your current ID chip and handprint. We'll work with you regarding these legal details. Please feel free to stay in the dorms and continue using the Clinic for your weight loss, free of charge. You may return to your own homes whenever you wish. We ask for your patience and understanding as we ease you into your new lives.

He makes everything sound easy and organized. Which is

not how it feels.

> Be assured that we are investigating the
> source of this crime. The perpetrators will be
> apprehended and dealt with severely. Thank you.

That's the end of the message.

I shake my head. Even if my ID gets changed to let all the scanners in the world know that this body belongs to Morgan Dey, it won't feel like me. I don't want to look like a Kowalczyk. I want to be Morgan Dey, inside and out. And the settlement payment? All the credits in the universe can't make up for the loss of my body.

The events of the day weigh on me, pressing and crushing me.

"Lights off," I say, the words cracking.

I let my phone clatter onto the desk. I'm so tired. Tonight, the soft gathering of stuffed animals looks more inviting than the bed. I drag a blanket to the window seat and curl up, then scoop a teddy bear into my arms. Surrounded by furry paws, legs, and snouts in the semi-darkness, I catch a glimpse of the green airbot hovering by the doorway. My gaze follows its bobbing shape for a minute.

Right now, I don't mind if the critter wants my company instead of air filtering.

"Down here, kid," I say, patting the cushion I'm lying on. "Lower. Right now I need you next to me."

CHAPTER 20

My room alarm speaks to me in a buttery voice. "Good morning, it's oh-six-hundred."

I moan, groggy with sleep. Why didn't I disengage the alarm?

"Turn off," I say.

The green airbot gives a cough-like whir and lifts off from a stuffed giraffe, floating toward the ceiling. Animals enclose me in a fuzzy hug, and I'm cozy for a split second until memories of yesterday scatter my comfort far and wide.

Bombs. Explosions. Destruction. *Death*. Stuck forever in Jodine's body, a body that's not mine—

I thrash from under the blanket and fling it onto the bed. Tears spring into my eyes. I slug a pillow a few times, then scream into it. My voice grows hoarse.

It's no use. No amount of head-bashing or screaming will change things.

I'm trapped. Forever.

I shuffle into the bathroom. My eyelids are puffy and scratchy, as if broken glass lies underneath. I'm not charged up about exercising this morning, yet at the same time I could use a session of sweating and slamming some weights around. Something gritty. Something numbing. Something to do until Dad calls and arranges our trip home.

I pull on sweats and plod downstairs. Surprisingly, the gym isn't vacant. Mrs. K. sits at one of the resistance machines, not moving, wearing turquoise sweats and a washed-out expression.

"I'll come back later, Mrs. Kowalczyk."

Mrs. K. turns her head in slow motion. "Don't. I'm not doing anything in here, anyway." Her gaze lands on my hair. "You cut it?" Her voice is stretched thin over the words.

"Sorry. I wasn't thinking. It's still long, just not as long." I'm so blazing stupid. I should've waited to cut it until I wasn't living with the Kowalczyks.

To my dismay, Mrs. K.'s face crumples, and she begins to cry. "I never appreciated her. Not her appearance, especially not her weight. Her vidgames, her clothes, her singing, her painting—" She breaks off, crying too hard to say more.

I take a seat on the base of the treadmill machine, my mind blank as to what to say.

After another minute, Mrs. K. blows her nose on a tissue. When she speaks, she sounds stuffy and nasally. "I wanted her to be slender, you know. I wanted her to be a painter like me. Not a singer, even though I knew her voice was lovely. I wanted to go shopping with her and buy stylish skinny clothes together, and she really didn't care about that. She had her own, more casual style. But after a while, she only fit into those revolting navy sweats."

"My mom likes to go shopping with me," I say. "Nothing personal, but it's more fun to go with friends."

Mrs. K. sniffles. "Jodine never had many friends, either. That snake of a girl, Noni, certainly didn't count."

I stay silent. I'm not supposed to know about Noni.

"The thing I feel the worst about," Mrs. K. begins, then stops. Fresh tears trail down her face and drip off her chin. "I—I can't believe how insensitive I was to her. She surprised me once, showing me the painting I told you about. It was her first try at a still life, the first time she'd painted anything besides abstract shapes and colors when I let her play around on old canvases. All I could see were the mistakes, not her effort. I told her it wasn't very good."

"If it makes you feel any better, I don't think the painting looks that great, either."

Mrs. K. snaps her head up, and her eyes squinch smaller. "How do you know?"

"It's hanging in her closet. I mean, I guess it's the same painting. White vase, some grapes, an apple."

"I want to see it." Mrs. K. rises like a shot from the resistance machine.

I lead her upstairs to Jodine's room. In the closet, I point to the painting. "There, see? It has my—I mean her—initials on it."

Mrs. K. makes a raw, animal noise. She takes the painting off the wall and cradles it against her chest. "Thank you for letting me know about this. I hope you can get together with your family soon."

I lean against the closet doorframe and watch her leave the bedroom with the painting. Something deep inside me rushes to the surface, and I feel my mouth curl into a broad, trembling smile. After all these years, she not only appreciates the painting, she *wants* it. All that work wasn't for nothing.

It's a belated but rewarding acceptance. And how nice Mrs. K. said she hoped I got back together with my family soon.

Wait a minute. I give myself a hard mental shake. *Oh, man, I'm going crazy.* I'm not the one who made that painting, and Mrs. K. isn't my mother. I drifted into major Jodine mode for a few seconds. Traces of her are much, much too alive and well in this body—that wasn't just a residual memory. I need to leave this house and get away from things that trigger this type of freaky blending. If that will even make a difference.

I sure hope so. I won't be able to stay sane if I'm not ever totally myself again.

Back in the bedroom, I find my phone and text Dad. He answers right away.

> I'm finishing breakfast. I got the okay from Mr. Behr to bring you home. Shall I meet you at the MT shelter at Alameda Street, by the Institute?

> Sure, if you want to ride that far.

> It's fine, kiddo. I can be there in about an hour. Uh, what do you look like?

I cringe. Weird question to hear from my own father.

> Heavy. Shoulder-length curly hair and freckles. Green sweats. Can't miss me.

> Okay. I asked Granddad if he wanted to come, but he's being reclusive. We just got notice he was awarded a room at the retirement home, and he's busy starting to pack. You can help us move him in on Saturday if you want.

> Sure. See you soon.

I sign off, trying not to think of Granddad leaving. Or what he thinks about my situation. At least I'll get to see him before he moves out, but I have an awful feeling he prefers packing to seeing me in my new body. I think he's as afraid as I am what his reaction will be.

I'm done here. Who cares about working out this morning? I send a text to Blair and Krista, force myself to clean up Jodine's room, and return the stuffed animals to the bed. I blow a sad kiss to the green airbot. In the kitchen, I nibble breakfast and discover a note that says Nettie is visiting her brother. Our hug last night was good-bye, then, which kind of sucks. I speak a message, thanking her for the friendship and food, then dictate a farewell for Dr. and Mrs. K.

I check my phone. It's ten minutes before my regular meeting time with Vonn at the park. If I hurry, I might be able to catch him before I ride to the Red Zone. If he even shows up.

I take the MT and rush down the sidewalk to our normal meeting place. The image of Vonn's real face bobs in my mind. *Superguy*. Do I care that he isn't ever going to be that hot again? A teensy bit, yes, but not as much as I would've expected.

Mostly, I just want him to be at the park.

"Please be there, please be there." I puff the words into the damp morning air. When I turn the corner and see him on our usual bench, I nearly short-circuit with relief.

He glances up. He looks as if he's been slugged in the stomach.

I halt beside the bench, gasping from my run. "I don't— I thought—" I take a deep breath and start over. "I'm glad you came. I wanted to say good-bye before I went back home."

Vonn stands. He touches my arm and lets his hand drop. His eyes have lost their spark, their impish glint. "Me too. I'm not sure where 'home' is anymore, though."

It's more difficult for him, living on his own. I almost feel guilty for having a family to go back to, even though going home won't be easy. "What about your mom? Is she in the Blue Zone where you usually live?"

"She lives there, but I dunno if I'll see her. Right now she's too busy saying 'I told you so' and yelling about how reckless I am. Like she says Dad always was. I'll let her unwind first. I can stay at Matt's until I'm ready to go back to my old apartment."

Words wedge in my throat. Not only is that sad to hear, I don't know what will happen to our relationship now, since we live far apart. I struggle against a powerful wave that threatens to flatten me, an unjust and extra shove from the universe when I'm already groveling on my knees. I'm not ready to lose Vonn on top of everything else. Hopefully he'll want to keep meeting with me, somehow. I try to regain control over my emotions so I can ask.

He scuffs his shoe on the pavement. "I keep thinking this is a bad dream, and I'm going to wake up soon. I feel totally upside-down. There I was, thinking I was Superguy to the rescue, helping people and improving national health, and now I'm stuck being boring old Matt Williams. My plans backfired, big time."

I don't know what to say to that. There may not be actual words that will help in this kind of situation. I give his shoulder an awkward pat. "Would you like my phone number in case you want to call, or my email to write to me?"

"You want to keep in touch, when we'll never be our real selves again?"

I tilt my head, pressure building behind my eyes. I will not cry. I *will not.* "Of course I do! We got to know each other in these bodies, not our real ones. You're not Matt inside. You'll always be Superguy to me."

Vonn slumps, almost wilts. "It means a lot to me that you think that. Thanks, Geekling." He fingers a coil of my hair. "You know, I'm sorry you've never liked this hair. It's cool, like a bunch of tiny springs."

That's beyond sweet, but I tell him my email address to avoid dwelling on the dismal thought that these tiny springs will be mine for the rest of my life. "I'll send you my new number after I buy a non-Institute phone. Since my old one got blown up in the bombing."

"My email is vonnderfuljerk@gridlink.com."

A cracked laugh erupts from my throat. His address is clever and kind of silly, just like he is. I slip my hand into his. "I gotta go meet my dad. See you around, I hope."

"Try to have a good Thanksgiving." He gives me a loose hug with his free arm.

"You too." We unlink our fingers and head off in opposite directions. I wonder how long it'll be before we get together again.

I'm done with the Institute, done being a Reducer. I don't know what my life will be like now, but I'm going to try as hard as I possibly can to take Vonn into the next part of it.

CHAPTER 21

I board the MT. It's time to find out what Dad thinks of me as my new self. I glance at my green sweatpants and melt into a slouch. Oh, no. I didn't think to bring other clothes, or even ask the Kowalczyks if I could borrow these sweats. I'm sure I don't have anything at home that will fit.

The MT approaches the Alameda Street shelter. I lean to look, and my heart races to see Dad striding along the sidewalk, his brow creased as he searches for me in the squares of the windows. While it's great to see him, I don't think I'm ready for this. I take some huge breaths and prepare myself as best as I can. When the MT halts, I step out the doors.

I trudge up to him, my hands tense at my sides. "This is the new me, Dad. Different, right?"

Dad encircles me in a tentative hug. "It's still you inside. I'm glad to have you back, kiddo."

I close my eyes. Thank goodness Dad accepts that I'm me somehow, even though I'm trapped behind Jodine's eyes and inside her body. After our hug, though, his gaze skitters away. No surprise. It's hard enough for me to reconcile my appearance with my real self, even though I've seen myself look this way for the last two months.

We sit to wait for the Express to the Yellow Zone. People mill around us. It's freezing cold, and the breeze smells bitter, like old rotten leaves. I wish I had a rewind button, to reverse my life back to the way it used to be. Back to the way *I* used to be.

"Are you okay?" Dad asks.

"Sorta. Not really. You?"

Dad folds his arms into a tight pretzel. "I'm not okay, either. It's totally unacceptable that the Institute wasn't able to prevent this somehow, or have some sort of backup plan."

"I don't think they expected the files in Denver to be destroyed at the same time. That *was* the backup plan."

"Well, it wasn't enough."

I sigh. "I shouldn't have done the program in the first place."

"It's not your fault. You were only trying to help this Loaner girl and pay our bills." He presses his hands over his eyes and scrubs his face. "It's your mom's and my fault for letting you earn credits for our debt. Living in The Commons for a few years wouldn't have killed us. It would've been better than losing your body like this."

I bite my lip, trying to keep my tears inside. It would've been horrendous to live in The Commons. He doesn't know that it *is* my fault. I ignored Granddad's warnings. I begged Dad to let me keep my assignment after my first WHA attack. I agreed to Leo's stupid plan to lie. I've ruined my own life.

We ride home, making bland small talk. When we get to our apartment, I stand helpless by the ID pad while Dad uses his handprint.

"We'll add you to the access list later," he says with a sympathetic glance.

Granddad is standing by the dining table when the door slides open, and he holds an unlit cigarette in one of his knobby hands. His bristly eyebrows bunch over his eyes like a pair of wary watchdogs. "Hello?"

"Granddad, it's me, Morgan."

Going blank, he stares, his cigarette dangling precariously from his fingertips. I wait for him to say something that will break the silence. He wheezes but doesn't speak.

Dad enters, and the door shuts behind us. "It's really her, Bob. This is Morgan's new body, the body she was a Reducer for."

Giving a rattled huff, Granddad backs away. "Doesn't look like Morgan. Doesn't sound like her, either."

"It *is* me," I say. "That's how I know your favorite books are *The Count of Monte Cristo* and *1984*. And that you like fresh peaches on your cereal."

"The government can find out anything about a person if they poke into his business. Nope, I'm not buying it."

"Granddad—"

"No! The real Morgan died in that explosion. Leave me alone, imposter." He stamps to the front door, snaps out a voice order, and stalks through the opening.

The door whisks closed.

"Dad?" The word is faint. A wrenching ache forms in my heart, under my ribs. A scream builds up in my head. I can't take this. I just can't.

"I'm sorry, Morgan. You know Granddad. He'll come around after a while."

The tears welling under my eyelids threaten to spill over. That's doubtful. I *do* know Granddad—he's more stubborn than I am.

A thin voice comes from Mom and Dad's bedroom. "Gregg? Is she home?"

Mom rushes out into the hall, not yet dressed, clutching her fuzzy blue robe around her. "Oh, Morgan, honey," she says, looking Jodine's body over from curly hair to tennis shoes. "This is you now?"

"Yes." I feel a hundred years old. "I still have at least sixty pounds to lose."

"I know you'll finish the weight loss," Mom says. "You always kept your own body so pretty and toned." Her lower lip trembles. She spins and runs back down the hall.

I collapse onto the couch and bury my face in my hands.

This is too much to handle.

"Things will get better, I promise." Dad pats my shoulder. "Give us a little time, kiddo."

He retreats down the hall, and my tears come out full force. I can't stop the flow. The wetness drips through the spaces between my fingers while Dad's murmurings to Mom seep through the walls. I feel like Frankenstein's monster, botched together with the soul and brainmap of one person, and the body of another. How much of me is Jodine, and how much of me is Morgan? I'm stranded with her body and her freaky residual memories. Will she eventually take over my habits and attitudes—or is my mind strong enough to hold onto the core part of me?

Who *am* I now? It's terribly confusing. I have to do something about this, except I have no idea what.

I cry until my eyes ache and my stomach hurts.

There seems to be no end to my tears.

My phone sounds out an alert, and I stare at it. I don't want to answer. I'd rather curl up in a corner, far away from everyone. But it's probably Blair or Krista. I smear my face semi-dry, draw in a wobbly breath, and speak a text greeting.

Krista answers.

> Are you home, Morg?

> Yeah. Just.

> Blair and I can meet you this afternoon, if you want. How about at the mall?

Too public. I need to take this slowly.

> I'd rather do the Peppermint Café.

> Wherever you want. At 1500?

> That works.

As we sign off, a tissue appears in front of my eyes, held there by Dad, who's back in the living room. I take it and blow my nose.

After a morning of watching mind-numbing TV with Dad and an early afternoon spent closeted in my room, I walk down the sidewalk to the café.

A knot twists in my stomach. Here goes my unveiling to my two best friends. I wish I were wearing something other than these green sweats.

Will Blair and Krista be able to see my real self behind this body?

I reach the Peppermint Café. Through the plate-glass windows, I see Blair and Krista perched at a table, their eyes lemur-round as they watch me walk to the door and open it.

Krista leaps up, her petite figure hugged by a sweater dress and striped tights. Her mouth is an orange *O*. "Morg, is that you?"

"How'd you guess?" My tone is woeful. A thin man and

woman sashay past me on their way to the counter. I feel like a watermelon in a crowd of carrot sticks.

"You sound different." Blair peers over Krista's shoulder. "Such a rich, sweet voice."

"Freaky," Krista says. "I feel really bad for you. I can't imagine being marooned in someone else's body like that."

Blair elbows Krista in the ribs. Blinking and trying not to think about what Krista just said, I follow them to their table, where a fruit drink already waits for me.

"I'm going to shed about sixty more pounds, obviously." My words come out choppy and rushed. I feel like I need to explain, to fill the awkward space. "And I forgot to ask my Loaner's family if I could borrow some clothes, so this is the only thing I have to wear."

"That's terrible." Blair pushes her hair back. A bright violet is now streaked through her usual honey color. "I bet Mom has some shirts or dresses you can use. She wears loose stuff, and they might fit. You want me to ask?"

I make a face. Wearing her mother's clothing isn't a cheery option, but at this point it's better than nothing. "Thanks."

Krista stretches out a careful hand and nudges one of my curls. "What fun hair. Great turbo action. You tried straightening it?"

"Hadn't thought of that. I did cut it. It used to be down to my waist."

"I like how you have it," Blair says. "A little of that kind of hair goes a long way."

"I know what we can do." Krista leans in. "After you've lost thirty or forty more pounds, we'll give you a makeover and experiment with your hair. It'll be great beauty school practice for me. We can also make Blair's mom's clothes more stylish. I'm good at alterations. You said I was last summer when I shortened that one dress for you."

"That should help," Blair says with an eager nod.

I try to smile, appreciating their support more than their ideas. They're trying to help, but I feel like I'm some sort of project. Like I need fixing before they can be totally comfortable around me. I guess I can understand that.

I just don't like it much.

"Krista, what's up with you and Randy?" I say in a blatant attempt to shift the spotlight. "You said he was acting hedgy."

"Mostly when I called him on Saturday."

"I think he has another girl," Blair says.

"You don't know that." Krista tosses Blair a peeved look "He just sounded distracted. Besides, Brad's not exactly hanging out with you twenty-four-seven anymore, either."

I shake my head. "Gotta keep an eye on those guys."

My words are flat, but Blair nods as if nothing's wrong. We talk about classes and the latest vids and music, topics that wash over me and leave a bitter aftertaste. It's hard to think about fun, trivial things when the rest of my life is so twistedly wrong. Nothing feels right. I'm not myself. I'm only Morgan on the inside, which is harder for all of us to see.

We're definitely going to have to flounder around for a while until we settle into a new rhythm in our friendship.

I'm different now. There's no getting around that bald, stark fact.

CHAPTER 22

I drum my fingers on my bedroom desk. Talk about post-Thanksgiving letdown. I've spent almost four days feeling like I'm walking around at a freaking funeral—in which I'm the dead person.

I don't know which is harder, dealing with Granddad's hurtful avoidance, tiptoeing around Mom's fragile psyche, or putting up with Dad's optimistic, trying-too-hard efforts at normalcy. Every little thing makes me want to burst into tears, and I hate that. I'm not usually this emotional and unsteady.

Monday's a school day. I don't want to go to classes. I can't. I won't be able to concentrate, looking like this, being like this. Maybe I can talk Mom and Dad into letting me hold off for a while longer. Like until April, after I reach my target weight.

Yes, I'm being a coward—and shallow. My appearance shouldn't affect who I am this much. But it *is* affecting me. On top of everything else, I miss Nettie's cooking in an extreme way. Yesterday I ate a truckload of poor-quality turkey and mashed potatoes with gravy, and haven't done much exercising. My body is as bloated and heavy as my mood. I need a gym, a place to do some weight training, burn some serious calories, and get my mind off this sucky situation. I can either go to the neighborhood gym or use the gym at the Clinic like Leo suggested. The local gym will cost me credits, but I'm not sure I want to go near the Institute—or what's left of the administration building.

The scene of my death.

Although it might be better if I stayed at the Clinic. Granddad leaves for the retirement home tomorrow, and if I'm gone, it'll cut down expenses and leave more for Mom and Dad to pay on the bills. I don't know how much my condolence settlement will be yet. We may still end up in The Commons.

My Institute phone rings. It's Leo. Not my favorite person these days.

> Hey.

I let the word fall out onto the screen by itself and hang there.

> I trust you're doing all right, Morgan.

He pauses for a few seconds, which is unusual for him. Why is he being hesitant?

> I was wondering if you were going to check in to the Clinic anytime soon.

> I was just thinking I needed a place to work out. Why do you care? Am I burdening National Health Care or something?

I'm being grouchy, but I can't help it.
Another few seconds' delay.

> Something has come up. A highly unusual situation, and it's throwing me into a bind. If you

cooperate, we can work through it. The first thing I'd like you to do is head to the Clinic sometime today so you can attend a meeting with the Kowalczyks tomorrow morning. I've set it up for 0800 in Meeting Room 3.

My heart skids into hyperspeed.

Am I in trouble or something?

No. Don't be anxious about it. I could fill you in on the details, except the Kowalczyks want to be the ones to have this conversation with you.

WHAT conversation?

The one at 0800 tomorrow.

Thanks, Leo, that's very helpful.

It's too bad he can't hear the sarcasm I'm not bothering to mop up from my voice.

Please, don't be difficult. When you go to the meeting, a representative from the Institute will be supervising.

You won't be there?

Another familiar thing, kicked right out from under me.

No, I've been appointed the new replacement director of the Seattle branch. I've been here since Tuesday. You'll be fine. Message me after the meeting, please.

I mutter a parting text and cut the connection. I'm puzzled about what the Kowalczyks want. It can't just be them wanting to say good-bye properly. Unless it *is* something like that, and Leo's so caught up on protocol that he's stressing over it.

I have to admit, it'll be nice to see Dr. and Mrs. K. one more time.

For a brief crazy moment, my heart flies high. Maybe the Kowalczyks want to invite me to stay with them for a while. After all, I have more in common with Dr. K. than Jodine ever had. It would be a way for them to keep Jodine around—at least the physical part of her. I can discuss physics with Dr. K. and learn to paint with Mrs. K. I can cook in the kitchen with Nettie, play HoloSports, and do karaoke. That'd be amazing.

I fall onto my side on my bed. To my annoyance, my eyes feel dangerously leaky. I squeeze them shut.

Amazing. Except for one big problem.

As good as all that sounds, I'd much, much rather spend time with Granddad and my own parents. Where I can be appreciated for myself, not the memory of Jodine.

That evening after dinner I pack a small bag for my stay at the Clinic. Along with my Institute-issued phone, I bring the new phone I bought on Wednesday, since I'll probably have to turn in the Institute one. I leave my room and walk by Granddad's at the same time he exits.

"Pardon me," he says, his words stiff.

I glimpse his room behind him, with its stacks of packed boxes waiting to be carted to the retirement home. His books have been taken off the shelves, his abandoned socks and shirts shoved into bins. It's the cleanest I've ever seen his room. It looks eerie, and it doesn't seem *right*. I won't get to help him move tomorrow, but I doubt he wants me around anyway.

"Bye, Granddad, I'm heading out. I'll miss you."

"I'm missing the real Morgan," he says. "Not you."

His reaction isn't surprising, but it stabs me hard. As I try to swallow it down, he ducks into the bathroom and begins sorting through razors and shampoo bottles. I lean against the doorframe as if my bones have dissolved.

Blinking, I try to control my quivering mouth. "Granddad. This is all the me that's left. I made a mistake joining up as a Reducer—or at least continuing the program when it got danger-ous—but I can't change that now. Please don't reject me."

He fumbles a razor, and it rattles across the sink cabinet and onto the floor. We both stare at it, not moving.

I take a deep breath and look up at his stricken face. His scruffy beard. The bushy white-gray hair that pokes out over his ears. The beloved bumpy profile of his nose. "I can't handle it if you don't talk to me anymore," I say in a near-whisper. "I can't lose you along with everything else. That would be a kind of Chateau d'If I couldn't handle."

He snaps his head up. Emotions detonate across his face. "You're wrong about whose mistake this is," he says, his voice clogged and raspy. "This is my fault, sweetie—if it really is *you* under there, in that body. I should've signed up for health care and not created this doggone debt. Admit it…you wouldn't have become a Reducer if it wasn't for me."

No way. I'm not letting him take the blame for my choices or my stubbornness. "That's not true. I could've prevented this. I knew the risks, and I kept on going. But you know what? Even now, knowing what I know, I'd do it all over again. For you." I barely get the last words out, they're so mangled.

He makes a gruff moan.

I can't tell if I fall into his arms, or he falls into mine. I hug his bony shoulders, and he gives me a scrunch that almost makes me feel like I'm Morgan again, my old self.

When he finally releases me, he wipes his hand under his nose and sniffs long and hard. "I gotta get back to packing. Don't forget to call and let me know how you're doing. I guess a brain clone of you is better than no you at all."

"I'll call, don't worry."

I take a wobbly breath and leave him to his sorting.

At the end of the hall, I find Mom and Dad navigating around the kitchen without much speed or energy. Dad grabs a knife to cut a slice of superstore-baked pumpkin pie.

I give him a sideways hug. "I'm going to the Clinic now. I'll call to tell you what's up after I have that mysterious meeting. I can keep using text instead of screen mode, since my face is unfamiliar."

"Whichever you're more comfortable with." Dad looks far from comfortable himself. "We need to get used to your new face anyway. Want me to cut you a slice of pie before you leave?"

"No thanks, I'm trying to lose weight." He's *so* not used to having me be this careful about what I eat.

Mom leans around Dad. "Good luck with the weight loss. Come back as soon as you can."

A formidable lump rises in my throat. "Yeah. Maybe we can do another song together."

Nodding, Mom studies the kitchen counter, then her fingernails. I know she's thinking of earlier today, when I sang a few verses of a song, and she complimented me on my voice. She acted surprised and a little spooked. No wonder. It's not the tone-deaf voice she good-naturedly used to tease me about.

"I'm outta here," I say quickly. "I love you both."

They echo my partings, although there's a pained look in their eyes.

I catch the Express to the Red Zone. My future looms before me, bleak. Now that I'll be staying at the Clinic, my days will be filled with weight loss, and there will be no credits for an extra incentive to keep going. That'll be miserable as well as dull, especially if Vonn isn't there to keep me company. I've only heard from him once on my new phone since we last saw each other.

His text was short and simple.

> Going to my mom's for Thanksgiving. Thanks for
> your number. I'll call you.

He hasn't called yet. Maybe I should ask him to come to the Clinic and lose weight with me—we could pretend we're just meeting each other, for appearances' sake. If I could see him again, it would help my mood. I need to stop thinking about depressing stuff, because I'm sick of crying and wiping my eyes. I've had it with all this emotion.

I need to think instead, be practical.

For a start, I check my financial statement on my phone. It doesn't look like my settlement has been deposited yet, but Leo sent a message yesterday saying it'll be ten thousand credits. Once I get that, plus what I earned as a Reducer for two months, I'll apply the total to Granddad's debt. He can't stop me. Although even counting Mom and Dad's share, we'll be three thousand credits short of meeting our end-of-December deadline. And there'll be nothing left over for my tech school tuition.

By the time I get off the MT in the Red Zone, a mass of

clouds has gathered in the sky. I hurry down the sidewalk. Rain begins to hit my sweats, and I wrap my arms around myself, wishing I had a coat. At the Institute grounds, most of the rubble from the administration building has been cleared away or bulldozed back. That's good, and a little less scary.

I concentrate on my feet thumping along the lit-up sidewalks. Enforcers stand guard everywhere. They scan my ID at both the gates and the Clinic entrance.

After I check in, I complete a strenuous workout in the gym, take a stinging hot shower, and fall into bed. The exercise helps me drift off to sleep despite the forlorn, stark efficiency of the dorm room. I dream of running a five-mile race without gasping or panting.

The next morning, after a quick breakfast, I trudge down the hall to Meeting Room 3. Outside, more rain falls, plinking like needles against the windows. I inhale through my nose and out through my mouth. Okay. Time to see what this mystery meeting is all about.

Dr. K. is standing by the door as it opens to my handprint. "How was your Thanksgiving, Morgan?"

"Great," I lie. "I'm sure I missed some of Nettie's super fantastic food."

Dr. K. nods. "We had a wonderful meal. Nettie's brother joined us, as well as a few of my colleagues."

I pull my sweatshirt away from my neck, which has begun to sweat and itch. Dr. K. sounds *off* for some reason. I look around the room to find Mrs. K. sitting android-straight with a polite smile on her face. A man in a suit, presumably the Institute's rep, sits a few feet from her. He introduces himself. As I sit down, he turns on a recording device.

Dr. K. throws a glance at his wife. "Thanks for meeting

us here, Morgan. We regret we weren't there to say good-bye when you left."

"I didn't like leaving without seeing you two or Nettie, either."

Mrs. K. rouses herself. "We were impressed with your work on Jodine's weight loss, and we thank you for it."

They need to stop the chitchat and get on with it. Why am I here?

"I should've spent more time with Jodine," Dr. K. says. "Our connection didn't have to be about technology or physics. Nettie tells me she plays chess with Jodine. I loved playing chess when I was younger."

The rep's gaze, ping-ponging from speaker to speaker, pauses for a second. My stomach churns like a laundromachine. I have no idea where this conversation is heading.

"Don't beat yourself up too much," I say. "No parents are perfect. Mine aren't. But I love them anyway." I halt before my control disintegrates.

Dr. K. takes a deep breath and presses his hands together. "At this point, it does make a difference. Because in our case we have an opportunity to make things right. To have a second chance."

That makes no sense whatsoever. "How will you do that?"

"Well, you see, before Jodine became a Loaner, I saved another backup of her brainmap file. We'd like to have that reinstalled into her body."

CHAPTER 23

I gape at Dr. K. while my heart whomps inside my chest. "You have a *what?*" I wheeze.

"We have another copy of Jodine's brainmap," Dr. K. says. "I didn't trust the Institute with the data storage. I insisted on being given my own copy before I agreed to let Jodine do the ERT procedure. For me, they made an exception. A good thing, as it turns out."

Mrs. K. sends Dr. K. a withering look, and me an apologetic one. "Charles made that copy without my knowledge, and I've just learned of it myself. We've been discussing this scenario for the past few days. We knew how this would affect you."

I fight a dizzying wave of lightheadedness. "But—but if Jodine gets put back into her body, where will I go? I don't have a body anymore."

Uneasy looks ricochet around the room. The rep's face settles into an expectant expression.

"As a precaution for the past year," Dr. K. says, "the Institute has been keeping a small number of extra bodies in suspended animation. They're called Spares. Reducers and the general public don't know about them, although Loaners are informed if they're persistent and ask the right questions. These Spare bodies are an insurance of sorts, in case a Reducer overexerts a Loaner body and it dies. Or in case of a fatal accident or illness."

"Where does the Institute get those bodies?" I ask, pretty sure I don't want to know. "What's happened to those people's brain activity?"

Dr. K. rubs the side of his neck. "This isn't something I'm fond of, but the bodies come from criminals on death row. Their brain waves are nullified and their brainmap file discarded. If you think about it, it's a more humane way to deal with them than electrocution or lethal injection."

"I'm going to be put in the body of a *criminal?*" I say, my voice rising.

"They're not criminals any longer," Mrs. K. hastens to say. "Their memories and personalities are gone. And the publicly recognizable inmates are never used for Spares. With a fresh ID chip containing your personal data, it'll be like starting over."

I squeeze my eyes shut, struggling to keep my breakfast down. I don't want to start over. I want my old life back. To think I'd daydreamed the Kowalczyks would invite me to live with them, and here they want to shove me into the body of a death-row inmate. A murderer, most likely. A body that might have residual memories of violent crimes. No way. Jodine's stray memories of cheesy songs, amateur paintings, and liegerdeens are bad enough.

This is worse than recycling a brain-dead body from a bad accident like Chad experienced with Vonn's friend, Steven — it's *creating* bodies with no brain activity.

"What if I don't want to do this?" I open my eyes and

squint. "I assume I have a choice."

On the verge of obvious tears, Mrs. K. clasps her hands in her lap. "Yes and no. We *can* turn this into an enormous legal battle. Loaners agree to the risks of joining the program, true, yet Jodine's body belongs to her. To us. But we don't want to go down that road. We'd rather you be comfortable with this decision. We're asking you—begging you—to agree to this. If you choose to be in another body instead of hers, Jodine can live."

The rep finally speaks up. "You wouldn't have to go into a Spare body immediately, Miss Dey. You can finish your assignment for Jodine, since her weight loss must continue in order to comply with Health Care regulations. Mr. Behr has told me you need the credits for tech school and paying off some family bills."

I can't process what he's saying. It makes no sense. I've lost my identity once. The thought of losing it again is just too much. At least Jodine's body is somewhat familiar to me.

I spring to my feet and back away. "This is all kinda sudden. I'll think about it. I promise I will, and I'll let Leo know soon."

The rep gives a reluctant nod. "We'd like to know within a few days, if possible."

"I'm sorry, Morgan," Dr. K. adds. "If it weren't for the WHA's irresponsible violence, we wouldn't be having this conversation. If it makes any difference, Janeth and I would be more than willing to add extra credits as an incentive, if you switch to a Spare."

I stumble to the door, ignoring the rep and leaving the Kowalczyks and their anxious faces behind. With my legs wobbling, I escape down the hall.

At the entrance, I snatch a plus-size raincoat from the

closetbot and dash out the doors. I have to get away from this place. I slosh past the Enforcers at the gate. The rain comes down in torrents, beating at my coat, drenching the streets, and pouring across the sidewalk in sheets.

My mind reels and my thoughts sting. *Breathe*, I remind myself. *Inhale, exhale, repeat.* I know the answer has to be yes. I have to allow them to take back Jodine's body—letting Jodine live is the only fair and right thing to do. But it doesn't *feel* that easy. Another part of me doesn't want to do this favor for the Kowalczyks. I'd rather say no and stick with what I have, chancing they won't win a legal case. Like Mrs. K. said, it was their gamble to take when they signed Jodine up for the program. Just as it was mine when I became a Reducer and got stranded in this body.

The idea of switching to a new, completely unknown body is apocalyptic-level disturbing. Especially when it belonged to a criminal on death row.

How can Leo and the Institute do this to me? And with a revelation this serious, why didn't he arrange for Mom and Dad to be there at the meeting? I wonder if it's because I'm underage for only another two weeks. Even if I tell my parents and they object, Leo can simply hold off until I'm able to sign a contract myself. I wouldn't put it past him to have that plan in mind.

I whip under a building overhang and pull out my Institute phone. Leo answers in a matter of microseconds.

> Leo Behr. I snap his name, saying it like a swear word. Too bad the effect is lost on text. I assume you've finished your meeting with the Kowalczyks.

Yes, and this whole situation puts me in a really tough spot.

Leo's words scroll fast.

Look at it this way. You're not in your own body, so you might as well be in one that has no existing owner. That way Jodine can be returned to her rightful body.

You knew about the extra data file all along, didn't you?

It's pretty much a rhetorical question, but I ask anyway.

Of course, but the Kowalczyks had to make their decision first. Did you agree to do the Transfer?

I told them I'd think about it. I don't like the idea of being shuffled off into the body of a MURDERER.

Spares aren't murderers anymore. Their minds were the criminal parts of them. Their bodies have been thoroughly examined and verified as healthy. Gene checks, blood tests, the works. No obesity or defects.

That doesn't mean they won't have residual memories. I don't want to have memory flashes of torturing or killing someone.

That's extremely unlikely.

I frown.

Can you promise me that?

There's a long stillness before Leo answers.

You worry far too much. Don't forget, you have the option to be placed into a Spare body right away. You don't have to finish your assignment. If you prefer, you can be switched to a new body and skip the weight loss.

My grip on my phone loosens. That *would* be nice.

Yeah, that's what the rep said.

And he's right. We can sign a new contract with another Reducer and let her finish Jodine's assignment instead of you. I know of a girl who could use the work. She's a few years older, but we can make an exception in this case. Jodine won't even know there was a switch.

My mouth opens, then closes. No more torturous dieting and exercising. No more dealing with Leo and his twisted Institute. I'm tired of his manipulations and his lies, his ugly secrets—flawed ERT procedures and residuals, surprise back-up files he's known about for weeks, and now a bunch of murderers being mind-wiped and turned into Spares.

What next?

On the other hand, I still need those credits. If I stick it out for four more months, we'll be debt free. I'm not going to let the Kowalczyks pay me extra to let Jodine live, though. That doesn't seem right.

I don't know. I'd like to finish up, but what if something else goes wrong? I'm surprised anyone even wants to be a Reducer anymore.

Leo's words scroll fast and vigorous again.

Nothing else should go wrong. Walter Herry, the

head of the WHA, has recently been arrested, which means the threat from that group is defused. We're also combing our employees for WHA sympathizers, as well as making plans to implant tracking chips in Loaner bodies to prevent sabotage from the inside. More importantly, you won't have to go to the Clinic or the Institute grounds. The Kowalczyks have insisted on a tech dropping by twice a week to record Jodine's weight and perform a health check.

Finally. Good for the Kowalczyks.

That's a great plan. Going to the Clinic makes me nervous.

I pause.

When I'm ready to be put into the Spare, will I get a choice about which body I get?

Absolutely. I can arrange that. So do you want to keep Reducing for Jodine?

I have to talk to my dad first.

I refuse to let Leo be pushy and call the shots like he usually does.

I've already contacted your father. Although he's not pleased, he said it's ultimately up to you, since you're almost eighteen. He said he's not a risk-taker, but he does feel better about you continuing since you won't be going to the Clinic for weigh-ins.

Right. Dad's robotics job for the last sixteen years has been safe, secure, and boring. On the other hand, look where my fearless risk-taking and so-called courage has gotten me lately. The urge hits me to fling my phone across the street and watch it shatter. I resist and try to keep breathing like a normal human being. I hate being in this situation, having to make this decision.

Whether I like it or not, I'm stuck trading in Jodine's body for a criminal model—unless I want to gamble on doing a legal battle with the Kowalczyks.

Which I don't.

So the big question now is when. Whether I want to continue being a Reducer for Jodine.

Man. I must be certifiable to even consider it. My family desperately needs the credits, but I don't want to be involved with the Institute anymore. Really, I don't.

> I need more time to think, I finally say. I'll let you
> know in a day or two.

Ignoring the sputtering text scrolling across my screen, I sign off.

When I arrive back at the Clinic, I leave the raincoat for the closetbot to dry and go up to my dorm room. For privacy, I text Vonn from my new phone.

> I'm at the Clinic and have to make a hard choice.
> Need to talk.

Pacing from the bed to the door and back, I chew one fingernail half off before I notice. I mutter a few swear words. Fingernail-munching is Jodine's freaking habit, not mine. Then I bite off the other half to match. Is Vonn going to answer, or is he busy doing something else? Maybe I shouldn't have bothered him with this right now.

My phone blings. It's Vonn.

Can you meet me at the park in 15?

I tap out a quick affirmative and dash downstairs, grabbing the raincoat from the lobby again. I run to the MT shelter and catch the next train to the park. My fingers twine in my lap. When I reach my stop and race to our bench, I find Vonn wearing a large hooded coat that looks like a poncho.

"Great to see you," he says, giving me a soggy but tight hug. A glimmer of his old mischievous self has returned to his eyes. "Let's exercise while we talk, if you don't mind."

I start with him along the path and tell him my dilemma.

"I can't believe they're asking you to do that," Vonn exclaims when I finish. "Do they really have that many bodies your age on death row? *Female* ones?"

I startle. "I didn't even think about how old they are, how many, or the gender. Leo didn't say."

"Of course he didn't, since he wants you to say yes. Anyway, you were never charged up about how this body looks. Maybe you can get one you like better."

I shove my hands into my coat pockets. "I don't really have a choice. Mostly, I need to decide whether to get the Spare body now or after I finish my assignment."

He throws his arm around my shoulders and squeezes. "To be selfish, Miss Fitness, I'd like you to continue your assignment so we can keep losing weight together. If you get put into a new body now, you'll be off in the Yellow Zone doing science experiments with your friends and club dancing with hot skinny guys."

I grin, a sudden warmth thawing me from the inside out. "It'd be sly to keep doing weight loss with you. I'm just really crimped at the Institute and Leo right now for springing this decision on me. That the Spares exist in the first place. Can you imagine if the WHA found out the Institute was stripping people's minds and inserting other brainmaps into their bodies?"

"I know. Major public outrage...and speaking of the WHA, yesterday the maintenance technician who worked at our Institute branch got arrested. He's the one who planted the bomb. One of his jobs was to repair and keep all the bots running well. He inserted the bomb into a floor-cleaning bot that travels through these little tunnels into the high-security room where our bodies were kept. The suspended animation room. The bomb itself wasn't huge, but the chemicals in the suspended animation solution caused a chain reaction that magnified the explosion. He did that on purpose."

I stare at Vonn's face under his dripping poncho hood. "Seriously? What the haze did he do it for, and what's that got to do with the WHA?"

"The guy's sister was a Reducer, and she got her contract terminated for illegal drug use. She wasn't paid for her assignment, so they both got mad. When she joined the WHA, he agreed to do the bombing for them if they provided the materials."

"That's insane! Because of a rightfully terminated contract? All those Institute workers who were killed, and all our real bodies—" I stop before I haul off and punch something, or cry. Or both.

"I know. It's warped and selfish. Of course the WHA denies it had anything to do with the bombing, saying the technician plotted it all on his own."

"Naturally. Just like it was a coincidence the backup files in Denver happened to be sabotaged on exactly the same day." I'm breathing heavily with a pain in my chest, and it has nothing to do with how far I've walked. I'm sick of dealing with the Institute, and I hate the WHA. Even if the WHA is right about some of their claims, there must be less violent ways of protesting those things. They'd really go ballistic if they heard about the Spares—

Wait a minute.

I grab Vonn's free arm so suddenly it makes him flinch. "Freak it all, *the Spares!* Remember when I was wondering whether the Institute was using Reducers in Loaner bodies for things other than weight loss? Spying on people and stuff? I think the WHA and I were on the wrong track. The Reducers aren't the ones who could do that. It'd be lots easier to insert someone's brainmap into a stripped-down *Spare* for those sorts of things."

Vonn sucks in a sharp breath. "You're right," he says after a tense second. "The Spares' bodies are anonymous, and no one would miss them. The Institute could pop people's brainmaps in and out of those bodies whenever it wanted."

"Exactly. Talk about major human rights violations. If the Institute has empty bodies from death row, it could use them to commit burglaries…or assassinations." I gulp. I'm sounding like Walter Herry in his freaking conspiracy vid. I hate to admit it, but he had some valid suspicions back then. "It could use them as disposable bodies for high-risk jobs. It could even sell bodies to wealthy people who don't want to die or who are tired of their own bodies. The owners' brainmaps could be kept on file while they checked out bodies like a lending library."

"Creepy." Vonn looks as if he has a bad taste in his mouth. "The identity shuffling that's possible is mind-blowing—and illegal. Do you think the Institute is really doing these things? Just because they *can* do it doesn't mean they actually are."

"I don't know. I'd sure *like* to know."

"And I'm not a fan of Leo after what he pulled with our TeenDom texts, but just because he knows about the Spares doesn't mean he's actively involved with anything shady about them. That's a lot more serious stuff to suspect him of."

"Leo told me to lie to my parents," I say, "and he didn't tell me about the residual memories and the Spares until he was forced to say something. Herry, the head of the WHA, also said Leo started working at the Institute a little more than a year ago. Dr. K. told me that's about when the Spares program started. It's also the same time the government increased weight fines and funneled more clients to the Institute…to Leo. Very coincidental."

"Definitely, but we have no *proof* any of that sinister stuff is true." Vonn guides me off the path to let two rain-drenched women jog by, and then he pins me with a concerned gaze. "The only thing we know for sure is that the Institute keeps a bunch of Spares tucked away that hardly anyone else knows about, just in case a Loaner's body expires. And that Leo is aware of them. The whole idea of the Spares is questionable, although for everything except maybe Chad's Transfer into Steven, it could all be perfectly legal."

"I know, I know." I chew on the edge of my fingernail. Vonn may be right, but if Leo fudged the rules for Steven, there's a huge likelihood that other things in the program are also shifty.

We stand there while the wet pounding of rain encircles us. No one else is around. Water drips from our faces as we study each other from under our hoods. Vonn's face is reddened from the chill of the wind. Everything around us except for the soaked grass at our feet looks as cold-gray as death—the sky and the sidewalk and the near-naked trees.

Vonn flicks a drop from the tip of my nose and gives me a lopsided smile. "I'm glad you texted me, Morgan. It's great to talk to someone about this stuff. Even if we don't have answers yet."

His tender words crack something inside me. I clasp his hands and pretend the sudden moisture on my face is from the rain. "It's nice to see you acting more like yourself. But I honestly don't know what to do about being a Reducer or getting a Spare. I'm so confused."

"What does your gut, deep down, tell you to do?"

I breathe in damp air through my nostrils and close my eyes. Tangled sensations scrape through me like metal claws. I'm tainted by everything that's happened in the past months. I'm scorched by burns of anger and betrayal, scarred by needles of fear and loss. Despite all that, in one distant corner, there's a small but bright torch of determination and forceful will. It's fanned by the powerful warm glow of Vonn's feelings for me.

No. Giving up and withdrawing at this point is not an option.

When I open my eyes, Vonn is waiting with an expectant and caring expression, still looking deep into my face.

"I've decided I'm going to keep being a Reducer," I tell him. "For my family and Jodine. For you as my exercise buddy. I'm going to earn credits for my family, no matter what the risks. And while I'm finishing my assignment, I'm going to start a personal crusade against the Institute. Against Leo. I'm through trusting him and doing what he says. I'm going to do some serious undercover sleuthing and find out what's really happening at The Body Institute."

CHAPTER 24

The following evening, I stand beside Jodine's bed and scan the poster-lined walls, the window seat, and the humongous deskscreen platform. I have to admit, being in this room again feels like coming home, like things have returned to the way they should be. I'm not sure it's my own self who's responding, or something deep inside Jodine's body. I suspect it's from Jodine.

Because I shouldn't be here, inside someone else. It's crazy to be Reducing again, even if I do want to do some sleuthing to take down Leo and maybe the entire Institute with him. Such a risky job. Yet here I am, after a long afternoon at the Clinic, getting a new backup brainmap generated, since I'm resuming my assignment. Jodine's body legally belongs to her again.

Now there's an eerie thought...right now I don't really belong to *any* body.

I place my Institute phone on the desk and pull out my own phone from under my shirt. Morgan Dey, phone-smuggler extraordinaire. Even though the Clinic personnel kept my bag before I left the dorms, they didn't get my phone. This will come in handy if I need to call Vonn or do something I don't want the Institute to track.

Making sure my phone is charged and on silent mode, I slip into the closet to hide it in the white box. Having another phone is against my contract rules, but there are more important things to worry about. I'll just have to be extra careful not to get caught and end up with my contract terminated. I'd lose all the credits I've been working so hard for, as well as my inside track on the Institute for more convenient spying.

I leave my phone in the closet and turn to leave. My glance is snagged by Jodine's fruit painting hanging over the doorway. Mrs. K. must've returned it there so Jodine wouldn't know she took it down. I wince. Jodine's going to notice the junk food missing from the white box, but that can't be helped. I'm sure she'll think her diary is safe, since it has a password, even if I possess her fingerprint for the bio-lock.

I'd really like to meet Jodine after this is over. We could compare notes and see if any of her residual memories accidentally got added to my brainmap generation today. Those memories aren't in Jodine's original backup file that Dr. K. saved—which means I'd remember the memory, not her. Which would be terrible. What if her special memory of painting that fruit or defeating the cyber-dragon got copied into my backup? Or even the memory of Gavin's music-room kiss? She would read it in her diary but wouldn't be able to remember it happening.

Even at the end of a normal assignment, any Loaner's residuals might be accidentally scooped up and privacy-deleted when a Reducer left a body. Gone forever, wiped out with the Reducer's assignment memories. *Neither* the Loaner nor Reducer would remember the memory.

Bad news. Faulty tech.

It's complex to think about, but it all comes down to Jodine possibly losing some of her strongest, most emotional memories. Permanently. Worse than that, I might have lost a few of my memories during today's backup if they stuck in Jodine's brain and didn't get copied. Also permanently. She'll keep them, not me.

I wonder if Shelby Johnson has any of my memories, random strays that stuck in her brain and didn't get canceled out with my Reducer memories in June. I can chase that angle tomorrow. I'll find Shelby's information online and see if she'll have a quiet little chat with me somewhere.

On my Institute phone, I sign into my financial account and discover my condolence settlement is there. About time. I apply all except one hundred of the ten thousand credits to Gramma's hospital bills and exit. That's what I can pay right now. Since I'm back to being a Reducer, I won't get the first installment of my weight loss credits until the end of December.

I shift the stuffed animals to one side of the bed rather than the window seat. They're good company after all. I'm adjusting a panda when a chirp comes from the ceiling vent, and the green airbot shoots out.

I straighten and smile. "Hate to say it, but I missed you, kid."

The bot emits a soft mechanical purr. As it drifts closer to me, my Institute phone rings. Cuddly critter-bot reunion interrupted.

Good evening, Morgan.

It's Leo, of course.

What's up in Seattle?

It's a good thing he can't hear my grumpy tone.

The usual challenges, he says.

Listen, I'm calling to see how it went at the Clinic this afternoon. I saw you signed the contract of intention to return Jodine's body and accept a Spare, but I didn't have a chance to check how your backup went with the replacement equipment.

There wasn't any problem. The doctor verified my brainmap file afterward with the computer, and said it looked complete.

As complete and accurate as ERT can be, anyway.

Good. And I assume you got your tracking chip implanted.

I rub my left forearm where the needle went in. That's one more thing added to my list of foul things about the Institute. Good thing Vonn's not a Reducer anymore, or he'd be chipped too, and Leo would know how much we hang out together. We'd get terminated, pronto.

Yes, and I'm not keen on it. It's like I'm some sort of tagged animal, set loose for observation.

If you want to be safe, you have to be willing to sacrifice a few things. That's the direction the world's heading, Morgan.

I bristle. I wonder what, exactly, he thinks the future world will look like and how the Institute will factor into it. The tracking chip might prevent things like the ERT equipment sabotage in Seattle, but it makes me feel like I'm Institute property. It's as though Reducers, Loaners, and even the Spares are Leo's personal chess pieces to direct and control.

Man, I'd sure like to know if he's involved in illegal activities with the Spares.

> Hey, those Spares could be useful in a future world, too.

I plow onward, hoping my text words come across more casual and innocent than I'm feeling.

> They'd come in really handy for someone who was dying and needed a new body. Like if the president or other famous person got a terminal illness. Or the FBI could use them to defuse a bomb or do a hostage rescue. The CIA could use them for spies, because there'd always be a backup of the brainmaps.

A brief pause happens before Leo's words scroll out.

> That might be true, but it's a more complex issue than you realize. Ethics, legalities, human rights, and so on.

That's a pretty careful, generic answer. Forget it. There's no point in trying to fish for more information, since he's not cooperating, and I'm tired. I mumble a parting and tap off the call.

"Lights out," I tell the room and slip into bed. A mild darkness envelops me while the humming of the airbot drifts into my ears. It seems content. Maybe it thinks Jodine is back.

I won't let on to it that that isn't true.

The electric blue and lavender of the Half-Moon Café surround me, along with people who are spreading cream cheese on bagels and sipping fruit drinks. I check the time on my Institute phone once more and chew on my lower lip, even though my first impulse is to gnaw off a fingernail. 1538 already.

Where's Shelby? She's late. The longer I sit here waiting to do something forbidden, the more my stomach churns.

I wait a few more minutes. A blonde with a pretty face wearing a short ski coat, fuzzy-topped boots, and tight jeans breezes through the front door. She scans the crowd and easily spots me. I wave her over.

"You look great." My envy isn't difficult to fake.

Shelby sits and smiles. "Thanks, Lucy. Lucy Callahan, right? How did you find my phone number to text me, anyway?"

"I went to CyberFace to get your dad's name and Zone, then the online Cell Directory. Sorry to act like a stalker, but I have to get some straight info. Can I buy you something to drink?"

"No thanks, I have my water bottle. So your text said you're thinking about joining The Body Institute as a Loaner."

I nod and flick a glance down at myself. "I'm really tired of living like this. I'm sure you know how people treat you when you're overweight."

Shelby gives me a gentle look. "Do I ever. It's like you're not a real person with feelings inside, just because you don't look the way they think you should."

"Exactly. Luckily my boyfriend doesn't care, but other people can't see past the pounds. They're surprised I even have a boyfriend."

Her low laugh holds a sharp edge. We chat for a few minutes about the positives of the Institute and her fantastic weight loss. Then I lean forward over my mango-pineapple drink. "I'd like to know about negative things, too. Is there anything you didn't like about your Loaner experience?"

She shrugs. "I'd say shallow people still being shallow people. Suddenly they want to be my friend because I'm on ad-vids and I weigh fifty pounds less. It's really annoying, you know?"

"I bet. What about ERT, the whole weirdness about having no consciousness the entire time some stranger is losing weight for you?"

"It didn't *feel* like three months. It's like going to sleep one night and waking up the next morning, except lots of things have happened in the world while you've been out of it."

I try to appear merely curious for my next question. "Did the ERT work okay, or do you remember some things now that might not be yours? Images or thoughts that don't belong, for instance."

An obvious inner war plays out across Shelby's face, with eyebrow and mouth twitches. "Oh, nothing too big of a deal," she says after a bit. "Mostly, the whole experience made me have strange dreams. Or thoughts, or whatever they are."

"Like what?" I need to know. I have to know.

She uncaps her water bottle, fingers tense, and takes a long swig. "Well, there's this one bizarre image that I get whenever my family goes over to my aunt's, and she drives us to the hover-skating rink in her car."

A compressed-air car. I think I know what's coming. "What's the image?"

"It's me, bent over a keyboard, happily typing an essay about air compression tanks and how they crack and not shatter upon impact. I mean, how would I even *know* something that geeky tech? It doesn't make sense."

It does to me. Because it's my memory—one I actually remember, since it was in my original backup file when I finished my Shelby assignment and got Restored.

"The reason I ask," I say, "is because someone told me ERT sometimes misses memories when it creates the Reducer's privacy brainmap file, the one that's used to cancel them from their Loaner bodies. It sounds like you got a stray memory from your Reducer."

Her mouth twists. "It's not going to go away, then."

"Probably not. I hope it's something you can live with. Does anything else pop up when you don't want it to?"

"Um, I see some really awful green chairs, like I'm sitting in the Clinic waiting room. And I see a beautiful woman with dark hair, singing to me while I'm snuggled up in bed. It's the most amazing sound, like the song of a husky-voiced angel. I can't make out what all the words are, but I know it's a Christmas tune."

My stomach pitches and drops hard. *Mom*. That sounds like a memory of her, one I don't remember. I can recall other images of her singing while I was young and in bed, but they didn't involve a Christmas tune.

No. Oh, no. I've lost that one to Shelby. That memory got downloaded into Shelby, and then it stuck in her brain when I got canceled out of her body. Not a problem for a Reducer normally, but that memory must've stayed in my real brain this time instead of being downloaded into Jodine, and I don't have my own body anymore.

Haze it all, ERT isn't even consistent with the memories it brainmaps from one assignment to the next.

Part of me is gone forever.

Shelby tenses up even more and leans so far over the table toward me, our heads nearly touch. "There's this one other scene that gives me the shivers. It's like I'm in a long hallway, following a silver robot shaped like a bell. I overhear a phone conversation spoken in some guy's deep voice. He's angry."

This is new, something I don't remember. "Yeah?"

"He comes out of a room and almost runs into me. He has

a black goatee. His face matches the words he just said—angry."

"Do you remember the words?"

"Yes, and I wish I didn't. He says, '*Then get rid of him, if he knows too much. Send him to Seattle.*' I don't know what that means, but it sounds light-years beyond creepy."

"It sure does." I try to keep a shiver from running down my arms, but a crop of serious gooseflesh springs up. Seattle. There's an Institute branch in Seattle. Leo's there now.

Shelby curls her hand over my forearm, and her fingernails press into my skin. "I hate thinking of that image. I figured it was just a bad dream until September when I was at the admin building waiting to plan a new ad-vid, and that *very same guy* came out of Mr. Behr's office. He's real!"

I grit my teeth, pat Shelby's hand, and extract her fingers from my arm. "I don't know if I want to join the program if I end up with memories like that."

She thumps against the back of her chair, exhaling long and hard. "Overall it was worth it, but I wish they'd fix their Transfer equipment and get it working right."

I shove my hair away from my face and close my eyes.

That, Shelby Johnson, is the understatement of the century.

CHAPTER 25

New park, new rendezvous bench. I stand on the sidewalk in South Park as the MT hums up to the Green Zone shelter and opens its doors. Now that I have this nasty tracking chip in my arm, Vonn and I have to meet at a totally different park to prevent Leo from making a connection between me and the park Vonn used to record in his daily log.

Vonn steps off the MT, strolls up, and gives me a hug so intense that it leaves me breathless. "Seems like ages since I've seen you instead of just yesterday. Come on, let's swap info. I'm dying to know what you've learned from Shelby."

We start along the paths, and I tell him what Shelby said. "That means the memory of the goatee guy must've happened while I was Reducing for her. That's why I don't remember it."

"Right, and it stuck in Shelby's brain during your cancelation mapping, so that's why she remembers it. I'd like to know what's in Seattle that's such a punishment."

"No kidding." Or maybe I don't want to know. "Have you learned anything with your WHA research?"

"Conspiracy news galore, most of it ridiculous. Maybe we

need to join the WHA to get an inside view."

I chuckle with him. Like *that's* going to happen. "Did you find anything about the Spares?"

"Not a whisper or a hint. I don't think anyone knows about them."

Which makes it more difficult to uncover the truth. I'm dying to find out what Leo knows. Too bad I can't ask him directly, or blackmail information out of him somehow.

"Where are all the Spare bodies kept, anyway?" Vonn asks. "In the suspended animation rooms? If that's true, a bunch of them got blown up in our branch's bombing."

"I never thought of that. Hey, do you think *Steven* was a Spare? The Institute could've stripped his brainmap and sold his body to Chad's mom. They could've lied to her about why Steven was brain dead."

Vonn's eyes are bugged as he spins toward me. "Do you realize you're implying that my best friend was the kind of guy who would end up on death row?"

"Sorry!" I say, my own eyes bugging. "I didn't think before I blurted it out."

"Don't worry, you're still my favorite Geekling," Vonn says with a lopsided smile.

I bump him with my elbow. "But maybe not all Spares are criminals on death row. A few of them might've just been in accidents and lost their brain function, like Steven."

We slow to a walk for our second lap. Vonn's silent for so long, I dart a look at him. He doesn't look mad, though, just thoughtful. Pale and thoughtful.

He veers off to a bench and accesses his phone, flicking info across the screen. "I'm looking up records for Steven," he says. "I was going to do it before, but then the bombing happened. There's gotta be something online that I didn't see back when he disappeared. Not that I was really looking. I just thought he forgot his email password again, since he wasn't the most organized guy."

I sit close beside him and rest my chin against his shoulder. He checks accident and death records first.

"Here it is," Vonn mutters. "A death record for the fourth of February. Sounds about right. Ten months ago is when I lost track of him."

"Is that the day someone did Chad's Transfer and inserted his ID chip into Steven? They're calling that the date of Steven's death?"

"Could be." Vonn scratches his chin. "Huh, check this out. He also has an arrest record. Dated in January, three weeks before his death."

I look and frown. The arrest is for trespassing and mild property destruction. "What's that's all about?"

"I can make a good guess," Vonn says. "Steven was really into animal rights and ran around with a bunch of frat boys who sometimes got a bit, uh, *passionate* when they heard about people abusing their pets. They'd go on aggressive rescue operations. Save starving dogs and stuff. Sometimes they'd trash people's houses while they were at it. Looks like Steven got caught."

"That incident or arrest wouldn't have anything to do with him being brain dead, would it? Like, he got injured or something?"

"Dunno. This record just says he was arrested, no hospital addendum. You know, it could be that the Institute has nothing to do with his Transfer. There might be a black market for bodies, and another group is stripping and selling them."

"Scientifically speaking, that'd be a stretch. It's really advanced tech."

Vonn's mouth is a tense line as he pockets his phone. "An Institute scientist or worker could be leaking classified data, selling it to underground groups. Something's going on, Morgan, something terrible. We just don't know exactly what or how."

"We'll keep digging," I say. "We should try Chad and his mother next. I bet she'd know if it was the Institute or another group who did their illegal Transfer, even if Chad doesn't."

Vonn curls his fingers around mine, and links them tight. "She's not going to tell us."

"We could convince Chad to ask her, and he could tell us. We need his contact info. Can I borrow your phone to do a bit of research without Leo having a fit?"

He digs it back out and hands it to me. "Needle in a haystack, Geekling. We don't know his last name, and Missouri's a big state."

Unfortunately, he's right. I run searches on CyberFace for "Chad in Missouri," and come up with hundreds of matches. Less for images, but too many to comb through while sitting on a hard park bench with a cold December breeze blowing in my face. "Ugh, I'll look through these tonight on my own phone. Chad might not even have a CyberFace profile. How about his mother?"

"We don't know her first or last name."

"Hey, don't spoil my fun." Not wanting to give up already, I type in *Chad, mother, National Health Care,* and *Missouri.* Chad did say his mother worked for health care. On the second page of results, my fingers freeze over an image on the screen.

Vonn sucks in a sharp breath. "Would you look at that…"

The photo is dated two years ago, taken at an annual health

convention dinner. A bony young guy with dark shadows under his eyes and no hair is labeled as Chad Moore, son of the councilwoman of the Missouri National Health Care Association. Chad's mother stands next to him, petite, auburn-haired, and fierce. A man stands on her other side, his arm wrapped around her shoulders in a comfortable and possessive way.

There's no mistaking the man's trim mustache, the precise styling of his hair, his determined salesman smile.

It's Leo. He used to work for National Health Care.

Not only that, it seems he knows Chad and his mother.

With Jodine's thick coat collar turned up against the spitting December rain, I join the flow of the crowd heading for the brick building across the street. There's a surprising number of people attending this WHA meeting. Vonn doesn't think I'll uncover anything worth the risk of being discovered, but I have to try every angle to dig up information.

If I'm caught, I can just tell Leo I was checking out the holiday lights in this area. It's decorated with glowing snowflakes and rows of crimson-draped trees.

"Excuse me," I say to a woman with tiny wreaths for earrings. "You're going to this meeting, right?"

"I am." She stops, boots poised at the edge of a puddle. "You're welcome to join us, although I'm afraid we're not too organized at the moment, with Walter gone."

"Did Walter Herry really have anything to do with the Institute bombing?" I restrain my words to keep them from coming out harsh. "That was horrible. No one's rights are protected when buildings and people are blown up."

The woman's forehead puckers. "Not all of us advocated violence like Walter. We agreed something had to be done, but we were split about what that would look like. He and his diehard followers decided the bombing was the best way to get the public's attention."

Ah. Herry *did* scheme with the maintenance tech to set off the bomb. As I suspected. I wish I could tell this woman about the Spares, how Vonn and I are 99 percent sure the Institute performed Chad's illegal Transfer—involving ID swapping that isn't sanctioned by the International Nations Council yet. Or at least Leo himself arranged for it, under the table. I'm super tempted to say something right now, but for that risky of a move I'll need to wait until my assignment is done and I'm out of Jodine's body.

"I'm thinking of signing up at the Institute as a Loaner," I say to the woman. "But I'm afraid of losing my backup file or having my body attacked by your group."

"Don't sign up," a male voice cuts in from behind us, before the woman can speak. "The program sucks. It's designed for a bunch of Ego-Heads who think they're better than you because they can lose the weight you can't."

I turn and discover two people in black sauntering up the sidewalk, a blonde with a star tattoo on one cheek and a smokin'-hot guy with spiky hair. "Maybe Reducers just want to help others," I say, my words coiled tight. "Not everyone is a shallow Ego-Head."

His gaze sweeps across me in a split second, and I can tell by the glazed look that follows that my round figure and overall appearance haven't made one tiny blip on his male radar. To him I'm a chunk of asphalt or a piece of furniture, nearly invisible as a female.

The blonde bounces in her buckled shoes. "Come to the meeting with us!" she says to me. Her voice is breathy, as if everything is beyond-galaxies exciting. "I've been a WHA member for more than two years, and we've done some really important work."

"The WHA helped murder a lot of innocent people," I say. "That didn't solve anything."

The guy shrugs one shoulder, barely a twitch. "It's a war dealing with rights, and there are always casualties in a war. Besides, none of those people were innocent, since they agreed to work for the Institute."

The blonde nods and starts listing off "valid" reasons for the bombing.

The woman with the wreath earrings spears the blonde with a stern look. "Don't make blanket statements, young lady. Not everyone in the WHA supports using violence to solve rights issues."

The blonde huffs, while the guy launches into a tirade to defend her. I've stood around here long enough. I'm not learning any new information. I hold up a gloved hand. "Sorry, I gotta go. Don't be late for your meeting."

The wind whips my face as I head to the nearest MT shelter. Man. I used to be deluded about a lot of things, people and beliefs alike. But I'll take one Vonn over a thousand hot-but-empty dudes like that WHA guy any day.

I've almost reached the Kowalczyks' house when Leo texts me. I feel like ignoring his message, but I don't want to get on the wrong side of him. He's formidable enough when we're working toward the same goals.

> Morgan. The auto-system just alerted me. What were you doing in the Red Zone tonight?

How I loathe my tracking chip.

> I didn't know being in the Red Zone was against the rules.

> Don't avoid my question. Let me state it this way: your chip placed you squarely in the vicinity of the WHA meeting scheduled there tonight. I want to know why.

There goes my excuse about the holiday lights, since anything related to the WHA is apparently flagged. This kind of linking to my location will really cramp my investigating.

> Don't you trust me, Leo? I hate the WHA! They ruined the backup files and blew up my body. It's not like I'm going to attend one of their meetings or become a member, if that's what you think.

> So what WERE you doing?

> Antagonizing them, apparently.

It's the truth, though not my initial goal.

> I was arguing about rights and the WHA going around murdering Institute workers.

> Ah, I see.

A slight pause.

> Don't engage them, Morgan. It's pointless. Concentrate on your job. You're not in Jodine's body to right the wrongs in the world. Do that on your own time.

> Fine. I'll wait until I belong to myself again.

Whoever "myself" is—or will be, by the time this job is finished.

CHAPTER 26

On the tenth of December, I awaken in Jodine's room and groan. I cover my eyes with one bent arm. It's Saturday, my eighteenth birthday. I don't see how this day will be enjoyable by any vast span of the imagination. My only bright spot will be meeting Vonn at the park later. Somehow I have to make it through my routine until then.

I throw on sweats. After an hour's workout, I trudge back upstairs and step onto the bathroom scale. A smooth mechanical voice informs me, "One hundred ninety-eight pounds."

Here I am, turning eighteen while imprisoned in someone else's body. And whatever I do today, thanks to my crimping tracking chip, the Institute will know where I am.

"I'm earning lots of credits, I'm earning lots of credits," I chant as I head to the shower, only pausing long enough to say, "Water on."

By the time I comb the curly nest that masquerades as my hair, I'm ready to strangle something. The green airbot hums and floats over the window seat, keeping its distance. A wise choice.

An incoming phone text announces itself, and I find another one besides that waiting. The first one must've arrived while I was showering. The new message is from Krista:

> Toot, toot! Happy birthday, Morg. You rock! Don't spend your day exercising, geek-girl. Have some FUN. Love ya.

Before I can respond, another text arrives. I connect with Blair.

> I'm glad you're up! Happy 18, she says.

> Thanks. Of course I'm up. I start exercising at the freaking crack of dawn. I'll miss hanging out with you and Krista tonight.

> I hate that you're gone again. I mean, we already know what you look like and everything, so I don't know why you can't get together with us.

That *is* pretty annoying.

> Leo, the director, said I have to stick close to the Zone where my client lives. You wouldn't be allowed in her house because of privacy rules, either.

> Then we'll do a night out when you come back. Doing anything exciting today?

> Not sure yet.

I refuse to complain about my dreary life.

> How about you?

> Brad and I are on the MT, going to the Shadow Realms. I can't wait! I haven't been there since that time I took you and Krista, 2 years ago. Too

bad you can't come with us.

The Shadow Realms. I love that place, with its real-life RPG quests spread over thirty acres in the White Zone.

Have a great time, I force myself to say.

If I could go *anywhere* with friends today, it would be an improvement.

The other message is from Mom and Dad, promising to celebrate properly with me when I return. I wonder if Granddad forgot, or if he just hasn't gotten around to sending something yet.

In the kitchen, Nettie putters by the stove. "Good morning. I'm making omelets. Will you fetch the onions and mushrooms?"

Obediently, I head for the fridge. This is *not* what I want to be doing today. I want to do something different and exciting. Not exercising, not chores, not even researching or spying on the Institute.

I spend the morning sweating at the HoloSports Center, then cooling down on the karaoke machine. I'm in the kitchen with Nettie, eating the last of a tuna-and-tomato sandwich, when Mrs. K. enters the autodoor.

"There you are," she says to me. "Happy birthday. Mr. Behr called to say you're doing well with the weight loss, and mentioned it was your special day."

"Wow. Thanks." Leo must be stoked I'm staying on schedule.

Nettie whisks our empty plates away. "I wish I'd known it was your birthday, Morgan. I could've made a cake." She darts a look at Mrs. K. "Or another more healthy dessert. Anyway, I'm glad to hear you're on track. I'm proud of you."

"Charles and I are, too." Mrs. K.'s tone is honest, though not quite as warm.

I thank them again and hurry off to catch the MT for my rendezvous with Vonn at the South Park. Finally. Despite the fact that it involves more exercising, I'm closing in on my day's bright spot. When I arrive, Vonn is already at our new bench. The thirty-one pounds he's lost gives him a more energetic look, even from a distance.

"Happy birthday," he calls. "The you inside that cute freckled body is officially an adult now." He gives me a vigorous bear hug that makes my shoulder pop, and I laugh. We start down the path, swinging clasped hands.

"You're awesome, Vonn Alexander," I sing out in Jodine's most triumphant voice. "I'm saying *you're* my present today, so thank you very much for your gift of you."

His face looks delighted and shy at the same time. "Nice! But what I'd really like to do for your Big Eighteen is take you somewhere to celebrate. Want to go dancing tonight?"

I snort. "Right."

"I'm serious, Reducer-girl."

It's a fabulous yet insane idea. "Only slender, athletic people dance in public."

"Stop stereotyping. I've seen bigger-size girls and guys at clubs before."

"I haven't seen very many."

"You probably weren't paying attention."

"I think I would've noticed."

Vonn grins. "It doesn't matter. The point is, you should give it a try. Come on, let's take a break from sleuthing and heavy stuff. We need to do something wild and entertaining after all we've been through. It'll be fun exercise. We can dance in a dark corner so we don't weird out anyone."

I giggle. If someone gets offended by our dancing, that's

their problem. "That sounds flippin' fantastic. I'd love to get out and think about something besides faulty ERT procedures and evil men with goatees. But Leo might not let me."

"You don't know until you ask. Just don't tell him you're going with me. I'll meet you there."

That might be worth a shot. What the heck—Krista told me to have fun.

"Meet you at nineteen hundred?" Vonn asks.

"Sure," I say, a trace of hopeful eagerness springing up inside me. "If it's okay with Leo and my Loaner parents, I'll text you on my personal phone, and we'll figure out where to go."

I smooth the sides of my black skirt as I approach the club. The pulsing bass coming from inside the building matches the rhythm of the flashing sign above the door. *Night Flight*, the sign announces. A crisp wind stirs the air, making goose bumps rise on my bare legs.

Still, even with my legs freezing and my skirt too tight, it feels wonderful to wear something besides sweats, T-shirts, and slacks. The thirty-seven pounds I've lost has expanded my wardrobe selection a little.

I clip my Institute phone to my belt and glance at the taxicab that's easing into a parking slot a short distance away. While I'm glad Leo agreed—reluctantly—to let me come here tonight, he insisted on a two-hour limit as well as a taxi escort. It makes sense not to take Jodine's body anywhere alone at night, but I feel like a two-year-old who needs hand-holding while crossing the street.

It's better than nothing, though. Leo and the Kowalczyks were more accepting of the idea after I pointed out that dancing would be helpful for Jodine's weight loss.

I turn on my exercise app, let the scanners register my ID at the door, and enter the club.

The thumping music surges. The melody rushes into my ears while the drumbeats shake me to my bones. Girls and guys pack the floor, a mass of rhythmic limbs, bouncing hips, and flipping hair. Holographic birds and dragons race overhead. Yes! I have *so* missed the feeling of being at a club.

Like anything is possible and I am free, free, free.

For tonight, I'll pretend my heinous tracking chip doesn't exist.

I spot Vonn standing off to my left. He looks sharp, wearing black pants and a violet shirt with thin white stripes. He gives a nod to show he sees me when I walk toward him. His gaze travels in slow-motion appreciation over my outfit, and I smile when a reckless grin spreads across his face.

Excellent. That grin just made it worth the tortured eighty minutes I spent pawing through Jodine's closet.

Vonn slips his hand into mine, and he pulls me toward a section where the dancers are less crammed together.

"Here's our reserved spot in the corner." He angles closer to my ear so I can hear him. His warm breath brushes the side of my face. "Just like I promised. Let's enjoy your birthday." He releases my hand and begins an energetic dance, accompanied by an exhilarated expression that blows me away. He's *really* good at this.

I push my hair behind my shoulders and join in. I have to admit, it is fun moving to the music in Jodine's body. Her figure does different things. Wider moves, more emphatic turns.

A tinkley little alternate melody runs through my mind as I dance, underlying the club's song. *Happy birthday to me, happy birthday to me.*

This day is improving exponentially. Granddad even finally sent a text this afternoon:

> Your mom nudged my memory about your birthday! Sorry I didn't write sooner. Special wishes to you, my favorite brain-clone granddaughter. Many hugs and much love.

Even though the occasion slipped his mind, he still cares.

Vonn and I dance for about thirty minutes before we collapse at a table in a sunken café area. We pay for beverages separately, ordering from a tabletop screen. While we wait for the drinks, I grab a napkin and blot perspiration from my forehead. "Good workout," I shout over the music. "I bet I've already burned a gazillion calories."

"At least." Vonn's eyes twinkle with their usual glint. "Hey, we should come back here and celebrate Jodine's birthday for her, too."

"Sure, if her parents and Leo let me — I mean, her." I laugh, not sure which is right.

We sip drinks and rest until the pulse of the music snags us again. Dodging the dancers, we resume our place near the corner.

Soon a song with a slower tempo winds through the room. Vonn leans in toward me, one hand settling like a large butterfly on my shoulder. "I hate it that we lost our own bodies, but I'm really glad we'll be able to remember each other now. Well, at least up until your new backup."

"I like that, too." His breath by my neck sends a zingy

shiver skidding down my spine. We hold hands, and I close my eyes. I love his touch. He's wrapping his fingers around mine as if I'm special, the center of his universe.

Vonn's voice fills my ear. "Are you thinking of me? I hope so, with that dreamy look on your face."

"Maybe, maybe not." Smiling, I open my eyes and look into his.

He moves even closer. All I notice then is his mouth, which is insanely lively and intelligent. "You know," he says, "I seem to remember saying something a while back about snogging at dance clubs…"

My smile widens and a soft laugh bubbles up. Vonn kisses me on top of my smile. His mouth is warm and intriguing, and we both press our lips more firmly against each other's at the same time. The room spins and disintegrates into a hazy background. Our kiss needs to continue on and on forever, it's so fantastic. It's as if all the words and walks and memories of our past eight weeks have come together in the merging of our mouths.

It's a connection I'm positive has nothing to do with how we look, but the people we are underneath. It stretches back to the waiting room when we first saw each other. It exists in the present, alive and intense. It springs way forward to a future I can't even see.

This is something I haven't felt before. It's a mind-altering drug.

"Oh, gag me and make me vomit!" a voice says, slicing through the music. "JO-dine is getting cuddly with Blubber Boy."

We jolt apart. I whirl to find Noni a few feet away, standing with hands on her hips. Decked out in dark leather, she looks brashly wicked. The color-change dye in her hair swirls from blue to red. Tibs, her minion, looks over from where she dances with a beefy-looking guy.

An instant storm churns inside me. This girl has no idea how special of a moment she just interrupted. "Shove off, Noni. Go howl someplace else."

"*What* did you say?" Noni's eyes widen behind her retro glasses. "You can't talk to me like that, Kowalczyk."

Vonn cuts in. "We're done talking." He pulls me away toward the sunken café. We squeeze through the crowd, the music thumping with my rapid pulse.

Noni follows us, her voice shrill. "Stop pretending nothing just happened, fat boy. Step outside and I'll kick your —"

"Let's get out of here," Vonn says to me. "Leo won't be happy if you get caught in the middle of a disturbance."

I shake my head. How can Noni do this to me, to Jodine? "We can't leave now. She just challenged you to a fight outside." We start to step down the four steps into the sunken café area, when a forceful shove against my back sends me tumbling forward. Vonn loses his grip on my hand, tries to catch it, and misses. I bounce into a dreadlocked guy and roll, landing on the floor with my skirt bunching around my thighs.

Titters run through the crowd. My hip hurts where I landed. I manage to get my legs under me and pull myself into a more respectable position while Noni cackles. Tibs saunters up.

"You ought to watch where you're going, J.," Noni says as I yank my skirt straight. "It's not good to be fat *and* clumsy."

I stand and glare at her sneer, at her shiny leather and flashy hair. The club fades from my sight. An image of a younger Noni appears in my mind, prancing around Jodine's bedroom, flinging Doritos onto the bed, the floor, the window seat. The echoes of her laughter stab me. Noni holds the chip bag up high, a dirty secret no one should see. *Give me your new gamebot, or I'm gonna tell, I'm gonna tell.*

The scene dissipates, but the hurt and anger don't. I've had enough of Noni. She's a horrible ex-friend, first stealing things from our house and then pulling cruel pranks on me at school. I shouldn't have to put up with her meanness. I'm sick of her stomping all over me, and I'm finally going to do something about it.

I march over to where Noni stands. As if on its own power, my fist shoots out and smacks her in the face. Her glasses fly off, skidding across a table. She staggers back and sits down hard, which causes the crowd to break out in a fresh wave of laughter and raucous calls.

"That's how you fight." I bite off the words one at a time. "Not sneaking up behind people and shoving them down stairs. I'm losing weight, but even if I wasn't, it's none of your business what I look like. Stop making a big deal out of it. If you do any more mean things to me or Helena or Gavin from now on, I'll deck you again."

Now I'm ready to leave. As I turn to rejoin Vonn, a muscular man strides up and blocks my path. A uniformed figure. A male Enforcer posted as bouncer for this club, judging from the badge on his shirt.

Oh, freaking haze.

"Your ID, miss, and your version of the altercation," the Enforcer says in a no-nonsense tone. People melt away, going back to their drinks and dancing with renewed zeal. The Enforcer holds out a device to scan my hand and record my statement.

I catch Vonn's eye over the Enforcer's shoulder and shake

my head to warn him to stay out of it. "That girl, Noni, insulted me. I walked away and started to go down these steps, when she pushed me. I fell into the café area. I'm lucky I didn't twist my ankle. Then she called me fat and clumsy, so I punched her."

"That's right," a guy with a crew cut yells with glee. "She punched that chick good!"

Noni lets loose a stream of caustic swear words. She staggers to her feet, aided by Tibs.

The Enforcer taps his device with a decisive finger. "You're on official file, Miss Kowalczyk, and your report will be evaluated alongside security camera footage." He gestures toward a second Enforcer arriving. "Upon confirmation, your ban from this club will last six months. You will now be removed from the building."

CHAPTER 27

I lie in the darkness of Jodine's room with the autoblinds open, watching the shadowy shape of the green airbot as it whirs near the closet. The night sky is inky and cold beyond the window frames. No stars tonight. I've stayed motionless on the bed for an hour after arriving from the club. If I remain still, I have no sensation of my body.

It makes me feel more like myself. The physical part of the old Morgan Dey, which no longer exists.

Happy birthday to me.

I thoroughly messed up my night out. When they discover my Reducer status, it'll be Morgan Dey the Enforcers penalize, not Jodine. I've never been in trouble like this before. So much for trying hard to be a law-abiding person, a good citizen who helps people. So much for enjoying a night where I can forget unpleasant things like my body's death, conspiracy theories, and my tracking chip.

Vonn looked really upset when I was escorted from the club.

What does he think of me now?

My mind replays our earth-shattering kiss. Yet the memory is distorted by the image of Noni's sneer superimposed over it. I can't bring myself to call him, to walk all the way across the room and get my personal phone from the closet. To bring up his number. To talk to him about the whole depressing part of the evening after we kissed.

The trill of my Institute phone breaks the silence around me.

"Lights on." As the room brightens, I roll over to the phone on the bedside table.

Hello?

This is Leo Behr.

That's all he says. The blank space below the words stretches out.

With an ugly sinking feeling, I push into a sitting position.

What's up?

I received a message from the Enforcer security system saying you were involved in a brawl at the dance club.

I snort.

A brawl?

Yes, and I'm quite displeased about the news. You endangered Jodine's body with your actions tonight. We've discussed this type of thing before.

That reminder grates on my nerves.

Endangered? How could I—

I huff and start over.

That girl at the club has picked on Jodine before, which Jodine didn't bother to mention to you in her prep report. I can't predict where these bullies will pop up.

I thought you could behave yourself in a public place. I misjudged you.

Seriously, *behave myself*? He's still treating me like a two-year-old.

It was out of my control. Everything was going fine until that Noni chick decided to barge in.

Jodine's hand could've been injured by the punch. Not to mention, slugging that girl can be defined as assault. Violence is prohibited in your contract, if you remember.

I'm not interested in being lectured.

She assaulted me first. It should be considered self-defense.

Was it?

Sure. I was sticking up for myself. For Jodine. Right before that, I had one of those residual memories, and the emotion from that made me hit Noni. It's the strongest one I've ever experienced.

Or you just lost your temper and were getting even. That's retaliation, not self-defense. I'm going to set up a conference call with the Board of Directors. I'll share the report from the club, and we'll determine if this is a breach worthy of assignment termination.

Termination. He's got to be kidding.

> Seriously, Leo, that residual memory pushed me over the edge. My fist and my arm moved before I could stop them.

> I doubt that, and mostly, I'm not sure we can trust your judgment anymore. At the very least you'll be put on probation and closely monitored. Restricted to the Kowalczyks' house unless accompanied by another person.

> That would be like living in jail! I'm practically a hermit as it is. This club thing is a one-time mess-up, and it won't happen again.

> That doesn't change what happened tonight.

True. I slump. Bleariness blankets me. Leo keeps texting while I stare at my phone.

> I'll let you know what the Board decides in the morning.

> Fine.

I tap the screen, growl the lights off, and fall asleep with my clothes on.

After the MT whirs away from me the next morning, the sidewalk leading to the South Park seems ages long. My feet walk, but they don't seem to get anywhere. The eggs and toast I ate for breakfast sit like stones in my stomach. The sky hangs crisp and gray overhead. Earlier in the kitchen, Nettie looked mournful and didn't say much. I assume Leo informed the Kowalczyks about my "brawl," and they told Nettie.

Termination.

That could be my punishment. Termination without pay.

How horrible. I'll take probation over being terminated. Otherwise, my last two months of weight loss will be for nothing. How could I have let that memory affect me that much? Honestly, I don't know where my emotions stopped and Jodine's began. Besides that tangle, I need to know what Vonn's thinking, whether I can make things right with him. He didn't answer the text I sent from my personal phone, at least not before I left the house.

I find our park bench vacant. Glancing down the street, I don't see him heading toward me, either. Maybe he's running late.

I sit on the bench. Five minutes pass, then ten. A trickle of serious worry leaks in. Maybe this isn't fixable. He might go to the city gym this morning instead of meeting me here. Maybe he never wants to see me again.

The day slips into deeper bleakness. The park stretches behind me, its expanse cold, its trees stripped of leaves. The air smells empty.

I sit for a while longer, the minutes creeping by. I wish I could carry my own phone in public so I could text him again or see if he answered my message. At least Leo didn't mention Vonn being in the Enforcers' report, which means our "date" is probably safe.

It's almost time to leave the park, and I haven't even broken a sweat. But why bother? If Leo and the Board end my contract, I won't need to lose weight anymore. A new Reducer will take over for me. Or if Leo puts me on a house-arrest type of probation…well, that's depressing enough to make me want to go back to the Kowalczyks' and eat a whole bag of Doritos.

I scan for Vonn again. A handful of people walk the sidewalks and park paths, guys with hooded sweatshirts, women with suit dresses and heels. A kid packing a hoverboard. By a wireless café, one figure moves along in a hurry. *Vonn.* The sight of him brings me to my feet in an instant. I jog down the sidewalk.

"I'm really sorry," I say in a rush when I get near him. "Are you mad at me?"

He struggles for breath. "I was…mad last night. Not now. Bummed, though. Sorry I didn't message sooner. Mom called this morning…tried to hurry to get here—"

He did text me! I just didn't get his reply before I left the Kowalczyks'. My relief swells, then vanishes. His face is flushed, and he's gripping his sweatshirt by his heart. "Vonn, are you okay?"

"Need to sit."

I help him to a closer bench than our usual one, and he lands with a thump. "Should I call for an ambulance? Are you having chest pains? Any tingling or lightheadedness?"

He shakes his head again. "No. Don't worry. I'm just winded."

Sitting beside him, I grab his wrist and feel for his pulse. "You have to be careful with this body. It's not in good shape."

He closes his eyes and draws in a long breath. "Don't I know it."

Not only that, he's not a Reducer anymore and has no backup brain waves.

His breathing evens out over the next ten minutes. Thankfully. When I feel sure he isn't going to collapse right in front of me, I dive into a flood of words. "I'm sorry I was such an idiot last night. I had one of those residual memories about that Noni girl harassing Jodine. Jodine's emotions fused with mine, and a huge reaction happened before I could stop it. Anyway, Leo's going to talk to the Board. I'll either get terminated or put on probation."

Vonn swaps a woeful look with me. "That's what I figured. If you're on probation, we'll be stuck with only illegal messages and no exercising together. You shouldn't even have that other phone. It's one more thing that'll risk getting you terminated and losing your credits."

Before I can respond, my Institute phone rings at my waist. I check the caller ID and mouth "Leo" to Vonn, who grimaces.

You're messaging early, I say into the phone.

Leo answers without hesitation.

I managed to contact the Board a little sooner, despite it being a weekend, and we've come to a decision.

Here it goes.

Okay, I'm ready.

We've decided you won't receive compensation for your assignment. That's the normal penalty for a contract violation.

A contract violation. I've been found guilty. Although I suspected the verdict, the news hits me with the force of a nuclear blast.

No pay at all?

No. Your parents, however, will be compensated

their portion, since the contract was fulfilled up
to the day you turned 18.

I'm terminated, then.

My voice is fractured. Vonn rests his hand on my arm.

I'm afraid so. Someone else will take over for
Jodine's weight loss. The next step is to insert
you into a Spare. Since we only house the Spares
in one location—this branch—it'll have to be done
here in Seattle.

Oh.

Nothing more comes out than that single word.

I've booked your flight for tomorrow afternoon.
The Kowalczyks will take you to the airport. I'll talk
to you after that.

I end the messaging and stare across the street. "Looks
like I'm going to Seattle tomorrow for a new body."

Vonn is silent for a bit, then he sighs. "That really sucks.
But at least I'll get to see you sooner than April this way."

A partial smile wavers on my face. "Good point. I'm just
kicking myself, hard. In one swift, stupid move, I've lost all my
payment credits. And not even for something I expected—like
secretly dating you, using my personal phone, or talking to a
former Loaner client. Who knows what this Spare body will
be like. Its looks, its memories. What it can and can't do."

"It'll be okay. Maybe there won't be any residuals in your
new body."

"That'd be an awesome change." A more dismal thought
hits me. "Oh no! My backup file is more than a week old. I
won't remember my birthday, or dancing with you at the Night

Flight. When you kissed me. Why I got terminated—"

Vonn pulls me against him, his arm snug around my shoulders. "At least we'll remember each other, and you'll remember up to last week. I'll tell you about everything after that, I promise. And I'll definitely kiss you again, even though it'll be a bit weird if you're in a different body."

"That's for sure." I lean my head on his chest. His heart beats in my ear, loud and solid even through the thickness of his coat. "I'm also worried that if any of my memories were hiding in a corner of Jodine's brain when my brainmap was made, I'll lose them for good. I lost that memory of my mom singing me a Christmas song. The one Shelby has now."

He twines the fingers of his free hand with mine. "You'll still be you, even without a few memories. If you give me your home address, I'll come find you. No matter what you can or can't remember."

I blink against a mixed swell of gratefulness and doubt. He sounds confident I'll be the same person without all my memories. I'm not so sure. My thoughts and my past make me who I am, and I don't want to lose *any* of me. Even if my appearance changes.

"I wonder what I'll look like the next time you see me," I say, tipping back to look into his face. "At least Leo's giving me a choice about my body. I don't want to end up ancient or mangled or something."

"No kidding." He gives me a mischievous look. "Make sure the new you has long brown hair, is about five-foot-seven, slender, sexy, big eyes—"

"Not funny." I whap his arm with my other hand, and he laughs. He kisses the side of my face in an exuberant way, and I get a strange double-vision of a music room with a guy wearing a silver eyebrow ring and wavy hair to his shoulders. An interfering memory of Jodine's kiss from Gavin, I assume. Freaky.

"Seriously, Morgan," Vonn says. "I'll like you no matter what you look like."

I throw my arms around his neck and move in closer to his mouth. "Then kiss me. This is your last chance before I turn into someone else."

CHAPTER 28

Rain streams across the thick oval of my window. The private jet I boarded an hour ago cruises through the sky like a featherless metal bird. My destination: Seattle. I've never traveled this far from home before. If the situation were a little different, I'd welcome the adventure. As it is, it's difficult to enjoy the thrill of the journey when I don't know exactly what lies at my destination. The future is a muddy, gray blur.

At the other end of the seating area, Dr. and Mrs. K. read from portables, surfing online with flicks of their fingertips. They look relaxed and content.

Of course. They're not the ones getting put into a Spare body.

After tonight this mess will be over, and I'll be glad. Mom and Dad couldn't believe it when I told them my job was terminated and that I was going in early for my body change. Blair and Krista sounded shook up, too. While they're all relieved I don't have to do the weight loss, they're worried about what I'll look like. It's a big question, all right.

I just want everything to be as close as possible to the

way it used to be, how everyone used to see me. Especially Granddad. I don't know if he'll be able to handle me being in a totally different body from the one I had at Thanksgiving. He had a hard enough time with the Jodine version. My hands twist in my lap, and I fight to keep my breathing steady. He sounds disoriented and angry in his texts. If I visit him at the retirement home, will he refuse to see me? Will he know who I am?

Mom and Dad are both thankful I'll be done dealing with the Institute, even if we have to go live in The Commons. I wish we could afford to buy a ticket so Mom or Dad could be here with me. Because there's a little more at stake than simply boarding a plane. I'm flying toward a body that will be mine for the rest of my life—for better or for worse.

I clamp my arms around myself. There's a potential it could be a *lot* worse. I'll be put inside a Spare, a person who has murdered another human being or committed a crime that's equally bad. I can't even imagine how bone-chillingly scary it'll be if I end up experiencing the strong emotions and images that could go along with a crime like that.

The memories could be bloody, grisly, violent.

My throat goes dry. As I reach for my in-flight juice drink, my Institute phone rings. I groan when I see who it is. Time for the official start of this whole Spares business.

> Hey, Leo.

> Your ERT is scheduled for 1930, Morgan. That's late, but it can't be helped given the short notice. The new Reducer for Jodine will be in Seattle by then. What I need to know is which Spare body to bring out of suspended animation for you, to make sure it's ready when you arrive. I've

gone through the database and selected some possibilities.

Thanks for letting me choose.

I have to warn you, there's not a big selection. Especially if we try to match age, ethnicity, and gender. Which I think we should.

I wrinkle my nose.

Yeah. I definitely don't want to be a guy.

We don't have a lot of female Spares under 20. Images of the ones we have are on the attachment screen. I'll wait while you look.

I expand the attachment screen. I have three choices. The first holo-image springs up, rotating slowly: the head and shoulders of a harsh-looking blonde with a square jaw and thick eyebrows. Not too feminine, except her eyes are a pretty blue. If she looks this harsh, I hope it doesn't mean she's more likely to have committed a really violent crime.

Once I'm inside her body, will some of the harshness of her expression go away?

The second image: a brunette with a pointed nose and narrow eyes. It seems I only have head shots to choose from, which is really limiting. I need an athletic body that can play paintball and jog in the park. I don't want to give up those things because my new body can't do them well.

I click on the third image: a girl with short sandy hair, her features washed out. She looks less harsh or sharp than the other two. The best option, if the body checks out.

None of the choices feel like me, but I'm stuck with making a decision. I suppose I could always let the sandy girl's hair grow out and dye it darker if I want to look more like my old self. I'd probably also want to give myself a better haircut and use a touch of makeup. Funny, how different personalities inside the same bodies would likely change their appearance, to match their ideas about what looks good. I flick back to the screen where Leo awaits.

> You're right. There's not a big selection. Guess I'll take the third one, the sandy-haired girl. As long as she has an athletic body.

> Great. I'll send the order to the Transfer room.

I'd still like to minimize potential grisly residual memories if I can—or at least mentally prepare myself for them.

> What did she do to get on death row?

> Trust me. The fewer details you know about this Spare, the less anxious you'll be. She's gone, and your brainmap will make a whole new person out of her.

I try to swallow, and fail. Maybe he's right, and it doesn't matter which girl. They're *all* on death row. I'll have to pretend any residuals are fragments from a gross horror vid I've watched, or some recurring nightmare. It's not going to be easy.

> Can my name be Morgan Dey?

> Of course. Since the Spares' original chips are removed before suspended animation, they're blank slates. We'll simply transfer your data to a fresh chip and inject it. Your accounts will be reset to that chip and your new handprint. I'll brief you more when you wake up.

Great, thanks.

I pause, my heart quickening. Leo's being slippery again—he didn't confirm the girl has an athletic body.

Wait, all I've seen is a head shot. I can't sign a legally binding contract without seeing the actual entire body you're putting me into. I want to check it out in person, not just on some dinky little holo-image.

There's one of those awkward blank time-spaces.

You need to just trust me that she's suitable, since we're on a time limit here. If we don't start the reversal from suspended animation soon, there'll be a longer wait before you're inserted into your new body.

Trust Leo? He must think I have the mental capabilities of a paramecium.

I'm really sorry if the nurses and the doctor will be delayed, but I have to be sure this body can do the things I love. I want to have some sort of preparation for what I'm getting into. It's not just about what I look like.

Oh...very well. It's highly unconventional, yet this whole situation is beyond normal protocol. I'll see you when you arrive for a brief detour to the Spares room.

Thanks much, Leo.

I end the messaging before he changes his mind, and let out a long breath. At the other end of the plane, the Kowalczyks remain absorbed with their screens.

I really hope this new body will turn out okay. Even not counting possible residual memories, who knows how long it'll take before I'm comfortable inside its skin. I try to imagine myself as the girl I've chosen—attending classes, crawling into my bed every night, looking in the mirror each morning. Combing through that sand-colored hair. Eating SpeedMeals with Mom and Dad. Hanging out with Blair and Krista and Vonn.

Visiting Granddad at the retirement home.

It's hard to envision myself doing those things, looking like that. That body is someone else's, not mine. People are more than what their bodies look like, but my new appearance may change me a little, create a slightly different Morgan inside. Being in Jodine's body sure has. Hopefully the core part of me will stay intact, and I can hold onto some version of me no matter how I look.

I've chosen to accept this Spare, and I have to make the best of it.

The jet plows on through the rainstorm. I can't help grieving for my real body and my original Morgan self, curling my hand next to my face to shield my emotions from the Kowalczyks.

When the jet lands in Seattle, my face is dry and I'm composed, at least on the outside. We get out and hurry through a covered walkway to a waiting Institute car, its headlights glaring like yellow eyes in the dark, wet night. I slide into its roomy, tomb-like interior carrying my bag, and clutch it against my chest as Dr. and Mrs. K. get in beside me. I'll need my bag when I become my new self tonight. The Clinic in Los Angeles gave me a set of smaller-size sweats to pack inside it, and I sneaked my new phone in before the flight.

The car carries us down unfamiliar streets while the Kowalczyks make light conversation with the driver. I listen to the tires hiss against the soaked pavement.

We reach the enormous Seattle branch building, its bulk tucked behind gates and a stretch of Enforcer-guarded fencing. Once we're escorted inside to the lobby, a hostbot glides up.

"Welcome, Dr. and Mrs. Kowalczyk," the hostbot says. "If you will please come with me, I will lead you to a private lounge."

"Good luck, Morgan." Dr. K. steps over and shakes my hand, holding it a few seconds longer than necessary, as if he regrets seeing me go. Mrs. K., to my surprise, clutches me in a quick hug. Is she grateful for my services, or is she just relieved that I let her daughter live?

"It was great to stay with you both," I say. "I enjoyed seeing the lab and painting the apple. Please tell Nettie good-bye again from me." I doubt they're happy I got myself terminated, but their farewell glances are amiable enough.

They stroll off behind the hostbot. As they disappear around a corner, another hostbot approaches. It leads me to a waiting room similar to Leo's old one in the Los Angeles building. Leo emerges from his new office almost at once.

"Let's get moving," he says without preamble. "Time is one thing I don't have a lot of lately."

I trail after him, gripping my bag with renewed determination. If he's trying to make me feel guilty, he's failing. I need to do this. What I decide now will affect the rest of my life.

He strides down the hall and leads me through the Transfer area, passing the beds and three nurses there and heading for a rear door marked "Suspended Animation." He signs in with his ID chip and handprint and ushers me into a dim room.

All human sounds cut off as the door closes. Cool air clings to my skin like clammy hands. A whirring, sucking noise of machinery fills the room, which smells odd, a sort of musty grease scent mingled with antiseptic.

Glow sticks hang by the door. Leo grabs one, activates it with a crack, and aims it down an aisle. Rows and rows of coffin-shaped capsules occupy the room, stacked three high like drawers in a macabre-style dresser. They make up a maze of walls a little taller than my head. I glimpse bodies inside the capsules, visible through the clear sides. E-tags with names and dates of initial storage mark each capsule, glowing with a bright crimson readout.

"These are Reducers," Leo says. "The Spares are in the back room."

I follow him down a long aisle, shuddering at the stacked bodies around me. These Reducer bodies have no complex brain activity. They're kept alive only by suspended animation fluids and machines. Back at the Los Angeles branch, my real body must've been in a room like this before it died. Lying so still, looking empty, sightless.

Soulless.

The thought makes my stomach churn. Why did I ever think switching bodies and belonging to the Reducer program were such fantastic things?

We pass shadowy bodies displayed lengthwise from head to toe. Male and female, African-American and Caucasian. Hispanic. Asian. Short, tall, pale, and tanned. They lie on their backs, fit and toned, wearing white hospital gowns.

My bag bumps against my thigh as I try to keep up. Leo directs me to an unmarked rear door that verifies his ID and demands an additional password, and we enter a room that resembles the first. Cold. Dimly lit. Lined with row upon row of tiered capsules.

Except in this section, there are no names. Just dates and simple numbers.

After a minute, Leo halts to consult his phone. "We're looking for F12."

I point. "There's a big E on that side wall. F12 might be in the next row."

He starts off in that direction, the illumination from his glow stick accompanying him. My gaze lingers on the murky forms beside me, my eyes adjusting to the shadows. There are a lot of these people, these inmates formerly on death row. I thought Dr. K. said the Institute had a *small* number of extra bodies available in case of Loaner deaths.

I halt. There, in a center drawer, lies a strangely familiar body. Male, middle-aged, and balding. Greenish stasis gel encloses him. His date reads the first of October.

I can't see all the details of his face, but what I do see makes my heart lurch.

It's the protester with the fringe of stringy gray hair.

CHAPTER 29

The world stops spinning, and my lungs lock up.

This is the WHA protester who stood at the gates when I finished my Shelby assignment, the one who held the sign about "goverment" control. He's the same guy who was there when I arrived at the Institute to become Jodine. What's he doing here, stripped of his brain activity? The first of October was the day following his arrest. He was put on death row and turned into a Spare *one day* after the attack?

My gaze drops to the body stored below the balding man. Wavy-haired, female. Also familiar. She's the stout woman who warned me not to come back to the Institute. Next to her capsule lies the bearded man who poked me and then hit me with his sign. Both of them have the same initial date.

Major freaking *haze*.

"I've located your Spare," Leo calls, his tone impatient.

I flinch and look down the aisle to see him leaning around the corner. When I bounce a glance at the capsules and can't get my feet to move, his irritation morphs into something else. His mouth evens out into a careful line. The muscles on his face tighten as though reinforcing themselves.

"What's your concern?" He strides toward me with slow steps, his dark suit eerie and side-lit from the glow stick in his hand.

"I was just looking at these Spares." My voice comes out soft. The thump of my heartbeat sounds louder than my words.

"What about them?"

Oh, man—what am I doing? I can't confront him about these people if what I think is true. Time to change gears, and fast. "They're zombie-creepy looking. Gives me shivers, knowing they're all from death row."

He makes an abrupt noise. "Come on. Your Transfer is already scheduled to occur past normal procedure hours, and we need to keep moving." Gripping his glow stick, he stalks back down the aisle.

I scurry to catch up, trying to compose my face to reflect something besides alarm and suspicion. I'm not sure what's going on. None of this makes legitimate sense, but I'd sure as heck better drop the subject and ponder it all in more detail later.

Around the corner, Leo pushes a button on a tiered wall. A middle capsule slides out like a morgue drawer.

"Here's your Spare," he says as I step up. "She's nineteen, a year older than you. It'll have to be close enough."

I stare at the girl, who wears the standard white hospital gown. Green-tinted gel encases her entire body, her head included. A transparent cup covers her mouth and nose, while an IV protrudes from her forearm, and monitoring sensors dot her body. She seems to have an average shape. Fairly toned-looking. Ordinary arms and legs. No extra fingers or toes. Quite normal, except the face looks more stark and bleached than the attachment image I saw.

"She looks dead," I say, taking a step backward.

"That's because the suspended animation solution is in her bloodstream. All her systems are suppressed, halted mid-breath. Are you satisfied enough so we can get the contract signed?"

"This body will be fine." I watch him tap on his phone, likely accessing the database to authorize the suspended animation reversal. "She's really young to be on death row."

He gives me a not-very-patient look. "Crime has no age limit."

"Sure, okay." At this point, I just want to be inserted into her body and go back home. To live my life and never, ever be a part of the Institute or ERT again.

"We're done here." He spins and marches away.

I scuttle after him. We re-enter the room where the Reducer bodies lie and navigate the ghoulish maze of beds without speaking. The thuds of our footsteps merge with the droning whir-suck-whir sounds of the room. I note the stiff set of Leo's neck and shoulders. It's hard to tell if he's annoyed or just in a big hurry.

When we reach his new office, he brings up a lengthy display on his screen.

"Here's the contract releasing you from Jodine's body. On the next page is an acquisitions contract for you to be inserted into the Spare. Since you're eighteen now, we don't have to worry about obtaining parental signatures."

"It's strange my signature is valid when I'm using Jodine's ID."

Leo jabs a finger at the security cameras near the ceiling. "In the director's office, we use audio along with visual vidfeed. It's documented your brainmap is in Jodine's body at this date and time. It's not the best scenario, but it's what we have to work with. Thankfully, it's a unique circumstance that won't be repeated."

I take care of the bio-signatures, and my fate is sealed.

"I'd also like your phone, please."

I retrieve the Institute phone from my bag, and he takes it without changing his businesslike expression.

I'm not about to tell him I have another one with me. I don't trust him or anyone working here anymore. In fact, what if he or someone else snoops around on my phone after I go out of consciousness? They'll see I know Vonn as more than a casual acquaintance, and more seriously, that I've been using a non-issued phone.

"I'll book your flight home as soon as the system generates a chip and coordinates your ID with it," Leo says. "There's plenty of room on Pac-West's oh-three-fifteen red-eye flight."

I nod. It figures. A public jet this time. The Kowalczyks won't be traveling with me.

He ushers me from his office, his smile a phantom of its usual intensity. He gestures to an arriving hostbot. "Follow this bot to the cafeteria. Eat dinner and then return here to be summoned for your Transfer."

I let the noiseless hostbot guide me to the cafeteria, where I place a distracted order with a servbot. While I wait for my food, I duck into a restroom to avoid security cameras, and call Vonn on screen mode since it's my own phone. I need to see his face. To my relief, he answers on the first ring.

"I'm set for removal at nineteen thirty," I say when he comes into view. "My insertion will happen later than that, since my Spare didn't get authorized to revive until a little while ago. My flight back is with Pac-West at oh-three-fifteen. I'll text you sometime after that. Listen, this is important. I'm going to delete your contact info and emails before the Transfer."

He frowns. "Are you okay?"

"I don't trust anyone here. I'm afraid someone will check my phone while I'm not conscious."

"Not sure why they'd mess with your phone, but I'll humor you. Anything else?"

"Lay low. Don't message or call until you hear from me."

"It sounds like there's more to this than you're telling me."

I glance toward the restroom autodoor and lower my voice. "I found out at least three of the Spares are WHA protesters who attacked me at the Institute. All the Spares are supposed to be on death row, but I don't think they are. I can't wait to do my Transfer and get out of here."

Vonn's eyebrows bunch together, hard. "I can't believe the Institute would do something like that with the Spares. That's really serious, Morgan."

A clunk outside the restroom makes me jump. "Gotta go. I'll miss you, Vonn."

"And I'll miss you. Long-distance hugs."

With a heavy heart, I end the call and delete his info. I chew on a fingernail. Have I done enough? I've heard it's possible to retrieve data from devices, even after something is deleted. It's not worth taking the risk.

I toss my phone in the restroom incinerator. I'll buy another one later.

When I've finished poking at my meal in the cafeteria, I return to Leo's waiting room. My mind replays the frightening image of the balding man, a shell of a human being lying in cold green goo. The guy didn't deserve death. Neither did the stout woman or the bearded man. A wave of guilt hits me.

What *did* they deserve? Last month, I wished for them to rot forever in jail cubicles.

An hour drags by before the silvery bell of a hostbot arrives.

"This way if you please, Miss Dey," it says, and rolls away.

It's about time. I pursue the bot down the hall, where it deposits me at the Transfer room doors. "Changing into a gown is not necessary," it says. "Proceed to your Transfer. Have a pleasant evening."

The scanner at the door verifies my ID, and I step inside. Of course I don't have to change into a gown. The new Reducer will continue Jodine's assignment in these delightful green sweats.

In the room, I'm surprised to find Irene, the nurse who worked at the Los Angeles branch. A thin man in a white doctor's jacket is the room's only other occupant. He stands across the room, flicking his fingers across a distant wallscreen, and then he walks through an autodoor into a side room. Dr. Gaunt-as-Death is here, too.

Irene checks a chart reader. "Morgan Dey, in the body of Jodine Kowalczyk?"

"Yes." I walk over and let her scan my hand. She's soft, smiling, and kind. I'll take all the calming vibes I can get right now.

"You're becoming quite the regular. You may place your bag on the shelf underneath and get settled." She pats a bed draped with white sheets. The curtains aren't pulled around us for privacy, probably because it's late and we're the only ones in here.

I stretch out. The ceiling lights glare into my eyes. "Did you get transferred here?" I ask to divert my skittering nerves.

Irene gives a gentle smile as she inserts an IV into my

forearm. "A core group of us got placed with Mr. Behr. The rest are assigned to other branches until the Los Angeles branch is rebuilt and operational again."

My fingers twist the sheet edge into a wad. I want this to be over with. Soon. "Do you know how long I'll be conked out before I'm placed into my new body?"

"I'll take a look." Faint screen tappings come from her direction.

I hear a sharp intake of breath. I lift my head and see her staring at the screen. "What, do I have to wait until tomorrow or something?"

"This can't be right," Irene murmurs. She sidles closer, her face pale, her dark eyelashes a jarring contrast against her skin. "Don't react. We're on visual camera. It seems your Spare's awakening from suspended animation has been canceled. The order was ready for authorization, until it was revoked by Mr. Behr ninety minutes ago."

Ninety minutes ago? When I was in the Spares room?

I gape at Irene and her chart reader.

"What?" I say, the word a dry croak. "If there isn't a Spare ready for me, what body will my backup file get downloaded into?"

She checks her reader again. "Oh, my word. Right now, you aren't assigned to a body at all. Your current brainmap will be discarded to comply with our usual privacy policy. And...it seems your backup file is also scheduled to be deleted. I—I'm not sure why."

The bottom drops out of my entire world, slashed into black nothingness.

My backup brainmap file is going to be *deleted*.

What has Leo done?

CHAPTER 30

I try to keep breathing so I don't pass out. If Leo has deleted my backup file, not only do I not have a body, I won't have a mind to put anywhere. Not after they delete my current brainmap for Jodine's privacy.

Surely this doesn't have anything to do with the protesters I saw…or maybe it does, and he's wiping me out to protect his ugly Institute secret. I don't know if it's smart to trust Irene, but at this point I have nothing to lose.

"I think I know why," I whisper, my words wavering. "Leo took me into the Spares room, and I saw three people who weren't really murderers. They were just WHA protesters."

Irene places a tense hand on my shoulder. "Oh, no. How horrible. But it explains all the Transfers into Spares that we've been doing during the two weeks I've been here. In and out of bodies like you can't believe. The system has also been generating entirely new data for their ID chips. Alternate identities, which is illegal."

"Help me—remove this IV," I say. "I have to get out of here."

"You can't just leave." Her gaze flicks around the room and rests on the door the doctor disappeared through. "This body belongs to the Kowalczyks' daughter. You'll be too easy to track when public readers scan your chip."

I shift into a shaky sitting position. "Then maybe you can undo the backup file deletion and the suspended animation reversal."

"No. Mr. Behr would be alerted if his orders are changed. Or even if the backup file is copied before it's deleted, since that's part of his order. But we could set the system to copy your *current* brainmap before it prepares a reverse-signal and discards the file."

"Will you do that for me?"

"If things like this are going on, it's much safer for me and my family not to be involved." Irene speaks in a low rush. "I can 'accidentally' leave my reader here for you, set to the Spares acquisition screen. After you order a copy of your brainmap, select a body and press Pre-Authorize. That generates a matching profile and ID chip, and gets your file ready to Transfer to the body when it awakens. If anyone reviews the vidfeeds later, they'll see it was you and not me who made the requests."

"So I'll wake up in the Spares room."

"Yes. The capsule will auto-open and drain. Try to slip out an exit. After twenty-one hundred, only the night crew and a few security guards are in the building."

"Won't they know which body is missing by looking in the database?"

Irene shakes her head, a slight movement. "As I said, using Spares with new IDs is illegal. The images and data for each Spare vanish from the master file immediately after an ID is generated and paired with a body. That way they're not traceable during audits."

A clunk comes from the doctor's room, sending fresh alarm through me. "I need to know how to get the ID chip."

"My extra coat is brown with a black furred hood, kept in the corner closet behind me. I'll put a syringe in the pocket, encased so scanners can't read the chip. Do you know how to use a syringe?"

"Yes." Thanks to one Catalyst Club experiment Blair and I did.

Irene gives a pinched smile. "Good luck. Before I start your drip, let me go ask the doctor your question." She says the last part louder.

The hard, flat surface of her reader bumps into my thigh. I look down at the screen as she walks away. My hands slick with sweat, I select the order for my current brainmapping and hit Copy Brainmap File. A confirmation flashes. Links for two groups of Spare bodies appear, male and female. Tap. I choose female. The link expands into a list.

> FEMALES: A1 female = age 43. A2 female = age 31.
> A3 female = age 36...

Where the haze are the younger Spares?

I hear Irene ask the doctor my supposed question, the words garbled.

Hurry.

My fingers tremble. I scan the list for younger bodies. Twenty-nine years old. Twenty-five. Double haze. I'm not going to make it. I need a body, no matter how old it is or what it looks like—I don't have time to click the links for more info. In my peripheral vision, I see the doctor enter the room with Irene and walk toward me. I select, fast.

G9 female = age 25. *Tap*.

CONFIRM? *Tap*.

PRE-AUTHORIZE? *Tap*.

END SETUP? *Tap*.

The gaunt figure of Dr. Death steps up. "The answer to your question is yes, Miss Dey," he says. "You'll remember everything until your backup a week ago, because we have no original brainmap file for you. That file got destroyed in the bombing. This goes against every privacy measure we've set up, so you must be extremely discreet about personal and household details you've learned about the Kowalczyks. We'll know it was you if there's a breach."

"I'll be careful." I scan his face, trying to decipher his aloof expression. Does he know Leo ordered my backup file deleted? Is he working with him to try to murder me? I swing my quivering legs up and recline as Irene deftly collects the reader from the bed.

"The system is set for Transfer and ready for authorization, Doctor," Irene says, with a single finger flick to her reader. I hold my breath as the doctor takes the device.

He pokes at the screen and adds his handprint. "Good. Let's proceed before it gets any later than it already is."

I'm on the verge of thankful weeping. I'm pretty sure he just unknowingly authorized a Transfer into my new Spare instead of the first one. He must not be in on Leo's murder plans, or he would've paid more attention. Dr. Death sets the reader aside and adheres sensors to my arms, abdomen, and ribs. I clench my teeth to keep my chin and jaw from shaking.

"Breathe deeply and relax," Irene says, stroking my arm. "I've started your drip. Count backward from one hundred. When you wake up, you'll be in your new body."

A zillion questions plow through my mind. I breathe as best as I can and stare up at the ceiling, powerless to move, fighting a desire to leap up and race down the halls. There are too many ways this plan could go wrong.

I swallow, hard. Ninety minutes ago, Leo Behr arranged for my deletion.

If this counter-plan doesn't work, he'll get his wish.

I will cease to exist.

My body grows weighty, lethargic. Thoughts slow and bumble around in my brain. I fold in on myself, compressing and folding again, until I feel as dense as a Black Hole. Then I dwindle into nothing, tight and dark inside a nameless chasm. The core part of my Self slips away without so much as a trembling whisper of a sound.

CHAPTER 31

Coldness hits me. Machinery hums and sucks and drones, while the smell of grease fills my head. I open stiff eyelids and see a shadowy world of walls and bodies.

The Spares room. I've made it.

I'm alive.

I blink in the semi-darkness. A hard plastic cup wobbles over my nose and mouth, its seal broken. I shake my head. The cup tumbles from my face and clatters to a stop beside my shoulder. I take in a grateful breath. Luckily, there's no gel surrounding my head. I seem to be in a lower drawer that has opened into the aisle.

My body tingles as nerve endings swarm into life.

I wiggle my new fingers and toes, then shift my arms and legs. When I awoke last time from suspended animation, it took twenty minutes and a hot shower before I felt normal. No chance to do that now. I need to collect my ID chip and get out of this building, fast.

With a grunt, I pull myself onto my side. The skin of my hand and arm is darker than normal, apparent even in the dimness of the room. Whoa—I've inserted my brainmap into a non-Caucasian body. And lost seven years of my life at the same time.

Can I *be* any more different?

"Focus," I tell myself. Nothing matters except getting out of here. I swing my legs over the edge of the capsule and leave a puddle of oily gel behind. The air stinks of musty antiseptic, but the residue on my skin has evaporated. I pluck off sensors. When I try to stand, the tug of an IV in my arm halts me. Since its flow has stopped, I pull it out and press my thumb against some oozing blood. As I stagger to my feet, a whoosh of an opening door echoes through the room. I freeze in place.

"This is Institute security," a female calls. "The system reported motion and a heat anomaly in this room. Come toward the door with your hands up, and I won't use my stun gun on you."

Oh, no. Adrenaline jolts through me. I hobble down the aisle and crouch by a wall of capsules. Thankfully, even though this body is stiff, it moves faster and with more energy than Jodine's ever did.

"Who's there?" Boots rap along distant aisles. "How'd you get in here? Show yourself."

I stay hidden. As far as I know, there's only one door, and I awakened somewhere near the middle of the room. Even in this ridiculous maze of bodies, it'll be difficult to sneak past this woman and out the exit.

"Lights on," the guard commands the room.

Nothing happens. I nearly faint with relief, and the Enforcer curses.

I skid around a couple of corners and sidle next to a wall. More footsteps. They rap down an aisle and halt.

When the footsteps resume, I dart out and flee down a

long stretch. The Enforcer speeds up and closes in. I flatten
myself against the end of a row. I don't know whether I should
go left or right as footsteps approach. I squeeze my eyes closed
and cover my mouth with the shoulder of my gown to quiet
my breath.

The guard stops one aisle away. The beam from her glow
stick casts a faint yet heart-stopping sphere of light nearby.
Her stun gun clicks on. Her boots tap a step or two.

Long seconds pass, and she swears again. Clicks and
shuffling penetrate the air, followed by a beep.

"I need backup," she says. "Someone's here in the Spares
room, and one of the bodies is missing. Get over here and
secure the door. And have someone see if there's an override
for the special lighting."

Oh, no. I'll never be able to evade two of them, especially
if the lights come on. I'll have to make a run for it.

The guard moves away from me, heading down an adjacent
aisle.

Creeping fast, I go the other way. I feel like I'm in a night-
vision paintball game, but the stakes are way higher than a few
bruises and a virtual splat of blood.

I inch forward and peer down another aisle.

All clear.

I leap out and run as fast as I can, forcing my sluggish
muscles to move. The guard shouts for me to halt. I hear the
electric charge of her gun sizzle somewhere behind me. I yelp
as I round the last corner.

"Open!" I yell at the door, and dive through before it
retracts all the way. I stagger into the Reducer storage room,
regain my footing, and keep going. At the other end, I order
the outer door open from thirty feet away, and almost leave a

toe behind as it closes behind me.

The Transfer room is vacant, shadowy and dark except for low security lights. I dart toward the closet. Someone bursts into the room—likely the second guard.

"Lights on," he shouts as I roll behind a storage cart. The room flares into brightness. I hold my breath while boots pound across the floor. He accesses the suspended animation entrance, and the door whisks open and closed. The room goes quiet.

"Lights *off*," I say. The room goes dark again. I grab Irene's long coat, shrug into it, and flip the hood up. I shove my feet into shoes and snatch blue pants from a shelf. I tear across the room.

Panting, I fly through the door into brighter halls. Behind me, the guards burst back into the Transfer room. As I race, I scan for an exit. Shouts echo at my heels. I don't dare look over my shoulder to see how close they are.

I careen down one hall and then another, and finally see an exit. I bounce off a wall without slowing, my shoulder hitting hard as I make my turn.

"Open!"

The door slides to one side. A loud deluge of rain and wind hits me. Staying far from the building's lights and exterior cameras, I use benches and bushes for cover, eyeing an Enforcer patrolling the building, walking away from me. His light bobs through the downpour. He doesn't seem to have gotten an intruder alert. Good. That means the grounds haven't gone into lockdown yet.

I wriggle into the blue pants behind a bench. My escape route has to be through the entrance gates, since the outer fence is electric. Can I pretend to be a nurse and simply stroll out? For that to work, the gate Enforcers will have to be only checking IDs for incoming people, not outgoing. Risky. And my only choice.

Leaping onto the sidewalk, I shove my hands into my coat pockets. I stride toward the gates with my head down against the rain. Under the furry edge of my hood, I see the Enforcers look up.

"Sloppy wet tonight, isn't it?" I call out. "I'm finally done, pulled a super late shift. Hate to see you four out in this."

The tallest Enforcer chuckles. "Yeah, rotten luck. Last night it wasn't as bad."

"No kidding." I give a bubbly laugh that sounds fake to my ears.

"We got three hours to go, ma'am," says another Enforcer. "You're the lucky one, going home."

"Don't I know it," I say, trying to keep the words from wobbling. "Stay awake!"

They murmur good-natured responses. Then I'm past them and hurrying down the sidewalk into the unknown depths of the city. My heart pounds in my ears. A sharp ache in my lungs makes my breathing shallow. Safe for the moment, but not totally safe.

I hunt for an MT shelter. I need to reach the airport and get away from Seattle. The Institute and Enforcers will expect me to go home to Mom and Dad, which means I'll have to fly to another region and stay there for a while. If I have enough credits in my newly generated account, that is.

At the bottom of one of my coat pockets, my fingers bump a hard cylindrical shape. Good—it's the syringe. Irene is a lifesaver.

By the time I locate an MT shelter, the rain has soaked my pants. That's okay. It makes them look darker. The display time reads 0252, already early morning. According to the readout, I have to board the next MT, ride five minutes south, and transfer to an airport-bound MT. I need enough time to do that before I'm traced.

I duck my hooded head as the train pulls up. Trying to act normal, I board. At some point the MT camera feed will be scrutinized, ideally not soon. I don't have an ID chip for the sensors to scan for the fare, but chips get blocked by metals and other things all the time. A missing fare alert won't automatically cue them it's me.

I get off at the second shelter, wait a few shivering minutes, and board the Express to the airport. The ride is tense, unreal.

"Now arriving at Pac-West Public Airport, Seattle," an e-voice intones.

Keeping my hood up, I merge with a group of adults carrying suitcases. I slip into the airport terminal past a frizzy-haired Enforcer who speaks into his comm-device.

"I got the image," he's saying. "Can't make out the face with the hood up. Female, you say? I'm looking at people getting off that MT right now."

What should I do? I try to curb my panic. If Enforcers are already searching for me here, I won't have a chance to buy other clothes to disguise myself. I can slip into a restroom, like the one thirty feet away, but I can't hide there for long.

The people providing me cover veer straight for a female Enforcer. I swerve and break off from them. I need another cover. *Quick.*

I scan other travelers and take a step toward an elderly couple with a bored teen. I'm not sure which way they're going. There's also that nice-looking heavy guy wearing a poncho—

Wait.

The nice-looking heavy guy wearing a poncho?

CHAPTER 32

I can't believe my eyes. It's Vonn. Of course! I told him about the red-eye flight, and he must've flown up to Seattle to meet me, even though I told him to stay in Los Angeles. He has no idea how serious this is. I can't put him in further danger.

He walks over to an information kiosk, and I force myself not to look up at the security camera pointed in his direction. *Careful.* We can't be seen interacting, even if I'm not caught talking with him right this minute, because our connection will be spotted later once the Enforcers review the security feeds. My throat goes dry. I step up to the brochure screen next to him, where he's scanning a city map display.

"Superguy. It's me, Geekling—but don't look over," I whisper-hiss, keeping my head down and my face covered by the furred hood. "Pretend you don't know who I am. Enforcers are looking for me, and I need to get out of this airport."

I sense him steel himself beside me. Trying not to look. Trying to process what I've just said. He sucks in a breath. "If you want to catch that oh-three-fifteen flight, you missed it."

"I don't think I can fly out now. Enforcers will be checking the boarding areas." I talk fast while my fingers make fidgety circles on the brochure screen. "I'm going to find some clothes and change in a restroom, even if I have to swipe someone's luggage to do it. I need you to leave the airport and follow the MT tracks left four blocks. Turn right, go down four more blocks. Wherever that ends up, I'll meet you there…just stop if you run into a dead end."

Vonn starts to protest, but then clamps his mouth shut and walks off.

I'm on my own again. I need alternate clothing, yet everyone I see is clutching his or her luggage, and it'd be a gamble as to what's inside the bags. Swiping one could also risk attracting an Enforcer's attention. If I buy clothes— whether from a vendorbot or a full-service store—my ID will be revealed and matched to my face when the vidfeeds are eventually reviewed.

What am I going to do?

A flare like pure instinct or adrenaline shoots through me. I slip into the nearest clothing store. In one second, I note where the security cameras are located. Blind spots assessed. In the next second, I'm angling down an aisle. Both the self-pay machine and the solo human cashier are serving other customers, so I snap the tag off a lightweight jacket and tuck it beneath Irene's coat. Next comes a pair of pants, also wedged under my arm. Then a baseball cap.

It seems my new body knows how to do this really well.

Footwear next. This store doesn't have sneakers, only flimsy slip-on flats. That'll have to do. I add a pair to my stash and head out. No one shouts behind me. I find a restroom, dash inside, and lock myself into a stall. It's a good thing security cameras aren't allowed in restrooms.

With cold and shaky fingers, I hang my stolen items on the door hook and peel off my wet coat. I remove the syringe from the pocket and ready it. Wincing against the prick of the needle, I inject the almost-invisible chip into the back of my hand.

There. I'm officially a new person, specific ID unknown.

I strip off my soaked shoes and pants, and roll them inside the coat along with the syringe. Shoes rap across the restroom floor as women come and go. The cold seeps up from the tiles and into the soles of my bare feet while I remove my hospital-like gown. I'm zipping up my jacket when a trio of young women comes in, chattering about the latest vids and fur-lined jackets. I put on the stolen shoes, and wait to leave my stall until they're in stalls of their own.

I emerge. No one else is at the sink area. On one wall, there's an incinerator installed, which is perfect. Time to dump my wad of incriminating stuff and get out of here. With frenzied fingers, I feed my entire coat roll and the gown into its metal throat. The machine hums, accepts my offering with zero fanfare, and turns it all into cinders.

Morgan Dey is officially dead, in more ways than one.

My knees buckle at the thought, but I grip the sink and hold on. The mirrors above the sinks catch my reflection—a shockingly unfamiliar one. A round face with a nubby nose. Medium-brown skin. Big eyes with irises so deep brown they blend with the pupils. The face is more plain and unremarkable than pretty.

That's totally okay. I love this body. I want it, no matter what it looks like. If all goes well, I'll get to keep it for the rest of my life.

I stuff my hair into the cap, adjust the cap low on my

head, and exit. My slip-on shoes are too long, which makes me stumble a little. My pulse pounds like a trapped animal's. I need to be extra careful. The vidfeeds could record part of my face if I tilt my head wrong.

I thread through the crowd toward the main terminal doors, passing two Enforcers studying the throng.

Casual. Act casual, I tell myself.

One of them marches toward me on my left, his eyes sharp. From under the bill of my cap, I see him look straight at me.

Swaying my hips, keeping my head tilted down, I wiggle my fingers in a coy greeting. A flicker of amusement touches his face before he passes me. In the next handful of seconds, I walk past another cluster of Enforcers, and I'm through the doors.

Outside, the rainstorm drenches me as I walk left into the darkness on a street paralleling the MT tracks. My teeth clatter against themselves after less than two blocks. My fingers and ankles and toes turn icy. I'm glad for the dark and the pouring rain, though. It'll make the public security cameras mounted on building corners less effective to identify me, maybe even worthless.

A few solitary figures pass me, intent on pre-dawn errands. I turn right.

"Four blocks to go," I mutter. I need to hang on just a little longer.

By the time I make out the dim figure of Vonn in his poncho, the cold has settled into my bones. Vonn leans against the wall of an office building, sheltered under a pillared entrance overhang. I dash over and throw myself against him. The sting of tears pricks my eyes, and a sob burbles out before I can stop it. He pulls me closer and kisses my cheekbone, my nose, my mouth.

"Shhh, you're safe now," he whispers into my lips.

I blink in quick succession at the tenderness of his voice. A strong shiver convulses me.

He rubs my arms. "You couldn't find something warmer?"

"I'm fine. Did you tell anyone you were coming to meet me at the airport?"

"No. Not even my mom. I was too worried about you and what was going on in the Spares room, plus scrambling to get a flight up here. As much as I'd like to know what all this is about, I bet you need to get somewhere dry and warm first."

I give a jerky nod. Vonn shields me from the wind and pulls out his phone. I close my eyes and lean into him, feeling a profound fatigue begin to replace my adrenaline. It's a relief to let him take over for a bit.

After a minute or two, he lets out a satisfied murmur and shows me a street map on his screen. "There are a couple of fairly cheap hotels seven blocks from here. I've checked into this bigger one, room 276."

"I'll meet you there. You go this way." I point at the map. "I'll circle around the other way so we're not seen on vidfeeds walking down sidewalks together. If I have enough credits I'll get a separate room, since I'll need to stay in Seattle longer than you. That way I'm not suddenly booking a room right as you leave."

"That's extremely careful." He gives me a troubled look before planting a warm kiss on my forehead. "See you in a bit. Be safe."

The billowing shape of his poncho disappears into the downpour. With my thumb, I massage the sore spot on my opposite hand where I inserted the chip. I'll stay here about ten minutes to be sure my check-in time won't coincide with Vonn's. I also need to know if my ID is going to work. I'd feel a lot better trying it out for the first time in a public area, rather than in an enclosed place where autodoors can lock and trap me inside if an alarm goes off. Maybe I can test the chip before I reach the hotel.

After a few more minutes, I plunge back into the rainstorm, keeping an eye peeled for a place to buy something.

Three streets down, I find a sheltered set of vending machines selling trail mix, sweatpants, and hooded souvenir sweatshirts. I select one of each, press "purchase," and let the scanner read my chip. I press my hand onto the bio-ID pad and brace myself to run. I flinch as the machine gives a scraping click.

A second later, the machine screen informs me: *Purchase verified. Thank you, Ana Maria Ramos. Balance: 1770 credits.*

Three objects land in the bottom tray with two *thumps* and a *thunk*.

Giving a throaty giggle, I slip the packages into a courtesy recyclable bag and trot down the street. It worked! How lucky the Institute's auto-system starts out new Spares with eighteen hundred credits. Or at least that's the total it generated for my body. It's not a huge amount, but if I'm careful, what's left will pay for a room, food, and even travel expenses at some point. And how interesting my name is Ana Ramos. The computer files must've registered my Spare's ethnicity in order to match my chip correctly. I sure hope no one expects me to be fluent in Spanish.

I keep walking. A few blocks later, two hotels come into view, the smaller one rising up like a cheesy-looking fortress. It's decorated with a flashing neon sign and a teddy bear hologram opening and closing its eyes. I'll go for that one. I step into the quiet building and try to ignore the fact that I have security cameras pointed at me. After checking in with the concierge-bot to pay for my lodging, I dart across the street to the bigger hotel and take an elevator pod to room 276.

Vonn answers when I tap on the door, and I slip inside. He's already removed his soaked poncho, socks, and shoes.

"I had enough credits to get a room in the other hotel," I say. "I'll pay you back for this room when I can."

"Don't worry about that." Vonn looks at me, from my soaked hair to my drenched slip-on flats. "Go thaw out in the bathroom, quick, before your chattering teeth make you bite your tongue."

Great idea. I scuttle off to take a steaming hot shower. When I'm done, the bathroom smells like raspberry shampoo, and my skin tingles, warm and dry at last. My new hair hangs in a thick black mane near my shoulders. I study myself in the mirror. What did this girl do to deserve a brain wipe? Was she a murderer, or just someone who opposed the Institute—or the government? She obviously was experienced at shoplifting, but that alone shouldn't have caused her to get turned into a Spare.

Shoplifting. I was the one stealing clothing today. I can't believe I did that.

I pull on my vending machine clothes. When I emerge from the bathroom, Vonn twists in his chair to face me. I flop into the other chair. "I feel *so* much better now," I say. Nowhere near normal, but better.

"What's up with all the secret agent clothing switcheroos, Morgan? I'm curious why all the Enforcers in Seattle are after you." One corner of Vonn's mouth quirks up. "Did you rob the

Institute or something?"

"Sorta. I stole this body."

His half smile fades. "That's not the one they assigned you?"

"No." I take a deep breath and give him a rundown of my frightening Spares discovery, and how Leo canceled my reversal and slated my backup file for deletion. "I woke up in the Spares room and barely escaped."

Vonn looks pained. "Leo authorized your file deletion on purpose?"

I nod and let the ugliness of that fact settle in. Leo worked hard to make something of himself, to reach his goals, but he sacrificed things like morals and integrity to get there. I clamp my arms around myself, fingers pressing against the bones underneath.

Leo tried to kill me tonight.

It's unreal. It's like I've been tossed into some warped action-adventure vid. When I first joined the program, Leo seemed supportive and sincere and caring. Somewhere along the line, he changed his mind about me—like I changed my mind about him. I was duped last spring, brainwashed into believing he had my best interests in mind. He didn't. His main concern was The Body Institute, period.

Back then I thought the Reducer and Loaner program was an awesome system to help people lose weight. But there are too many glitches with the brainmapping, and too many ways the ERT procedure can be twisted into something evil.

Spares, illegal ID chips, even murder.

"Your backup was more than a week old," Vonn says. "Leo didn't have to delete you. You wouldn't have remembered any of what you learned about the Spares."

I frown. "I hadn't thought of that. Talk about overly vindictive."

Vonn makes a gruff noise. "And now you probably can't go back to the Yellow Zone or live with your parents. Do the Enforcers know what you look like?"

"I don't think so. At first I had my coat hood up everywhere except the Spares and Transfer rooms, where it was pretty dark. Then I wore a baseball cap, and now I have this hooded sweatshirt. I think all they know is I'm an average-height female. I'm going to lay low in Seattle a couple of weeks, since they probably expect me to run far away from here, and soon."

"Won't they know which body is yours when they check the Spares database?"

"The nurse said any data and images about the body are wiped after the new ID is generated, since it's illegal."

"Then I'd better not blow your cover. I'll go to the Space Needle today, since I've always wanted to see it. I'll stick around town for a day or two to make it look like a legit vacation."

"Delete everything about me on your phone, too," I say. "I'm going to leave in a few minutes. I'll take a side exit to the stairs where there's only one camera instead of two or three like in the lobby."

"I hate to let you do this alone. This is a really scary situation."

Yeah. I wish he didn't have to leave Seattle. The next two weeks will be stark and empty without him. And like he said… scary.

"I won't be able to see you until I get to the Blue Zone," I say. "That's a safer place for me to stay than the Yellow Zone, where everyone else I know lives."

Vonn breaks into a full smile. "Great. We can get jobs and pretend to meet each other at a café. Start up a hot whirlwind romance."

I smile back. The tension in my shoulders eases a little. "Absolutely."

He scans me, head to toe. "You know, I love your new looks, but it'll take me a while to get used to the difference. One day I'm hanging with a girl who looks like Jodine and I'm calling you Morgan. The next day I'm hanging with a girl who... What's your new name, anyway?"

"Ana Maria Ramos. You won't be able to call me Morgan anymore."

"That'll take a while to get used to."

For me, too. I get up and sit on Vonn's knee, curling against him. He's warm. He's here with me. That's all I want right now. "Thanks for flying up to Seattle to make sure I was okay."

"I had to do it, Ana," Vonn murmurs, and tips my chin up so he can kiss me.

CHAPTER 33

I blow out a determined breath into the January air. The handles of the grocery bag I'm carrying bite into my fingers, and I shift the bag to my other hand. Vonn and I are having chef salads tonight. He's done stacking crates of apples and cauliflower at his new produce job, and we have just enough time to throw together a dinner at his apartment before I take off for my restaurant hostess job.

Ugh. I hate my job, but there wasn't much available when I arrived in the Blue Zone last week. I'm still living in a nearby hotel instead of an apartment, until I get one more paycheck. Welcome to the real world. No more basic-level schooling for me. My records say I'm twenty-five and have already earned an education certificate.

Once I'm inside Vonn's megacomplex and on the tenth floor, I press my hand to the ID pad by his apartment door. It slides open, since he programmed the pad to recognize me.

"The salad lady has arrived," I call. "Get your veggie-chopping hands ready."

He pops out from a back room and smothers me in a hug.

I stand on my toes to kiss him. "Hi, new boyfriend."

"Greetings, old girlfriend."

"Funny." He doesn't miss a chance to remind me that I'm now a few years older than he is—at least according to our ID chips.

He grabs the grocery bag, and we start chopping. "Mom invited us for dinner Sunday so she can meet you," he says. "If you don't think you can survive that, I can make up an excuse."

"No, I'll give it a shot." Might as well get it over with. His mom sounds nice enough, though nosey and full of unsolicited advice.

"Do you think it'll ever be safe enough for you to see *your* mom?" Vonn asks.

"I doubt it." I blink, and the wetness in my eyes isn't because of the onions. I wish with all my soul that I could see Mom, Dad, and Granddad. It's so wrong I can't see my own family. I'd like to "happen" to bump into them somewhere, someday. Just once, to tell them I'm alive. But it wouldn't be safe. Leo or the government might be tracking my friends and family. Monitoring their calls, reading their texts. I wouldn't put it past him or the Enforcers.

I have to let Mom, Dad, and Granddad mourn and move on. Having me appear as Ana would only endanger them. It really sucks they think I'm dead. In a Seattle newsvid, Leo spouted about how he sent me to the airport in an Institute vehicle after my Transfer, and that's the last he saw of me. The driver and four Enforcers lied to verify his story. Later, the body of the sandy-haired girl was found by the river.

Yeah, he and the Enforcers lost track of me at the airport, all right. That part is true.

Leo hurt my friends by arranging my fake death. He destroyed my life and the lives of my family. As soon as it's safe for me to do something—and as soon as I figure out what to do—Leo and his prized Institute are going down.

I sure hope Mom and Dad made the December payment deadline for the debt. Maybe with Granddad and me gone, they were able to move into a cheaper one-bedroom unit, even if Dad's wages got garnished.

An abrupt pounding rattles the front door, which makes me drop the onion knife. I shoot Vonn a glance. His eyes are wider than mine.

"Open up, by orders of the U.S. government," a man shouts. "Your emergency door is also guarded, so don't try to escape out the back."

Enforcers. Have they discovered my real identity, or is Vonn the one who's in trouble?

It doesn't matter. Neither one of us can escape.

Vonn opens the front door to a pair of male Enforcers, one weathered and steely-eyed, one young and pimpled. They enter without being invited, and the door closes behind them. The pimpled one scans our IDs and logs our names.

The weathered Enforcer studies me. "Our main business is with Mr. Alexander. For the record, Miss Ramos, state your relationship with him and why you're here."

"Um, girlfriend," I say. "Making chef salads. Has Vonn done something wrong?"

"How long have you known him?"

"Eight wonderful days." My palms and the back of my neck begin to sweat.

"Mr. Alexander, I'll get straight to the point." The weathered Enforcer takes a visual sweep of the apartment, his blue eyes sharp. "We've combed Institute surveillance feeds and discovered you talking with the late Morgan Dey in the Clinic weigh-in room. Using facial recognition matches, we then found you on public Green Zone cam-feeds for October, November, and December. We recorded you entering an interactive vid theater, patronizing the Half-Moon Café, and walking with her in two different parks while holding hands."

Oh, no. They've made the connection to Vonn. What if they suspect *I'm* Morgan?

The pimpled Enforcer folds his arms. "Of course, these things were done while Miss Dey was in the body of Jodine Kowalczyk."

"And now Morgan's dead," Vonn says with a bit of a growl. "What's your point? Sure, we became friends while we walked in the park, and then we found out we were both Reducers. We decided to keep walking together. I didn't think it was a crime to be friends with someone."

"As a Reducer, your interactions offsite were restricted," the weathered Enforcer says.

Somehow, I need to steer them off any possibility that I might be Morgan. I narrow my eyes at Vonn and pour my nervousness into a glare. "You didn't tell me about this other girl, *honey.*"

"I didn't have time to!" Vonn says.

The pimpled Enforcer holds up his hands. "Don't be getting all riled up, you two."

I step toward him. "I want to know about Vonn and this other chick. Did they just hold hands, or did they kiss?"

"That's not the issue here," the weathered Enforcer cuts in. "Mr. Alexander, state the last time you saw Miss Dey."

Vonn pretends to think. "Uh, I saw her in the Green Zone's

South Park, just before she went to Seattle to get a new body. Well, after that I also went to Seattle to try to surprise her at the airport, but she wasn't there."

I jam my fists on my hips. "You told me you took a vacation to Seattle last month to see the Space Needle. Not to see some old girlfriend."

"Miss Ramos," the weathered Enforcer snaps. "Be quiet, or we'll cite you for impeding an investigation."

I sink onto the couch while the Enforcers continue to grill Vonn. Time inches by. I don't dare bring up the fact that I'm going to be late for work. After they're done with Vonn, they question me, and it's a good thing I studied my personal file so I know my background. One deceased parent, the other in a long-term coma in an Orange Zone care home—who I suspect is a legit person the auto-system connected me to. No siblings, as is usual these days. Born and raised in Phoenix, Arizona. Luckily, the Enforcers don't ask specific questions about where I supposedly grew up.

"What made you move here to southern California?" the weathered Enforcer asks.

Careful. My records state I worked in a parts-assembly factory for a year in Seattle—which is smart of the Institute to give Spares a reason to be in the area—but it might look too coincidental that I've ended up where Vonn lives.

"Have you ever been to Seattle?" I say with a brittle laugh. "It's about the gloomiest, wettest place on earth. Well, plus I had a bad breakup with my ex and wanted a fresh start somewhere far away from him."

"State the reason you checked into the SnooZee hotel three weeks ago."

Whoa. I guess they know that fact from scanning my ID

earlier and pulling up a search. "Post-breakup. I left my ex and let him have the apartment until the end of the month. Since it was already paid up, and all."

"Noted," the pimpled Enforcer says. "What do you think of the Institute and the WHA?"

I shrug like I don't care. "The Reducer program sounds good. Vonn did a great job for his client, until the WHA blew up his real body. I wish the WHA wasn't violent and fanatical, because if they weren't, they'd be a way better organization. It's not against the law to want my rights protected, is it?"

"No," the weathered Enforcer says with a grunt. He taps his comm-device and moves toward the door. "That's all the questions we have at this time for either of you. Mr. Alexander, you will be fined five hundred credits for violating offsite restrictions in your Institute contract. This amount will be auto-deducted from your account."

Vonn struggles not to look peeved. "Yes, sir."

After the door whisks closed behind the Enforcers, Vonn and I stare at each other. A muscle jumps on his jaw. My appetite is gone.

"That was close," I say and get up to wrap myself in his arms.

The late April wind whips my hair back from my face as I wait for the MT. I flex my fingers. They're sore after my work shift, and so are my arms. If it wasn't for earning time-and-a-half pay, I wouldn't work Saturdays. But the extra income from the assembly line drudgery gets me closer to tech school, one meager credit after another.

Enough of that crimping hostess job. I'm holding onto one of my dreams, even if it takes me years to get there.

Two older teen girls approach the shelter, their lively voices snatched up by the wind and tossed into my ears. A lilac-scented puff of air accompanies the blonde as she passes me to sit on a bench. The other girl joins her, blue-eyed and sporting orange lipstick.

I stare. Oh my gosh. *It's Blair and Krista.*

This is the first time I've seen them since Thanksgiving. They don't recognize me, of course. To them I'm just a random stranger standing by an MT shelter. Krista's hair is cut in chunky layers; Blair looks about the same. I wonder why they're way out here in the Blue Zone.

"That was fun," Blair says to Krista. "Thanks for helping me pick out my perfume. I'll smell awesome on Friday."

Krista tilts her face to the sun. "Lilac is so romantic and feminine. Maybe I should've bought some."

"I'll share mine," Blair says.

Ah, that explains why they're here. There's a humongous perfume store in the Blue Zone mall. I try to concentrate on the pavement a few feet away instead of staring, but it's no use. I want to keep looking. Their faces are heart-achingly beautiful. I'd like to memorize every last inch and pore of them. Who knows when I'll ever see them again.

"What time does the party start?" Blair asks.

"Everyone's gonna be at my apartment around seventeen hundred. We'll hit the Flash Point after the pizza and cake." Krista taps her foot to music from a nearby building's vidscreen. "Let's dance until oh-three-hundred when the club closes."

I can't believe Krista's birthday is next Friday, and I'm not going to be a part of her celebration. I'm tempted to show up at the Flash Point. Stay close by, soak in the celebration vibes. Pretend everything's the way it used to be. Or better yet, I could walk over right now and start a new friendship with them as Ana. Maybe I could even tell them who I used to be.

My daydream bubble bursts. No. That would be foolish, since Enforcers might still be keeping an eye on Vonn and me. Maybe on Blair and Krista, too.

Blair scans the MT shelter area, and our gazes meet. There's no recognition in her eyes, like I'm invisible. Krista starts to say something to Blair, when a news flash erupts from the building wall beside us. We turn toward the vidscreen. A reporter materializes there with a jubilant expression.

"We interrupt this viewing to announce that the State of California has convicted Walter Herry, the mastermind behind the WHA attacks on The Body Institute," the reporter says. "Herry's increasingly violent measures were a serious cause for concern, especially last fall when he teamed up with a maintenance technician for the horrific bombing of the Institute's Los Angeles branch building. Herry was arrested in December after—"

My heart twists. On one hand, I'm glad they caught the man who's responsible for the death of my real body. On the other, who knows what they'll do to him now that he's been convicted. Lucky for him, he's too well-recognized to be brain-stripped and turned into a Spare.

"According to the WHA, a new president has been chosen," the reporter continues. "He'll speak tonight at the Crowl Auditorium in the White Zone at nineteen thirty. This man, Russell Alleger, has condemned Herry's violent measures in the past. He vows to reform the WHA and take down The Body Institute by peaceful means."

The reporter and his smirk fade, replaced by an ad-vid for children's indoor play equipment.

I turn back to Blair and Krista, who seem to wilt against each other on the bench.

Blair tucks a renegade wisp of hair behind her ear. "That awful Institute and its Reducer program. I wish Morgan could be at your party. I miss her so much."

Krista doesn't answer. She looks close to tears.

My hands ball into fists. I can't stand this. If they only knew the truth…

"I just don't want her to be dead," Blair says in a near-whisper, so low I barely hear her. "I want to know what happened at that airport. She wasn't on any of the flights. Was it really her brainmap in that girl they found by the river?"

"Please. Don't talk about it. Going over and over that stuff doesn't change anything." Krista bites her lip and stares off across the MT tracks.

An urge seizes me to run over and enclose both of them in a giant hug. To tell them I'm alive. To say how terribly I miss them and that I'll always be their friend, no matter if I never see them again. I think they'd be comforted to know I have a good life as Ana. That I'm working toward tech school, and Vonn is my sweet and devoted boyfriend. My Superguy.

I take a step toward the bench and freeze. My mind wars with my legs. I want to do it so badly, but it's not smart. Not smart at all.

Blair scoops up her shopping bag and nods toward the street. "MT's coming."

I shrink back. I'm out of time. Which is probably a good thing.

Krista rises to her feet. The solar-activated colors of her skirt do a dancing kaleidoscope in the sun as the MT to the Yellow Zone whirs to a halt in front of us. She boards with Blair. I lean to keep their faces in sight for as long as I can through one of the windows. Their images recede as the MT resumes motion, a square snapshot of one sassy orange smile and one ex-Catalyst-Club partner.

Three words pop into my mind. *Adiós, mis amigas!*

Good-bye to my friends, in the language of the girl who used to occupy my body. Phrases like that spring into my brain a lot. It's just as unnerving as constantly singing this one unknown song I'm sure comes from Jodine, but there's nothing I can do about it.

I wait for my connecting train to arrive on the other tracks as the energy of the encounter seeps away. It hits me full force that I'm no longer Morgan Dey. My life is forever different. I'm stuck with listening in from the outside, a stranger to my friends' and family's lives.

The newsvid words claw at me. Walter Herry's conviction. That Alleger guy who vows to lead peaceful protests. The timing could finally be right for me to do something about Leo and the Institute. About the Spares. I've been hiding out while all those bodies lie like gruesome pickles in a room that stinks of grease and antiseptic.

Vonn and I highly suspect his friend Steven was turned into one of those Spares. His minor arrest only three weeks before Chad was Transferred into his body is mighty coincidental. Chad did say he woke up in Seattle—where the Spares are housed. Death-row inmates…what a flippin' lie. It's body recycling, tossing out people's minds and replacing them with "better" ones, as if their first minds were worthless.

Yes, I think I'll join with Alleger in taking down the Institute. Especially since Leo and his Spares will go down with it.

I call Vonn and let him know I'm heading to the White Zone, a journey that takes the rest of the afternoon. My nerves writhe inside me. It's hard to believe I'm thinking about joining the very organization that attacked me and helped destroy my Morgan body. Will Alleger's leadership make a difference?

At the Crowl Auditorium, I take an aisle seat near the back of the room. The place fills with people, young and old, male and female. The brisk aroma of coffee fills the air. Conversation buzzes.

A woman in a bright green jacket plops down beside me and peers at me. "You're Rosa, right? You went off with Herry's 'army' to storm The Body Institute, part of that Los Angeles riot. Did you get arrested?"

A bolt of shock runs through me. *Rosa.* That name sounds personal, close to my heart. I lean away from the woman. "No, that wasn't me. My name's Ana, and this is my first WHA meeting."

The woman scrutinizes me a little longer and gives a bouncing nod. "Sorry. My mistake. Rosa had a thick accent. She looked sadder around the eyes, too. Welcome to the WHA, Ana."

"Thanks." My tension eases—until a scene flashes in my mind. A security fence. The irritating blue of Enforcer uniforms in my peripheral. I'm running. Breathing fast. An obese man lumbers into my path: a Reducer. Anger churns inside me. These stupid, stupid people who help the Institute abuse rights and force their ideals about perfect weight on everyone. We can't all look like athletes in a freaking sports vid. I shove the man, hard, and he tumbles to the ground. His legs flail. I start to step past him, but a shock of pain slams into my spine. *Ay!* Everything goes blurry as I fall. *I've been shot—shot by a stun gun—*

The vision clears. I shake my head, and the woman next to me throws me a puzzled look Whoa. I think that was a memory of Rosa's. Probably because I'm here in her old territory, mingling with the WHA. Is her involvement in the riot the offense that got her turned into a Spare? I haven't had any other residuals beyond bits of Spanish. Certainly nothing murderous. I'm betting she was never on death row, like the protesters never were.

That's a relief, but it also means the Institute is stripping brainmaps from anyone who gets in the way. Not a good revelation.

My attention shifts to a tall, bronze-skinned woman who takes the stage and gives a brief background of the WHA and Herry's last three years. She beckons to someone offstage. "At this time, I'd like to present the new head of our organization, Mr. Russell Alleger."

Alleger strolls out to wild applause, all stringbean legs and gentle-eyed in a suit, his graying hair tied back into a neat ponytail. He speaks for a few minutes against Herry's violent strategies, and in support of privacy, freedom, safety, and choice.

He spreads his arms wide. "I'd like your help in joining our new campaign, which is to gather enough signatures to shut down The Body Institute. We also need funding for ads on TV and city vidscreens. On that subject, I'm pleased to announce we've received a donation of a million credits from one of our new members, Dr. Charles Kowalczyk. Please acknowledge his generosity and welcome him and his family."

The Kowalczyks are here. I sit up straighter as the audience cheers and three people stand in the front row: Dr. and Mrs. K., and Jodine. Jodine walks up the steps behind her parents wearing a ruffled blue dress. Her body is toned and curvy, and she has a glow about her. She flicks a long coiled strand of hair behind her shoulder.

I do a quick calculation and smile. Yes. Less than three weeks in her real body, it really is Jodine up there. I hope that glow means she's enjoying making scrumptious meals with Nettie again, and she's getting some quality face-time with her parents. Seeing her look healthy is awesome, but it kind of grates on me that she's been *forced* to look like this. She'll be on Leo's "strict" maintenance program for the entire next year. I'm sure her weight will be closely monitored for the rest of her life.

Rosa's right. We can't all be buff athletes. The government and the Institute are defining what makes a perfect body, forcing us to look a certain way.

Dr. K. accepts a microphone from Alleger. "Thank you. I'm excited about this campaign, and I fully support Mr. Alleger and his new direction for the WHA. There's a lot of potential for ERT technology to go awry, and we need to neutralize it. My daughter Jodine would like to speak about this." He wraps an arm around her shoulders and hands her the microphone.

Jodine clears her throat, the sound coming out velvety. "Um, hi. I was nearly a casualty of the Reducer program," she says in an eerily familiar voice. "I've lost weight, but in November my original brainmap file was destroyed. The backup files too. If my father hadn't insisted on keeping a copy, I wouldn't be standing here tonight. Another girl would be inside my body, living an entirely different life. ERT's too risky of a procedure to keep using."

A chill ripples over me. What they say is true. As brilliant of technology as ERT is, it needs to be banned. There has to be a better way to solve the health care crunch.

This is a Jodine I'd love to talk to sometime, maybe even tonight. See what else she knows about the Institute. How she feels about the Spares. Find out if she has any of my memories, and if losing weight has changed her life or made her different inside.

I'm not sure about myself and my own life. I seem to be a confusing blend of Morgan, Jodine, and Rosa. Partly because of residual memories and partly because of everything I've been through, but also, as Granddad said back in September, maybe I act differently because I *look* different.

I'm Ana Ramos, a whole new person.

Alleger murmurs in Jodine's ear. A rosy blush spreads across her face under her freckles.

"Mr. Alleger would like me to lead you in singing the national anthem, as a pledge to keep this country safe and free. Please rise."

Members of the audience surge to their feet. Dr. and Mrs. K. look happy. Proud. Jodine begins the song, the words flowing rich and resonant. The crowd joins in. There's no musical accompaniment, only the sound of raised, passionate voices. Jodine sings into the microphone, her words coming out strong. And just like when I first tried out the Kowalczyks' karaoke machine many months ago, her voice gives me the absolute freaking shivers.

CHAPTER 34

The crowd swarms the Crowl Auditorium, alive and humming with conversation. As people filter out the doors and into the night, I scan the room, trying to keep an eye on Alleger and the Kowalczyks. I struggle to move closer, but too many people block my way, clogging the aisles. The Kowalczyks shake hands with Alleger and head toward a back exit.

My hopes sink. I won't be able to talk to Jodine like I wanted. Well, maybe I can do that another time if she attends more WHA meetings.

That leaves Alleger. I have to tell him about the Spares. But a group of people is knotted around him. I'm about to give up when I notice the bronze-skinned woman a few feet from me. I motion her closer.

"If I could," I say, "I'd like to meet with Mr. Alleger to tell him something serious and dangerous about The Body Institute."

Her eyebrows go up for a second, then she directs me to an empty room by the stage. After about ten minutes, she ushers in Mr. Alleger and leaves.

He scoots up a chair and leans forward, his eyes intent. I tell him everything. The Spares room. Leo's involvement. The protesters who aren't really death-row inmates.

"Is there something we can do about this?" I ask. "The government is involved, so we can't get help from there."

"We could appeal to a higher authority," he says. "The International Nations Council is headquartered here in Los Angeles, but I'm afraid they might not believe anything I tell them. Herry hasn't exactly made the WHA a credible source of information the past few years. We really don't have hard evidence of this, either, just your personal experiences."

I frown. No way. I refuse to accept that nothing can be done. "Dr. Kowalczyk can verify the existence of the Spares and that they're housed in Seattle."

As Alleger nods and taps his finger against his chin in deep thought, a hard and cold weight settles over me. No. I don't want Dr. K. or even Alleger to be involved with this. There's only one way to do it.

I rise to my feet. "Never mind. It's not safe for you or Dr. Kowalczyk to be the one to blow the lid off this illegal stuff. With the government and its Enforcers involved, it's not safe for *anyone*. It has to be done under the radar, totally anonymous. I'll get the info and some proof to the Nations Council myself."

"Are you sure? Please assess the risks and be careful, Miss Ramos," Alleger says. "If you really do go ahead with this whistle blowing, your best contact there will be Ambassador Bowman."

"That's helpful, thanks." With my mind already spinning with plans, I shake his hand and leave the room.

Over the next week, I prepare for my trip to the Nations

Council headquarters. Vonn helps me. We make sure we don't do anything related to the task on our phones or with our ID chips, to stay untraceable. To plot my course across the city, I study MT schedules while standing at bus shelters. For my anonymous letter, since I can't send an email, I visit a local pawn shop and select an old-fashioned print book like the kind Granddad keeps on his shelves. I don't use my ID chip to purchase it. The shop owner agrees to swap me for the earrings I'm wearing.

At my apartment, I slice a blank page from the back of the book and compose a letter with snips of words and letters from the novel. In a ransom-note style that I once saw in an old movie, I glue the words onto the page with a paste made from flour and water:

Ambassador Bowman—

At the Seattle branch of The Body Institute, a high-security area exists behind the suspended animation room. This area houses bodies called Spares that Director Leo Behr uses when a Loaner body dies. He claims these bodies are all harvested from death-row inmates. THIS IS A LIE.

If you will compare numbers of inmates with the high number of bodies in that room, you'll find they don't match. Also, the bodies of at least three WHA protesters who attacked a teen girl at the Los Angeles branch on September 30 are stored there: A balding man, a stout wavy-haired woman, and a bearded man. The date on their capsules read October 1, just one day after the attack. They can be found in Row E. Judging from online articles about their arrest, their names appear to be Peter Sandella, Marcy Willaby, and Rick Leymund.

I am writing anonymously, since the government and its Enforcers seem to be involved. Please help correct this wrong.

—A concerned citizen who knows too much.

I make an envelope from more blank pages from the book, seal the letter inside, and inhale a tired but resolute breath. I'll incinerate the tattered book somewhere, soon. I have to say, right now I agree with Granddad about the inconvenience of a society that uses virtual credits instead of paper currency. But the hassle of finding paper is better than the risk of using anything electronic.

The day before my trip, I cut one of my T-shirts into a headscarf. At my job, I temporarily snitch a tube of dark pink lipstick from a co-worker. Vonn gives me extra hugs and kisses for luck when I go over to his apartment for dinner. I try to ignore the worried shadows under his eyes.

"Don't get caught, 007." He hands me a pair of his old white sneakers as I leave.

Before the sun rises on the morning of my day off, I'm up and dressing in layers that I plan to shed along the way. I pull on my hooded sweatshirt and wear Vonn's bigger sneakers over a pair of plain flats. Under my shirt, I tuck a belly pack containing small disguise items.

I slip downstairs to the nearest MT shelter. My double shoes pinch my feet. During the first part of my journey, I ride with my hood up to cover my hair. A wide metal bracelet overlaps my hand to keep the fare scanners from reading my ID. It's a risky move, riding without paying, but I don't want any record that I'm trekking across Los Angeles today.

The envelope with its incriminating message crinkles under my shirt. It's like a bomb against my ribs. My heart pounds against it, and I lick dry lips. But I can't back out now—I have to do this. To protect people against getting turned into Spares, to help wipe out this part of the Institute.

When I arrive at a mall, I get off and duck into a restroom to transform myself. I whip off the hooded sweatshirt and my jeans, revealing a shirt and black leggings. Makeup follows: heavy eyeliner and eye shadow. As much as I hate to, I toss my sweatshirt and jeans in the incinerator, along with the makeup. The dark pink lipstick goes on next. Then hoop earrings. I press stick-on cloth bows onto my flats. Pink ones.

My hands tremble as I pull my hair back and cover it completely with the scarf. This trip is giving me bad déjà vu of being in the airport four months ago, trying to escape the Enforcers in Seattle. One sloppy mistake, and they'll catch me now, or spot me on public vidfeeds later on.

I add a slouch to my walk, exit the mall, and board another MT. Again, I make sure my ID chip is blocked. By the time I transfer one more time and reach the Nations Council building an hour later, my jaw aches from clenching my teeth so hard.

Here it goes. Time to deliver my letter.

The steps leading to the double doors of the entrance stretch out in front of me, long and nerve-wracking. The autodoors whoosh open. I pass through, sweat prickling under my arms. I don't know if the building has scanners built into the sides of the entryway, but I keep my bracelet low on my wrist just in case.

Once I'm inside the lobby, that's when I see the security checkpoint.

Oh, no. This is as far as I can go.

My footsteps slow as my mind races. Stern-faced guards flank a trio of high-tech scanners. Not only ID chip sensors, but full-body machines and the works. I won't be able to hide my identity with a simple wide bracelet now.

A woman with a tight ponytail waves me forward. "Metals go in the plastic tray, shoes on the conveyor belt."

I shake my head and pull the envelope from under my shirt. "I'm not going inside. Some guy in the coffee shop down the street wanted me to deliver this to Ambassador Bowman. He said it's urgent."

The guard goes into instant alert mode, face tense. "What's in it?"

"An important letter. No bomb or anything laced with anthrax. He bought me an iced caramel latte with whipped cream, so I said sure, I'll come here and hand this to someone."

"You should never do things like that," the woman says with a growl. "Why didn't he deliver it himself?"

I place the envelope into a tray and shrug. "I dunno. He looked scared, like he didn't want to be seen coming here. Will you give it to Ambassador Bowman, or make sure he gets it?"

The woman picks up the tray without touching the envelope. "We'll take care of it. From now on, be less trusting or you'll end up regretting it."

I manage to jerk out a nod before I walk away and leave through the autodoors.

At this point, the situation is out of my hands. There's nothing else I can do. I hope they don't dump the letter straight into an incinerator.

On the return trip, I take a different route and stop at a high-traffic hover-skating rink. I transform myself back into Ana Ramos, wiping off makeup, shedding my shirt and earrings, and incinerating the shirt and scarf. I comb out my hair and peel off the black leggings. There's a pair of tan ones underneath, and I un-scrunch my final T-shirt from around my waist and pluck the pink bows from my shoes.

Time to hop an MT and go home.

CHAPTER 35

Three days later, Vonn's TV murmurs distant nothings in my ears, its holographic forms moving above the platform in my peripheral vision. I'm not really watching it. His mouth is much more interesting. Warm. Swimmy and dreamy. His kisses are part of his personality, and his personality is mega-*mega*-octane.

"Ana, look." He shifts, trying to untangle our arms and sit up.

"No, I don't want interruptions." I wrap my arms back around his neck. I'm addicted to him. There's no such thing as "stop" right now.

"Seriously, you gotta see this." Vonn grabs the remote from the arm of the couch and cranks the volume.

I sigh, mock-growl, and twist around to view the images in front of us.

My head clears in an instant.

It's a live broadcast held at The Body Institute in Seattle, Washington. Troops from the Nations Council wearing gray uniforms march through the gates, past saluting Enforcers.

"—pending this property search for evidence of crimes against humanity," a newsvid reporter is saying in the lower corner of the display. "Apparently a large number of bodies are kept here in a high-security suspended animation room. These bodies, called Spares, are a questionable reserve against accidental death of the Institute's Loaner clientele. Death-row inmates are presumably stripped of brain activity to provide these bodies. However, according to an anonymous tip, the Spares far outnumber the total of recent death-row inmates. Where have these other bodies come from? The International Nations Council has sent in troops today to search out answers."

"It worked!" I breathe the words into the room. "Ambassador Bowman got my letter."

Vonn gives a straight-lipped smile and slides his arm around my waist. "You did it, Geekling. The proof came down to the numbers. Way too many bodies in that Spares room."

I watch the 3-D figures march across the platform, and it's as if I'm standing right on the grounds in Seattle. I can almost feel the light rain pattering on my shoulders and head. I'm glad I made this investigation happen, for Vonn's sake especially. It's a belated justice, even if it doesn't make up for Steven's wrongful death. Or anyone else's, like that Iowa woman's brother, or the unlucky guy who got sent to Seattle by the man with the goatee.

The reporter angles her umbrella, her expression growing intense. "I've just gotten word that the unaccountably large number of Spares has been verified. Troops have confiscated this portion of the Institute's operation, and will ship the bodies to a neutral location. Reserve bodies will now only be issued in the case of actual Loaner deaths. No new Spares will be created."

"It's about time this happened," I say. "Great start. We can take the Institute apart, piece by piece." Further words stick in my throat as Nations Council troops file out from the main doors of the Seattle building, escorting a trim man in a dark suit. Snatches of the reporter's words reach my ears. *Arrest. Director. Responsible for this atrocity. Extensive knowledge and involvement over the past year.*

I stare at Leo Behr. His body appears to grow larger as he walks closer to the camera, until he's a three-dimensional part of the living room, right in front of me. His shrewd gray eyes are hard, drilling straight into mine. It's almost like he can see me, and he knows it's my fault he's wearing restraint-cuffs. His dark eyebrows knot across his forehead. I lean back from the image.

Vonn tightens his arm around my waist and breathes with me. There aren't any words to react to what we're seeing. My heart pounds, loud and slow. Leo moves away across the platform, growing smaller as he's ushered toward a waiting security transport. Eerily, the sensation of his glare stays with me, like I've been irradiated.

The reporter continues. "The White House has sent official word that it had no knowledge of Mr. Behr's mismanagement of these bodies."

I grunt and nudge Vonn. "Sure. Just like the WHA didn't have anything to do with the maintenance tech's bombing of the Institute."

"And sadly," Vonn says, "I bet it's still not safe for you to contact your parents or friends."

"No…I'm sure the government will be keeping an eye on them for the rest of their lives."

I can only do what I can while living under the radar, and the only thing left for me to do now is to make sure the Institute is shut down. Completely, not just the Spares room. As Granddad said many months ago, this body swapping stuff just isn't right.

The winding sidewalk leading up to the Pleasant Hills Retirement Home reminds me of a park path, except the grass blades stand unusually still in the breeze. The same for the bushes. That's because the entire landscaping on the grounds is made of fake turf and shrubs.

Only the best for this country's senior citizens.

I climb the steps toward the brick buildings. The corner of the WHA signature reader I clutch digs into my ribs. Here at the far edge of the Blue Zone today, I plot a dual mission. One mission is dedicated to the WHA and its petition to close the Institute. The other is something I've been wanting to do for myself for months, but never had good camouflage for my actions.

I check in at the entrance. The small wallscreen by the door responds in a snippy, tinny voice: "ID verified and logged. Security cameras are posted at this residence to prevent theft and vandalism."

I roll my eyes and start canvassing in the west wing. Working my way along the first floor, I try to breathe like I'm cool and composed. I stop at an inner courtyard. A chatty gathering of elderly people plays horseshoes there, and I collect a dozen easy signatures.

"Thank you," I tell them. "If we don't protect our rights,

they'll be taken away."

They nod their gray heads in solemn agreement. Their bodies look wonderful, their wrinkles telling stories of lives lived long and full. I promise them I'll come back another day to play horseshoes. If all goes well with my second mission today, I'll sign up to volunteer here on evenings and Saturdays to mingle with people. That'll provide additional cover for any future visits.

I return to the echoing halls. Odors of floor cleaner and ancient wooden furniture sift into my nose. Security cameras lurk every ten yards, perched high on the wall like evil metal bats. The building directory listed my goal as room 1382. I have three or four rooms left before I get there. I work my way closer, then finally reach my ultimate destination. Tucking my reader under my arm, I twist my fingers together so hard my knuckles crack.

1382: Bob Sanders.

Here it goes. Will he talk to me or throw me out? He hates petitioners.

I knock instead of using the ringer on the keypad, since he prefers quieter interruptions. The door slides to one side. Granddad sits across the room in his old plaid armchair, his bushy hair and beard framing his face like an aging sunflower.

"What is it now?" he says. "It'd better not be another shot. If this place spent as much time with the food as they did pushing pills and shots, it'd improve a hundredfold."

I can't help laughing, and the tension in my gut dissolves like sugar in water. Same old Granddad. I've missed him something fierce.

"No, Mr. Sanders, I'm not giving out pills or shots. I'm collecting signatures for a WHA petition to shut down The

Body Institute. Have you heard of us, or the Institute?"

"I sure have, young lady." He whaps a gnarled hand onto a thick printed book that rests on his knees. His eyes go watery. "That Institute murdered my granddaughter."

"Really?" I try to sound detached, but my voice falters.

He waves for me to sit on a folding chair opposite him. "Well, indirectly. That foolish technology of theirs. Had no right messing with brain waves and all that swapping nonsense. They had her convinced it was safe. Then they said she disappeared in Seattle—or her brain clone did, anyway. Some other girl's dead body was supposed to be her, and they'd already deleted her backup file since she was done being a Reducer."

"I'm sorry to hear that. I've had bad experiences with the Institute too."

"So here you are at a government retirement home, trying to get signatures to take down one of their big-shot funded programs." Granddad chuckles. "That takes guts. I like that. It's about time the WHA did something besides set things on fire. I wasn't fond of that guy…what's his name? Henry or Harvey, or something. It was his fault my granddaughter was murdered—her real self, not just her clone. Good as snuffed her out himself in that burning building."

His face crumples, his chin quavering. He gathers himself with an effort. "What exactly is this petition about?"

I try to focus on his fuzzy hair rather than his sad eyes and shaky chin. He doesn't remember Herry's name or that the incident was a bombing and not a fire…more of his memories are becoming lost forever. But it doesn't matter. Even if he doesn't remember everything, he'll always be Granddad to me. "If we get enough signatures, it'll convince the Nations Council to stop government funding and close the Institute. A lot of people agree the Reducers program is too dangerous to balance out the good of helping people lose weight."

"My kind of petition. Hand it over."

I present my reader to him. He adds his ID signature and handprint to the screen with a zesty flair. My glance falls on the book in his lap. Brown and bulky, with worn edges. It looks vaguely familiar for some reason.

"What's that you're reading?" I ask.

A smile wreaths Granddad's face. "One of my favorite books, *The Count of Monte Cristo*. These days I've forgotten some of the details, so I started it again yesterday. Have you ever read it?"

I snatch at wisps of possible memories in my brain, but they flee, as elusive as clouds on a windy day. We shared lots of books, but not this one. "I don't think I have. What's it about?"

"Betrayal, true love, God, justice, revenge, and reconciliation. It's all in here. Good stuff, though it's old and the words are more poetic than books nowadays. Don't live your life without reading it."

"Then I guess I'll have to give it a try." If the book is important to him, I'll make it important to me.

Hunching forward, Granddad points a knobby finger at me. "There's something about you that I like, young lady. Can't quite put my finger on it. What's your name?"

I desperately want to tell him my real name. But I can't. Once on a government radar, always on a government radar. Leo was a key figure in the nasty Spares business—but not the only one. Someone had to provide him with all those bodies.

"I'm Ana Ramos."

"Nice to meet you, Ana. Do you want a sneak preview of this *Monte Cristo* book? I can start over at the beginning with you. I'll even let you do the reading, since my eyesight's not what it used to be." Granddad scratches his head. "If you like the story, maybe you can come back another time, and we can keep reading."

A broad smile breaks out across my face, straining my muscles something wicked. It's a glorious feeling that makes me want to shout, to rattle the security cameras in the hall right off their posts.

I lean back in the folding chair. "I'd love to do that, Mr. Sanders," I say. "It'll be a perfect way to get to know you."

ACKNOWLEDGMENTS

First, to my made-of-awesomeness agent, Kelly Sonnack, for her unflagging belief in this novel despite its ugly duckling beginnings, and her perseverance until it finally grew up into something that more resembled a swan. For her knowledge, guidance, and general overall sweetness.

Undying gratitude to Stacy Abrams of Entangled Teen. You chose my book! And you edited it to make it so much stronger than before, knowing just what it needed to round it out. Thanks to everyone at Entangled Teen, from cover design to publicity (answering my incessant questions) to copyediting and more.

Grateful appreciation to Mary Kate Castellani, whose revision notes on spec shaped this novel into a more reader-friendly and vital story. Also to Amanda Rutter, my almost-editor at Strange Chemistry (and her team!), for also choosing my book, and making revision-useful comments.

Endless gratitude and hugs to my critique partners and other long-suffering souls who've read part or all of this manuscript — at various stages and often multiple times: Carolyn Lee Adams, Kathe Anchel, Nazarea Andrews, Patricia Bailey, Deanna

Carlyle (Gwen Ellery), Rosie Connolly, Trish Fletcher, Chantee Hale, Rachael Harrie, Stina Lindenblatt, Stephanie Sinkhorn, Al Sirois, Emily White, and Debby Zigenis-Lowery. Extra thanks to Stina Lindenblatt, who advised me on exercising and toning details. With MEGA-SPECIAL endless gratitude and hugs to Lynda Young, Aussie critique partner and friend extraordinaire, who wasn't afraid early on to tell me the novel had major structural problems. You rock, Lyn!

To my online blogging community—you know who you are, and while there are too many to list individually, I appreciate your ongoing encouragement, generosity, and support. Likewise to my friends in the Fearless Fifteeners group, as well as the Oregon and northern-California SCBWI. Hugs to all. You've made my journey to publication that much more enjoyable.

Much love to my husband, Dennis, who generated the geeky details of ERT, and got the book kickstarted from my premise. For his unfailing support, as well as making it possible for me to stay home and write, write, write. To the creative writing teachers who encouraged me: the late Jim Rainey of Marshfield Senior High in Coos Bay, Oregon, and Mike Steele of Pacific University in Forest Grove, Oregon.

To my niece, Emily (Pritchett) Beasley, who encouraged me by eagerly reading my early novels and sharing them with her friends. To my mom, Betty Hazel, for taking the time to help me proofread. To my daughter, Janelle Henderson, for her enthusiasm and thoughtful comments when I described my book to her. To my other daughter, Megan Henderson, for her advice on what teens do NOT say, so this book wouldn't sound like it was written by an old fogey (even though it was).

Most importantly, heartfelt thanks to God, who gives meaning to my writing and my life.